I0576390

FOXHAWK

Part of the
'Remember Time Never Was'
Anthology

The First Book in the
Charlie Foxhawk Carter Series

By
Frank Cervarich

Copyright © 2019 Frank Cervarich all rights reserved.

Editor: Margaret Blain Cervarich

Photography:
Robert Campbell photos of images created by Frank Cervarich: pages 17, 21, 61, 113
Frank Cervarich: Cover, back cover, and pages 25 ,31, 47, 52, 99, 125, 139, 165, 177, 201, 209, 229, 236, 253, 265
Frank Cervarich and Robert Campbell, page 277

Design Elements: Great Northwest Phantasmagoria
Layout: Kayleigh Montgomery-Morris

www.foxhawk.org

This story is inspired by real places, events and people; however, this is a work of fiction. I have taken broad imaginative latitude with the real places, events and people so much so that these places, events and people are a product of my imagination in service of an invented and fabricated story.

Published in the United States by Cervarich Enterprises LLC
Frederick, Maryland in 2019.

Library of Congress Cataloguing-in-Publication Data

ISBN 978-1-7328754-0-1

IN MEMORIAM:

Mary Peacock
Linda Peacock
Sharon Litwin
Lhary Meyer
Jim Lesan

CHAPTER ONE

I, CHARLIE FOXHAWK CARTER, BEGIN

Richmond, Virginia.
1948
I am very young

What happened? Why am I here, and there? Am I dreaming? I was, am happy. I'm on an outing with my father, just the two of us. He told me, "Just us guys." Abruptly I was not the same me. I mean I'm somehow removed, distant, in a faraway place all the while observing and recording the everyday world with an understanding that is not me. This strange state, sensation, feeling makes me more and more frightened as it takes me over more completely, all embracing. Sitting in the front seat with my father helps me to reassure and quiet my gnawing panic. Everything is unknown yet ordinary, everyday. I watch the streets of Richmond slide by, the outside world. I observe, calm and clear, from that place which is somehow not me, a removed watching me. My forehead is wet and clammy. My palms are damp.

The feeling persists. I hold my father's hand as we enter through the unlocked back door of an apartment on Grace Street which leads into a small kitchen and head into the living room/dining room area. I see more clearly than ever before yet still far away a bespectacled bald-headed elderly man sitting in an armchair, back straight and head looking intently downward. In his hand he holds a puzzle piece poised above a card table on which a half solved jigsaw puzzle and the loose pieces lie. His face is without expression yet intense with concentration. Light from a front window causes a glare on his glasses, obscuring his eyes.

A chunky, kindly woman rises from her armchair putting down her sewing as she does so. She smiles making a slight curtsy to us and laughs with pleasure at our arrival. She stoops down to get a better look at me after my father introduces us. The elderly man seated at the card table working on his puzzle, mysterious and grave, watches without comment.

My father greets him. "Hello, Mr. Vitolinich. I want to introduce you to my son, Charlie."

My father pushes me forward. "Say hello to Mr. Vitolinich, Charlie."

He does not have to add – just as you have been taught to do. I am obedient, eager to be a good son. I tip my head in a slight bow in his direction and raise my hand in an awkward half wave; Mr. Vitolinich takes my hand into his with a firm but pleasant grip. We shake hands. He does not smile. I see something in his eyes, the reflection of my eyes.

Mrs. Vitolinich takes me into the kitchen and feeds me homemade sugar cookies and milk while my father and Mr. Vitolinich talk. I finish my cookies on the tiny back porch of their apartment which looks out on the treeless shared lawn for the apartment complex. A parking lot, in which our car is parked — a big, black Cadillac, the latest model with all the options — borders the yard. A newly built television tower dominates the immediate skyline. It is sited less than two blocks from this apartment complex in an empty lot next to the WTVR-TV Channel 6 building, the first television station in the South. Who, what am I? Where am I? What's happened to me? Why am I here yet there, far away?

My father is chatting with Mrs. Vitolinich in the kitchen when I go back inside to return my empty glass and plate. I follow them back into the front room. Mr. Vitolinich is completely absorbed in his task. There is something ritualistic, sacrosanct about this task of his. And I am eager to take part in his ritual. But I think that to take part would violate somehow the unwritten rules of his puzzle solving exercise. An indescribable feeling rushes up, down and around my body making me light-headed, abstract yet still clear. I am carried even further away, out of my body and am reduced to a speck in a blindingly white everywhere light that soothes as it makes me tremble before I am drawn back by Mr. Vitolinich's poised hand holding a puzzle piece. The rightful place for that piece is being determined and Mr. Vitolinich will put it in that place only when he has divined it. In this clear, distant yet new understanding place, I vow that one day I too will divine rightful placement of puzzle pieces that will solve mysterious problems.

My father takes my hand in his. I look up at him. He does not look down at me. I want to be just like my father when I grow up. In the back parking lot, he starts the powerful and authoritative engine of his new Cadillac after we close the well-fitted doors. In the rear view mirror, we can see the small porch which leads to the Vitolinich apartment. But I watch my father. He does not speak, just stares straight ahead. Leisurely, he puts the car in reverse but still has his foot on the brake. He is thoughtful. He turns to me.

"I'm going to tell you a secret that you must tell no one," he says to me. "Can you do that, keep a very important secret? Can I trust you?"

I nod my head gravely.

"That man, Mr. Vitolinich, is your grandfather."

Is this a dream? It seems real. Why am I here...there?

The Cavalier Hotel
Virginia Beach, Virginia.
Summer 1955

The Lester Lanin Orchestra's scintillating dance music merges with the hypnotic ebb-and-flow of surf at the Cavalier Beach Club. I have agreed to attend the Tea Dance with my parents held on Wednesday and Friday *afternoons at the outdoor pavilion. A partner in my father's law office and his family has come down to the beach, as has my father, for a long weekend. Their daughter is my age. We have met, on more than one occasion. On our first meeting, the daughter made it abundantly clear that she had no interest in me. But both of our parents refuse to honor her decision. 'Wouldn't they make a darling couple,' I overheard my mother say to the girl's mother on a previous, equally dysfunctional meeting of the two of us.*

My mother, my sister, my nanny and I traveled to the shore earlier in the week to begin a two-week holiday at Upper Magnolia, one of two rental apartments stacked one on top of the other on the Cavalier grounds. I have been body surfing, playing tennis and golf, and brooding since we arrived.

I mumble an incoherent soliloquy of regret before I depart from our table beside the parquet dance floor shortly after my parents' friends and daughter join us. My father, deep in colloquy with his business partner, dismisses me with a wave of his hand and a nod; my mother blanches but does not object. The daughter graciously accepts an invitation from another vacationing peer to take a turn on the dance floor. The three of us attended the fashionable Miss Donnan's Cotillion the previous fall where we were instructed in the social graces.

The breeze is fresh. A tropical storm, still to the south, is moving rapidly up the Eastern seaboard of the United States as sometimes happens in late summer and early fall. The angry sky grows angrier by the minute. The surf pounds onto the sandy shore. Standing on the wooden boardwalk high above the beach, I breathe in the cleansing air.

The boardwalk passes in front of a row of cabanas, small changing areas with a shower for Cavalier guests who opt for this privilege. Lunches can be ordered using a phone in the cabana. They are brought to guests and served out on the table in front of each cabana by African American men wearing white coats and black pants.

In our cabana, I pull on my swim trunks, still damp from our morning swim. I left them hanging up on the shower rod. Then I scamper down the wooden steps to the beach. The dance music dwindles to a remote irritant, relegated to a distant memory by the turbulent waters that draw me toward them. The potential for a stormy sea with wild, furious, thunderous breakers tantalizes me, a boy on the verge of puberty and his unruly teen years. A wild excitement, a heady rush, consumes my consciousness. This is the music I yearn to bring to life in my future, not dance music brought to you courtesy of Lester Lanin. The haunting, throaty roar this turbulent call of nature makes suits my vision of myself as the hero in some Western epic of the silver screen. It is combined with other more nebulous roles that emanate from my very private Invisible World within.

I sprint up the beach and back, the wind hindering my advance in one direction and propelling me in the other. I have been working on my conditioning during the summer with the hope that I will make either the football or basketball team at Westhampton Junior High School. I rejected the suggestion of my parents that I transfer to St. Christopher's, the private school most members of the Country Club of Virginia set choose for their boys to attend despite the argument that the transfer would increase my chances of getting into a 'good' college. I go against that good advice because I fantasize that attending Westhampton will somehow manage to change the fact that I'm a loner, an outsider, who will never be part of the "in" crowd. Making one of Westhampton's teams, I imagine, will go a long way toward overturning what is in fact an internally accepted outsider status.

At the end of my run I happen to stop near a woman who is anxiously looking out toward the water. I am so self-consumed that I, at first, don't recognize her look as one of concern.

"Is the undertow strong?" she asks as I come close enough for her to speak without shouting.

The wind is blowing our hair. Saltwater spray seems to dance in the air. Sand fiddlers are scurrying over odd bits of seaweed and around compressed balls of sand towards the precarious holes which lead to their lairs. Just before sunset, I often pour water into one of these holes hoping to force one of them to emerge. I love to watch them, particularly as day turns to night on a summer evening.

"Have you just taken a swim?" the woman continues with a friendly but anxious smile trying once again to attract my attention.

"No ma'am. But I did go in this morning."

"Oh."

It is then that I note the pinched look on her face, a tortured look that is heightened by the bits of air blown sand that rocket through the air. I follow the direction of her gaze and discover the object of her concerned attention. A head is bobbing up and down just at the point where waves begin to be defined from ocean swell. On a rough afternoon like this that point is closer to shore than on warm lazy days. This is a dangerous dividing line, sharply defined by the undertow, which ripens in stormy weather. Beyond the swelling waves one is relentlessly dragged out to sea; inside, one is tugged with disturbing caresses that thrill some and chill others shoreward.

This day's waves are, for the Virginia coast, large and their violence is dramatic as they come ashore. The pebbles on the shoreline are fairly dancing with clattering song caused by the waves; shore birds are busily engaged in the business of feeding as they race on spindly legs up and down the dampened and ever-changing strip between water and sandy beach.

"Do you think it's safe for him to be out that far? The undertow..."

Her voice trails off. She clasps her hands in front of her. My mother, all mothers, my nanny, come sharply to mind. My emerging self-image - the hero, the anointed one – given velocity by my advance toward puberty, shapes my immediate decision. Without a word, I head towards the incoming surf. Foam surrounds my ankles as I look out, hands on hips, to the place where the bobbing head, the mother's son, is floating. I enter the swirling, tugging water. The menacing undertow sends strong messages to my ankles, my knees, my thighs, my whole body. The potential peril of this son rapidly crystallizes as I, myself, begin to wonder whether it's "safe." Will I too become a helpless pawn in this grasping, gulping mass of water? Am I truly a blessed being, a special case, a hero?

I am a strong swimmer, have been on the swim team this summer. I briskly knife my way through the water until I am within easy hailing distance of this son. But I don't call out at once. I observe a skinny, blue-eyed runt, decidedly younger than I, determination and panic etched in equal parts on his freckled face. This situation calls for diplomacy and tact. I know whereof I speak. I am undersized myself but I make up for it among my fellows by my athleticism and aloof demeanor. Or, at least, I like to believe I do.

"Great waves," I offer after an appropriate period of shared space has passed and I can no longer ignore the meaning looks of his mother from on shore.

"Yes," he answers, his mouth sinking below the water line briefly as he responds.

He shakes his head and paddles more briskly.

I look seaward, the direction the undertow is drawing us both towards.

"Storm looks like it'll hit soon."

No answer. I can almost smell the panic rising from his body above the brine that surrounds us.

"Was that lightning I saw out there?" I ask.

The boy jerks his head around and he is forced to swallow another mouthful of water. He's tiring fast. But I don't offer to haul him in despite the fact I have taken a swimming safety class at Boy Scout summer camp and have earned my Life Saving merit badge as a result.

"Hey, let's dive down. It's really neat," I suggest.

"Okay," the boy responds after a brief pause.

We both dive under. He's a good swimmer too, just not as strong, not as old, as I. We surface. I shake my head tossing aside droplets of water and then look out to sea again.

"Another bolt of lightning," I comment.

No bolts of lightning are striking anywhere that I can see.

"Lightning..." the boy answers, slightly refreshed by our dive and more focused.

"At Boy Scout camp we were told to get out of the water fast when lightning strikes."

"Why's that?"

"The water acts as a conductor for the lightning. We could be

electrocuted."

"You think we should head in?"

"We might just catch a really cool wave on the way in. You up for it?"

The boy nods and turns, willingly agreeing now to what his pride had not allowed him to accept seconds earlier.

"Dive under the water. See how far we can go. I'll race you," I shout.

The boy is game. He energetically dives. I catch up to him and purposefully bump into him as we surface. That gives me an opportunity to shove him shoreward without seeming to offer help. We are still under the strong influence of the undertow. I begin to wonder if this rescue thing might involve me as well.

"You won. Hey, want to try it again? I bet I can beat you this time."

The boy's teeth chatter. He's beginning to suffer from hypothermia. But he's still game. He nods his head, smiles shyly and ducks under water before I have a chance to dive. But I catch up to him again. This time I grab his arm and pull him with all my might shoreward. We surface. The boy does not object.

"Here comes a wave. Let's grab it," I shout, not giving the boy time to respond.

The wave passes us by as we paddle furiously trying to catch it. But we have made shoreward progress, not enough but still a significant move forward.

"Darn. Let's catch the next one."

The boy's teeth chatter some more and his freckled face is bluish but he smiles nonetheless as he nods. His blue eyes sparkle. I haven't fooled him at all about my intentions. We swim as briskly as we can toward the shore, making this our be-all or end-all effort. To our surprise, we get caught up in a great roller that thunders rocketing towards the shore. I hold my body straight with arms forward imitating an arrow. As the wave crashes, we are both forced into the sandy bottom with terrific force. My chest, my elbows, my shins are scarped raw and bloody. I have the uncomfortable feeling that I will not make it to the surface before my lungs collapse. We emerge in the foamy aftermath of the wave our bathing suits pulled well below our waists. Sand heavy, we jerk them up, embarrassed, gasping for breath, exalted, surprised, self-rescued heroes standing up in the surf. We are well and truly saved, set apart – delivered for some higher purpose? We look at each other. He smiles and sticks out his hand.

"Tony Vitolinich," he states.

I take his hand with the firm grip my father has trained me to produce. "Charlie Carter."

Approaching the intersection of Haight and Ashbury Streets
San Francisco, California
October 1968

Turn on the radio.

The Beatles are singing "Tomorrow Never Knows" from their Revolver album.

Change the station.

Bob Dylan is singing "Like a Rolling Stone" from his album Highway 61 Revisited.

Change the station.

The Mamas & The Papas are singing "California Dreaming."

It's a winter day and I'm cruising down the foggy streets of San Francisco.

Change the station.

"Former Vice President Richard Nixon and his running mate, Spiro Agnew..."

Why am I here? Left behind in Richmond, Virginia are predictable seasons; my family; my friends; all the old familiar haunts and hang ups; and Isobel, the object of my long term romantic contemplation...In their place a foggy, cold, wet, inhospitable assortment of people, places and events... Am I here because I am forwarding a career path that will bring me security and an enviable position in society, or is it because I am a seeker yearning to apprehend the Universe and my place in it?

Change the station.

The Animals are singing "We Gotta Get Out of This Place."

Can't leave right now... I'm being broken in as an insurance claims investigator.

Change the station.

The Lovin' Spoonful is singing "Did You Ever Have to Make Up Your Mind?"

I was hired by Life Beneficial and fast tracked into their management training program. Six months in, I'm transferred from their home office in Richmond, Virginia to their newly expanded Northern California office and rotated into my current position. Prior to working at Life Beneficial I worked as a lowly office researcher and copy writer for a secret, never mentioned governmental agency – The Office. When asked, I told people I was fulfilling my two years of military service working for the Defense Department. The Office handles top secret intelligence operations purportedly relating to military concerns that are more often political in nature, be they international or national, using cutting-edge, sometimes experimental techniques during their operations. That background may have influenced Life Beneficial in their decision to send me to fill this opening but they are dead wrong to think that that background will give me a leg up. I don't care what their reasoning is. What I do care about is the ever-present question of influence – my father's – on me, on those who hired me, on all my decisions. Follow my lead – that's what I've been doing since childhood. I followed my father's lead when it came to courses to study in college, when it came to agreeing to employment at The Office, accepting an offer of employment at Life Beneficial. Is that how I want to lead my life? I am living in turbulent times and those of my generation are questioning authority, searching for answers that will lead to a better world more attuned to these changing times.

Change the station.

"Doctors report the birth of a deformed baby to a young woman in Iowa who took LSD-25 during pregnancy. There is speculation that the drug can trigger severe chromosomal changes..."

Change...

Jimi Hendrix plays "Axis: Bold as Love."

Shifting waves of fog cling to wind-bent trees attached with ferocity to precipitous hillsides. Water drips from every porous opening in the earth. Mud slides are on everybody's mind as buildings, sidewalks and streets sag, shift and, hopefully, don't end up at the bottom of the hills on which they are perilously perched.

Change...

The Rolling Stones sing "19th Nervous Breakdown."

Why am I here?

Barry McGuire sings "Eve of Destruction."

Martin Luther King has been assassinated.

Why am I here?

Robert Kennedy was assassinated.

Why am I here?

Riots have broken out on city streets and at the Democratic National Convention.

Why am I here?

We are still embroiled in an unpopular war in Vietnam.

The Byrds sing "Eight Miles High."

And I have arrived on the San Francisco scene after what journalists the world over called the Summer of Love. Happenings and Human-Be-Ins are taking place in Golden Gate Park. Acid tests, where the Grateful Dead play and LSD-spiked punch is served, are being conducted by Ken Kesey and his Merry Pranksters. Flower power is rampant. Celebrities and tourists flood the already crowded streets of Haight-Ashbury picking up on the vibe – George Harrison wearing heart-shaped, rose-colored glasses; your mom and dad riding in the cool comfort of a tour bus as guides point out the sights.

Freaks to the left of me; freaks to the right of me; craziness, madness, wacky lunacy suitable for a TV sitcom set in an insane asylum surrounds us. It's 1968. Free love, free food, freedom set to the beat of ear shattering rock-n-roll. Young people are speaking their minds, if they still have one that is intact. They have tuned in, turned on, and dropped out. That's how all the press clippings read.

Across the San Francisco Bay, students riot and demonstrate for free speech near UC Berkeley and cruise the teargas stained streets of Telegraph Avenue while reading the Berkeley Barb. Meanwhile, in Oakland, the Black Panthers demonstrate on the steps of city hall in full battle attire including automatic weapons. Racial tensions are high and city streets have been turned into infernos patrolled by billy-club wielding, anger-and-fear driven police officers – the pigs, to the youngsters.

The kicker – a cousin still uninformed of his relationship to me, Tony Vitolinich, is part of the clamoring crowd of 'hippies' congesting the streets and byways of the San Francisco Bay Area.

_____

"We can work it out" The Beatles tell us in song while
The Doors suggest that you "Light My Fire."
Marshall McLuhan proclaims "The medium is the message."
Why the hell am I here, parking my car after circling the block a few times?

My raincoat clings to my backsides. I'm a wind-blown swarthy, slight but sturdy, brown haired, brown eyed, five foot nine piece of flotsam being driven down a near empty side street. I'm looking for, no propelled toward, a grubby backstage entrance that is reached by making my way between two rundown houses - past garbage cans and weeds - towards emptiness. I look up at the narrow slit of sky above. Featureless...Slate gray... a raindrop causes an eyelid to jerk closed and then pop open. Groovy...Far out... Shake it away...I knock on the backstage door.

The Rolling Stones song "Paint It, Black" is playing loud enough inside the theater to make the dented grey metal door rattle on its hinges.
Why am I here, forced to beat on a stage door in a dead end alley to gain entry, nervously playing with brand new business cards, tied to a company supplied 24-hour answering service...

Will this door open? Do I want it to? I'm probably the only one my age in this neighborhood wearing a coat and tie. Most of my peers are probably still in bed – with pleasant company by their side and a favorite form of transformative substance to help them get out of bed with a smile on their faces.

The Stones continue to drone on about painting everything black.

Why am I at a murder scene? I'm an insurance investigator for Christ sake, not a homicide detective.

More "Paint It, Black." Good grief.

Why am I here?

Why, in God's name, did I take this job, accept this transfer?

"Name's Carter... Charlie, ah C. F. Carter, insurance claims investigator," I prattle by way of introduction to the patrolman who finally opens the stage door.

Does he hear me above the incessant wailing of the Stones' "Paint It, Black?"

I'm a native Richmond, Virginian, Georgetown University graduate, desk job in lieu of military service misfit, a loner, an outsider, a wannabe mystic, a seeker who imagines he would like to be out on the outer edge of Edge City who has always obeyed and remained sheltered, protected, even though or maybe because my folks belong to the right clubs, go to the right church, attend all the proper functions and live in the right part of the capital of the Confederacy, the state in which the first permanent English settlement was established in 1607.

The music comes to a sudden, screeching halt after the patrolman has spent what seems an eternity staring at my card, then staring at me. During the deafening silence, I'm politely but firmly directed to a short, barrel-chested detective with salt-and-pepper hair in a neat crew cut. He's smoking a pipe and wearing a beat up raincoat.

"C.F. Carter," I repeat for him as I hand him one of my cards.

He looks at it and then at me before stuffing my card in his already overloaded raincoat pocket. I stick out my right hand; the detective shakes it.

"I'm Cooper... Detective Everett Cooper, SFPD. But everybody around here calls me Coop. What's your game, Mr. C. F. Carter?"

"Well, ah, insurance. Claims... Investigation..."

"Don't see many claims investigators on a murder scene. What gives?"

I shrug my shoulders. Get back to you when – when I've solved one of the eternal questions of existence and get a clue, any clue, about the meaning and direction of my life. But I reply, "Well, you see, Life Beneficial likes to be proactive." I remember hearing that during my orientation class after I was taken on at the company.

Coop is noncommittal. "You must be new in town. Haven't seen you around..."

"They've been keeping me under wraps. Top secret stuff..." Coop almost smiles, then snickers. He chews on the end of his unlit pipe, fires it up again with a lighter. "What you got on this case, Detective, ah, Coop?"

"Just Coop is fine... As far as the case is concerned - what you see is what you get for the time being," Coop answers, scratching his chin after taking his pipe out of his mouth. "Makes you feel like Sherlock Holmes, don't it?"

A somber silence lingers over the tattered theater. Center stage, Robert Randolph White, Jr., lies in a tangle of theatrical rigging surrounded by a pool of blood and hundred dollar bills. Some are blood drenched; others have been made into paper airplanes. His arms and legs are twisted unnaturally. The attacker tried to make it look like Bob White had a nasty fall from above, very unlikely since there's nothing up there from which he could have fallen. Spotlight highlights this nasty work, very arty. As Coop says, real Nick and Nora stuff.

The coroner's report will reveal the pooled blood is not Bob White's - pig's blood, most likely from a butcher shop. The multiple stab wounds in his body were inflicted ritualistically, whatever that means. The proverbial blunt object was applied to the back of the head and could be the cause of death if it's not the stab wounds. Nasty bruise on his face...knuckles raw...No sign of the blunt object or the knife. Time of death, approximately midnight... If Bob White had been murdered on this stage at midnight, there would have been about two hundred stoned witnesses out in the audience to observe his life ending fall.

Dust clings to his clothes, his face. So does the smell of pungent incense. He'd been a tousled-headed beanpole. Pale, blue eyes... Bit of a dandy... Never had a chance to fill out, put some meat on his bones. His hand is clutched as though he had been holding something. A weapon of some sort, a flower: make love, not war. Another lost hippie soul that the media idolizes every day as captured on the magical streets of Haight-Ashbury? Definitely not

Major warning bells went off in my head when the Big Boss himself, Mr. William Hancock, called me up to assign me to this investigation. No one in my department, not even my new boss, Mr. Meade, had ever chatted with or seen the Big Boss. And out of the blue, Mr. Hancock, the Big Boss, calls and asks for me by name. I've never met the man...

And Mr. Hancock is on a first name basis with the policyholders, Randolph and Edwina White.

I'm willing to believe these policyholders are clean as a whistle. They only have about ten million reasons to see their son, Bob White, dead. They took out a policy on him less than two years ago and will receive double indemnity if their claim is honored.

The reason stated for the five million dollars in protection money is a trust fund that Granny set up for Bob White, the heir apparent, just before she died some years ago. The provisions in Granny's will made Bob White the family golden goose . He controlled the sizable family purse strings. Think that rubbed his well-heeled, pampered parents the wrong way - Bob White holding the purse strings? Granny must not have trusted Mommy and Daddy with the family jewels.

Okay, so Life Beneficial wants to make certain the claim is clean, meets the terms of the agreement. Which is that Bob White was not killed by the claimants or agents of the claimants, that his death was not due to natural causes, that his death was not a suicide, that his death was not drug induced, that his death was, in fact, due to suspicious circumstances, in this case murder. Furthermore, if the cause is murder, that the suspect or suspects have been arrested and/or put on trial for that murder. You see, Life Beneficial is tight-fisted, not eager to fork out big bucks to pay off a claim of this magnitude without making claimants jump through extremely awkward hoops, lots of them. At least that is what the Life Beneficial rule book dictates. I've got a feeling the hoops in this case will be strictly formalities if the big boss, Mr. Hancock, has anything to say about it, based on what Hancock told me – 'follow the rules, fill out the forms, due diligence, touch the necessary bases, wrap it up in a bow, pass on the findings to Mr. Meade, your immediate superior so that he can pass it on to,' you got it, Mr. Hancock 'looking forward to it, in a timely and efficient manner.'

I have to admit that it's not completely clear to me how I'm supposed to go about "investigating" this claim. I'm new to this game and I haven't gotten what I consider to be complete instructions on the process so I'm a little nervous here, lost, awkward.

None of this is Bob White's concern. He's stretched out on the stage floor dolled up like a cowboy matinee idol — leather jacket with lots of fringe, tall black boots, mustache and goatee Buffalo Bill style, bolo tie in place of a bandana around his neck.

"Don't mind if I do some poking around, do you Coop? Just looking to close the books on this one, you understand."

"You'll keep us informed?" Coop replies with a wry smile sneaking into the corners of his mouth.

"Wouldn't have it any other way..."

I don't mind Coop making this request. Solid guy... I like him right off. Hope the feeling's mutual.

It has already been made abundantly clear that I not disturb the crime scene. That's okay by me. My job, as I see it, is to get information which will help me to close out my insurance claim, not find the person who murdered Bob White. Nonetheless, I will need to get involved with the criminal investigation to do my job. At least that is what I think I should do. So I ask a few questions, looking for background.

Turns out the Straight Theater had been a neighborhood movie theater back in the day but it closed down ages ago and nothing took its place until a fellow named Luther Green leased it about six months ago. As far as anyone knows, the event staged last night – during which half naked people stomped around while tripping on bad acid as an ill-prepared rock band nobody caught the name of played to a near empty house – was the one and only use that has been made of the space since Green leased it. At this event, magic incantations were uplifted to old Satan himself by a fellow named Ronald "Rotten" Outrage, the impresario of the event. The cops have never heard of him but I have. He's an underground filmmaker with a reputation for the bizarre and a cult following on the college film circuit, particularly in the Northeast. The Great Northwest Phantasmagoria provided visual interpretation for this listless devil dance. Great...

The grandson of Mr. Vitolinich, the boy I rescued, my secret cousin, Tony Vitolinich, is a member of this wayward band of visual interpreters, light show artists all.

Coop gives me his blessing to question Green, Outrage and Tony. Just background stuff, leave the criminal investigation to the cops, they remind me. No problem. Keep in touch, they remind me. Right on.

Outside through the front door rather than the back, the sun is trying to glare through the fog. It's pretty chilly though. Lots of lost souls mill about on the street — teenage runaways, meth heads, heroin dealers, innocent eyed fledgling hippies. A dog humps a parking meter near two chopped Harley hogs. Hells Angels lounge nearby. Guy drifts past me mumbling, "Hash, grass, acid." Doesn't bother to stop...

Street vendors lay their wares out on the filthy sidewalk. Barefooted strangers, filthy-footed, pass them by. A bedraggled hippie plays a guitar on a street corner. The proverbial tour bus passes by, guide murmuring to bug-eyed tourists inside.

Pass a head shop filled with drug paraphernalia and "far out" doodads — lava lamp in the window, DayGlo posters of Jimi Hendrix and Janice Joplin. No sales people present. No customers either. The front door is wide open.

Coffee house next to it is filled with lots of different kinds of tea and cookies. Great way to satisfy that horrendous sweet tooth that develops when you're high... They have plenty of business. Looks warm and cozy inside... The Electric Prunes' song "I Had Too Much to Dream (Last Night)" is playing.

Can a grandiose dream degenerate into this sordid triviality so quickly? Is that the fate of all utopian visions?

Why am I here?

Why did I leave Richmond?

"Charlie...Hey, Charlie..."

That's my name — to my friends. I turn around figuring I'm not the 'Charlie' being hailed, but what the heck.

"Tim."

It's Tim Montgomery. We go way back. I'm not surprised to see him. He has a way of showing up in my life at odd times. I really looked up to him when we were kids. With the passage of time, he's become something of an enigma to me, prescient at times, at other times a thorn in my side.

"Charlie. How the hell are you?"

Tim grips my hand, just as if we are greeting each other on the patio of the Country Club of Virginia, not in the middle of this congested Haight Street intersection. He hasn't changed a bit – same dark hair and mustache kept neatly trimmed, same pale skin and five o'clock shadow (he had to start shaving when he was fourteen), same tall and lean look. And he has on the same clothes – a tweed sport jacket, tan slacks, blue work shirt and heavy wool sweater. We're a pair. I'm still wearing the club tie and blue blazer I wore at the university and then to work at The Office.

"What brings you to this happening place?" he asks looking me up and down with mild amusement.

"Looking for a cosmic connection, a synaptic flash in my evolution..."

"Still very much the tortured philosopher, I see. But Herman Hesse beside the point here...Old hat. Hey, did you know that Dangerfield is in town? I was just on my way to see him at the Oracle office. He works there as a graphic designer. Really heavy into meth these days...You wanna tag along?"

"Well. .."

Marijuana wafts through the air. The Beatles reappear on a passing transistor radio as a singing postcard that reminds me "Love Is All You Need" and ever present peace signs signal that we should all "make love, not war." What what has brought the masses to this intersection in revolt against authority, the war, parents – to do a tribal stomp as Janis Joplin torch singer wails "Piece of My Heart."

People pass by us, around us and through us as if we were shadows living in a parallel universe. A streetcar rumbles and rattles towards us. Stopped, we are identified as – not part of the scene - yet here we are. Am I like the rest of them – an innocent making a first tentative step forward in the quest to realize the Ultimate Experience that will devolve into a flirtation with rebellion followed by a relapse into staid conformity and obedience? Or is my quest sincere, authentic?

"Talked to Isobel lately?"

Naturally Tim would ask me that.

"Ah, no, not really..."

"Well hell," he throws his arm around my shoulder. "Let's see what kind of trouble we can get into. Meanwhile, we'll catch up."

I hand Tim my card and mutter, "Can't right now. Got some things I need to do."

Tim looks at the card then back at me. I jerk it away and pull out my pen so I can write on the back of it.

"This is my home address. Call and leave a message at my service. We'll catch up with each other later."

"Right..." Tim answers.

There is an awkward pause. Neither of us takes our leave just yet.

"Say, if you haven't got any other plans, you could crash at my pad tonight. Give us a chance to shoot the shit."

"Won't put you out too much, will it?"

"Call... Leave a message. We'll get together tonight, later."

CHAPTER TWO

Powhite Creek
Chesterfield County, Virginia
Very early spring 1951

I'm headed for the creek, one border of the ten-acre tract on which sits my mother's ancestral home in Chesterfield County. Her heritage - Indian blood mixed with solid English stock. A scrubby five-acre forest of second growth trees leads into a floodplain area at the creek. This is, in my mind, my personal sacred ground, the place where I am freed from all contacts with the outside world, the place where flights of fancy become reality, the place where my own private religion is practiced, the place where my Indian blood calls out to spirits known and unknown.

The creek is the most sacred place within this holy area. I walk out onto a spit of sand that juts into a bend in the rambling creek, now flush with run-off water from winter snow. The creek sings with pleasure and chuckles over the rocks in shallow areas. Deep spots are easily identified by the seemingly dead calm surface. The whole of the creek's essence is alive and pulsating amidst still barren tree branches.

I look upstream, then downstream. The sky is gray, dull and muted. The air is crisp and fresh, no longer frigid. I am alert, alive, totally absorbed by the moment.

Out of the corner of my eye, I see a movement as I am turning to leave the spit of sand. It comes from the surface of the water near one of the deep pools. I look closer. At first, I can see nothing. Then I see them – water bugs with long, delicate legs sitting on top of the water. I kneel down and bring my face level with the water's surface in order to see these amazing creatures from a better perspective. The God of Nature, the God of All, manifested these water bugs in the here and now, I think. They are immobile on the surface of the water. Suddenly, they walk rapidly across the creek's surface as if it were solid earth. Startled, I jerk back. They stop only to glide with the flowing current. Then they move again. I am hypnotized, frozen to the spot for an indeterminate period of time.

Thank you Lord, I mumble to myself, for allowing me to witness this wonder of Nature.

I have merged my Nature God and the God of All with the one extolled in church.

Reverently, I retreat and walk along the banks of the creek. The path I take is one I have taken many times before. It is lined with moss, a velvety carpet that enhances the impression of holy ground in my mind. I sit down beside the soft moss, leaning against a sturdy tree that seems to cup my body. I am relaxed, swimming in a marvelous state of near suspended animation. I neither think nor marvel. I am.

With wonder, I notice that the moss nearest to hand has stalks. Bell-shaped flowers crown the stalks. I inspect these appendages, antennae for dispersal of spores, up close. I thank the Lord once again.

Within and beginning to manifest itself without, I hear a voice on the edges of my consciousness. I know it is the approaching sound of the Lord. I raise my head slowly towards an opening in the trees between which can be viewed unobstructed the leaden sky. The voice becomes more distinct and my entire being begins to tremble. I am shaking with fear and apprehension. Descending precipitously into this incomprehensible and shattering visionary moment, my consciousness, my attention is made aware of -

A girl standing on the top of the bluff that rises abruptly on the other side of the creek…

She has on a tan fringed leather jacket and her dark hair is braided Indian style. Her pale skin and delicate features send shock waves through my mind. In what way if at all is this maiden linked to my secret world and the gods that rule over it? Is she a messenger sent by my Indian ancestors, ancestors never talked about at family gatherings but always on the edges of my consciousness? What-why-how does her appearance at this time and place mean? I am without words, without the ability to initiate thought. I only know that this Indian maiden is the most enticing creature I have ever seen.

She does not see me, is gazing off toward an horizon I can't see from my position in this floodplain encircled by still barren trees. She has a faraway look in her eyes. What is she thinking? What is she feeling? Is she in a vision state as was I? I, rooted to the spot, do not want to attract attention to myself. But, in a flash, she, as I beheld her, is deeply etched into my mind. She steps back from her survey of the landscape and disappears I know not where.

The maiden, I will discover much later, is Isobel Cunningham.

Note pinned to the front door of Luther Green's impressive Victorian house reads - 'Be there or be square - At the Park.'

Great... Golden Gate Park is only one of the largest city parks in the good old U S of A. Fortunately, finding the location of Mr. Green and his cohorts is a piece of cake. There's some sort of open-air concert in progress. Possibly one of the Be-ins I've heard so much about? At any rate a public party where folks get together and "let it all hang out."

It's a hike from where I have to park my car. I put on an old hunting jacket I keep in my trunk and a floppy hat. I'm beginning to feel self-conscious about my coat-and-tie and it's brisk in the city. Sun is no longer peeking through the haze. Thick fog is rolling in overhead bringing much cooler, moist air in its wake. Looks like it might rain. I'm dead wrong to think something as mundane as the weather could put a damper on the festivities.

An elevated stage, constructed from risers, has been placed in an open meadow that I find out is called Pony Pasture. I'm impressed with the size of the crowd. They fill up the pasture and a good part of the surrounding woods. On-the-move participants weave through the crowd, using the irregular openings created by people clumped together as a path. The audience smokes weed, drops acid, meditates, chants, laughs, sings, talks, whirls, dances, frolics – and are generally too-zonked-to-move. The collected crowd is 'making the scene, where it's happenin', man.' Goofing on others gawking at them. Far out...Too much...Groovy... Out of sight...

No one seems to be in charge. No organizers shepherd groups on and off the stage or try to make money on a concession stand. In fact, there is no concession stand. I even wonder if this is an authorized event until I see that there are park police stationed throughout the crowd. They look very uncomfortable, not certain what they should be doing. Arrest one person for smoking marijuana and you'll have to arrest the whole crowd, might end up with a riot on your hands. Best to go with the flow and keep a low profile... One cop, or is he a spectator in costume, has long hair and a beard.

Identifying Mr. Green takes time. I do so while a band called the Sons of Champlin play. Without meaning to, I find myself moving in time to the music as I mutter, "Luther Green. Luther Green. Luther Green" just like the drug dealer on Haight Street was doing only he was chanting "Hash, grass, acid." And I feel decidedly out of place, warm under the collar, until someone takes pity on me and points a finger in the direction of a group of folks gathered under a tree dressed in outlandish Victorian garb.

They're sitting on a large blanket onto which the contents of an old wooden picnic basket have been emptied out. Camp chairs, on which no one sits, complete the portrait of Victorian splendor. One dude sports a monocle that keeps popping out of his eye each time he laughs, Teddy Roosevelt gone berserk. A fetching young lady holds aloft a frilly silk parasol to protect herself and her broad brimmed hat from the elements. Are they mimicking Impressionist paintings they studied in museums for art appreciation classes in college?

"Luther Green?"

A natty young man wearing a bowler hat, pouring wine into glasses, ever the gallant host, and wearing a spiffy suit and tie and sparkling brown boots turns to me with a twinkle in his eyes. Did I meet him at a debutante party during the season or at the Club soda fountain slurping a vanilla coke while waiting for a triple-decker club sandwich?

"I already told the constabulary all I know about the sad demise of Mr. Bob White, my good man," he states with disconcerting alacrity.

Wonderful...I had hopes I'd seen the backside of his type when I arrived in wild and wacky San Francisco. But karma rules as do cosmic jokes, at least in my universe.

"Not a cop, just an insurance investigator, Mr. Green."

I hand him one of my cards. He looks down at it then back at me.

"You guys don't waste any time."

"Could we talk in private for a moment?"

Green springs to his feet in one agile movement. Flips his bowler hat down his arm and catches it in his hand, then tilts his head in my direction. His audience gives him a round of applause. Thanks for that, really.

We move to the other side of the tree. A girl in an Indian costume meditates there. Is she part of Green's group? Didn't pick up on the dress code if she is... One thing's for certain. She's a knock out. Has long, straight blonde hair, model's high cheekbones. No makeup. Penetrating eyes... Fresh, vibrant, voluptuous... I'm gobsmacked, rooted to the spot. While I'm feeling this thunderclap of charged sexual awareness light up my body, a smooth humming sound (Ohm) issues from her mouth.

"You know Bob White?" I ask Green to deflate my turbulent heart rate. Green laughs then smirks.

"Bobby? Who'd want to know him?"

Not going to bite on that one, Mr. Green. Not a chance. I wait him out.

"Only thing he loved was himself and the ever changing role he assigned himself in life. One day he's a great writer; the next he's an internationally renowned filmmaker. Day after that he's a rock star. Never had the time or inclination to try becoming something, you dig?" What is it I'm supposed to understand? "Just another lost soul on the scene... Took lots of uppers and downers... Wasn't really into consciousness expansion... You get where I'm coming from?" Not really. But he doesn't care or expect me to. He's on a roll. "Your typical loser, you understand. No disrespect for the dead intended, just a fact."

Some obit... Tough audience... Most of us learn better as we get older.

I say this from my ancient perspective of 26. I can't be trusted, you know, even though I'm not over thirty.

"You know anything about his family?"

"Should I?"

"He was worth a considerable amount of money, had a trust fund that pretty much made him independently wealthy. And, through our insurance company, he had a seven-figure double indemnity policy on his life."

"That so..."

Green is not impressed. Probably has his own trust fund and his own ideas about how to spend his money and his time. And Green, hip to being cool, obviously thinks White was uncool, the ultimate put down for people in this set. Green's long dark hair is stylishly clipped - just like the Beatles. He's the focus of a scene. Probably has a stable of creeps that toady to him.

"Life Beneficial will pay off this claim once we sign off on the cause of death, in this case, if we certify that the cause of death was murder and that none of the claimants were in any way involved."

"My, how blood thirsty. Were his relatives in great need, axe murderers, devotees of wicked deeds?"

"That's part of what I need to find out."

"Why talk to me?"

"His body was discovered on property that you lease, the Straight Theater, during an event you rented the space out for, some sort of saturnalia."

"Well, yes."

"So you neither know anything about Bob White nor have you heard anything about or had contact with his family or are familiar with any dealings that he was involved in that might have an impact on this claim?"

"My, how easily you do get touchy."

"Okay. What was this satanic party all about?"

"Bunch of psychos into some bad head trips: Black magic, Voodoo, Mumbo jumbo. Hey man, I'm thinking about becoming a wizard myself. Might be a real trip..."

Green's eyes twinkle in amusement. Did he take the booking because he thought the scene was camp? He certainly didn't do it to make money. Or did he? Did he think people would come in droves to listen to bad music and garbled chants?

"Not much of a turnout."

"I got paid — in front. Outrage didn't seem to mind. He had other irons in the fire."

"Like what?"

"Maybe he wanted to film it. He has a real cult following on the college circuit, you know. But, for sure, he considered it worth his while to splurge on the devil worship game, if you dig where I'm coming from."

"Okay, Outrage has plenty of bread to throw around." Hey, two can play at this hip lingo game. "And he likes to party. What else do you know about him?"

"East Coast... Heavy vibes... Flamboyant professor type... Practically run by his lover boy Bernie Toucan, the leader of the shitty band that played for the event, in case you didn't know."

So that's how the band got booked.

"Outrage know White?"

"His name never came up in my conversations with him."

"And you know nothing about his death or who might have had a hand in it?"

I know. I'm over the top. This is a question the cops should be asking him. But this guy presses my buttons, the wrong ones.

"Please."

"You know anybody tight with White? Mad at him? That talked to him at this whatever you call it last night?"

"He was hanging around that lightshow group. The Great Northwest Phantasmagoria, they call themselves. From Oregon, so I heard... Bobby told me he wanted to represent them. Said he could get them gigs. What a joke. Guy hardly has the sense to come in out of the rain. Figures he'd choose a bunch of losers like them. Said they were different. The next wave in lights... I saw him talking to the real skinny one with the long hair and the granny glasses, the one on the overheads in the group, at the break."

Tony. Tony Vitolinich. My secret cousin... Shit.

"Who hired this group?"

"Outrage..."

Green is losing interest. Fast.

"Hey, Green. Get your butt over here," someone shouts.

The Sons of Champlin finish their set amidst scattered applause. Great billowing clouds of marijuana mixed with incense rise from the crowd. Continued frolicking in the mud... Space cadets abound. Dervish dancers very much in evidence... Plenty of tie-dyed clothes, god's eyes and peace signs too.

"When you ask the question 'why' and the external world complicates existence, trust your inner voice."

It takes me a moment to realize the meditating beauty made this comment. She looks like she's high as a kite. Rocking back and forth on her lovely feet with her hands pressed together at her chest in a prayerful attitude, and what a chest it is...

How long has she been standing there? Did she eavesdrop on our conversation? Down, boy, down. This girl in costume probably wouldn't give me the time of day if I asked for it. Besides, I can't think of a clever response. Never have been quick on the uptake... Isobel has been for the moment completely obliterated from my brain.

Green laughs out loud. I laugh with him.

Is what she said a joke? Am I the joke? Looks like it. Realize I'm blushing. Sure sign that a woman has penetrated my tongue-tied defenses. My brain is warning me, watch out. She's trouble. I can't wait to get burned. Isobel, well, we're talking about apples and oranges here. Or are the two of them that different? They both introduced themselves to me in American Indian garb. They both are connected to spiritualism in my mind. Oh, how quickly secret and magical worlds crumble, childish fantasies are shed, long term romantic entanglements fade, when confronted with a wild and wacky San Francisco vixen.

"You got any more pro forma questions before you dole out the big bucks to the grieving parents?" asks Green, trying to tuck the girl in the Indian costume into the crook of his arm.

She wiggles free of his grasp and throws the hint of a smile in my direction. I bask in the potential of her encouragement. The flesh is weak — and eager. Green puts himself between us. Gives what is probably a characteristic smirk. Jerk. All right, I get it. I'm not with it — an outsider with East Coast vibes wearing a beat up hunting jacket that barely covers a coat-and-tie. I represent a stodgy, probably war mongering insurance company, must be in favor of might-makes-right military industrial complex operatives, in a word 'uncool,' i.e. dealt with and dismissed.

Allen Ginsberg begins reciting a mantra-like tone poem on stage. Some Hare Krishna cats whoop it up in front of him clanging bells, snapping hand cymbals and beating drums, singing up a storm. More dancing dervish demons... Ginsberg chants away.

"Hare...Muscle...Howling...Chant...Descending...Flower... Tumescence."

Something garbled along those lines floats in our direction. The PA system is off, must have belonged to the band. Distance does strange things to chants.

"You'll find the answer. But it'll cost you dear," offers the Indian-costumed one.

Lump in my throat. Or is that lump only in my pants? Hand her a card. It disappears somewhere inside her costume. Force myself not to figure out exactly where.

"In case you happen to know anything about Bob White. I'm working on an insurance claim due to his death."

She looks deeply into my eyes. I reluctantly turn back to Green.

"Mind if I ask your guests a few questions?"

"Mr. Carter here is trying to solve a murder mystery and he has some questions," Green announces to the group at large. Then he gives me a full-of-shit smile, nods. "Tell us all about it. We love detective stories, particularly ones with a twist at the end."

"Hoping you all might be able to help me out," I start, trying to ease into the conversation the way we Southern boys like to do. Stony faces confront me. I plow forward.

"Anyone here hang out with Bob White, meet his family, know anything about what he was up to?"

Someone snorts then giggles. A billow of sweet smelling smoke drifts my way. The rest of the picnickers burst out laughing.

"We thought that's what you were going to tell us about – the people with the motive, means and opportunity – the murderers. You're no fun," answers Green after everyone present has had a good long laugh. I'm a pleasant diversion during a lull in the festivities.

"Maybe some of you might like to contact me later," I'm not going to get anywhere with these creeps. "I hate to interrupt your day at the park."

Another billow of smoke... A young lady rips open her blouse and exposes her robust breasts. A loud hoot goes up. A pimply fellow mutters "right on." The girl closes her blouse then sticks out her tongue. Real schoolyard stuff... Green goes on.

"No problem at all, Mr. Carter. Love the cloak and dagger stuff. Just makes our day. Particularly when there are, as you have informed me, big bucks involved. Makes it so much more an authentic American tragedy, don't you think?"

A small American flag materializes out of nowhere. The owner waves it in front of my face.

"Why do you think Bob White's murder revolves around money?"

Group of Victorian dandies sing a cappella, "We're in the money. We're in the money." They throw their arms over each other's shoulders and sway in time to their song, then collapse on the blanket in a giggling fit. They're hilarious, really. A laugh riot...

"Doesn't it always end up being about money in this fair land of ours? The root of all evil I'm told," Green adds shaking his head and clicking his tongue.

There's more giggling from the crowd. Some 'Oohs' and 'Ahs....' Score another one for Mr. Green. Well done.

"We're talking about another human being here who was brutally murdered. That bring to mind anything that struck you as odd about Mr. White, the people he was hanging out with or the scene he was into?"

The picnic crowd snickers. I'm a running gag. Young man pulls down his pants and moons me. Hilarious, really...

"You'd be doing his parents a service," I add.

That's a corker, a real zinger. Howls, no gales, of laughter erupt. A young man rolls on the ground as his friend tickles him. He babbles, "Mommy, Mommy, Mommy..." It's a much more diverting act than Allen Ginsberg and the Hare Krishna devotees up on the stage.

"Guy probably stuck his nose in where it didn't belong. Got it chopped off for his trouble," offers one who does a disappearing nose trick that was old before the days of vaudeville.

He gets a mild laugh. A chorus jumps right in.

"Nothing but a weasel anyway..."

"A fucking loser... "

"Fill out the death certificate and move on."

"Live in the Now now..."

"The past is deader than dead."

"The future's a wet dream from heaven."

Oh, they are clever - a singular chorus of uninspired infantile cynicism. I hand out my card all around. They laugh - shoot me the bird on the sly. That's right, I'm a horse's ass. Thanks for pointing it out. Turn away. Take my leave.

Now I know what the people were thinking in those Impressionist paintings: nothing. They were all hedonistic jerks only interested in their own preoccupations.

Another band has taken the stage. Didn't notice because I thought roadies were trying, unsuccessfully, to tune the musicians' instruments. Surprise... What seemed like tuning becomes an improvised riff. From the looks of it, this number could last for quite some time. They're still working out on one chord. When they put two together, they'll really take off. Unstoppable... The whine of their guitars echoes throughout the glen... Somehow appropriate to the off-center mood of the crowd. They're called the Grateful Dead, I discover, and are a favorite of the crowd.

Did I ask the right questions to get the answers I need to adjudicate this claim? Is Luther Green an example of a typical interview subject in far out San Francisco? Why the hell did Mr. Hancock order me to handle this claim? Why ask why — because I am a seeker looking for the truth, because I am insecure and need reassurance, because I am anal-retentive and like to clean up messes, because cosmic jokes are my cross to bear and I'm a mystic in training, because I am an obedient and unquestioning boy pliable as ever to the wants of my elders, because I'm a schmo still learning how to walk through a cow pasture without getting anything unsightly on my shoes, because I am a puzzle solver looking for answers, the solutions, for the eternal questions and resolution of the insurance claim I have been assigned to handle?

CHAPTER THREE

A small but well-attended Episcopal Church
Chesterfield County, Virginia
1955

Our family drives out to the country every Sunday to attend services at the church my mother attended as a girl. We maintain a modest country home on land passed on to us from my mother's side of the family near the church. That suits me fine. It allows me to roam in my sacred woods afterward and it gets me away from people who make me uncomfortable, people living in the West End of Richmond, who are members of the Club, who send their children to private school and who, invariably, attend services at St. Andrew's Episcopal at the intersection of Grove and Three Chopt Road just a few blocks from the Club and a stone's throw from where we live.

On this particular Sunday, a meeting of the congregation is planned after the service to discuss plans for a new meeting hall put forth by the Building Committee on which my father serves as chairman. My mother, a past president of the Women of the Church, is particularly radiant today. The light from the modest stained glass window near the pew in which we always sit shines down, bathing us with celestial light. Kneeling in prayer, I have no difficulty connecting my nature God with the God of my parents. I offer a humble prayer and succeed in transporting myself to my private worship realm.

How long I remain transfixed I do not know. What I do know is that my trance is jolted when I see, walking in the line headed towards the altar to receive communion, the same girl I saw at my sacred creek two years earlier.

Just as before, the girl is unaware of me. I tell myself - how could she not somehow be aware of my presence even if it's on an astral plain? We are star crossed, destined to meet.

After the service, when the meeting begins, I wander outside. It's a glorious fall day and I, as I have done many times before, take a turn in the small cemetery at the side of the church, reading headstones and enjoying the delightful weather.

"Hi, Charlie..."

It's Tim. His parents are Club members and he attends St. Christopher's. Even though he fits in there, he remains perfectly willing to hang out with me – the loner, the weirdo, the outsider. That's great as far as I'm concerned. He's a cool guy, a great athlete, approachable yet somehow set apart. He's almost a year older than I am. I look up to him, put great credence in what he says and thinks.

"Hi, Tim..."

Tim matches his steps to mine and we inspect a headstone together.

"Let's topple it," Tim suddenly says.

"Why? I like it like it is."

"I don't know. Something to do... Don't you ever feel like doing something just for the heck of it?"

"Rebel without a Cause" might be a sensation in major metropolitan areas this year and J.D. Salinger's "The Catcher in the Rye" might be required reading in places where literary trends make headlines, but here in the Richmond I am familiar with their influence is non-existent. I am reading books by people like Alexandre Dumas and Robert Louis Stevenson, a series for school kids called Landmark Books, and I am heavy into Western movies and books, the product of my father's passion for Western movies. None of the heroes in those books or movies would want to topple a tombstone just for the heck of it. I kick a rock down the graveled pathway at the edge of the small cemetery and decide to change the subject.

"Hey, do you know a girl a few years younger than we are who was at the service today? She has dark hair and pale skin, big eyes and wore a blue dress and black patent leather shoes."

Tim puts a hand to his chin as if reflecting. Then a suppressed grin breaks out on his face.

"Sure. I know her. She's my cousin, Isobel. Well, not really a cousin, but our families are very close. We grew up next door to each other. Why?"

"Oh, no particular reason... Why haven't I seen her at church before?"

"Because she doesn't usually attend this church, dummy... What's the matter? Have you got a crush on her or something?"

"Heck no," I answer much too vehemently.

"You've got a crush on her. I can tell. I'd introduce you but you might beat my time."

"Is she your girlfriend? Honest? Or are you just funning me?" Tim gives me a sly smile. "Come on now, you idiot. Don't kid around.
Okay?"

"Who's kidding?" he responds.

From behind us, Isobel appears as if by magic. Tim starts to clown around and dazzles us both with his sharp wit. Who knows what he says. Who can remember? It's childish chatter, seemingly forgotten the minute it's spoken but registered in some hidden nook of consciousness that influences people the rest of their lives.

Thomas Jefferson High School
Richmond, Virginia
Fall 1957

"Suck it up, Vitolinich, and stuff him!" shouts our football coach.

The coach has a beer belly nurtured by years of belching forth mighty Rebel yells after downing multiple Bud six packs with army buddies, Civil War re-enactors, and other Troglodyte types.

"Hup," grunts the coach.

Tony lunges toward a starting offensive lineman who outweighs him by fifty pounds and is eight inches taller than he is. The lineman swats him away.

"Holy Christmas, Vitolinich. What are you, some kind of pansy? Can't you get more into it than that?" The coach speaks loud enough for all those within range to hear and probably loud enough for even some well beyond the field on which we practice. "Pitiful," he comments to no one in particular and looks back at Tony. "Leverage... It's all about leverage, Vitolinich. What's the matter, momma's boy, afraid you might get hurt?" Tony makes no comment, does not make eye contact with the coach or the rest of the squad.

"Let's try it again. Hup..."

Tony surprises the lineman with a ferocious hit that catches him in his flabby gut and upends him. He hits the ground with a thud, barely missing landing on Tony.

"That's it, Vitolinich. That's the ticket. Now you're getting it."

Tony glares at the coach in response to his praise – hatred and something much deeper animates his being.

"And you, Slade, get your lard ass off the ground," the coach continues.

Everyone laughs. Well, they smile to themselves.

I noticed Tony right away on that first day of practice but didn't speak to him. He's a sophomore; I'm a senior. What do we really have in common, other than a bizarre meeting under unusual circumstances at the beach? We didn't pal around after that day at the beach. The turbulent changes of puberty have half obscured, half obliterated from my mind what my father told me about Tony's grandfather – that he was my grandfather too.

But, after practice, when I step out of the locker room, I hear the disturbed muttering of a group of guys. A fight's in progress. Although I usually avoid messy moments like these, no good can come of them in my opinion, I am drawn to this confrontation.

Garry Slade, the lineman, upset that he has been made a laughing stock in practice by this nonentity, this puny example of real manhood, has jumped Tony and is now sitting on top of him holding both of his hands in one great paw and smacking him with the other paw.

"Cry baby. Cry baby," he taunts, as the rest of the group cheer Slade on uncomfortably. Who wants to be next in line for Slades's ire? He's not only All City but on the student council. Next year he'll get a scholarship to the college of his choice, probably some well-respected institution like VMI. And then he'll go into his father's contracting firm, one of the largest in the region. Who needs that kind of grief?

I rush Slade, catching him off guard, and jar him loose from Tony.

"What the..." snorts the lineman, not yet comprehending what has just taken place.

Has this ever happened to him before? Someone has opposed him and in so doing is pointing out that he's a bully. The assembled guys giggle nervously. Slade comes to life fast.

"You little..."

He rears back to strike. Before he lands the blow, I butt him in his soft spot, the stomach, with my head as hard as I can. "Umph," he responds as he grabs his stricken gut and doubles up. From the nearby parking lot comes a shout.

"Hey, what's going on there? You boys break it up."

It's the coach.

Slade, Tony and I get demerits and have to report to detention, study hall after school, for a week. That causes us to miss football practice, no big deal for Tony and me but deadly serious for Slade. Tony and I are on Slade's shit list and we are persona non grata to all the cool kids and many of the teachers in school from then on. I don't mind. I've already nominated myself part of another club – the outsiders, the loners, those so dismissed they are invisible, beyond ignored.

Tony never says a word as he dusts himself off. He just looks at me and nods in silent thanks. We're cousins, I remember thinking at that moment, even if Tony isn't aware of it. From that day forward I made it a point to get to know Tony better.

————————

Ronald Outrage lives in the "Russian Embassy" at the corner of Scott and Fulton. Coop, who gave me that info, had no idea why the house was called the Russian Embassy. All he knew was that a hippie commune once occupied the house. It's across from Alamo Square Park. The park is a squalid collection of hard-packed dirt, languid trees, a rusting swing and sliding board set, green benches bolted fast in concrete blocks. Dog poop everywhere. Garish, multicolored paint jobs have been transforming a smattering of the many Victorian houses that surround the park.

The Russian Embassy jumps out and grabs your attention. It's a cold, forbidding, massive Victorian perched on a lot at the crest of a hill. A drooping, probably dying, palm tree hangs menacingly over the steep front steps; an elderly Ponderosa pine in the backyard obscures a tower room that commands a three hundred and sixty degree view of the city. Is that peeling gray paint on the house, or is it mildew and mold? A gracious curiosity has, over the years, become a hideous monstrosity.

Up the steep concrete steps to the oversized front door I go. I lift and drop the large, shiny-new brass knocker several times. Hollow echoes boom inside the house. Notice a note pinned to the doorframe. Have to look very close to read the tiny, cramped scrawl.

"Rotten Outrage is home to no one — alive to no one. Stricken... Taken... Entombed... Your knock will not be answered. Go away — to the eternal dance in Hell. Amen."

What happened to Satan? Got a cold, a nosebleed? Decide to try the back entrance. Big mistake... Confronted by a yard full of weeds in full growth ringed by a rusting fence... Yard littered with broken beer bottles, rocks, bricks, nails, old tires. Has a smell that's more than just urinal. Chemical, covered in a layer of light mist. Not enough to cleanse this abomination. The rickety, almost falling down, back steps lead to a wooden porch in dangerous disrepair. Barely escape several loose and rotting boards. Nothing moves but the wind.

Back door is open. Walk cautiously into a kitchen. It's bathed in half-light from the hall. Air so thick I can almost see the molecules swarming. Oppression hangs heavy. The stove is in use. Something vile bubbles in a massive pot on its ancient surface - warlock brew? I'm sweating for no good reason. Place gives me the creeps.

"If you're here on Office business, in future, use the front door and the phone just like the rest of us."

I whirl around. A man dressed in a ratty kimono. Gold and black... Half open. He's naked underneath. Very hairy...broad chest...about five-seven...hundred and sixty...brown on what was once all brown. In good shape for a man who could be nearing sixty... Has a striking face. Must have been a real pretty boy when he was young...

"Ah, no one answered the front door."

"If you're not with The Office, who are you and what do you want?"

The man seems to float across the floor. Maybe it's because he's not wearing any shoes. Maybe it's because this house imposes a certain mind set. Maybe it's created by the fetid odor from the stove that matches the smell on his robe. Pull out one of my business cards. Hand it to him. He takes it without looking at it.

"Office... What ah... Ah, no. That is, I'm C.F. Carter, insurance investigator... with Life Beneficial...working on a claim on the life of Bob White...looking for Ronald Outrage. Understand he lives here."

A reaction rushes across the man's face. Is it anger, horror, pain or all three? Then a stony-faced mask that warns off trespassers replaces it.

"So you're working for The Office and your cover story is that you are settling a life insurance claim on Bob White — and your name is C.F. Carter... Is that it? You got any relatives that used to work for The Office? I don't appreciate sick jokes. Go away."

"All I want to do is talk with Ronald Outrage. He does live here?"

"And if he does live here, what information do you want from him?"

Irrational thoughts fly through my head. Is he about to turn into a vampire? Is he the resident Office vampire? Wouldn't put it past The Office... Will he bite me on the neck, turning me into one of the living dead, a toady now employed carrying out this man's Office operations? This guy not only gives me the willies; he never bothered to ask what kind of accident Bob White had last night.

"Just the usual... Questions about how well Mr. Outrage knew Mr. White. Whether he saw him last night... Anything he could tell me that might help me make a determination in this case."

The man looks speculatively into the cast iron pot on the stove. A paddle-like spoon sticks out of it. He dips in a finger and pulls it out to taste the vile liquid. I cringe mentally, realizing that's just what this man wants me to do.

"Mr. Outrage has left town and will not be returning," the man finally answers.

"Robert Toucan. He around..."

"Also gone...Permanently... Back to the slime pit from which he emerged."

"Ah..."

"Los Angeles."

"Your name is?"

"A friend... Of long standing..."

"Well, friend, anything you can tell me about Bob White? Anything at all..."

"He was, if you really want to know, a lovely but troubled child who got more than he deserved but never received what he most earnestly sought and needed."

"Something that could have gotten him murdered?"

"That would be speculation on my part."

"Well, his body was discovered on the stage of the Straight Theater this morning. Mr. Outrage rented the Theater to stage some sort of ceremony last night. Were you there?"

"I was involved in the ceremony."

"Druid..."

"Hardly... You know anything about satanic ceremonies, Mr. Carter?"

"The band playing, was that the satanic part? Or was..."

"You laugh...but you also tremble before the throne."

"You see Mr. White there? Was he acting strange? See anyone talking to him?"

"He...his mouth moved but no words came out."

"He know anyone who attended the ceremony..."

"He knew his loved ones."

"Sir..."

"The lightshow people... He spoke with one lightshow member, Tony Vitolinich."

"Tony Vitolinich?"

The man's eyes, filled with unspeakable rage, drill into me. Then they settle back once again into the mask, the mask this man presents to the world.

"Have you ever lost a loved one, Mr. Carter?"

"Ah, no... That is, yes. I mean, I...You get a message to Mr. Outrage?"

Something - a door - bangs open on an upper floor. A floorboard squeaks. A toilet flushes...Seems to snap the man in the kimono out of his spooky trance. Until I know much more about what's going on here, I need to beat a hasty retreat, but first for a delaying action...

"Yes sir. That's right sir... And well, I don't want to alarm or offend you but you might want to mention to him that playing voodoo games in a seedy old house, you know like mixing up nasty smelling brews and stuff, might make the authorities suspicious, might make them think he's implicated in Bob White's murder in some way. Detective Cooper of the SFPD and most of the guys at this Office you keep mentioning might possibly fall into that category. Just a thought, you know."

I push past the startled man. He follows me towards the front door down a central hallway. Rooms off it look empty. Man in the kimono, I assume to be Outrage, lets his robe come undone.

"Button up. Please."

"Insults do not become someone who has just broken into a house. I could call the police, you know."

"I should get a medal for daring to deal with your backyard. And your backdoor was open. And, not to put too fine a point on it but, Southern hospitality just seems to be a lost art for some people."

Outrage barks a hostile and tortured laugh.

"Save the attitude for the girls you try to impress at those well-heeled Southern country clubs and debutante parties you attend," he answers, slamming the door in my face.

CHAPTER FOUR

I, CHARLIE FOXHAWK CARTER, CONTINUE

San Francisco Bay Area
Early summer 1968

I call from Sacramento during my drive across country and Tony suggests we eat at a Chinese restaurant, surprisingly located at the edge of Japantown. The place has enclosed wooden booths with draw curtains at the entrance to the booth if additional privacy is desired. We so desire. After ordering — I know nothing about Chinese food so I let Tony do the honors — the curtains are closed and a joint is lit.

"Whoa. Slow down there," I comment, raising my hands palm outward as Tony takes a deep tug on the joint.

I just want him to put the damn thing out. No such luck. He holds in the smoke and passes the joint to me. All the lightshow guys and Tony's girlfriend, Jane, watch. One of them even makes a motion for me to get on with it. I fold. After all, I'm no virgin. I've taken plenty of 'mother's little helpers' in college to get me through exam week and the writing of term papers. And I've smoked a few marijuana cigarettes stuffed with admittedly low-grade Mexican weed. I have even smoked hash from a cool brass pipe - once...But this...

In no time we are smashed out of our gourds.

"Acapulco gold," announces Harry passing the joint back to me smoke leaking from the edges of his mouth.

I nod knowingly, even though I have no idea what he's talking about. Jane and the rest of the lightshow folks nod solemnly acknowledging Harry's sage comment. The first few dishes of our order are discreetly shoved in through the closed curtain as our heads bob up and down in unison.

"Try the sauce, Charlie," Dumas suggests sliding the spice jar in my direction after adding some of the sauce to his dish.

"Yeah," agree both Jane and the rest of Tony's lightshow buddies. They've already added sauce to their dishes.

What the heck? 'When in Rome,' as they say... They all watch as I fumble with my chopsticks but manage to take a bite of food after putting some sauce on my order.

"This is great," I enthusiastically state, picking up my plate to make it easier to shovel more food from my plate into my mouth.

I'm new at this chopsticks thing and it seems easiest in my present state to just use the wooden sticks as shovels instead of tweezers. I mean, picking up individual pieces of rice with these things... No way. Grinning faces meet my gaze as I survey the folks in the enclosed booth with me. Gosh, this is fun, an authentic San Francisco experience. Without warning, my mouth, my throat,

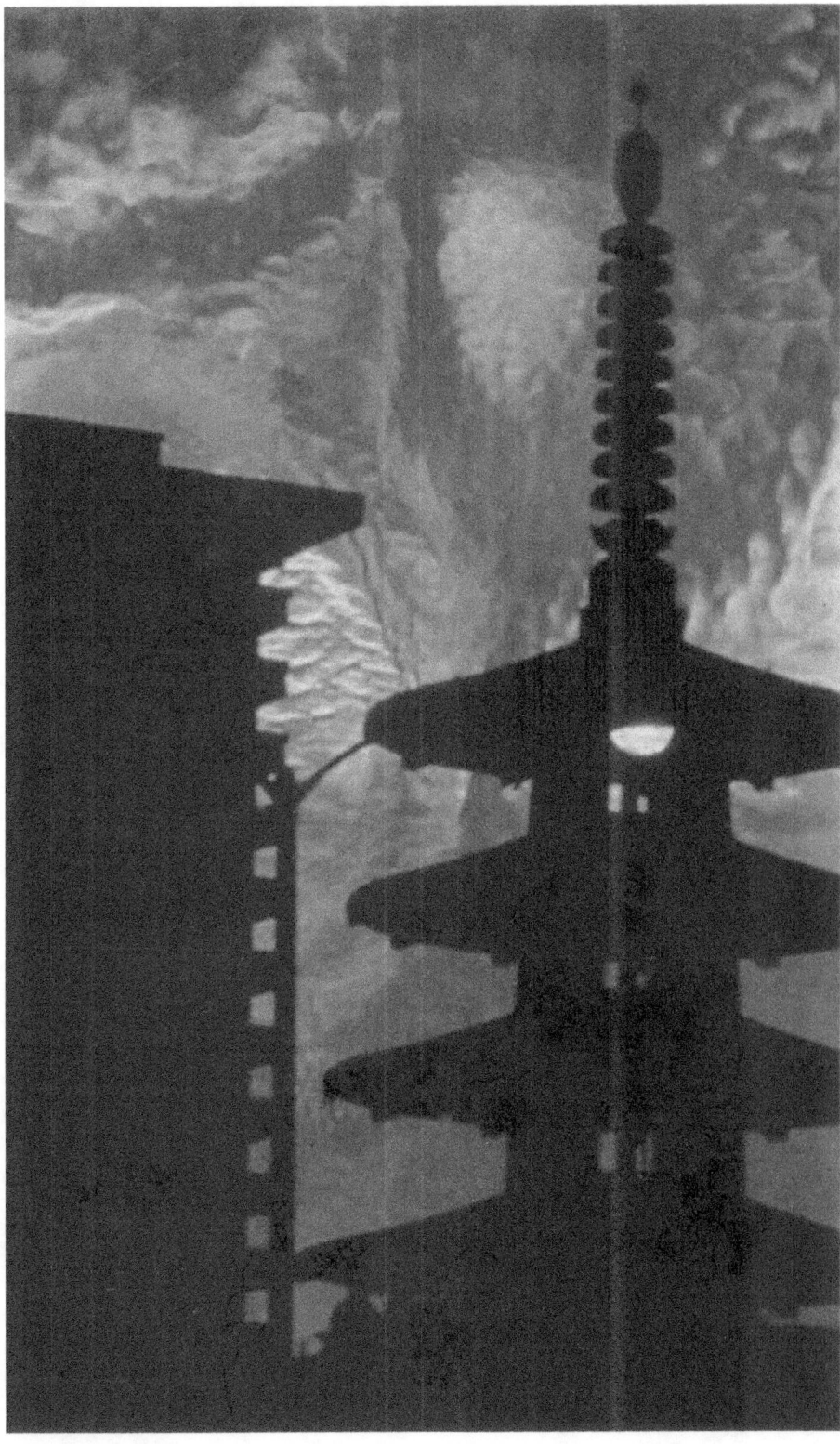

my stomach, my body are on fire. Sweat begins pouring down my face. I slam down my plate so I can take a gigantic gulp of the Chinese rice beer I ordered.

"Hot," I manage to squeak out, embarrassed, trying to find my voice.

Everyone laughs. The initiation is over. They've probably pulled this stunt on other newcomers before me. I'm willing to be initiated. This is one heck of a restaurant. And the pot – wow…What is it called again? As the meal progresses, they regale me with a running narrative of lightshow adventures past and present.

"I met these guys, with the exception of Harry, through David. He's the married one of our bunch," comments Tony.

"His wife and kid live with us in our group house," adds Dumas before Tony continues.

"One thing led to another," Tony carries on.

"We played the Armory in Portland and in Eugene we had our regular gig at Maxie's. Not bad for just getting started," Dumas jumps in to say.

"Should have stayed in Eugene where we belong but we got bit by the bug, took the plunge and headed down to San Fran," Bracken replies.

Dumas and Bracken laugh. They're like peas in a pod. They have the same first name, Jim. Their hair is shorter than most guys living in San Fran these days. They wear battered cowboy boots and tan work shirts. Bracken even sports a corduroy sport coat. They both wear old fashioned looking granny glasses.

"We're lucky to be afloat after the start we got," laughs Tony uncomfortably.

"John Paul got us down here for a three-day gig at the Longshoremen's Hall."

"Never got us another gig…"

"We moved into a group house in the Mission without another gig lined up."

"On Army Street…"

"Some neighborhood…"

"Making the rent was a real hassle…"

"Lived on brown rice and stolen chocolate chip cookies…"

"Hey, we got a regular gig with Kitty."

"She owns the New Orleans House over in Berkeley. She's also our landlady now, a real lifesaver – no rent," comments Rodney, a Brit who attached himself to the group no one seems to know how.

"We've gotten fill-in work at the Avalon and the Fillmore," Harry jumps in to say.

Harry's from New York and has plenty of street smarts. He wears thick prescription glasses and has long, curly red hair that is starting even at his young age to recede. A slight paunch likely to increase with age is easily ignored when confronted by his penetrating eyes and his overall appearance of strength and intelligence. Dumas and Bracken don't think much of him. The feeling's mutual.

"And we've done lights for debutante parties, fashion shows, total environments and, of course, rock concerts," Tony proudly adds.

"If I never have to attend another rock concert, that'd be fine by me," Bracken kicks in.

"Hear, hear..." in chorus from the table at large.

"The Fillmore gig looked like it would be a real high water mark," Harry throws in to get them back on track.

The native Oregonians in the group are getting a little weary of living on the edge in the San Francisco Bay Area. They liked the rhythm of the great Northwest where a small group of loyal followers considered them to be the coolest of the cool. In San Francisco, they're nobodies and their social life is a big fat zero.

"That's right, the Fillmore gig should have been a high water mark," Bracken repeats with an edge.

"Until no less than Jimi Hendrix put us in our place," Tony puts in.

"How did that happen?" I ask, still in a marijuana fog and suffering from the hot chili sauce.

"Well, you see, our lightshow gear isn't exactly powerful enough to light a space as large as the Fillmore," Harry starts.

"Yeah, that's right. So get this. At one point just after 'The Experience' had finished a tune, Jimi Hendrix was doing some amazing shit, by the way, and we were going crazy with our lights trying to match his licks..."

"And we were really getting off, you know, hey, we're rocking with Jimi Hendrix. Holy shit..."

"And Hendrix talks with the guys in his group in between songs then steps up to the mike."

"Everybody wanted to hear what he had to say..."

"Probably something cool, special..."

"Something he would only say to the audience at this gig..."

"Maybe he'd say something about us, the lightshow artists transforming the music of Hendrix and the Experience into far out images..."

"And what does he say?"

"Hendrix says right into the mike, 'Could someone up there operating the lights give us a little more illumination on the stage? We're having trouble seeing.'

"We thought we'd pulled it off, thought maybe nobody had noticed...fat chance."

"Man, we wanted to be anywhere but where we were right then."

"Well, Dumas throws everything off of one overhead and turns it onto the stage. Just a big, ugly blast of white light... Christ, it was horrible."

"What else could he do? Our projectors were so weak the audience could hardly make out our images and the musicians couldn't see what they

were doing."

"The miserable house lights were out competing us."

"Anyway, Hendrix thanked us and they roared into the next song."

"We did some neat stuff on the wall to the side of where his band was playing after that."

"If anyone saw it or cared..."

That calls for another shared joint and the ordering of more dishes from the kitchen. I have already offered to pay, which might have spurred them on to order more food. The group members don't look like they've been eating too regularly. By now I'm getting the hang of the hot sauce and I liberally add it to each offering.

"Tell him about the Reno gig with Blue Cheer," Bracken requests of Dumas.

Dumas pushes his glasses up with his thumb. Then he clears his nose with a large red handkerchief that he pulls from his rear pocket before fulfilling the request.

"Well, you see, we drove up in the lightshow van with all our gear on our own nickel and worked our hearts out."

"Yeah, we had to hang Mylar up behind the band stand. It took hours."

"Mylar is very reflective. It brightens our images," Tony explains.

"Right... And then we had to deal with the union electricians for the building. Bunch of cretins..."

"And we didn't even have time to eat before the show began."

"But that wasn't the clincher."

"Oh?"

"Yeah... The gig ended and we were told that we'd be paid back in San Francisco."

"We'd already booked a motel."

"Which we tried to cancel..."

"But we had to pay a cancellation fee."

"So we drove back to SF because we didn't have enough money to pay for rooms without being paid for the gig."

"Turns out we're not the only one in town that had been burned by him."

"The Jefferson Airplane had him as their manager and they still haven't gotten a cent of royalties because of him."

"Thank goodness for Kitty."

"Hear. Hear."

Dumas was an art major for a time at the University of Oregon and still thinks of himself as an artist. His conceit has rubbed off on the rest of the group. The group members are lightshow 'artists,' not hippies. They entertain the crowds and retreat to their studio to create. That studio, by the way, is in what had been the dining room of the group house they live in.

And so it goes until we are headed out to the lightshow van, the only vehicle large enough to ferry us all at one time. And I begin to feel a strange tingling feeling. Before I know it I go down in dazed slow motion, chipping my tooth against the curb as I do so. I'm only out for a few seconds but it seems like an eternity, an indeterminate length of time in the void beyond human awareness, a true out-of-body experience, another in a long list of weird states that come upon me from time-to-time.

"You all right," Tony asks as he and Jane help me to the van.

"Yeah... Just kind of zoned out right now..."

In point of fact, I'm relaxed and dreamy, in a faraway place that has no boundaries, no beginning or end, no time or place. No 'I,' just eternal non-existence. Buddha-like, I listen to the car fan shooting out its heat emitting rays as the van makes its way to the lightshow group house in Berkeley where I have parked my car. With a distant nod, I agree to stay the night and am helped up the stairs to Tony's room.

"All right, I admit that graduate school might not have been at the top of my list after finishing my undergraduate studies if there hadn't been a draft," Tony tells me much later on while Jane is down in the kitchen making tea. "But then again, it might have. I mean, getting an MFA in Creative Writing, teaching on the college level while writing the great American novel, has appeal. And some pretty cool guys have chosen that route. But, holy tomato, I wasn't interested in more English classes. I just wanted to write."

Jane comes back with tea. Tony picks up his guitar and asks, "Did you bring your guitar along?"

San Pablo Avenue in Berkeley
Just after sunset
October 1968

I park my Volvo S122 two-tone (gray over blue) sedan near a deserted taco stand with a flickering pale blue neon sign. It has outdoor seating at picnic tables illuminated by a single harsh streetlight. Off into the distance in both directions, similar streetlights cast pools of light that reveal rusted out car hulks, graffiti, and cracked sidewalks. The moon rising over the Berkeley hills fails to penetrate to the small, untended yards of blue-collar cottages and squat workshops but highlights the stunted, brown-leaved palm trees regimentally planted every thirty feet or so on both sides of the street.

I'm a few doors down from the New Orleans House. It has no sign. A Pabst Blue Ribbon neon sign is in the window. Inside, dark, narrow, cave-like. Bar on the left... A small stage along the back wall... Over the front door a platform on which the lightshow sets up their gear. Three lightshow artists hunched over in the confined space run the hot equipment. Looks pretty damn uncomfortable to me... Fame, such as it is, has its drawbacks.

The lightshow displays its work on a sidewall. A Chicago boy relocated to the Bay Area, Charlie Musselwhite wails the blues. He has a gravelly voice. Dark glasses and dark clothes... Plays guitar and harmonica and mumbles into the microphone as he wobbles on a stool.

A dozen or so patrons sit at tables, six or seven at the bar. They're mostly Berkeley residents, locals, with a few hangers on. Nice crowd for a Wednesday night in a dive like this.

Take a pew at the bar near the door. Right next to the ladder down which the lightshow artists will climb when the set ends. Order a draft. Get carded. Order a basket of corn chips and salsa with my beer. Focus my attention on the lightshow images created by my secret cousin and his pals. Trying to visually interpret Musselwhite's music is a serious challenge.

What do these college kids, lured to this happening scene on the coattails of LSD, marijuana, and hashish who are still faking their hip credentials, know about grubby big city vibes? Probably about what I know – what they have learned from reading Burroughs and trash novels, and watching tired police procedurals on the silver screen and TV.

And why do these guys insist they are lightshow artists? Do they have a death wish, a burning desire to crash and burn? I tried to tell Tony he wasn't cut out for this life but he wouldn't listen. Why should he? He knows better. I hope he's right. I hope I'm wrong in thinking that lightshows are a fad that will be dropped like a hot potato by dancehall owners and promoters in general when the masses move on. "That's irrelevant," responds Tony and his

lightshow buddies. They honestly believe their work will transcend dancehalls and rock concerts. Lightshow creations are the vanguard of a new, happening way of using light to create high art with overhead projectors, slide projectors, film projectors, color wheels, strobe lights, various mixtures of colored oils and water, artistic transparencies, masks, photographs, motion picture film and Polaroid material. From the outer rings of the cutting edge, these deluded space cowboys fuel themselves on dreams and hallucinogens. More power to them; I wish them well.

Light applause draws the set to a close. As the lightshow images are shut down, the house lights, such as they are, come up - three ugly flood lights target the now barren side wall, throwing off a disgusting glare and making the down-at-heels space look even more depressing, if that's possible. The lightshow artists, among them Tony, crawl down from their perch. Musselwhite has somehow managed to disengage himself from his stool and heads backstage. People wander by me towards the street to get a breath of fresh air and maybe smoke a joint. Typical sounds of shuffling feet, flushing toilets, glasses clinking against each other, and the murmur of conversation accompany me over to the lightshow table.

"Think Musselwhite ever sat in with Howlin' Wolf back in Chicago?"

Tony looks up, smiles, chuckles. I introduced him to blues, rockabilly and jazz while I taught him the basic guitar chords. Tony shakes my hand and slaps me on the back as he gets up from his seat. The rest of the lightshow guys give a vague nod of recognition.

"What brings you to this side of town?" Tony asks.

"I'm sizing you guys up for the competition. They're nervous. Better keep your material under heavy guard," I respond, taking a seat.

"They better be nervous," Jane jumps in to add.

Tony gives her a loving look. She's a Whiskey-A-Go-Go girl, fresh off the Strip, a knockout with long blond hair. Well built. Still sporting some baby fat that somehow enhances her healthy good looks... Wearing a magenta miniskirt and white leather boots that come up to just below her well-formed knees...

"Better raise the skull and crossbones if you plan to board and take us," tosses out Tony, still glowing after the tribute from his girlfriend.

As always, Tony, you're right on target, particularly when you're unaware of the connection. I've done some research and have discovered our common ancestors came from Vis, an island that is part of the Dalmatian Island chain in the Adriatic. These ancestors are rumored to have made their living raiding passing ships.

"You settling in at your job?" Tony asks after I order a round of beers for the table.

"Life Beneficial has thrown me to the wolves. I'm investigating my first claim."

"No kidding. Is it interesting?"

"It's a real humdinger, I'm sorry to say."

"Ah, you'll show 'em."

Tony's eyes sparkle with reassurance. I'm about to rain on his parade.

"You here on business or pleasure?" asks Harry, his long, reddish blond hair partially obscuring his thick coke-bottle, wire rim glasses.

Harry has already seen through my introductory remarks. He's bright, brighter than anyone else at the table. He's a graduate of Bronx Science and a Bard College dropout. His brash New York manner can put people off. The rest of the group hooked up in Eugene, Oregon where most of them, including my cousin, were attending the University. Harry became a lightshow member in San Francisco after he and Tony fell in together. In fact, Tony met Jane because Harry dated her sister, Linda.

"Well, it's always a pleasure to see you guys and, of course, Tony. But... well, I'm here on a business related matter."

"The other shoe finally drops, huh," comments Dumas with what he must think is a witty remark.

Being a rube from the sticks and not so secretly proud of it, he tends to have a suspicious nature, particularly of strangers. And I fit his criteria.

"I'm not dropping any shoes, just offering a heads up... I'd get my story straight if I were you. You might have visitors."

"Why's that?" asks Dumas, on alert and now uptight.

"You guys do a gig at the Straight Theater the other night?"

"Piece of crap gig... And we haven't been paid yet. What else is new?"

"Guy turned up murdered there this morning. He's had some dealings with you guys, or at least that's what I've been told. Name was Bob White. His parents are the claimants in the case I'm investigating."

"What?" Dumas is incredulous. "Shit."

These guys don't read newspapers or own a television. The White melodrama was on the front page above the fold this afternoon and led the six o'clock news. Grief stricken parents were caught arriving at the airport on their way to the St. Francis Hotel and the morgue, not necessarily in that order. A high school yearbook picture of White looking all scrubbed and clean captured audience attention, just the kind of guy any gal would want to bring home to Mom. Not the same guy I saw lying in a pool of blood on a dirty stage floor.

"That's right, Bob White, the guy two sources told me talked to Tony last night. Is that true?"

Tony flushes, looks around the table.

"Well sure. I mean, while we were setting up, he turned up but...we all know him. Anyway, what does that..."

His voice trails away. His hand grips Jane's vise-like. I know that look. Guilt...Caught with his hand in the cookie jar. Oh Lord, what will happen to him when he makes that face in front of the police? Trouble, real trouble...

"You guys knew him too?"

"Asshole... Said he wanted to represent us," mutters Harry.

"That's right. He said he wanted to represent us. Said he'd be in touch. Had big plans... Vegas. LA. New York. London. Paris. We blew him off. Just a creep," Dumas mutters.

"They're calling it murder?" Jane mumbles.

Her voice slides down into the ether. She's very far away, must be really stoned out. Pupils pinpoints of light. She uses Tony's arm to pull herself up. Tries to rouse herself, fails. Blurts out what comes to mind.

"Just because the cops think Tony was the last one to talk with Bobby is no reason for them to suspect him?"

"They might want to question Tony. That might lead to a few questions for the rest of you to answer. If you've got nothing to hide, I wouldn't worry about it. Just prepare yourselves and get your story straight."

The round of beers is forgotten; so is the gig. As one, they turn inward. There's an uncomfortable shifting about in seats. No eye contact. Those who smoke cigarettes take a deep drag. I plunge ahead.

"What kind of contact you guys have with Bob White before Wednesday?"

"That creep," repeats Dumas after taking a sidewise glance right and left to see if anyone is watching or listening.

"He might have dropped by the pad once or twice. Lots of people do that," Harry allows.

People shush us; another act has come on. Comedy group called the Congress of Wonders. They fire off zany one-liners and race around like madmen. Three guys talking fast. Cosmic zaps for this stoned out crowd. A real crackup, particularly if you're high.

Nobody at the lightshow table laughs. They're looking over their shoulders - with good reason. Front door swings open and in walk the cops. Make a stop at the bar; bartender points in our direction. They head to our table. Everyone at the table looks from the approaching cops to me, then down at their laps. Too late to disappear...

"Which one of you is Vitolinich? Tony?" growls a plainclothes cop with disdain.

He's chewing a stogie. Looks like a real sweetheart.

"Me," squeaks Tony in a high-pitched voice, tight, constricted.

He clears his throat. Coughs... Jane clutches his arm convulsively. It dawns on me that she's been in a little hot water herself at one time or another.

Congress of Wonders winds down their skit early tonight. Crowd, distracted by the arrival of "pigs," gives them a light round of applause. The trio disappears backstage. Where the hell did they go? This place doesn't have a back room. The crowd disperses fast.

"Like to ask you to come down to the station to answer a few questions if you don't mind...Just routine."

The stogie guy's act, low-key, just-doing-my-job-dirt-bags, is getting him off, that and the fact that he's clearing the house and fast. The cops would like nothing better than to pin this murder on Tony. "Spaced out hippie goes wild in ritualistic killing," that kind of headline is tailor made for the Chronicle and its readership. And it might give dreams of a promotion a shot in the arm for the arresting officers.

"He hasn't done anything wrong," whines Jane.

"Never said he did, ma'am," answers stogie evenly.

"C.F. Carter. Insurance investigator working on the White claim... Can't this be handled in the morning? These people are working..."

"Put a lid on it, Carter," mutters a beat cop.

He must work the neighborhood. Showed stogie where this place was.

"If you don't mind, Mr. Vitolinich..."

Haunting riffs from a twelve-string guitar, almost classical in nature, fill the room. John Fahey starts to play. No introduction. Must have sneaked onto the stage somehow...

Dumas and Harry snap to. The gig... Good reason to leave this bad vibe table. Tony looks at his buddies' retreating backs longingly, then stumbles out of his chair.

"Sure. Okay. Ah, I'll be right with you."

His chair screeches across the floor, threatening to fall over, and is rescued by providence. What little audience that's left pretends they don't notice. Fahey plays on, oblivious. Got several nodders and one or two deer-in-the-headlights gawkers as an audience to our performance at the table... Stogie grabs Tony by the elbow.

"Where you taking him," I ask.

"Back to the city... Downtown..."

I won't be a welcome sight there. Tough... Stogie pushes Tony. On his way to the door, he looks back over his shoulder at us, panic in his eyes. Ready to piss his pants... Jane is too perturbed to wave. The front door slams shut, sounding like a jail cell closing.

Fahey cranks up his meandering musical monologue as the lightshow images try to latch onto his drift. The music, dark, introverted, wild, tumbles off of his guitar strings and tries to evaporate but somehow lingers, a haunting impression remains.

The murder, the scene at the park, Outrage, the mood of this joint - is this what flower children think of as peace and love?

"Tony didn't have anything to do with this...this murder. That's crazy talk, crazy. Can't they see that?" Jane sputters trying to shake her drug induced daze away.

I see, all right. I see a stoned-out little girl whose body grew up fast and whose brain is struggling to catch up. I see a candle burning at both ends. I see disaster sooner rather than later. I see a fast end to a dream of good times and pleasure eternal.

"They'll figure it out sooner or later," I answer with little conviction.

Someone in the audience shushes us again. I take Jane by the arm. Fahey's virtuoso performance on the twelve-string continues. He's taken his audience, much in need of diversion, away from their immediate cares and concerns and down into his intricate musical maze. We pause by the door just below the lightshow platform. Bracken, the only lightshow member not at work, waits there, in case of need or emergency.

"Did Bob White get you the Straight Theater gig?" I ask in a stage whisper, looking from one to the other.

"Nay..." Bracken mutters. "Outrage... We did some lights for a movie he's making. The Straight Theater thing came up after that. After the gig, heard his boyfriend, Bernie something, the band leader, stole all the band gear and the van Outrage bought for him. Outrage nowhere to be found. Probably never get paid for that gig either."

I put my arm on his shoulder in commiseration then turn towards the door. Jane grabs my arm just as I'm leaving. Surprise, she's coming with me

———————

On the Bay Bridge with Jane in the shotgun seat...As we emerge from Treasure Island, the city skyline greets us. Full moon peeps through high clouds far above. Fog that slithered in through the Golden Gate late in the day has now settled over the whole bay and is moving up the shoreline towards the hills. Coit Tower and the Ferry Building, local landmarks, slowly being engulfed, dissolved. Clock on the Ferry Building reads almost midnight. A gigantic Hills Brothers coffee billboard near the end of the bridge interrupts contemplation of the view.

The city streets swirl in and out of focus. Through the fog and mist a glow from the moon above, like a streetlight, turns darkness into shiny gray areas of glare and deep pockets of illuminated particles. We're riding in a cocoon...Gliding through fantasy streets towards a dungeon in an imposing castle - police headquarters.

The streets are downright cold on the south side of Market, the warehouse section of town. After parking the car, we hunch up our shoulders and drift down Bryant with the rest of the vagrants and no-accounts towards the Hall of Justice at the intersection of 7th. Jane, as moody and quiet as the night, moves fast, matching my long stride with ease. Inside at the front desk, I ask for Coop. He's off duty.

"Looking for a man brought in for questioning, name of Tony Vitolinich," I inquire.

Desk sergeant points down the hall to a waiting room. Jane turns in that direction. Shoulders slumped. She's pale and wan, an inmate shackled. Brain closed down until further notice.

"I'm working the case. Insurance investigator for Life Beneficial... C.F. Carter."

Show him my newly issued license and business card.

"Like to have a word with the on-duty officer in charge of the investigation..."

"That'd be..." He looks down at a duty roster lying in front of him. "Johnson. Down the hall to the stairs and up to the third floor...Room 317... On the back near the head. They just pulled in about twenty minutes ago. With this Vitolinich character, I presume. They'll be able to fill you in – if they've got anything for release to an insurance investigator, that is."

Very polite but distant – maybe a hint of disdain mixed with weariness.

It takes a gentle push on Jane's back to encourage her down the hall. She's in a near terminal funk. I put my arm around her. Whatever drug she'd been high on at the New Orleans House is a memory now.

The fluorescent lights in the hallway flicker, making the dirty wooden paneling seem more dingy than it really is. The marble floors echo to the click of our heels. Glass paneled doors rattle when they bang shut. Lonely conversations echo throughout the building sounding like the plaintive wails of spirits from beyond.

Room 317...Homicide investigation... Bunch of beat-up old wooden desks randomly scattered in a large open room. Nobody around... Wall of windows at the back of the room provide a great view of the jail in the next building.

"You people lost," asks someone behind us. We jerk around.

"Looking for Detective Johnson," I answer, extending my hand in greeting.

Guy ignores my goodwill gesture.

"He's in Interrogation Room Two at the moment talking with a suspect. Can't be disturbed... Maybe I can help you."

Just a kid really...Looks like he works out regularly...Big neck. Bulky shoulders and forearms... Plenty of pimples... Got a face only a mother could love. Maybe he's been downing something a little extra to help him put on those muscles, probably responded to one of those Charles Atlas ads when he was a kid and discovered some short cuts to bulk.

"Is he talking with a Tony Vitolinich?"

"Who wants to know?"

I pull out one of my cards. Hand it to him. He smacks it against the back of his fingers as he listens.

"Carter. C.F. Carter. Licensed insurance investigator working on a claim on the Bob White policy...was getting background information from Mr. Vitolinich when a detective smoking a big stogie came in and hauled him away...Like to have a word with Detective Johnson when he has a free moment."

Muscle bound stops slapping the card against his fingers...Looks Jane up and down.

"This is Mr. Vitolinich's girlfriend," I inform him.

I can see he reads hooker, drug addict, piece of meat. Sneers... I move down a notch in his estimation.

"Swell of you two to take the time," he answers.

Did he hear that line in a melodrama that first played in movie houses in the 1930s?

"Mr. Vitolinich did speak to the victim on the night in question in a public place with hundreds of witnesses. He then left the Straight Theater with Miss Preen. She was with him all night and will swear to that fact."

"Is that so?" Implying that this piece of news isn't worth the time it took me to state it. "Why don't you take a pew? I'll see if Detective Johnson is available."

Probably going to community college in his spare time, majoring in Criminal Justice... Do his plans include becoming a hotshot lawyer so he can toss all the bad guys into a deep, dark cell for a very long time, or does he just want to beat on them when the opportunity arises?

He sneers over his shoulder again as he retreats down a darkened hallway. Hope his bunched up calves get cramps. I force Jane to sit down with me on a hardwood bench.

"That is your story, isn't it?" I ask.

"Lot of good it'll do."

"You got something you want to get off your chest?"

Jane shakes her head...Looks guilty as hell.

"Whatever you might have been hauled in for in the past isn't going to rub off on Tony, if that's what's bothering you."

Jane gives me a strange look but softens.

"They'll lock him up just for kicks. He won't last an hour in the same cell with the animals they've got here. He's a gentle soul."

"He's not under arrest. They just brought him in for questioning."

"They don't need a reason to lock people up."

A tear for Tony, a tear for herself, a tear for the human condition rolls down her cheek. Grim and gloomy but determined for all that, she stares straight ahead. I don't have to worry about her cracking. She has a core of steel. But she's right about Tony. I've got to get him out from under as soon as possible. People like that are the first ones to be used up and tossed aside in situations like this – a first rate victim, has the letter 'P' for patsy pasted on his forehead.

"He'll talk with both of you – when there's a break inside," growls the muscle-bound young detective from across the room, jerking his thumb over his shoulder towards Interrogation Room Two.

He doesn't even bother to walk across the room. Where are his manners? Miss Donnan, my cotillion instructor, and her ever-present partner, would never condone such behavior. What a bore. It simply is not done.

Johnson, the stogie man, barges out of Interrogation Room Two, almost running into the muscle-bound one while he's still doing his tough guy act. "Christ," I hear him mutter under his breath before he coughs and heads down the hall. There've been too many stogies, too many long nights, too many shots of straight Scotch in Johnson's past. He looks at my card...Looks up at us.

"Know your boss, Carter – Meade - Good man," he states. I extend my hand. Johnson turns to Jane. "And you are?"

Jane looks up. "Preen, Jane," she barks brittle and defensive.

Good grief. Why not put on cuffs and a striped shirt? Why not beg for a beating?

"Mr. Vitolinich is just answering some questions," Johnson says to me after looking Jane up and down. "Following up for Detective Cooper... You touch base with him yet?"

"Saw him at the crime scene...Got filled in with enough info to start my investigation. Talked with Mr. Green, the owner of the Straight Theater, and Mr. Outrage, the man who put on the event at the Straight the night White was murdered. They both mentioned Mr. Vitolinich. That's why I was talking with him at the New Orleans House when you arrived. Brought Miss Preen here down to the station because she was with Vitolinich all of last night. Thought that might save you the trouble of following up on his alibi."

"You've been busy. Why, when you know this is an open police investigation and there's little or no need for you to poke your nose in until we say so? We might want to choose our own time to let persons of interest be clued in on facts in the case, you know?"

"When you're right, you're right, Detective. So I'll be honest. This is my first investigation and the Big Boss himself called and spoke directly to me asking that I settle this claim...Called Mr. and Mrs. White, Bob White's parents, by their first names."

"That would do it."

"You better believe it...What's this about 'facts in the case'?'"

"One thing the Big Boss must not have mentioned is a check dated yesterday in the amount of twenty thousand dollars written out to Tony Vitolinich from the victim's account. That's not for public attribution, by the way."

"Why would Vitolinich want to kill White if White had just written him a check?"

"That's one of the things we're trying to clear up." Professional courtesy time is over. "You're welcome to wait if you want. I've got to get back."

I'm waiting. This is Tony we're talking about. Jane follows me into the break room. We serve up for ourselves some lousy, bottom-of-the-pot-late-at-night coffee and stale donuts and head to a hard wooden bench in the hall. Even that's cozier than the break room. I use a pay phone down the hall to check in. Jane also makes a call. Whoever tipped Johnson off to this check written out to Tony hasn't passed the information along to Life Beneficial or, at least, they didn't bother to fill me in. I have only one message. Tim will drop by my place later. He fails to specify a time. Great... An answering service is a big help. I rejoin Jane on the bench. She doesn't fill me in on her call. Would she call her mother?

We don't say much but I'm convinced there's more to Jane than her outfit suggests. I am beginning to wonder about myself, though. I mean, what the hell am I doing at goodness knows what time in the morning at a police station trying to bail my secret cousin out of trouble when I'm supposed to be at work bright eyed and bushy tailed first thing in the morning? What can I do for him here and now? And, what am I doing here with Jane Preen? Good grief. Will I ever allow myself to tell Tony about our mutual murky, ancient family history? And what good would it do if I did – more harm than good? A regular swarm of confounding questions circle about in my head, keeping me on edge and churning up my gut. Why the hell did Tony have to get mixed up in this mess? What is the role of karma and the role of fate in life? Talk about an innocent fool – who else would speculate on eternal questions at a time like this or get mixed up in a murder investigation when the prime suspect has a connection, a good one, to you?

Clicking heels rush down the hallway towards us. Man and a woman. Well dressed. I make them as the bereaved parents of Bob White.

I think I might know why I was chosen to handle this investigation. I know the man. I'm up off my chair in nothing flat and catch the approaching couple's eye as they approach.

"Randolph and Edwina White," I ask.

I'm recalling that Bill Hancock, the Chairman of the Board of Life Beneficial, congratulated me on my 'service to my country.' I thought it was odd that he should know about my stint in Washington, D.C. Now I see the connection – Mr. Randolph White. Bill Hancock and Randolph White – how are they connected to The Office? And my father, is he mixed up in how I came to be selected to investigate this particular claim…seems like he's in some way behind most every change that comes down the pike in my life.

"Yes?" they ask, pausing.

"Allow me to express my sincerest regrets over the death of your son. Tragic…A devastating loss…" They acknowledge they are receiving their due but remain aloof. I press on. "Also allow me, as a claims investigator for Life Beneficial, to express the company's deepest sympathy." Mr. White smiles… Does he see that I have recognized him? I only saw him once briefly in a hallway at The Office exiting a high official's office. Mrs. White seems grateful for my solicitude but there is also now something that hints at pride in her look. What is her relationship to Bill Hancock and Life Beneficial? I pull out one of my cards and hand it to them. "I'm C.F. Carter. Anything I can do to help, give me a call, day or night."

"Bill, that is Mr. Hancock, told us he had spoken to you," Mr. White replies, looking up from my card.

He smiles again as though challenging me to recognize him. I smile right back at him offering nothing but a firm handshake. The Office did teach me one thing – few circumstances in life are accidental. Mr. White, ever the well-bred one, breaks the awkward grip-and-grin moment.

"What can we do for you, Mr. Carter?"

"To tell you the truth, we came down to chat with the on-duty officer about Tony Vitolinich."

"The man Bobby wrote that check to," Mr. White begins.

"It turned up in Bobby's belonging," Mrs. White adds.

"Bobby never wrote Tony any check. And he had nothing whatsoever to do with Bobby's murder," Jane blurts out, interjecting herself into the conversation.

"Allow me to introduce Jane Preen. She's the particular friend of Mr. Vitolinich," I supply.

"I'm sure," mumbles Mrs. White dismissively, nose in the air.

Mr. White gives Jane the appraising look of a connoisseur with extensive experience and something else that I haven't the time right now to analyze.

"Miss Preen was with Mr. Vitolinich all of last night," I add.

"What, did your lover boy blow his cork when he found out you and Bobby were playing house - not very nice after Bobby had just written him a check for twenty thousand dollars. Is that the story on your not-so-smart hippie boyfriend?"

"Yes, he has long hair" Jane fires back at Mr. White, hackles up and guns blasting before I can launch a counter offensive. "Just like your son did. But Tony is good and kind and honest. He's a writer, an artist, and never a murderer."

Indignation, righteousness, her shoulders thrown back and head held high - what a woman. Tony might not need my help with a protector like this. Or, then again, they might both need my help. Mr. White nods thoughtfully, then turns to me.

"We'd like to talk with you about this unfortunate situation at a more convenient time, Mr. Carter. Say nine o'clock tomorrow at our hotel. We're staying at the St. Francis."

I know Mr. White. His kind is arrogant, aloof, powerful, privileged. He expects, no, demands, things be done his way. I know him because his kind have dominated and ignored my independent and loner nature from childhood; I know him also because his kind are those in front of whom I have kowtowed and been a good, obedient child, a good Scout, my whole life.

It occurs to me to call my father. He was the one who suggested I apply for the job at Life Beneficial and he is the one who used his pull to get me the job at The Office. It wouldn't hurt; in fact, it might clear up many unanswered questions while opening now closed doors. But this is something I have never done, not even on the day my father introduced me to my grandfather, not ever. I do not ask; I accept and obey. Our mutual silence, in my opinion, is not as golden as some portray silence to be.

This method of coping — silence that is moody, brooding, internally anguished just like my anti-hero heroes — has protected my insulated world filled with fantasies despite the fact that it likely has no tangible impact in the 'real' world. Do I maintain this pose out of pride? Is it arrogance? Is it stupidity? Is it stubbornness? Or is it associated with something else, some act that I, the seeker, must maintain in order to reach another, higher level of reality, of realization? Or am I just once again seeing my place in life in grandiose terms when in fact I'm just a second rate version of the sensitive young man character rehearsed by novelists? I sometime make myself sick. I laugh in contempt, cry with frustrated anger. Is it possible for anyone to believe this posturing including myself, most particularly myself? Is this approach to life merely the masturbatory rationalizations of a selfish white boy brought up in comfortable circumstances surrounded by supportive people who are ready, willing and able to create and maintain an invisible barrier that has protected me from seeing the real world as it really is? What the fuck! I'm the outsider here, the loner, the scorned, the seeker, aren't I? Get used to something and stick with it for Christ sakes.

CHAPTER FIVE

Georgetown
Washington, D.C.
Winter 1963

After several long and torturous phone conversations and an exchange of high-sounding, ambiguous and unsettled letters, Isobel and I come to an understanding. She will take the train up from Richmond to visit me for the weekend. I've just graduated from college and am settling into my new job. She will share in my new-found freedom and sophistication. A visit to my one-bedroom apartment off the beaten path in Georgetown would be the perfect conclusion to that weekend, in my estimation.

"Oh Charlie... look who I ran into just before I left town."

Tim smiles, standing at her side. The train station makes me feel like we are in a bad World War II movie. Exhaust from the trains. Steam every time we breathe... Cigarettes in our mouths... Car coats and scarves and leather gloves - bundled up. Stiff and formal... A brief kiss on the cheek from Isobel... before the end of this movie, one or more of us will die, if this really is a movie. After a noticeable pause and several changes of expression, I extend my hand to Tim. We nod without speaking. I'm afraid what I might say if I open my mouth. Isobel overlooks our interplay. Boys will be boys.

"I just felt I had to bring him along. The three of us together again... Like old times... I hope you don't mind."

Yes. Isobel and Tim and I — the three Musketeers...All for one and one for all...Right. Isobel has a huge crush on Tim and I have a huge crush on Isobel. Tim? Yes, there is always the question of Tim. I can't really say that he has a crush on Isobel and I can't really say that he is trying to outflank me. Quite the contrary... He's always there to offer advice and fellowship. Anyway, Isobel seems to have gotten over her flirtation with him. I guess it would be more appropriate to say that she gave up hope because she saw the situation was hopeless.

"Are you the new American James Bond?" asks Tim with one of his patented sly smiles.

"Oh Tim," Isobel playfully punches his arm.

I regain my composure or at least like to think I do.

"I had planned to pick you up in my Aston Martin but it's in the shop. Here. Let me take this for you."

I reach down and pick up Isobel's bag before they have a chance to laugh at what I hope is a cool, confident joke. Then I cast aside my cigarette, crushing it out with the heel of my shoe. It's cold in Washington, D.C. A very long night awaits us.

Isobel grabs my arm and Tim falls in line beside her. Yes, the three Musketeers ride again.

"Did you have plans for dinner? Can you get a table for three so Tim can come along at this late date?"

I had planned to take Isobel to dinner at a seafood restaurant my parents like to visit when they come up. It's right on the Potomac. And there's a very good wine list, so I'm told. I wouldn't know. I'm really not that interested in alcohol.

"I'm sure the restaurant can accommodate us."

I'm right. We dine overlooking the Potomac, talk about Washington movers-and-shakers, mostly politicians or politically connected people we don't know, and my new job. Mutual friends and relations back in Richmond fill in the gaps. We share a bottle of wine and then another as oysters on the half shell are followed by fresh caught rockfish. Over desert, I casually suggest we visit a Georgetown nightclub – the Blue Note. Mose Allison is the headliner.

"I feel like a hick from Hicksville," *Isobel comments after we are seated at The Blue Note.*

The nightclub has low ceilings, exposed brick walls, small tables that have trouble accommodating drink orders. The room is packed. Smoke fills it, hanging heavy and suspended in the space between the ceiling and the tops of heads in the audience. Waitresses make their adventurous way to tables bearing refreshments of all types held high above their heads. Beats, cool above all else, snap their fingers and nod in time to the music. Some even drift off into what seem to my innocent eyes like drug-induced stupors. But the audience is overwhelmingly composed of upscale young elites making the Georgetown scene. They are chic, witty jet-setters-in-waiting.

"Well, we're sure not part of the 'in crowd' to these people, that's for sure," *Tim comments sarcastically.*

"Hey, I'm a Washington, D.C. resident now, aren't I?" *I answer.*

"You sure are," *Isobel agrees.*

"And I have a cool job in government."

"Right again," *agrees Tim.*

"So we are part of the scene – with it, part of the 'in' crowd, whether you know it or not."

We all laugh. Part of what brought us together in the first place was our shared belief that we were outsiders – and the posture we took was that we chose to be that way.

Mose finishes his set to cool applause. He drifts away. It's almost midnight and his next set isn't scheduled until almost one o'clock in the morning.

"I've got an idea," *Tim submits without previous warning.* "If you're up for it..."

"What?" *Isobel asks.*

"I heard about this party in Georgetown. It might be interesting."

"You have an invitation?"

"Well, not exactly. It's not really that kind of 'do' if you get my drift."

"How did you hear about it?" I ask.

My grand design – getting Isobel in the sack, professing my love and her responding in kind – have now officially gone up in smoke. I'm trying to be a good loser but that's too much to expect of me for the moment.

"To be honest – my Richmond drug connection."

"What kind of party is this?" Isobel asks.

"I really don't know but there should be some interesting people there, if you know what I mean."

"Beatniks and hipsters and creative types?" giggles Isobel, intrigued.

Before we know it we're headed up the hill, up Wisconsin Avenue towards the party. As we approach this 'far out' gathering, we grow quiet. The street in front of the pad and the steps leading to the apartment are littered with guests despite the blustery weather. No one seems to mind. I have no idea what to expect inside.

Don't get me wrong. I've been to my share of late night parties in Washington, D.C. and Richmond. I've hung out with Beats, radicals, and creative types. I, of course, have read Kerouac and J.D. Salinger and Kurt Vonnegut and Allen Ginsberg and Mallarme and Cocteau and Herman Hesse. I majored in English at college, for goodness sakes. I am an avid fan of Fellini and French New Wave films and British Black Humor. But – I am still a long way from hip. And I know it. I can listen to bebop music and praise Pop Art and think about growing a goatee until I'm blue in the face. I could...

My mind stops in mid ramble as we ascend the front steps. I escort Isobel into the party as if this was an exclusive debutante party. And Tim is right there with us.

The front door is unlocked. We walk into the hallway of a railroad apartment typical of turn-of-the-century townhouses. The first door to the left leads into what must have been the front parlor. In the dimly lit room, there is a sofa and a few armchairs fronted by a coffee table. On a cluttered side table is a battered television set. The volume is turned down and the reception is poor. Whatever is playing attracts the attention of several obviously stoned out guests. The TV image wavers and flickers. It's more a wavy impression than an image. The antenna must need adjustment. Jazz music fills the room coming from a source that I cannot identify.

None of us speak to each other; nor does anyone else speak to us. The room is in shadows. A shawl has been thrown over a table lamp. We drift into the connecting room. It must have been the main dining room at one time. Now the room is empty save for a few wooden chairs. Mose Allison sits in one of the chairs smoking a joint. No one dares speak to the great man. He's on break and talks to himself while jerking his head first one way and then the other with a long slow-to-change scowl. Everyone in the room turns their back on him. It *would be un-cool to crowd the great man. Tomorrow, they will all be able to say to their friends, 'I was at a party last night. Mose Allison was there. I was right in the same room with him.'*

Ten minutes or so of this kind of tension makes the room unbearable. We drift back into the hallway and end up in the kitchen at the very back of the house. The sound system doesn't penetrate to this room and there's room for conversation. Someone is picking out a folk tune on a guitar. The room is filled with smoke. A bottle of cheap red wine sits on the table. No one seems to mind if you sample it. I don't know how, but Tim and Isobel disappear while I'm being overwhelmed by the crowded crush pressing up against a round kitchen table.

When I realize they are gone, I, for no known reason, hesitate before going in search of them. The evening bears no resemblance to the one I envisioned. Is it even worth pursing them? And what would I discover if I did follow – them necking in the corner? Worse yet, would they have escaped from the party and left me to my own devices with a group of people I don't know?

I stand by the kitchen table for an indeterminate period of time contemplating my navel, looking over my options, being indecisive and uncertain. I am full of nervous energy, not really defeated, I have pledged never to give up my crusade to win the hand of the fair and amazing Isobel, but I'm definitely brought down.

It is then that I notice sitting on the table a pack of Murad cigarettes. That's my brand. I like the oval cigarettes and their Turkish tobacco. The pack is cool too - hardened so you can open the top and take out a cigarette from inside. Without thinking, I open up this pack and take one out. Maybe it's just for something to do. Maybe it's a rebellious act. Maybe it's a cry for help. Maybe it's a lot of things - but it definitely is an impulsive act, out of character for me.

I light up, put the pack back on the table and take a few anxious drags. As I do so, a man in his late twenties or early thirties comes up to the table, picks up the pack and puts it in his shirt pocket. Embarrassed, I lean over to him.

"Excuse me."

The man turns to me. He is about six feet tall with blond wavy hair and light blue eyes - nothing special about him at all.

"I hope you don't mind. I took one of your cigarettes?" I confess.

He smiles a pleasant smile.

"Not if you don't mind that those cigarettes are laced with AMT," he replies quite casually.

It is then that I vividly recall that Tim mentioned he found out about this party from his Richmond drug connection. A rush, a tingling — is it fear, is it uncertainty, it definitely is a clear clarion from the unknown — permeates my being. I put out the cigarette.

The man is gone — just like that. Uncertainty roots me to the spot. I listen without comprehension to the folk song being played on the guitar. At long last, how long I stood there I do not know, I turn and wander out of the room.

I will go in search of Isobel and Tim, I tell myself. We will leave this party... Now. In the front room people are still watching the soundless, flickering wavy-image TV while jazz music plays. In the next room Mose Allison is gone. Only a few stragglers remain. The apartment, the party, is covered by deep, threatening shadows. Gloom and uncertainty — a bleak painting hung in a forgotten corner under a dank staircase — grips me by the throat.

I feel a wave rush over me. Am I about to be sick? I need some air — immediately. I stumble out onto the front stoop. It is crowded with people. A police patrol car comes up the street and slows in front of the house. I am shivering but it is not from the cold night air or the now retreating patrol car. I move down two steps on trembling legs and flop down onto a step. I feel like I am going to come out of my body. I am hyperventilating. I am certain that I am going to pass out. I put my head down between my legs, trying to catch my breath. No help.

I look up. Everything is moving in slow motion. Cars jerk by in single frame motion. Each new frame leaps ahead, skipping forward as cars go up the street. Someone beeps a horn that transforms into a Doppler effect, eerie and somehow everlasting. Someone laughs. A girl shouts something. A shriveled leaf falls on the cobbled sidewalk and joins others lying desolate, only to be blown and scattered in the wind. I rise on shaky legs, pulling myself up with help from the metal handrail. I don't know how but I make it to the sidewalk still covered with snow on the edges from a snowstorm several days before.

I think — if I can just get to the car, I'll be all right. If I can just sit down inside my own car, I'll get through this.

I float down the street, downhill towards streetlights and away from the party and people and smoky rooms and the Murad cigarette soaked in AMT. Turning my head, the Wisconsin Avenue scene strobes in slow motion, big black blotches between the strobes. I look back up the street. The steps leading to the party seem distant. On them is someone shouting — Charlie, Charlie, Charlie. The name echoes in my brain way back in the distance, far away, far away.

The person on the steps shouting is Tim. Isobel is at his side. As they start coming down the steps, I stumble into a pile of snow curbside. I stagger and then ever so slowly, ever so magically, ever so peacefully, I collapse into the gutter between two parked cars as Tim and Isobel come rushing in slow motion towards me.

Blackness...The Void...Peace everlasting...The end of my weekend plans and the introduction of new twists and turns, a change in my relation to the outside world...

Later, an eternity later returning from a time and place beyond meaning, height, width, depth or dimension, I am in my car. It is still parked but the engine is running. My head is in Isobel's lap. She is stroking my hair gently saying, "It's okay, Charlie. It's okay. We've got all night. Don't rush. Don't rush." Just bubbling up - my ego - saying in my head, "I'm not interested in you as a mother figure or a friend." But that is neither here nor there. So far away...I relax into a cushion of otherworldliness mixed with the odor of never-to-be-realized sex.

This mysterious mystical experience, without many mental twists and turns, links up with my creek side one. I recall other moments, not as intense or as memorable as those two but still connected. It seems to me they are all indications of the visible world leading toward or connecting with the invisible one, the Beyond, the Almighty. I ponder how these puzzle pieces fit, seek solutions to universal questions, and try to integrate my life path into the puzzle of existence.

On the many lonely nights I spent while living in Washington, D.C., I checked out books about mysticism and mystics and Buddhism and Beat Poets and William Blake and Herman Hesse and so on and so forth and so on ad infinitum. It was just what I needed to put a space between my work at The Office and my private life. It took me over completely. That's part of the absurdity and goofiness and wild eyed innocence that is my life, sort of my trademark if you will. Oh yeah, and I really got into believing I was a seeker trying to solve the puzzle, the eternal questions of life. I was a stranger in a strange land meditating, observing, trying to realize...

This transformation fit my persona like a glove. And I wore that glove like a fetish, a talisman. Don't ask me how a continually horny and clueless guy matched up in the real world with this new persona. I made a joke of my new obsession daily. Anyway...that was an added part of the long and short of it, of my life at that time and place – Washington, D.C., at the height of the war in Vietnam, protesting in the streets, peace and love brother, J. Edgar Hoover, etc. etc.

And, oh you bet, Charlie Foxhawk Carter was working for The Office doing research and creating plausible stories of deniability, i.e. re-imagining history for the heads of a top secret agency in the most powerful country in the world. I liked to think I got the irony of my situation while at the same time I kept doing my duty like the good scout I had aspired to be since my childhood. Of course that included being a devoted son of an upright father who shared his love of Western movies and their values with me and side-by-side repeated the Boy Scout oath and the Pledge of Allegiance to America.

I couldn't stand the lie I felt I was living and I made my feelings known to those in charge of my fate at The Office. I suspect these higher ups were not eager to lengthen my stay and just wanted to make sure my father wouldn't be hurt that they had allowed me to leave. At any rate, at the end of what I had been calling my required service to my country, I loaded my car up with my few worldly possessions and drove down Interstate 95 to Richmond.

I wanted nothing to do with my old Richmond friends. They were

phonies, living a meaningless life, not going down the path I felt I needed to take
– or so I liked to believe – but, yes, because of my father's influence, I allowed
myself to be roped into the management training program at Life Beneficial.
I'm sure that old friends and family smiled a knowing smile, thinking, "So much
for high ideals. Charlie will soon be one of the gang who hang out at the Club
and marry and have kids and live in the right part of town and so forth and so
on." But my fortuitous transfer took care of that kind of speculation in a hurry.
Goodbye Richmond, hello San Francisco.

I notice in my rear view mirror a nondescript Volkswagen Beatle. Is it making the same lane changes I am? I'm jumpy and tired. Probably nothing...

"How did Tony meet Bob White in the first place, you know?" I ask, lighting up a Murad.

Jane fires up a joint. Where the hell did that come from? Was she holding in the police station?

"He just showed up at a gig the guys were doing. And Bobby sidles up to them like he's King Shit and announces that if the lightshow guys make him their manager, he'll get them gigs, help them to realize all their dreams. The guys got really fired up even though they tried to play it cool."

"When was that?"

"Oh, I don't know. Some gig. I wasn't there. It was one of those gigs where the Airplane and the Dead were supposed to play and Big Brother and the Holding Company without Janis show up instead. The only interesting group was It's a Beautiful Day. David LaFlamme is a fantastic violin player."

"Yeah..."

"I took lessons when I was a kid. Mom's idea... I wasn't any good... Didn't practice enough."

Fog grows thicker as we enter the Haight-Ashbury District. Waif-like flower children drift through pools of light created by streetlights. Trees in the Panhandle dangle down out of foggy clouds.

"You called him Bobby. You knew him, I mean before?"

"I knew him. You know. I know a lot of people." Her voice is muted. She takes a long hit on her joint...Looks out the window. Takes another quick hit, then snaps out of her odd funk and without warning launches into a punchy, rolling marijuana high monologue. "Bobby shows up on our doorstep with some blow, see. And the guys end up turning on their equipment. Before you know it they've got all kinds of lightshow shit happening. Really wild, out there stuff. And Bobby is playing around with the images too. And they're doing more blow. And the music is blasting and that room is hot. And Bobby gets really pumped, see, and lays a couple of hundred bucks on the guys to show good faith, he says. Hell, the guys take it and run. Times are tight. Believe you me. Claims he'll be back ASAP...Then nothing. The guys figure - just another blowhard - too bad. Great blow...No show...The end. Then he makes the scene again, if you can call it that, at the Straight Theater gig." There's a change in the pitch of her marijuana high monologue here that I can't quite identify. But she's still on a roll and blasts to the finish. "Bobby says he's got it all together. Says he'll drop by tomorrow and bring them up to speed on the deal. Tells them their lights are killer shit. The guys are like, yeah, yeah. But I can tell. They're stoked. They want his shuck-and-jive act to be real. They need someone to bankroll them, to believe in them, real bad. We're talking about down to the short strokes here." She's run out of gas. She takes another hit from her joint but discovers that the joint has gone out. She doesn't bother to relight it. Then she looks at me. I can't read her look. I'm concentrated on the road. And she adds, "Next thing we know you come waltzing into the New Orleans House telling us Bobby was murdered."

We've driven into the Park. It's another world. No streetlights. Inky blotches of manicured yet abundant vegetation snap into and then out of sight. Dense tendrils of earthbound clouds swirl around, over, and under the car. We creep past the Arboretum. A group of hippies with backpacks and sleeping bags jump into view. I swerve to miss them. Getting ready to spend the night in the park, I guess. Not my idea of a good time. Dive deep into more all-encompassing fog. Lose my sense of direction.

Suddenly, we intersect Park Presidio. Turn right and head towards the Golden Gate Bridge. The fog is still heavy but it doesn't cling to the car. I plan to steer Jane back to this conversation when we settle in at my apartment. Pull into the basement parking lot of my apartment building near 19th and California. Vapor lights lead me to my designated spot. Tim is standing where I should be parking my car. Seems unlikely that I'll be able to pump Jane some more with Tim around... We head up the stairs to my new place. It's a pricey efficiency that I've cluttered up with unpacked weights, books, records, stereo equipment, my guitar and clothes piled around at random. Cheesy stuff the place came furnished with makes it look like a motel. A deck about eighteen inches wide that looks out over 19th Avenue opens off of a French window. I keep the window closed to muffle the constant traffic noise. Most of the residents on my side of the building do the same.

"You guys hungry? There isn't much in the frig but you're welcome to whatever is there," I holler as I veer off to my bedroom closet to hang up my coat.

Tim has his head in the refrigerator when I return. Jane is in the middle of the room with her arms crossed over her mid-section. I'm undoing my tie and opening my collar.

"How were you figuring this to work?" she asks me with tired tension in her voice.

"I don't rightly know. But," I look at a clock hanging above the counter that separates the small kitchen from the main room. "It's three thirty now. I'm guessing they'll release Tony sometime after eight when Detective Cooper comes on his shift. That doesn't leave us much time for sleep before we'll have to get a move on." We both survey the room. "Why don't you take my bed and Tim and I will take this room."

Tim ambles into the middle of the front room with a peanut butter, mayonnaise and banana sandwich in his hands. We used to gobble those up when we were kids.

"Good idea, Tim. You want one, Jane? I'm going to have one."

Jane makes a face.

"I'll pass. I'm just going to crash."

"Okay. I'll give you a call in the morning."

She nods. The bedroom door closes and locks behind her. I get out the makings for a sandwich and turn my focus to Tim. Christ, I'm bushed. If this is an example of a typical day working for the San Francisco branch of Life Beneficial, I'm not sure how long I'll last.

"You had a chance to settle in here in SF?" I ask just to make conversation.

Tim shrugs heads over to my stack of sides and evasively comments over his shoulder, "I've hung out on several scenes. But, for one reason or another, they've all gotten kind of complicated."

He searches through my sides after he turns on the radio, moving the dial from KJAZ to KMPX. He ends up selecting 'Sketches of Spain,' one of my favorite sides, and switches the tuner from radio to phonograph. Tim's side spinning skills are a specialty of his.

"Don't mind if I roll out my sleeping bag and crash out, do you? I'm really done in," I ask.

Tim nods. He's hunting through my sides for more selections. I try to close my eyes and drift off. Tired as I am, that's impossible. I prop myself up on one elbow.

"I know I'm being rude, crashing and all," I begin.

Tim has an MJQ album in his hands and has been inspecting the list of tracks on it. He looks over at me.

"Hey, when you're beat, you're beat," he states. "We can catch up tomorrow."

"That's the problem. A whole pile of shit has fallen on me and it's likely I'll have to use all the energy I have dealing with it." Tim is listening just like he's done in the past. "Jane's boyfriend, Tony Vitolinich, you may remember him, he's from Richmond too, is being held for questioning in the murder for which I'm doing an insurance claim investigation," I blurt out with a sigh, the weight of this revelation again takes hold of me. "The more I find out the worse this thing gets."

"Get some rest. Sounds like you'll need it."

A parade of phantoms clash — my father, Tony, Tim, Isobel — and new ones, some with ghastly overtones — Bob White, Luther Green, Ronald Outrage, Randolph and Edwina White, Mr. Hancock, Jane Preen — band after band of hippies in colorful costumes, San Francisco police officers in official blue, the lightshow folks — and the phantasmagoria of my new surroundings — the Straight Theater, Haight Street, Golden Gate Park, the old Russian Embassy, the New Orleans House, San Francisco Police Headquarters, the lightshow house, a banged-up Volkswagen Bug - suck me down a maelstrom with ever increasing violence and intensity. Whirling, rocking, tossing, nauseous, threatened, I suddenly no longer exist. Goodnight Charlie.

In my dreams where time and space have new and constantly changing meanings...

Isobel and Tim are traveling with me on a road trip through glowing countryside. We stop at a house or roadside inn. Next morning I am packing in my room. Bright sunny daylight floods the landscape outside and creates velvety shadows inside. We are preparing to move on. I see Isobel across the room. She is also packing. As I see her, I am again transfixed by her beauty, her luminous soul. She beckons me into the next room, a bedroom. Tim is there. They open the closet door. Inside are cell bars. Inside the cell Tony clutches the bars pleading to be set free. He is screaming, screaming for release.

My father sits in his favorite chair talking to me. At first I believe he is angry. Then I note his unwrinkled, undisturbed pale skin and deep-set eyes. He speaks with great concentration but I am unable to hear what he is saying. We communicate at a level beyond words. He points downward below his throne-like chair. I realize his chair is perched on top of a treeless hillside. At the base of the hill, at the edge of a valley, is a cabin.

The golden light of sunset drenches the hillside, the valley, the cabin. As I approach the cabin, I realize this is my mother's domain. Her Indian ancestors chant holy songs amid the tingling chimes of the glorious last flashes of light in the day.

The door to the cabin magically and silently swings open as I approach. The golden light of sunset attempts to penetrate the black void within. Sinister and inky darkness contrasts sharply with the soft golden rays of sunset... I am paralyzed with fear and foreboding.

I have had this dream many times before, I realize, even as I dream the dream. Maybe that is what keeps me from waking in a puddle of sweat and panic - my usual reaction. Instead, I am taken over by the darkness within the cabin. In this realm, I began to discriminate shadows and gray areas. It is then that I discern a trap door in the floor. When I open that trap door, I understand it will lead to sub basements that I must explore. At this point sweaty panic begins pulling me toward unsettled consciousness.

CHAPTER SIX

My phone is ringing. It takes me more than one shake of the head to bring myself back to consciousness and tuck that consciousness back into the shell now stretched out on the floor in a sleeping bag. Then it takes me even longer to disengage myself from the sleeping bag and make my comic way to the telephone.

"Hello," I mumble my throat constricted and my nasal passages blocked.

"Charlie. It's me, Tony."

Tony's voice, a wake-up call, explodes in my brain.

"Tony. Are you all right? Where are you?"

"I'm still being held by the police for questioning. Detective Cooper let me make a call while he gets us some coffee."

He's on the verge of hysteria. I can hear it in his voice. But he's still hanging in there – for now. How long can he last?

"When are they going to release you? Do you know?"

His words come out in jerky phrases as he answers. What will he be willing to say just to get out of the clutches of the police if there seems to be no relief in sight?

"There's this thing about a, ah, check...I ah, don't know about any... It's a fucking nightmare, Charlie...Kafkaesque... Not sure what, how that..."

"Hang in there, partner. Just tell them the truth. That won't get you into trouble because you've got nothing to hide. Right... And you don't have to worry about forgetting it, because it happened."

"Well, yeah. But..."

A door closes in the room from which Tony has made the call.

"It's Detective Cooper," Tony comes back on the line to say. "He wants a word with you."

"Put him on. And remember this... I'm with you all the way on this. And so is Jane. Hang in there."

"Yeah... Okay. Thanks."

"Charlie Carter?"

"That's right, Detective Coop, eh Cooper. We met yesterday — at the crime scene. I'm the insurance investigator for Life Beneficial assigned to investigate the claim..."

"Right... C.F. Carter — the new guy in town, if I remember correctly. How do you happen to know Mr. Vitolinich?"

"We're both from Richmond, Virginia. Met when we were kids."

"As I understand it, you vouch for Mr. Vitolinich?"

"Well, I can tell you that in my opinion Tony wouldn't hurt a fly. And I can also tell you that a Miss Jane Preen told me she was with Tony all night after he left the Straight Theater gig."

"Have you run this by Life Beneficial? That check..."

"I'm just talking now as a private citizen. I haven't spoken with Life Beneficial yet. And, as for the check, I just heard about it last night. I'll be meeting with Mr. White this morning and I assume it will come up in conversation. And I will, of course, be in touch with my office. But getting back to holding Tony in custody..."

"Those are orders from on high, son. Your Mr. White has some very powerful friends in very high places, it seems."

"I see." There is a pregnant pause while both of us ponder authority and the people we must report to. "Here's a thought," I then offer. "Jane Preen told me last night after we left the station that Bob White showed up at the Straight Theater gig and told Tony that he was ready to back the lightshow with cold hard cash. Maybe what White had in mind for the lightshow guys was that check for twenty thousand dollars."

"Then why would he make it out to Mr. Vitolinich?"

"Good question." I'm trying to think fast without my morning coffee and first cigarette of the day. "Correct me if I'm wrong...you can hold Tony for forty-eight hours without charging him?"

"You got it."

"And that is what you are planning to do?"

"Well, we are continuing to check out Mr. Vitolinich's story and are holding him for questioning. That's the department position."

"And you have no problem if I continue with my insurance claim investigation?"

"Well, it's your job, son. As long as it doesn't hinder an ongoing criminal investigation..."

"Oh of course...and I'll be sure to tell you if I uncover something I believe might shed light on your investigation."

"I'm sure you will."

"And would you be willing to pass along anything that might help me complete my investigation?"

"Within limits... yes. I'm willing to keep you in the loop sort of off the record. Let's call it professional courtesy. Meantime, you make it a point to get in touch with your company and your claimants. And get back to me if you turn anything up."

"No problem. You still got my business card?"

"Yeah, somewhere..."

Someone rings the front door bell. I'm trapped on the phone. Miracle of miracles, Tim pops right up and opens it for me. All I know is, it's a woman. I can hear her voice but can't see her. She's asking for Jane.

No sooner do I put the phone down than it rings again. I pick it up. My apartment door closes. Tim heads into the kitchen. I know him. He's looking for his first cup of coffee. Hope he thinks of me too.

"Carter."

"Yes sir."

It's my boss, Mr. Meade, my San Francisco office boss.

"I want you in my office on the double."

"I'll be there right after I shave and shower..."

"I'll give you thirty minutes and not one minute longer. We get an early start at the San Francisco office of Life Beneficial — that's West Coast time, not East Coast time. The home office likes it that way. Got it?"

"Yes sir."

What time is it, I wonder as I put down the receiver. Six o'clock. Jim is grinding up coffee beans. The tuner is still on but all the records have moved from the top to the bottom of the spindle and the record player has shut itself off. I turn off the receiver.

"Bad news?" asks Tim.

"Tony is still being held for questioning. He may be there for some time."

I knock on my bedroom door. No answer from Jane. She must be a sound sleeper. Then I hear the shower start to run...Looks like a shower is not in my forecast for this morning. I straighten my tie and try to shake the wrinkles out of my sport coat. Tim is leaning over a cup of coffee he poured for himself.

As I race down the stairs to the parking garage, I remember I forgot to ask Tim who was at the door. Pulling out of the parking garage, I spot a black VW Bug parked on the street in front of my apartment. Was that the Bug I saw in my rearview mirror last night? Probably not... There are lots of black Bugs on the road.

"I got a call from Mr. Hancock this morning, Carter. And he tells me that you were at police headquarters late last night standing up for that deadbeat hippie Bobby wrote a check to for twenty thousand dollars. Is that correct?"

I'm standing at near attention in Mr. Meade's office in our downtown office, located in a high rise near the corner of Powell and California. Meade is practically foaming at the mouth. Is that fear, anger, or disgust or a combination of all three that I hear in his voice?

"Well sir, I was talking with Mr. Vitolinich when the police picked him up for questioning. It only seemed reasonable to..."

"And that's another thing. We are not in the business of solving murders. We leave that to the police. Our business is to settle insurance claims. Period... And have I got it right that you know this, this individual, this Anthony Vitolinich?"

"Well, yes sir. We both grew up in Richmond and..."

"Let me make this clear as well, Carter. Your loyalty is to Life Beneficial and their customers. That comes first. Have you got a problem with that?"

"No sir."

"Let me finish." What a weasel. Probably almost had a coronary when Mr. Hancock got him on the horn first thing this morning... "Let me finish."

"Yes sir."

Looks like I was wrong to assume a job at Life Beneficial, headquartered in my hometown, a backwater of prejudice but a known quantity, would free me to 'do my own thing' in some limited but acceptable way.

My father comes to mind again. I dismiss that line of thought for now. Mr. Meade plows on with the party line. Like it or lump it. My way or the highway... Suck it up time, mister. Buckle under. Be a good scout. Yes, sir.

"I told you and Mr. Hancock told you. We want this claim handled with tact and efficiency. We want our claimant to be pleased with our service. We want a fair and prompt disposition. We want to make certain that no ill winds blow back from this claim to harm the company. And we want to make certain that we are fiscally and morally on solid ground just as the confidentially agreement you signed when you joined us stated. Now, are you in agreement with what I have just said and can you carry out your duties in the manner stated? Can you, Carter? Do you understand what I am asking of you?"

To be honest - no, I am not clear at all what my new boss is asking me to do. I mean, what exactly is the relationship between the Whites and Life Beneficial, more specifically to Bill Hancock. And if I stand up for the stated moral code of the company, where will that leave me? Out in the cold? And where does this leave Tony? And on a more mundane but very practical level, what the hell am I specifically supposed to do in order to close a claims investigation so that the investigation is fair and thorough? Shit. They say we are all destined to keep making the same mistakes over and over. Do we - ever learn? If we do, then what - more mistakes to correct? What? More to the point, how can I learn when I don't have a teacher, a textbook, a manual at least?

"I understand completely sir. And I will do my best."

"Your best has nothing to do with this. Can you settle this claim in a satisfactory manner so that Life Beneficial and our claimant are more than satisfied? And will we here at Life Beneficial and claimants like the Whites continue to see you as a golden boy, a bright one, on the fast track at Life Beneficial? Or should we part company here and now?"

"I will do my very best to live up to your confidence in me, sir."

And I will. But I'm beginning to have second thoughts about this "Do it the Life Beneficial way" line. Is holding down a good job, security with benefits, all that really matters? I mean, all of us get old and get sick and many of us have kids and take on a mortgage. I mean, shit. I get the message. Straight arrow time — don't ask too many questions. Suck it up and knuckle under — for the good of...

I realize that Mr. Meade is glaring at me.

"Get the hell out of my office and clean up this mess — before the end of this week at the latest. You hear me, Carter?"

"Loud and clear, sir..."

I am left to my own devices in my windowless cubicle down near the water cooler. I dial a familiar number.

"Walter. How're they hanging?"

I need a pal. If I learned nothing else while working at The Office, it is that knowledge is power. And, believe you me, The Office guys have that old standby aphorism down pat. So why not work that source? And Walter is my pal at The Office.

"Charlie. Heard you dropped out and moved to San Fran. Getting any tail on that commune you joined?"

"Got a harem full of hippie chicks... Not like those uptight D.C. babes."

"You just have to know where to look."

"Like you'd know..."

People like Walter and I will never be swingers. We're brooders and tend to bring party animals down, particularly those who are members of the opposite sex. But that doesn't stop us from dreaming.

"Hey, look. I've got my first claim to investigate — and it's turning into a very sticky wicket."

"Lots of loose floorboards to fix, huh..."

One of our "in" jokes — you had to be there. I chuckle in appreciation.

"Right on. Why ask why."

"Really going native, are we?"

"Too much and far out man to you too..."

"Send me a picture postcard."

"Thing is, I need to check out some people."

"You've come to the right place for that one, partner. And since we are supposed to be public servants, I'm now asking — how can I be of assistance to you, sir?"

"I've got a long list. You got a pencil handy?"

"Right behind my ear and moving now to a legal pad on which I will make notes. Shoot."

"Okay."

I rattle off Jane Preen, Luther Green, Ronald Outrage, Robert Toucan, Bill Hancock and the Whites. Then, as a kicker, I add Tony and my father.

"Geez, Charlie. Take it easy."

"Yeah, I know. Stick to babes and swinging communes."

"My thought exactly. Peace be with you, my brother. Call me back tomorrow same time?"

"You bet."

I pick up the San Francisco Chronicle when I get off the phone. The Bob White murder story makes page one above the fold. It appears that 'Bull'

White and Bob Jr., as Mr. Hancock called them, are both model citizens. Tony Vitolinich is no-good hippie trash – looking good to take the fall. Our men in blue will find a way to keep this vermin behind bars and close the case. Stay tuned for further developments. Of course, there is a sensational description of the murder scene and the tawdriness that pervades the story. The Chronicle knows what sells papers in SF.

I dial my apartment number. It rings and rings and rings and rings. Where the hell are Tim and Jane?

I need to clear my head. I go into the bathroom with the Dopp kit I keep in my desk drawer. For the first few weeks on the job, I did most of my morning routine at the office. I wash my face, brush my teeth and shave. Want to look presentable for the Whites. Company policy would dictate that, wouldn't it? You bet your ass.

I'm muttering to myself as I pull out the multitude of claim forms required to settle the White matter with Life Beneficial and begin to fill them out. Is this job just about filling out forms that will settle a claim, rubber stamping the marching orders of the day from on high? Do I now believe that getting Tony off the hook is my top priority, the job and the claim come in a weak second? I mean, who cares whether some fat cat gets paid off big bucks on a life insurance claim post haste if my secret cousin is thrown into the clinker for the rest of his life for a murder he didn't commit as a result? I could never forgive myself if that happened.

I hop the Powell Street trolley to get to my meeting with the Whites at the St. Francis on Union Square. I hang onto a pole and lean far out from the side as we rattle up one of the famous, precipitous San Francisco hills. The trolley bell rings at cross streets. Brake handle in the middle of the aisle is tall so the driver can tug on it and ease the trolley to a stop. Packed with people... Most of them with cameras... What a tourist attraction. And I'm using it for public transportation. Glorious...I get the eye of the guy driving the thing. Give him the high sign. He rings the bell. We both laugh. Just like the Rice-A-Roni commercial. Clatter over metal plates. Cable makes weird noises. People talk in several different languages. A radio plays from somewhere on the trolley. Cars move around us on both sides. A click-click-click sound as we begin our descent. Stopping causes a big screeching sound. In no time, I'm in front of the St. Francis Hotel.

"Mr. Carter. So nice of you to take the time..."

I'm three minutes late. Mrs. White has her hand out to guide me into the room. She looks like she diets constantly, probably so she can wear designer clothes to charity balls. Her bone structure is excellent, classic. Her skin is neat, tucked. She is tall, an ash blond going gray. Her bearing...regal...

Her eyes... alert, active. With something else in the corners of them... concern.

The room is glamorous. Just like a set for a Rock Hudson and Doris Day "Pillow Talk" sequel. No. Not quite that "Hollywood." But the same vacuous feel, an unlived in, managed space, decorated to look like something a decorator deems appropriate for well-heeled clients. French windows open up onto a balcony that looks down onto Union Square. Hubbub of activity outside shut securely away when they are closed. "Ding-ding-ding went the trolley" a dim memory... Sirens a low-level momentary ringing noise in your head... Moneyed guests of this staid and venerable institution would brook no tear gas to intrude or revolution to disturb their tranquil stay.

Mr. White, sitting at a writing table, is on the phone. He is smoking a small, sturdy cigar. He raises his eyebrows in recognition and waves me to a seat then makes a motion to indicate he'll be off in one minute. Dressed in an impeccable gray suit... Soft leather Italian shoes... Conservative club tie... He's shorter than his wife but solidly built... Looks like a former football player, probably the captain of the team. Still in excellent trim...Dark skin, dark hair, darker eyes...

Mrs. White has on something simple but elegant, i.e. expensive. Since I'm no expert on women's fashions, I won't try to describe it. Only thing I can say for certain is the skirt comes down to just below the knee. Miniskirts, so popular with younger women, are not as popular with women Mrs. White's age.

"How long have you lived in San Francisco, Mr. Carter?" asks Mrs. White as we await the end of Mr. White's phone call.

"Three months. Moved here from Richmond, Richmond, Virginia..."

"Of course... Life Beneficial headquarters... The capital city at the headwaters of the James... Lovely place... We're New Yorkers and part time Floridians."

"Richmond has its own special appeal."

"Yes, we know," she answers, picking up a cup of coffee from a side table.

She has something on her mind she wants to say. But she's holding back. I'm in no hurry – not sure I want to get chummy with her.

Mr. White laughs a great big guffaw. "Don't you worry, Bill. I shall." Dramatic pause... "As a matter of fact, he just walked in the door." Another significant pause... "I will and you do the same for me."

Mrs. White and I smile woodenly. White and Peter Lawford would get along famously. It occurs to me that they might actually know each other. Maybe Lawford picked up some of his screen moves from White. Stranger things have happened.

White hangs up the phone, puts aside his cigar as he rises, and walks toward me, hand extended. I get up. We shake hands. For the second time, he waves me to a seat. Very lord of the manor...Self-absorbed prick...

"Edwina, have you offered our guest coffee?" he asks, looking at his wife.

Mrs. White holds up the silver coffee pot and smiles graciously in my direction after freshening her husband's cup.

"Mr. Carter?" she asks.

"Thank you."

Mrs. White turns over another cup into a saucer. The silver service rattles ever so slightly.

"Mr. Carter was just telling me he's from Richmond - in Virginia."

"A little slower paced than the life we are accustomed to but it makes up for that with its grace and charm," oozes Mr. White with a twinkle in his eye.

I nod, add a tight-lipped smile, take a sip of my coffee, clear my throat. Was that comment intended to put me in my place, reassure me, or set me up for what's coming? I don't have to wait long for the answer.

"Well, Mr. Carter, what have you to report?"

He leans back in his chair and crosses one leg casually over the other, picking up his coffee cup as he does so. Great – elegant, athletic, cosmopolitan and a son-of-a-bitch all rolled in one neat package.

"I beg your pardon?"

A momentary glitch in the program of obedience that has been drilled into me since childhood slips out. Sorry about that. Or am I? And if I'm not, what am I willing to do about it?

"Hope you don't take offense – company policy and chain of command and all that. But Bill told me to ask you."

I determinedly fail to take the bait and respond to his not so subtle mention of "Bill."

"Bill Hancock," he prompts me after a pause. "The chairman and president of Life Beneficial... I was talking to him on the phone when you came in. Funny how those things work out, isn't it?"

"Yes sir."

As The Office instructed me, I remain neutral while engaging a potential opponent, and a dangerous one at that. I'm now convinced that Mr. White was not just a visitor to The Office. I am certain he was staff. Will Walter confirm this suspicion soon? If he does, just how high up is our Mr. White in the food chain at The Office? And how would The Office fit into this situation? What the fuck is going on? Maybe I should just sign off on this thing, do the paperwork and forget it. Would the powers that be forget about Tony as well? We've all got better things to do with our lives.

"I'm not trying to put any pressure on you. We want you to be as thorough as possible, you understand."

"Bobby was an impulsive child. A disobedient child on occasion, if you really want to know.... Always getting hurt," throws in Mrs. White, trying to soften her husband's demand.

I smile and take another sip of coffee thinking, "this time Bobby really went and did it. He got hurt for keeps" as alarms are going off in every chamber of my brain.

Why are the Whites putting me in this position? What are they trying to hide? Is this why Tony was glommed onto with such fierce determination?

I should have known that taking a job with a conservative organization like Life Beneficial would put me in this position — standing up for the rights of people who give me the creeps, falling in line with their prejudices, kowtowing to their worldview and peculiarities. One would think I didn't grow up in Richmond or was too dumb or slow witted to get the message at a very early age. I have always preferred to think I'm too much of an idealist, not enough of a pragmatist — I root for the little guy, the woebegone and forgotten. Maybe that's what drew me to Tony in the first place and what has me up in arms now. The protective shield I have donned is chafing me now — being a good boy, a straight arrow with a few crooked lines that offend no one and add interest to my otherwise dull and easily dismissed life. What is it that young people are chanting in the streets now according to someone or other — we want the world and we want it now...

"At any rate, we are hoping that you have just about enough information to close the books on this one," picks up Mr. White. "I mean, that Vitolinich boy — well, Bobby was not very smart about choosing his friends, now was he? Look where it got him — murdered by a common hippie and left on the stage of some shabby establishment."

I add some cream to my coffee and take yet another sip. It's fresh, hot — made with exceptional beans.

And I wonder — would I really achieve the seeming goal of all good Americans, of humanity in general, to be happy, if I learned my lesson and knuckled under, put in my thirty years with the company, at the Country Club, sent the children to the right schools, made appearances at the right time and place in society, kept up with and surpassed the Joneses?

"Bill told me you worked in Washington before joining his firm," Mr. White prompts me.

"That's right."

But you already knew that. You knew that because you checked me out just like I'm checking you out. And Bill Hancock did the same thing. That's why I got this assignment. I'm a member of the club, The Office club, and, as such, I should be more than willing to overlook minor and not so minor indiscretions. In short, I will be willing to play along with whatever game that needs to be played for fellow members of this club.

"Then how can you be sympathetic to war protesters, draft card burners, bra burners, rabble rousers?"

"Our country was formed by rabble rousers, sir. Revolutionaries, they were called. We fight to protect their, our, right of protest."

"Of course," jumps in Mrs. White. "But you wouldn't make any connection between our Founding Fathers and this bunch of...of....persons, would you?"

Mrs. White has the good grace to be uncomfortable in her role. Her eyes reach out to me. They plead, beg, scream, yell...

"Whatever the case may be," Mr. White's voice barks with well-oiled authority. "Bill has asked me to pass on to him what you have learned and how you intend to proceed on this claim. Are we clear on that, Mr. Carter?"

I put my coffee cup down and it must seem to them that I now snap to attention, waving away my passive-aggressive demeanor, perpetuating the double standard myth we all share in America that this is a classless society; and the myth that words like "freedom," "equality" and "democracy" really do have meaning.

"My report sir...yes sir. In order to meet the criteria of this claim I believe it is necessary to investigate how this unfortunate event occurred. Knowing these facts will allow Life Beneficial to eliminate you, the claimants, from all culpability. I am, of course, relying on the police to investigate and bring to justice the perpetrator of this heinous act and will benefit from their excellent work. I have asked for and received the go ahead from the police to interview people connected to your son's murder, not to help in finding the perpetrator but in order to ascertain information that will help me to settle this insurance claim.

"First off, I interviewed the lessee of the Straight Theater where your son's body was found, Luther Green. He has no obvious means of support yet he has leased this theater and lives in a large Victorian house. He was flippant in his response to my questions and less than forthcoming with his answers. I may find it necessary to speak with him again but am not planning on doing so at this time.

"Second, a man named Ronald Outrage, probably a stage name, who is an underground filmmaker and college professor, rented the Straight Theater the night of the murder. Possibly you have heard of him – from mutual acquaintances in Washington, D.C.? After talking to him, it seems to me Mr. Outrage might know something about or be in some way involved in these tragic circumstances. He lives a decidedly unorthodox life. His boyfriend, Bernie Toucan, is someone that particular note should be made of. It has been asserted that Mr. Toucan absconded with all the musical equipment and a van that Mr. Outrage owned after the performance. And it has been implied that Mr. Toucan may have been involved in some very underhanded and illegal dealings, all of which would be a matter for the police. I am particularly puzzled, though, that Mr. Outrage made mention of a top secret agency of the federal government, The Office, when I spoke to him and wonder what bearing if any this revelation may have on my investigation. I think following up this interview might prove fruitful.

"Third, I was interviewing Mr. Vitolinich when he was taken in for questioning by the police. Full disclosure, Mr. Vitolinich and I were acquainted in Richmond, Virginia where we both grew up. As an aside, I personally find it difficult to believe that Tony could commit a felony murder crime. However, the twenty thousand dollar check you uncovered certainly bears further investigation. I'm not sure whether or how that check might relate to the insurance claim I am investigating but since it was presumably written by your son it might have relevance. I will add that the check might have been the first installment on a business investment your son claimed he was going to make in the lightshow. That is what your son talked to Tony about at the Straight Theater on the night of his murder, according to Miss Jane Preen, Tony's girlfriend and the one who supplied to me an alibi for Tony on the night of the murder. Miss Preen was with Mr. Vitolinich the whole night after Tony packed up from the gig at the Straight Theater. Since your son was involved in some sort of negotiations with this lightshow, the Great Northwest Phantasmagoria, I believe it behooves me to inquire further about this relationship."

I look from one White to the other White. They greet my explication with stony silence. I plunge on.

"I might be wrong. This is the first case I have worked on. But it seems to me that I am 'proceeding by the book' based on the training I have received and that I still have due diligence to do on this matter."

I pause again and look from one White to the other White. They await the exciting conclusion of my report without comment.

"So, I'm hoping that both of you will be happy to provide me with all the pertinent data that is required on the multitude of forms that I must fill out in order to close out my investigation and to bring me up to speed with any information you think will help. You know Life Beneficial policy insists that we dot all the i's and cross all the t's. Thoroughness eliminates most future calamity, as they say. In conclusion, all of us at Life Beneficial wish to express our sincerest regrets for your loss."

Mr. White has paid very close attention to my report and has chosen to make no comments while I do so. And, I am surprised to discover that he makes no comment now.

"And you are planning to wrap this up in...."

"A timely manner... Life Beneficial is a highly- regarded company and sloppy work on my part should not be allowed to stain their pristine record of service and dependability."

Mr. White relights his cigar, giving nothing away.

"Quite so...Quite so... Very good, Carter...Very good... Then we'll be hearing from you regularly until you finish your investigation?"

"Unless Mr. Hancock says otherwise, sir..."

"I'll ask him about that."

"You do that sir. I'd appreciate it."

I stand, as Mr. and Mrs. White do. Mr. White and I jab hands forward for the ceremonial handshake. Thank goodness for small favors, he remembers not to thrust forward the hand in which he holds his cigar.

Before I can retreat to the door, Mrs. White leaps forward and takes my hand in both of hers with unnatural solicitude. Smiles... Gracious. Puts on what I would call her Southern charm.

"Please don't think we're ogres, Mr. Carter. It's just that this is our son...We, we need to find a way...I mean, our love, well, he would want us to find a way to put this behind us as best we can and move forward. I, I know that in my heart."

"I understand," I answer.

She's passing me a slip of paper as she carries on with this nonsense. Mr. White does not move. Has put one hand into his smoking jacket a la Napoleon... I have an inspiration.

"About that twenty thousand dollar check, sir..."

White freezes, lifts his eyebrows, chomps down on his now unlit cigar.

"Yes?" he allows after a long pause.

"You wouldn't happen to have it handy. I'd like to see it. Just for the record, you understand."

For this, he has an immediate and definitive answer.

"Your job, Carter, is to settle our claim with Life Beneficial. That check has nothing whatsoever to do with settling that claim. And it is now evidence in a crime that may help bring the man who murdered my son to justice. Speaking of which, I am unconvinced that your approach to settling this claim is the right one and will seek clarification on that when I speak to Mr. Hancock."

I nod without comment. White is on a roll now. He's not going to allow the hired help to interfere in his plans, his sense of what is appropriate.

"Oh, and another thing, Carter, that alibi witness Vitolinich has — Jane Preen — I don't think I'd place my trust in her reliability. She just might let you down."

Before I can respond to this jab, White concludes.

"Be sure to give your father my best, by the way, when next you speak to him."

I get the message. Stay in your place. Take your orders and obey. Be a good scout. How can I do that when Tony has a noose around his neck? If I do my job as White prescribes, that noose will almost certainly get tighter.

How do Bill Hancock and Life Beneficial fit into the White universe? And my father — what does he know and will it make any difference to him when he is informed about Tony's part in this affair?

Tony. Jane. Bob White, Jr. — these are the current targets and victims in this case. I'm not including myself because we all view ourselves as the hero of our own dramas, our life story. Didn't I rescue Tony that day at the beach?

Didn't I come to his aid after football practice?

I am older now — grown up — or so my parents and people of their generation say with one breath, while with the next they tell me to tuck in my shirt and speak only when spoken to.

My loafer-clad feet sink into plush hallway carpet. My blue blazer coordinates with the cream-colored walls lined with sconces and heavy room doors that have French door handles. My neat haircut blends in with the small crystal chandeliers hanging from the ceiling at regular intervals.

What am I — hero, youngster, grown up, servant, outsider, chameleon, phony, difference maker, seeker, chump...

I stab the elevator button. I'm going down. Mr. White is a bastard. All those feelings of dis-ease that assailed me in the waning days of my employment with The Office and that caused me to leave come tumbling back into my mind with added force. Wasn't I the perfect candidate to investigate this insurance claim for Life Beneficial with my background? That must have been the thinking of those in positions of authority. Right...right...right...

Outside, it's raining — what northern Californians call mist. I'm glad I'm standing under the portico for the St. Francis Hotel. My mind is doing somersaults; my emotions are working overtime. I'm pissed. No way am I going back to my office in this condition. I get off the trolley near my office and head for my car in the parking garage. Reaching into my pocket for my car keys, I feel the note Mrs. White passed to me. Later...Jane Preen first.

I light a cigarette. Ornette Coleman lays into some progressive jazz licks on KJAZ as I navigate the city streets. In the past I've been put off by discordant sounds. But now I wonder if expelling irritants while performing might cleanse the performer and his audience as well. Purging yourself of impurities has definite appeal. I plan to give it a try when I get back to my apartment.

"Hello, anyone home?" I hoot into what turns out to be an empty apartment as I enter.

There's no note. The refrigerator is still empty. My spare apartment key is gone. A pile of wet towels in the bathroom is all that remains of my visitors. Jane Preen — and whoever picked her up at my apartment — are a finger in the hole of my dike of protection for Tony. I must talk with them. I must know what they know. Because I, just like my father, am a firm believer in the maxim — what you don't know can hurt you — and Tony.

As I leave, I stick my hand in my pocket for the door keys and come up with the note from Mrs. White. It reads —

"Must talk to you... Call at the St. Francis at five this afternoon. I'll be alone."

CHAPTER SEVEN

I, CHARLIE FOXHAWK CARTER, GET CARRIED AWAY

Forget Mrs. White for the moment. I'll be there if I can make it. I'm in Berkeley, headed up Ashby toward Telegraph. Sun is shining. Amazing how the weather can change from one place to the next in the Bay Area. I'm eager to take off my slicker and my sweater.

Palm trees don't look out-of-place and threatened in the East Bay. Squat stucco cottages with tile roofs line the streets. I try not to think about the maze of people about whom I know little or nothing that will influence this mess I'm in, try not to remind myself that Tony is still in jail, try not to panic and call Detective Cooper so I can whine, curse fate. I have trouble keeping my car within the speed limit, even more trouble keeping my mind on the road. Somehow I've turned on KMPX. Traffic took me across town and over the bridge. Procol Harum guides me upward, deeper into the heart of Berkeley.

Suddenly I'm coughing. Feel like retching. I put out my cigarette. Turn on the car fan. Something stinks. The air looks thicker. This is not my imagination. A roadblock appears out of the gathering gloom. A cop directs traffic down a side street.

"What's the problem, officer," I ask as I creep by. He's waving his arm, looking distracted, tired, stressed out.

"Gone crazy at Sproul Plaza again... Spilled over onto Telegraph... Real mess..."

I'm past him before I have a chance to ask more. Follow the car in front of me. Don't know where I am. Wind around. Pass Alta Bates Community Hospital... Get mixed up in several dead-end streets. Switch the radio to AM and find a news station airing a bulletin.

"Rioting has broken out on Sproul Plaza at the UC Berkeley campus. Police have confronted the demonstrators. Roadblocks have been set up. Please avoid the area if you can. We will update you as more information comes in. But first, we've got to pay some bills."

A catchy jingle comes on. I switch off the radio and pull over to the side of the road. In my glove compartment I've got a set of maps. I discover I'm only a few blocks from the lightshow house. My destination... Might be simpler to walk... I get out. It is deceptively quiet. Birds chirp in the trees. Children not in school play in their backyards. Mothers hover nearby to keep them from harm. A small market is open. Has some fresh produce in boxes near the entrance. I buy a likely looking peach to munch on.

On College Avenue — shops, people having lunch at a sidewalk cafe, meeting and greeting... Busy. Street tree-lined. A bookstore and a record store look promising.

Go down Stuart Street towards Regent. The smell of teargas makes my eyes water. I can hear shouting in the distance. I see, several blocks down the street, people in ones and twos coming my way. They are running, stumbling, helter-skelter — victims of the fray. Most of them are young — college students. They are dressed in street clothes — hippie attire.

I pick up my pace. How are the lightshow crowd making out? Are any of them involved?

Their large three-story Victorian house towers over the street. The driveway at the side of the house, two strips of concrete for the tires with grass in between, goes up a steep incline from sidewalk level, then flattens out passing by the side of the house as it leads to a dilapidated detached one car garage in the back yard. In front of the house an unmarked car that has cop written all over it is parked.

The smell of teargas is much stronger. Bullhorns blare. A crowd in pandemonium murmurs nearby. I recreate newsreels I've seen and hear in my imagination the cracking sound of billy-club on cranium. The Student Movement still thrives in Berkeley — not so much in San Francisco — more of an East Coast vibe here. Whole world has gone crazy over this war. Clash of the generations worldwide, or so the media tells us...

I start looking for a back way into the house. Detective Cooper seems okay but I'm not so certain I want to alert the cops to my movements. An alley runs behind the houses on this block. I peek in a back window of the lightshow house. The room is empty.

I try the backdoor. It's unlocked. I enter as quietly as I can. Molly Kovauc, the de facto den mother of the lightshow, is reading a book at the kitchen table. Her long dark hair is tied together in back. Wears glasses...Has big dark eyes... About five foot three tops. Olive complexion... Rory, her child, big, healthy, happy, looks at me solemnly. He's playing on the floor.

"Hi, Molly... What gives?" I ask in a conversational tone.

She looks up, cool as a cucumber.

"Cops woke us up at eight this morning. Good thing you warned the guys last night. Dumas and Bracken unloaded the gear from the lightshow truck, packed their bags and headed out. Harry disappeared into the night as well. He's a draft dodger, you know."

"What did the cops do?"

"Oh, they searched Tony's room and made a lot of noise. Then they packed up some of Tony's stuff and took it away with them. Said it was evidence..."

"Rioting down on Telegraph..."

"Really..."

"Walked down here because of roadblocks... Saw a few stragglers on the way. Did you know an unmarked cop car is parked out front of your place?"

"They want to talk with Jane."

"So do I... You know where she is?"

"Probably at her mom's house, but don't tell the cops I told you. What's the word on Tony?"

"Still being held by the cops for questioning... And things don't look good for him."

A wave of amplified rioting sounds penetrates to our sanctum. But there's no knock on the front door. The cops are sitting tight.

The kitchen is large enough to hold a wooden table and chairs. It's the most lived in room in the house and it has the most furniture, including the bedrooms upstairs and Dumas' room in what was a detached workshop out in the backyard. Coffee's on the stove. A bowl of fruit sits on the table. Fresh uncut bread sits on a small butcher block next to a cutting knife. A black wall phone is right next to the chair that Molly sits in. Rory leans forward, then takes off crawling. He's an explorer. Molly reaches into the nook below the phone and pulls out a phonebook. Hands it to me...

"Jane's mom should be listed. She lives up in the hills above Oakland somewhere," Molly comments as I start thumbing through the book. "Want some coffee? I just made it."

"Thanks."

Danger encircles the house. Molly and I are, momentarily, excluded from the chaos outside. How long will that last?

"How's Tony holding up?" She asks, pouring my coffee, getting some milk out of the refrigerator.

"Well, you know Tony."

"That's what worries me."

"You got it. And they have orders from high up to hold him the full forty-eight hours they are allowed without pressing charges."

"Why?"

"Bobby's father says he found a check made out to Tony from Bobby for twenty thousand dollars."

"What? A check Bob White wrote?"

"That's what his father says. You know anything about it? I mean, I was told Bobby was making noises like he was going to back the lightshow, get bookings, help them make it big."

"But you just said the check was made out to Tony."

"If the check is legit, what other reason would Bobby have to write Tony a check of that size? Maybe some of the other guys might know something."

"If they know, they haven't clued me in. And they're so freaked out now who knows when they'll surface or what they'll be willing to talk about when they do. But I'll ask them when I see them if you'd like."

"Hey, thanks. I'd like that. And, if you don't mind, I'd love to hear your take on Bob White — anything you might know and, of course, how he fits into the whole lightshow scene."

"That bad, huh..."

Molly takes a sip of her coffee, looks over at Rory to make sure he's safe, then leans back in her chair. She sighs.

"I might have to stop pretending to be an insurance investigator and work fulltime trying to prove Tony didn't kill Bobby — the hell with the consequences."

Molly nods before she answers, takes another sip of coffee.

"I don't know much about Bob White. But I do know he got our attention by fronting us some money and promising us the moon. Still have some of his cash left in the cookie jar. You don't often see hundred dollar bills. Novelty... Could be a drug dealer...probably just some rich kid looking for cheap thrills... He definitely was born with a silver spoon in his mouth. Lots of energy but very scattered...I don't know. There was something about him that was off, something in his past, some weird something he was involved in or something not quite right inside his head that you don't run across every day. I can't put my finger on it."

"What makes you say that, anything in particular?"

"It was just a feeling I got from things he said that didn't add up right. You should ask Jane. She used to date Bobby before she met Tony."

Molly and Jane are never going to be very tight. Molly graduated from Barnard College with honors; Jane dropped out of community college after the first semester of her freshman year. But Jane is family, nonetheless, because she's Tony's girlfriend.

"When was that, that she dated Bobby?"

"I don't know for sure. It was while she lived down in Los Angeles. Jane's kind of vague about all that."

"Really, why...too high...too painful..."

"Ha, the rumor is she was too busy driving around in her yellow XKE all dolled up. Making the scene on the Strip... Making the scene at the Whiskey-A-Go-Go... Hanging out with the high rollers... That's the story, at any rate."

"How'd she get hooked up with Tony? Seem a little unlikely as a couple."

"Tell me about it," Molly agrees. Then laughs... She has a wicked chuckle. "Her sister dated one of the lightshow guys for a while - Harry. Don't know how he got hooked up with Linda. That's Jane's sister. And Harry's not one to talk. Tony and he are tight. That's how Harry hooked up with the lightshow. The two of them even took an extended trip down to LA in our van. Said it was on lightshow business. Came back with a half-pound of Nepalese hash that I'm told came from the house of one of the Monkees. Stayed at the Buffalo Springfield house out in Malibu... Use to be Vincent Price's place. So much for a business trip... But you asked about Bobby and Jane. Wish I knew more."

The coffee's good. I find Jane's mom's address and phone number.

Shouldn't take long to get there with my trusty map...

"Mind if I check in for messages? It's a local call," I ask.

Molly nods. I dial. No messages. Is that good or bad or both? I give my service my current and next location with phone numbers for each and inform them of my five o'clock meeting with Mrs. White at the St. Francis. I'm striking up a relationship with the woman who takes messages at my service – the only benefit I've seen so far to this service. Rory pulls up on the side of my chair. Wants to see what's going on.

There's a knocking at the front door. We look up. Who else could it be but the cops? I let myself out the back way while Molly picks up Rory so she can answer the door.

―――――――

Jane's mom lives at the neck of a canyon in Piedmont. On a winding back road...Lots of eucalyptus trees. Brought in from Australia years ago, I'm told. They've really spread in northern California. The canyon is steep, long and narrow. Can see all the way down to Oakland and the Bay far below...No teargas here, just clear, refreshing air coming up the hill from the Bay...

No cop cars in evidence either. Jane's mom's garage is at street level. Garage door is open. Inside is parked a brand new Cadillac Eldorado. Red with a white ragtop... Real showboat...

Down a paved path with a step every twenty feet or so as it cuts back and forth down the steep descent... Through a hillside landscaped with native plants... To a house that's a prime mudslide candidate during some heavy rainstorm in the future. Kind of thing you see on the national news every year or two. Jane opens the door after peaking at me through the glassed side panel. She has on tennis shoes and dungarees. She looks jumpy, on edge.

"Where's Tony?" she asks.

"Still in the can... Like to talk to you if you don't mind..."

She hesitates but then opens the door wide. I'm led into a living room with a cathedral ceiling that goes up two full stories. Long, narrow panes of glass on the side walls reach toward the ceiling. A gigantic deck opens out from three sets of sliding glass doors. Has a great view down the canyon.

All the living room furnishings and the carpets are in various shades of white. The walls are natural, ash-colored wood. Huge stone fireplace that looks like it's never been used. Wouldn't want to get ashes on the pristine white surfaces surrounding it would we... Is it really okay to sit down in this room? Should I take off my shoes before I enter?

Jane lights up a cigarette. I follow her cue. She's obviously been sitting alone in the living room for quite some time. Cup of coffee next to her... Ashtray filled with lipstick-stained butts.

"I only come here when I know my mother's away," she tells me. "To feed the cats," she adds as if to answer my unspoken question.

Then without preamble Jane states, "Tony hates Richmond."

Wind is blowing, even in the middle of the day. Banging at the side of the house... Bet the sound it makes can be really impressive in the dead of night.

"You ever been to Richmond" I toss out, just to keep the conversation going.

She fidgets with her hair. It could do with a wash.

"Never been east of the Rocky Mountains... Mom says that's where all the real kooks live, on the East Coast. Of course, that's probably just a slam at Dad. He's from Boston. We're third generation Californians."

"First native Californian I've met since I've been here."

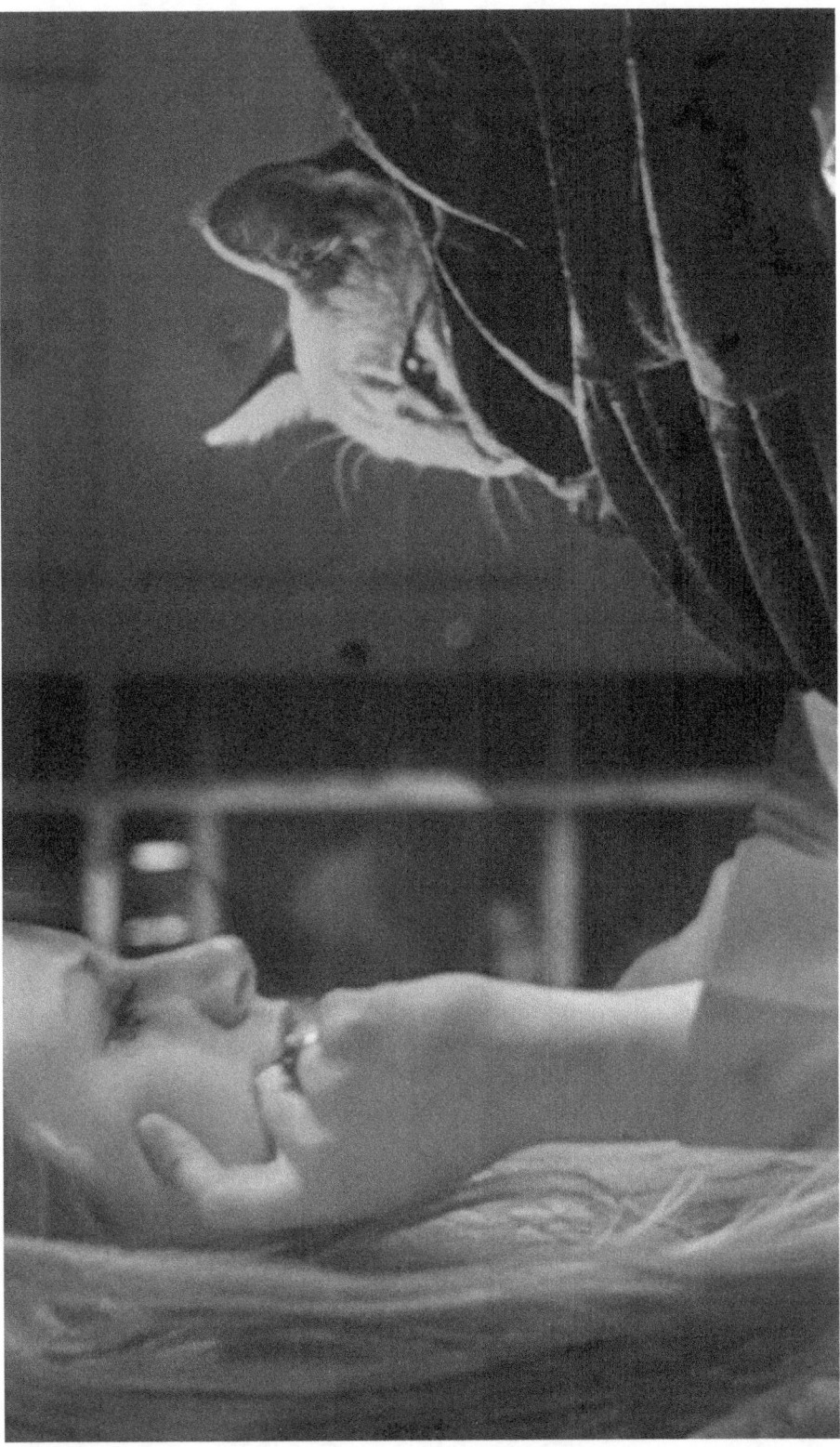

"We're around. You just have to look."

Christ. She's even defensive about her home state.

"That your dad's car in the garage?"

"My mom's latest boyfriend... She bought it for him. A birthday present..."

"Your parents separated?"

Her eyes shoot up. I've landed a blow when I had no intention of doing so. She sees I'm not the enemy — not yet. But we might tangle sometime in the future, her eyes say.

"Dad disappeared. Never came back. Mom had him declared legally dead a few years ago." The anger in her voice is palpable. Her eyes flash, jets of piercing violence. Jane loves her Daddy. Mom isn't going to be forgiven any time soon. "That's when we moved into this house," she continues, trying to appear neutral. You could cut the hostility with a knife. "His assets bought the place. Probably that car too, for all I know. Mom's real good with money," she adds diplomatically.

I nod. Raise my eyebrows. Pick a piece of tobacco from my lip.

"I don't take a cent of her money," she concludes. "I don't want it."

Right... Where did that fancy yellow car come from and your expensive clothes?

"Bob White," I interject. "I'm told you used to date him. True?"

"Who told you that?"

"Molly."

"Figures..." Jane takes a drag on her latest cigarette. She moves slowly, deliberately. Some might call her sensuous. I'd say angry, defiant. Still a kid really... Maybe time will wear down that gigantic chip on her very shapely shoulder. I'm tempted to take a shot at that chip. Nobody wants a dream girl to turn petulant. Shatters the image... "Yeah, I dated him. So what..."

"That the real reason why he got so interested in the lightshow?"

"I was as surprised as the rest of them. I told Bobby to get lost. He laughed. Came around the very next day... He flashed his roll at them. That's the only way he knew how to make friends. Show them your trust fund money. Buy them."

"You weren't maybe a party to his scheme to get rich on the lightshow?"

"For the record, I love Tony. And I'm planning to marry him. You can tell that to all those snotty friends of yours and his in Richmond."

I won't have to. You'll do it yourself by marrying him, I speculate. I nod and wrinkle my lips with a 'you go girl' look on my face. Take a drag of my cigarette. The wind continues to moan and batter.

"Tell me about Los Angeles. I assume you met Bobby down there."

"He showed up on the scene just like here waving his roll. Staked all comers... The crowd ate it up. Aren't quite as idealistic down there as they are up here... 'Peace and Love' just a joke really down there, a thing you say as you raise two fingers in a 'V' and smirk as you do so."

"How long did you date him?"

"Date him? I lived with him. You satisfied?"

"Should I be?"

"I was a teenager practically living on the streets. He offered me the moon. I let him have his way. No crime; no foul. Moved out later... He'd tell you he kicked me out. So why did he call me every five minutes and accidentally run into me every time I turned around? Guess he found it hard to believe that someone would turn down the high life he was offering."

"When was he, the two of you, how long were you an item — a few months, a few weeks?"

"Almost two years, the whole time I was in L.A. He actually followed me up to San Fran."

She pushes out a self-conscious chuckle and stops cigarette in mid-air, eyes looking off into the middle distance, smoke floating toward the high ceiling and dispersing. The furnace comes on somewhere deep in the bowels of the house. You can clearly see the once pudgy and insecure little girl beneath her tough, street-wise, sexy exterior.

"Was he a dealer? What?"

I'm not at all sure she's going to answer — until she does.

"He'd disappear for days at a time. He'd claim he was away on business. He'd get calls at all times of the day and night. He took them in his 'home office.' And, of course, he had long conversations with his dad and the family legal advisor. Was all of that about business? He never convinced me it was."

She peeks at me for just a moment, long enough for me to recognize that what she has told me isn't the whole truth. She knows plenty — and that plenty might make Tony's troubles go away or get worse, might put her in jail or exonerate her. Getting her trust is all that matters at the moment. So I'm taking it very slow and easy.

"We had some hilarious scenes - in retrospect. Really...He grabbed me once. Ripped apart an expensive dress he had just bought me. Hit me. I threw him down the stairs, the little twerp. He tripped, actually. We were stoned out on downers. He probably never knew how he got the bruises.

"You name it; we did it. High on the best weed, the finest speed, the purest heroin... Yes sir, Bobby had himself a come-to-life Barbie doll put on earth to bring him pleasure. Why talk business with someone like that? Why talk about anything serious or important with them? Why show them any respect at all?"

"Any of the people around him have reason to hold a grudge?"

"Mostly just suck ups... All of them despised him or so they said. Would they kill the golden goose? I don't think so."

Yes. There's more, much more. Do I really want to get the real inside scoop? Back off. Do the obvious – that's what everybody is screaming at me to do.

"Did you ever meet either of his parents?"

"His father... Came on to me... Trying to be a real swinger, he thought... Making suave Peter Lawford moves. It was gross. I mean - he must be at least forty-five."

"You can't remember anything, anything at all that might get the spotlight off of Tony and on to someone else?"

"Well, there was this one time. He got real high on some angel dust and thought he'd bought the farm. While he was crashing, he went on a talking jag - the fact we shot up some meth to bring us down might have had something to with that." Jane shakes hair strands out of her face. Takes a drag of her cigarette... Seems to be looking at the clouds moving across the pale white sky overhead... Her eyes, her jaw, are locked, rigid, angry... Why - and for whom? She snaps out of it. "The legal advisor... Maybe..."

She leaves this remotely speculative fragment hanging.

"You sure this legal advisor wasn't his father?"

"No. Bobby isn't...wasn't... No, that wasn't Bobby and his father's scene. Maybe..."

"What?"

She leaves that one hanging too.

"I don't know," Jane states in exasperation. "Anyway, who cares? He's dead. He's gone. That's the end of it. Pay the parents off and forget about it."

We're back to square one – with a difference. Jane doesn't just have a chip on her shoulder; she's frightened of someone or about something. What is she hiding? Do I really want to know?

"Mr. White told me not to trust you to stick with your alibi for Tony. Why would he say that?"

Fear turns on a dime to anger, open hostility. What knowledge would frighten this girl one moment and turn her into a hellion the next?

"Fuck you. Fuck him and the horse he rode in on," she spits in my direction, springing from her chair, dropping her cigarette precariously on the edge of the ashtray.

That pristine white carpet is in danger. So is the white leather sofa on which Jane had been sitting. Hands raised in supplication, I get up with her. Secure the cigarette in the ashtray.

"Okay. Okay. Just cool it. I apologize." I'm not sure she's buying my mea culpa but her body looks like it might relax – given time. "Hey, you mind if I use the phone to make a long distance call?"

The idea seems to amuse her. Yet another way to stick it to her mom...

"Ah, sure...In the kitchen...On the wall by the door...In the nook..."

She stops me as I'm almost out of the big, boxy, high-ceiled room.

"Charlie?"

"Yes?"

"You won't tell Tony any of this stuff, will you? I wouldn't want to hurt him, not ever."

Too late for that now, kiddo...Before this is over lots of messy secrets are going to get splashed around in places where they can cause the most damage. That's for sure.

"No, Jane. I won't tell him."

Despite the fact it's the middle of the day, the windowless kitchen is full of shadows. It's clean. It's dark. Looks unused... The telephone nook is on my left. I take a step towards it.

A loud hiss and a growl followed immediately by claws lashing out at a wire cage make me jump back. Jane is in the room in a shot. I'm reaching for the light switch at the same time she is. We're bathed in light. I look below the tabletop jammed into the alcove in which the phone is mounted. I see a cage. Back in the shadows, a form...a dog? No, a cat... A very muscular cat bearing its teeth at me...

"Margay... Type of ocelot," Jane states matter-of-factly as she nods her head and smiles. "One of mom's cats... Did you hear the puma on your way in? She lives under the house."

The margay uncoils and strikes again with fierce intensity as I make a slight move toward the phone. The cage wires rattle. Claws wrap round the wires of the cage. Nasty little bugger... There's not an ounce of fat on him and every ounce of his fifty pounds is wrought up, madder than hell.

"Puma's in heat. Neighbors are having shit fits. SPCA dropped by. Been here so often we know the staff by their first names..."

"Why?" I ask shaking my head.

"Don't ask," she answers.

I take one careful step backward.

"You have another place I can make my call?"

"Upstairs in my mother's bedroom... First door on your right after you hit the top of the stairs." I nod and start to turn. "If you want, you can watch me feed the mountain lion. She's got a much nicer temperament than this one."

She points to the margay.

"I'd like that," I answer with a smile, hoping I mask my misgivings.

First friendly overture this woman has made.

Mom's room, done up in white with gold trim, has an oversized king size bed. Round... On a pedestal...A dressing table with mirrors that looks like something out of a cheesy bordello by way of Frederick's of Hollywood. The boyfriend must be a real clean machine. No underwear on the floor. No shirts on the backs of chairs. Can't even get a whiff of either of them in the room... The phone is in the French style. The receiver, done in gold and white, has a gold cradle on top of a white inlaid box. Feel like a jerk using it.

"Carter, Williams and Smith," the receptionist states after I punch in the number.

My father, thank goodness, is in the office and not meeting with a client. He comes on the line almost immediately.

"Charlie. What a pleasant surprise. How's the West Coast treating you?"

"You got a minute, dad?"

My father isn't recognized as a top attorney in Richmond for nothing.

"Give it to me straight – clear and concise."

"Dad, Tony Vitolinich is being held for questioning in a murder investigation. And I have been assigned by Mr. Hancock to handle the insurance claim resulting from the murder."

Dad does not react to the name – Tony Vitolinich.

"Bill Hancock? Isn't that a little unusual?"

"Very."

"Who is the victim? Do we know him?"

"Robert Randolph White, Jr."

"Bobby Junior..."

"You know him?"

I hear my father take a deep breath before he continues. He does not often give away even that much to indicate what he is feeling. I'm impressed, concerned and uneasy.

"I know his father," Dad admits. "Bull White, they called him in college. He was the hero of the famous 1938 Yale-Harvard football game. Ran for the winning touchdown with fifteen seconds left... First time Harvard had beaten Yale in a decade. That pretty much assured his future, particularly when you consider his heroics captured the heart of a rather excitable boarding school student in the stands, Edwina Hancock."

"You mean Mr. White's wife?"

"And Bill Hancock's cousin. She inherited a large piece of the family fortune. Still owns a large block of the company stock. Sits on the board with other family members... They've condescended to visit Richmond on occasion. I've had some business dealings with Bull."

"What kind?"

"Privileged... Sorry. You know how it is."

My father had more than just contacts at The Office, contacts that helped get me my job with them in lieu of military service. He worked for them during WWII, or so he informed me when I asked him how he knew about the opening at The Office. Now I'm thinking, did dad continue to have a relationship with The Office after the war was over, right up to the present day?

"You think our mutual association with a certain governmental agency might be why Mr. Hancock called me personally to assign me this case, my first by the way?"

"What do you think?"

We both ponder in silence for a moment.

"Wouldn't Mr. Hancock want his best investigator to handle his cousin's claim, not somebody on his first case?" Dad does not react. The wheels are turning in his head. But what is he thinking? "And now Tony's gotten sucked into it." Still silent... I go on. "I've been told specifically by my boss to settle the case and to forget about Tony. I'm supposed to report to Mr. White what I turn up. Failing to toe the company line is not an option if I plan to stay with them, I get the impression."

"And you have already violated those direct orders?"

"Yes sir. Tony's my cousin, isn't he, and my friend?" Silence... "I think he's being railroaded." More silence. "Mr. White claims his son wrote a twenty thousand dollar check to him. That's the main reason the police are still holding him." Yet more silence. "Oh yeah, and Mr. White used his pull to keep Tony locked up."

I hear the intercom come on in my father's office. He turns his head away from the receiver to answer then comes back on the line.

"I've got to take this call, son."

"Dad..."

"Yes?"

"I need your help. I don't think I'm going to make much headway here without it."

"I'll see what I can do."

"And let me know?"

"This is a family matter – and you are my son."

The line goes dead. I'm drained yet refreshed. This is the first time I've had the feeling that my father and I might someday talk as two adults who don't agree on everything but still respect and appreciate each other. That's a satisfying but unsettling thought. I don't really understand my father – and I desperately want to do so. I yearn for his blessing and his support. I pray my call for help will be viewed as a sign of maturity, not a sign of weakness. Dad is very Darwinian in many ways.

Downstairs, Jane has a bowl full of fresh meat on the counter.

"You ready," she asks, heading for the door before I have a chance to answer.

We go down a set of stairs that take us under the house. Hillside has some shrubby underbrush amidst the eucalyptus trees. Mostly, though, it's dirt... We swing under the sturdy metal girders holding the house on the hill, only to be confronted by a solidly-constructed cage about seven feet high that runs ten feet in either direction. The mountain lion is inside. Jane turns to me before she opens the door. The cat watches.

"Never turn your back on her. She might decide to jump up on you. She likes to play. Doesn't know her own strength... If you do go down, she might get carried away."

I nod, my heart pounding. The cage door opens. Jane coos baby talk to the cat. They're pals. She introduces me. The cat looks much larger from inside the cage. Must be well over one hundred fifty pounds... All muscle. Nice eyes. Smart. Bored...in heat...Believe you me I don't take my eyes off of that cat.

Jane puts down the food. Pets her... Continues talking... Wind never seems to let up in the canyon.

Suddenly...A car pulls up in the turnout in front of the house. We both look up. Coop and another cop get out of the car. I pull Jane to one side. The cat growls and paws the air. Thinks I'm about to hurt her.

"It's all right," Jane purrs at the cat trying to calm her. "Now back out of the cage, nice and easy."

Jane guides me to the door then clicks the lock closed on the cage. The cat growls, then roars. She wanted more than just food; she wanted attention. The doors on the cop car slam shut. We hear the sound of leather shoes on loose gravel and the murmur of voices.

Jane says, "You stall them. I can get away through the neighbor's yard."

"It'll make you and Tony both look guilty."

"If you need me, leave a message at 9010 Gough Street."

I let her go. Why? I don't know. I hear a knock at the front door. I hustle to circle around the outside of the house.

"I thought we had a meeting of the minds," Coop states before I've had time to catch my breath after making my awkward climb from the back yard to the front door. There's no well-worn path.

"There's nobody home," I reply, deflecting Coop's query.

As Coop is poised to tear into me, a car pulls into the garage. Out of it steps a middle-aged woman. Her blond hair is neatly done up in a bun on top of her head. She wears expensive and well-fitted clothes.

"Who's that?" Coop asks.

"No idea," I reply.

She descends, her heels clicking rapid fire down the path to the front door. She's in control of the situation. This must be Jane's mother.

"May I help you?" she asks as she approaches us.

"You are?" responds Coop reaching into his pocket for his wallet onto which is attached his gold shield.

"Alice Preen. This is my house."

"Mrs. Preen, I'm Detective Cooper, SFPD. This is my partner, Detective Ramos."

"And I'm C.F. Carter, an insurance investigator for Life Beneficial."

I reach into my pocket for a card. Mrs. Preen looks guardedly at us and keeps her mouth shut. She doesn't even bother to inspect the card I hand her.

"We're hoping you might allow us inside to see if your daughter, Jane, is there," Coop begins.

"I need to ask her some questions about an insurance claim that relates to the murder of Bob White that Detective Cooper here is investigating," I hasten to add.

"Robert Randolph White..." Mrs. Preen asks.

I nod. Mrs. Preen is quick with her response.

"Gentlemen... My house is a mess and my daughter no longer lives at home. The maid won't be here to clean up until Thursday."

"We'll just be a minute," Coop inserts hopefully.

"This is the last place my daughter would choose to visit. Besides, I changed the locks since her last visit. There was a wave of break-ins in the neighborhood."

"Maybe she mentioned her boyfriend, Tony Vitolinich, to you. He's a suspect in the murder," I interject.

Detective Ramos gives me a dirty look. Coop smiles but I don't think he's too happy. Mrs. Preen unlocks the front door then turns to face us before she enters.

"I understand the urgency of the situation, Detective — and you too, Mr. Carter. I will be happy to give you both a call if my daughter should show up. I really can't help you myself. Now if you will excuse me?"

Coop mumbles "yes ma'am" and hands her a card. With a quick smile from eyes of steel, the door closes in our faces. Mrs. Preen is a very cool customer. I think Jane's judgment of her might be very wide of the mark. She protects her children with fierce intensity.

"What the hell do you think you're doing?" Coop asks when we are at street level.

"I'll be honest with you, Coop. I'm not sure. Like I said, this is my first case."

"That explanation is getting a little old, particularly when you add that Tony Vitolinich is a friend of yours.

"What did your office have to say? What about the Whites?"

"You get your marching orders about Tony from on high. I get my orders from Life Beneficial and Mr. White." Coop looks me right in the eyes. I see something there that tells me this is a cop who routinely drives himself to do more than just what is asked of him. "I'm going to be straight with you, Coop. I know this is my first case and I'm green as hell. And I know that having Tony involved has influenced my behavior. But..."

"But what..."

Coop pulls his pipe from his pocket and a tool to tamp down the tobacco in it. His partner waits patiently by the unmarked car from motor pool.

"Well, why would Mr. White refuse to let me see that twenty thousand dollar check when I ask him for it? Has he shown it to you?"

Coop lights his pipe. I pop open my Murad box and lift out a cigarette.

"We have a Photostat of it."

I light my cigarette and take a drag.

"You verify that the handwriting is Bob White's?"

"Not yet."

"And why would Bob White write Tony a check in the first place – if it really was written by Bob White? And why would Tony want to murder Bob White if he knew about this check? I'd want him very much alive if I were Tony, so I could cash that check."

"Anything else stuck in your craw?"

"Why are Mr. White and Life Beneficial so insistent on holding Tony in custody? He's not going anywhere and you can still build your case."

I take another drag on my cigarette. Coop plays with his pipe. We both stare off down the hill. Hell of a view.

"And why would Mr. White tell me that Jane Preen was unlikely to stick to her alibi story?"

"I got one for you. Why did you cover for Miss Preen so she could give us the slip?"

I shrug and give a lame laugh. I'm new to this game and Coop is good at his job. Keeping him on my side seems like more than a great idea, it's the only bright spot I've seen in this mess so far.

"What this investigation needs is time and a wider scope, in other words a breath of fresh air. Not likely to happen with Jane and Tony in custody. Every person I've talked to raised more questions than supplied answers, wearisome questions that deserve good, solid answers. There's Luther Green, Ronald Outrage..."

"Tony Vitolinich, Jane Preen, members of the Great Northwest Phantasmagoria..."

"And Mr. White..."

"Is that it? Is it?"

"What I'm looking for is help. Hell, I know I'm a babe in the woods here."

Coop lights his pipe again and takes a thoughtful toke. I take a last drag of my cigarette and grind out the butt with the heel of my shoe. The wind is picking up. Afternoon weather pattern seems to include that in the Bay Area. Coop looks me in the eyes.

"Okay, son," Coop begins. "I get the message. You're concerned – and you have a right to be. Too many things don't add up in this case. But they will – trust me."

"How can they if our bosses don't let us do our jobs?"

Coop lowers his voice and steps in even closer.

"I'll get that handwriting analysis in the works. Okay? And I'll do my best to get Tony Vitolinich released."

"Thanks Coop."

"And you – I'm going to give you some latitude here. And I'm sticking my neck out to do it. But you keep me – I mean me directly – informed. You do that?"

"I'll do my best."

"Even if it means losing your job..."

"It seems like that might already be in the works."

"Truer words were never spoken. Oh, and do me a favor, try not to get yourself shot or arrested while you're doing your best."

All of this run-around about a murder, the "who-done-it" factor raising its nasty head at every turn. And the big joke on me is I don't give a shit who killed Bob White, I just want to get Tony off the hook and get me the hell as far away as I can get from the mention of murder because you see I'm a seeker on a quest for higher consciousness puzzle pieces that will solve, well you get the idea. And that's the truth...or what I would like it to be...I think... maybe...

———————

"Why didn't you tell me you were related to Bill Hancock?"

I bypass the good manners I was taught. Edwina White raises her eyebrows.

"What possible bearing does that have on my son's murder?"

"I know he's just a first cousin to you. But he's the top banana in the big corner office to me. And he personally assigned this case to me — my first, by the way. And you don't think your relationship to him and the company has a bearing on..."

"Okay, I get the point. But the insurance claim has to be handled by someone inside the company. I mean the policy was with them. And it has no bearing on the crime. So..."

Mrs. White stops in mid-sentence lost in her own web of thoughts. She sighs. I pace back and forth. Refuse coffee. I stop, look out the window. A trolley pulls up in front of the hotel. People mill about in Union Square or walk briskly in and out of upscale stores. Cabs block traffic. Cars crawl towards the underground garage. A large neon sign - City of Paris - looms above the palm tree infested Square.

Mrs. White is sitting, hands in her lap. Seems composed... I break our awkward but somehow companionable silence.

"You wanted to see me?"

"Yes." Mrs. White immediately dispels the impression she's cold as ice. She shifts in her seat. Nervous as a cat... That makes two of us. "You see. It's, well, it's about my husband."

I force myself to sit down. I take a cup and saucer and pour some coffee. Tête-à-tête time with Mrs. White... She lights a cigarette and immediately puts it out. Not ladylike to smoke in public, my mother used to say. Then she takes a leap off the high board. The water is cold and bracing.

"I...I am worried my husband had something to do with our son's murder."

I put down the cup and saucer on the coffee table. Try to let her know with my body language, my eyes, I'm here to listen sympathetically without judgment.

"Why?"

It comes out in a rush now. Those nasty thoughts have been clogging her brain for years.

"My husband has his faults, as you are by now aware. The years of working on very top-secret government projects have changed him, not for the better in my opinion."

"Does he work for The Office?"

"I...I really don't know...I...What does it really matter what... Anyway, he also loves a pretty face," she states, getting back on track. "I...I'm not proud to admit it but I've learned over the years to ignore his peccadilloes."

Mrs. White's lip curls up ever so slightly. She's going against the grain of everything she holds dear, everything but mother love. She holds her head high and proceeds.

"The thing is, I'm relatively certain Bull had an affair with one of Bobby's girlfriends."

"What makes you so sure? And how would that connect to your son's murder, if it's true?"

Mrs. White does not acknowledge my rude interruption. But she's made a note of it somewhere deep inside her for future study. She coughs and clears her throat before continuing.

"He comes out here on business, frequently. Well, we do own some property down in Palo Alto near the college. At one time, there was hope Bobby would get into Stanford. Managing the property wouldn't account for... Well, he claimed the visits gave him an opportunity to visit Bobby. We both knew that was a fabrication. Anyway, after his last visit, he came home upset. I could tell. You don't live with a man for twenty-five years without figuring out his moods. I...I heard him talking on the phone. He was angry. I've never heard him quite that angry. I tried to block it out. Didn't want to listen, to know... Habit I guess... developed over the years to protect..."

She stops. Looks out the window dry-eyed and tight jawed.

"Who was he talking to? What was he talking about?"

There is a longish silence. The traffic continues to make noise outside. A vacuum runs in the next room. A TV is on somewhere. The room is stuffy. Needs a good airing out...

"Bobby. He was talking to Bobby. Well, you see, Bobby and his father have not always seen eye-to-eye...There's a considerable amount of rivalry between them. Even open hostility. I won't bore you by airing all our dirty linen."

She sighs again, possibly thinking of tabloid journalists or maybe the baby boy she once held in her arms, now lying in the morgue.

"What? What did they say?"

"At first it was about some girlfriend of Bobby's. Then, without any warning, the whole conversation changed. Must have been something Bobby said. I had the impression it was about some business deal, a scheme, a plan gone awry - I don't know. I...I went out into the garden to get away. Just like I always do when I need time to think..."

"Can you remember the girl's name?"

"It didn't come up."

"This business deal...can you remember anything specific about it at all?"

"It was more of a plan, a scheme of some kind that must have included Bobby or something Bobby did or had something to with. That's what was so strange about it all. Bull never let Bobby anywhere near his business deals. Thought he was a..."

A tear rolls down her cheek, a tear for all the lost moments in her life, all the sorrows that can now never be rectified. Her son has been taken from her. Her husband has been unfaithful or worse - and friction of some sort between father and son might have led to her son's death.

"What do you want me to do?"

"I, I need to know. Take all the time you need. But find out what happened to my son."

"And if your husband turns out..."

She stops me by raising her hand. Where is her garden retreat now, poor woman?

"I know you will do what is right, Mr. Carter. I saw it in your eyes the first time we met. And it was confirmed when I found out who your father is."

Christ, I'm tethered by a rock around my neck called family, loyalty. Does it all lead back to home and family for everyone, or just those who grew up in the provincial and insular South? Or is it that the South is just a superb example of the phenomenon?

"I'll do my best."

I'm again condemned by a promise made in awkward circumstances that I might not be able to keep.

"Do you happen to have a letter, a card, anything with your son's handwriting on it? The police need a writing sample for verification purposes."

"A letter — it's a keepsake. Something I'd hate to have damaged or destroyed."

"I'm sure they would be careful with it and return it as soon as they've finished their verification."

"Well, if it will help."

I write Coop's phone number and name on the back of my card.

"Deal directly with Detective Cooper — no one else. You'll call as soon as I leave?"

She nods. The heat comes on in the room. The vacuum cleaner in the next room stops running. The TV nearby is playing a soap opera. The gray sunlight falls on the carpeted floor. Mrs. White's world is stifling, claustrophobic, turned upside down. God bless all mothers.

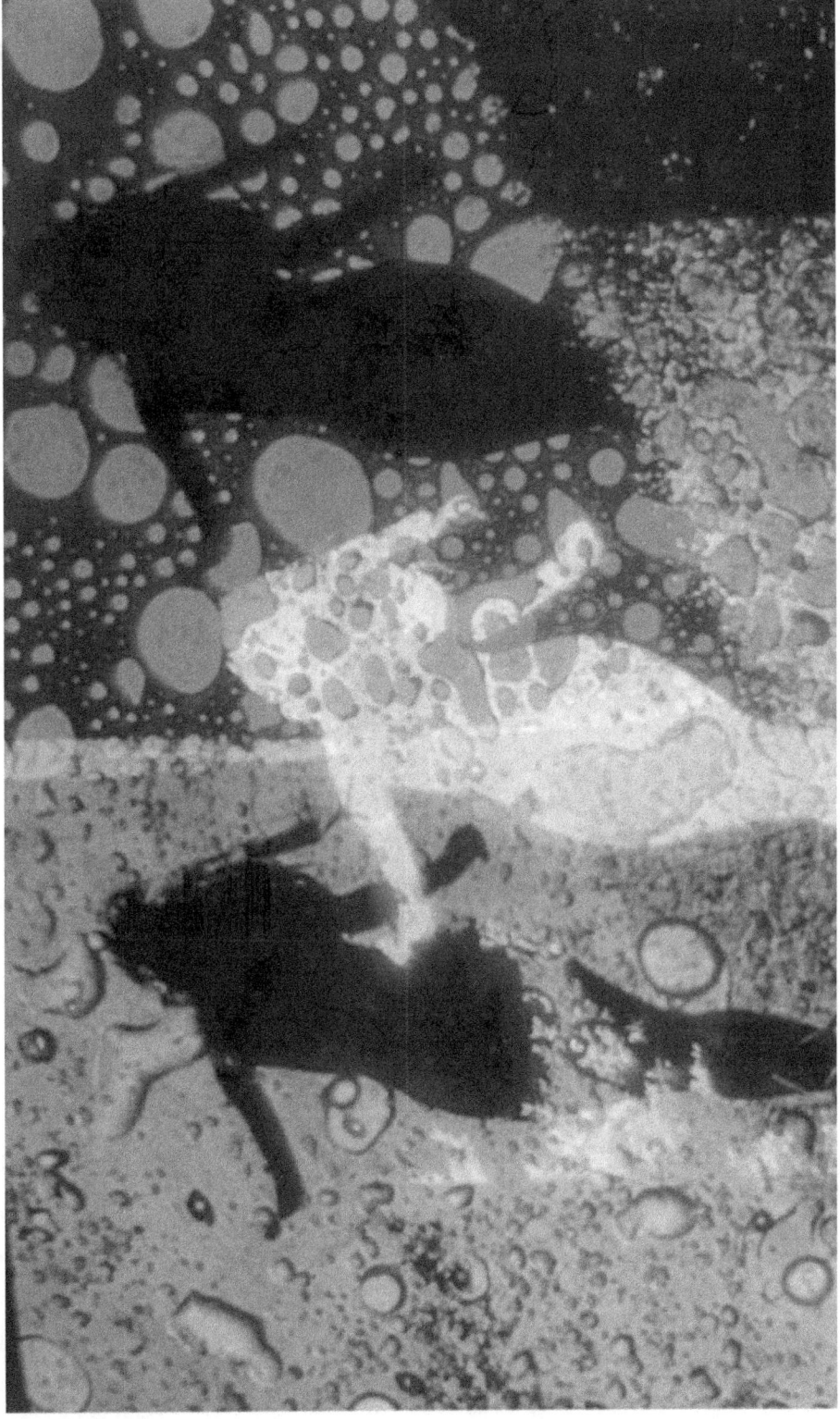

CHAPTER EIGHT

I spot her immediately sitting in an armchair in the lobby as I'm looking for the pay phone to check in. She sticks out like a sore thumb. Young woman in an Indian outfit... From the tribal stomp in Golden Gate Park...No red blooded American male is likely to forget her. She spots me and makes a beeline in my direction.

I'm not handsome, rich, or famous, so why...

She holds up my business card.

"I called your answering service. They told me you were meeting a Mrs. White at the St. Francis at five."

She grabs me by the elbow, muttering another fortune cookie line into my ear that blocks out the lobby murmur in the St. Francis, "Your worst fears will be confirmed, but none of that will matter."

Before I know it, we are outside and across the street looking back at the St. Francis from Union Square. It's raining. What else is new? People are rushing by, umbrellas raised and collars turned up on raincoats. This windy city brings heartaches to all umbrella users and sends rainwater down the necks of raincoat wearers. The doorman at the St. Francis is still looking at us with suspicion even though we are across the street.

"We've got to hurry. Timing is everything," she states, tugging at my sleeve.

She's driving.

"I know the city better," she commented, taking the key out of my hand.

My Volvo flies up and down the streets of San Francisco, makes turns crossing over bumpy trolley car tracks, avoids double-parked cars with a smooth snap of her wrist.

KJAZ came on when she turned the motor over. With a flick, she changed the station to KMPX. "Quicksilver Girl" by a group called The Steve Miller Blues Band plays.

"Okay. I'm as susceptible as the next guy but..." I begin.

She puts her finger to her mouth, then puts it on my lips before backing out of our parking spot.

"Your heart is pure. The body is weak. You will learn. But that is not why you must indulge me now."

We are driving out of the underground parking lot.

"Okay. So why..."

We turn onto the street.

"First off, I have known Jane Preen long enough to know that she got that cut on her knee when she fell off her bike at nine trying to learn how to ride it. Shh..." she insists before I can interrupt.

We are headed away from downtown.

"Number two. You will want to know about things that only I can reveal to you."

She's driving. Good thing. She does know the city one hell of a lot better than I. My car continues to fly up and down the streets of San Francisco.

"Tony..."

"Shh...so young, so innocent, so pure... That is your starting point. Now listen. First stop is a visit to Ronald Outrage."

She makes a turn, crossing over more bumpy trolley car tracks as she does so.

"Am I allowed to ask why you think I should visit Ronald Outrage?"

She avoids more double-parked cars with a smooth snap of her wrist.

"You will see. You will learn," she answers.

The gritty late afternoon light of winter changes to darkness. Angry clouds and rain boil in the sky.

Country Joe and the Fish singing "'I-Feel-Like-I'm-Fixin'-To-Die" comes squawking on the radio, then segues to the Beatles' "Help."

Am I going to let this happen? Is she diverting me or directing me? And am I rationalizing just on the off chance that I can get into her pants? Isobel – she's on the East Coast – and what does she have to do with this anyway? Okay, okay. So I have been pursuing Isobel doggedly for years.

That takes us to a parking spot about a block from Outrage's place. We've not spoken another word.

I do need help and beggars can't be choosers. So if it comes in an attractive package I should reject it out of hand because of the packaging? She's kooky but convincing in her role as an oracle arising from the hippie-crowded streets of San Francisco.

That takes us up a street crowded with cars sending up spray as they head home from work. It's cold, damp, unpleasant. I walk with my hands jammed into my soggy raincoat pockets. Even my sport coat and tie are damp. I look up at the inky sky above. Non-stop precipitation... The Indian costume walks at my side, matching me step for step – coatless, in paper-thin moccasins.

"What's your name," I ask.

"Heather. Heather Chicago. The windy one... Blow in and out of a scene before you have time to say 'Hey, who was that girl.' That's my theory, anyway."

The penetrating chill doesn't seem to affect her. We walk next to a concrete park wall holding back a threatening hillside as we approach the Russian Embassy. A local passes us with a dog on a leash searching for a place for the dog to do his business.

"You know Outrage?"

She stops and looks up at the gloomy monstrosity across the street — the Russian Embassy. I think I see a light on in a downstairs window. Has to be a candle if it is... Mighty low illumination... She lets out a purifying breath as though ending meditation exercises and re-engaging with the external world.

"Bobby drove by once. Told me Outrage lived here. Never been inside though..."

"Bobby? You knew him? He knew Outrage?"

"I think he was trying to impress me. Outrage has quite a cult following on college campuses, you know — with good reason. Art films with far out images... And his subject matter — death, angst, black magic, outlandish sex... Classic shit."

A car passes. It backfires going down the slope towards Divisadero. What appears to be a liquor store has its lights on at the bottom of the hill. It's dark, windy, ominous, wet. Typical San Francisco, so far as I can tell...

Am I ready for this? Am I wasting time when I can't afford to? Is this a trap? Am I being ruled by what's in my pants?

I take her arm and guide her across the street. I can hear music playing as we walk up the steep front steps of Outrage's place.

"Sympathy for the Devil," mumbles Heather. "The Stones..." Is that a sign? Is my brain turning to mush created by Heather Chicago, a true hippie-trippy-dippy San Francisco original who is taking over my insulated, fragile world?

The music has a resonance with this house, this time, that's unmistakable. Cold chills run up and down my spine. I rub my hands together before I lift the knocker and let it fall crashing to the door. The 'thunk' it makes echoes down the empty corridors I know are behind the massive door.

We wait. Nothing... The music continues to blast away. That knocker would wake up the dead. But what about the undead...Heather reaches out to the doorknob. It turns. The door opens.

No need to stand on ceremony if you're a hippie, I guess.

It's colder inside than outside. Frigid...Like a morgue... Heather isn't impressed. She walks confidently down the hall. I'm by her side.

The music is much louder. Dust...Emptiness...Angst and anger palpable in the air... We have entered what - a vault, an underground grotto, a grave. Has an odor I can't quite put my finger on. Oppressive, the latest hot fragrance to hit this camp vision of hell...

There are no squeaking floorboards, no cats to step on, no furniture to bump into, no doors that slam shut. Heather slows.

We both peek in a doorway. The raucous music originates here. There is an altar of sorts inside, the base of which is covered with black velvet material, making the altar appear to float in space. In front of the altar, on the same riser as the altar, is a bed with gold satin blankets and red sheets trimmed with gleaming black. The bed is circular. Pillows are tossed about.

The altar — does it honor the Dark Forces, the Evil One? An unholy collection of profane objects each more disgusting than the last lie artfully about. Some sort of horned animal mounted above the bed. Prominent "666" painted on a gold and red shield. What looks like a monkey's claw, a clump of long black hair strands, an evil eye, a leather pouch that must be filled with charms and appropriate amulets...Sticks of incense burning...

The bed and the altar are spotlighted. The rest of the room is in shadows. From the ceiling hangs a mirrored dancehall ball, sending multi-colored sparkles of light around the room. I place the smell. It's the brew I discovered on the stove during my earlier visit to this house.

Then we see him. Outrage... He has on ceremonial robes. Long. Flowing... Majestic... Black... He is kneeling on the floor watching a motion picture projected on a bare wall. The clattering 16-mm projector is showing a movie that depicts lightshow images filling the wall, the floor, the ceiling of an antiquated entryway — the one we just passed in the hallway. Down the stairs with the rickety railing, the stairs of this house, through the phantasmagoric liquidity of light, walks a young man. He is scantily clad. His walk, his whole attitude, is a sneer, a raging assault. This is a dangerous man. It has to be Ronald Outrage's lover, Bernie Toucan.

"Mr. Outrage," I foolishly inquire, stepping towards him.

Outrage doesn't respond. I bend down towards him.

"Mr. Ronald Outrage," I repeat again in as normal a voice as I can muster above the raging music.

He is very far away. Hands outstretched in supplication. His head turns slowly. His eyes blink twice, then focus to pinpoints of anger at my intrusion. I realize tears are rolling down his cheeks. His hair is in disarray. He looks old and wizened. We have interrupted a sacred ceremony, looked behind the mask. That is not allowed.

"Who the hell..." Outrage starts as he struggles to rise from his kneeling position on the floor. He staggers as he rises. Catches himself...

"The door was opened," Heather offers making a motion with her hand over her shoulder.

Suddenly, a wild man bursts into the room. Knife raised and ready to strike. Crazed killer... Bernie Toucan, the guy in the film.

"Watch out," shouts Heather.

Toucan's knife slashes downward towards Heather. I dive, grabbing Toucan's hand, managing to change the direction of his attack. Toucan falls off balance and staggers toward the floor. I am pulled with him. Outrage cowers in the corner. Heather is slammed into the wall with a deadening thud. Our bodies have sent her flying.

"Bernie," Outrage shouts.

I roll in a tangled struggle with Toucan on the floor. The knife clatters out of his hand and slides under the raised dais. He's moving on all fours towards it in a flash. He's a cloven-hooved creature, danger on the prowl.

"Bernie. No," shouts Outrage.

I leap on Toucan's back. He throws me off like I'm air. I slam into Heather. She does not move; she's out like a light. A tall candleholder topples over next to me. I pick it up and advance towards Toucan. He leaps at me. I brace myself, then jump into his surge. We're like two linemen in a football game. He slips and tumbles against the profane altar, screaming like a banshee. A bowl of that disgusting stuff that was bubbling on the stove has splashed onto his arm. I knew it smelled pretty rank but I had no idea it was so potent. Toucan is beside himself. His eyes grow large. He throws down the knife which he has retrieved from under the altar and zooms out of the room, all the while holding his arm. He's screaming in terror now. What the hell got into him? Hell?

"Are you all right, Heather," I shout, leaning over her slumped body, shaking her shoulder.

She moves. Then groans... "Yeah... Think so."

No blood that I can see. She's moving her limbs so nothing's broken. Just got knocked out...

"Bernie. Bernie. Come back. Don't leave me. Please, don't leave," shouts Outrage.

I hear the front door slam shut. I throw back blackout curtains in front of the bay window. Toucan is jumping into a black van parked under a streetlight. He's still decked out in his exotic regalia. Gold sandals... Long black robe that matches Outrage's... Some sort of crown in his hair... He's wearing makeup – garish lipstick, rouge.

Take my handkerchief out of my back pocket and pick up the knife old Bernie boy was wielding. He looks good for all sorts of mayhem in my book.

"You sure you're okay?" I ask Heather as she begins to stir on the floor.

She nods, getting up slowly. She's a keeper.

Outside, the van explodes into life, turns onto Scott Street in a crazy swerve, and makes a left onto Divisadero against the light. Cars slam on the brakes to avoid him in his hell-bent-for-leather exit.

"What the hell is this all about?" I bellow at Outrage.

"You've screwed with destiny, Mr. Carter. You'll pay for that. You'll pay."

Outrage is now standing by the door with arms crossed, legs akimbo. He has regained his composure and now has donned his wrathful chief devil persona.

"Yeah, well I better not find out that your boyfriend has any connection with Bob White or his ass is grass. It's not polite to go around pointing knives at people."

I hold up the assault weapon.

"You surprised him. He was defending himself. He thought you were robbers, intruders, which you were. I'll say that in court."

"And I suppose you two were spending a quiet evening at home."

"This is still a free country. And you two are trespassing. Give me that knife."

Outrage takes a decisive step forward. I take a step away from him, putting the knife in my coat pocket. It sticks out awkwardly.

"Not a chance," I answer pulling Heather to my side. "I suppose you never had any dealings with Bob White or his family either, back in your East Coast lair. And your boyfriend hasn't listened to your pointed and aggrieved gossip about them either. Am I right?"

"Mr. Carter, I have no idea what you're talking about." I've hit a nerve. Outrage, in control but just, glares at me... "I'm telling you. Leave. Now...Take your heroics, Pocahontas, and yourself and get the hell out of here. Are we clear on that?"

Outrage has given up his claim on the knife. A concession... But I've not seen the end of him, I have a feeling.

"I'm going to get to the bottom of whatever voodoo mumbo jumbo you're into, Outrage. And if it connects to Bob White's murder..."

Heather pulls me by the arm towards the door. Outrage and I exchange foreboding stares. The record comes to an abrupt end. The film gliding through the motion picture projector runs out at the same time. The film, now on the take up reel, goes slap-slap as it spins round and round to the hum of the projector. A harsh white light, once a movie image, flickers on the peeling-paint wall. The smell of a hot projection lamp collides with Outrage's warlock brew. I restrain the urge to gag.

Will the forces of light overcome those of darkness? Will innocence prevail over evil? Christ, I've been enchanted by Heather, by the whole San Francisco scene, by mumbo-jumbo voodoo.

Outrage stabs at a light switch. The glaring white blotch where the motion picture image was fades, the room goes dark, and the humming of the projector slowly dies. The power has been turned off at the Russian Embassy. It's time to go.

Outside, the damp, foggy weather seems balmy. This peace-and-love business can take some very nasty turns. If the parents of the kids who are loitering on this city's streets knew this kind of stuff was going on, tanks would roll down the streets of this free love city to rescue their babies. This whole nonsensical scene would be history in a week.

I open my car door for Heather. She slides into the shotgun seat without comment. I circle round to the driver's side of the car, get in, hold out my hand for my keys and, when Heather puts them in my hand, start the engine. While the engine warms, I lean forward and look up the hill to Outrage's solitary Victorian house.

"You knew the guy with the knife."

Heather looks me right in the eye then puts her hand on my cheek. Her touch is soft, lovely.

"You saved my life," she answers.

I pull away slowly, reluctantly. Look out into the pouring rain. We're both cold and wet. The heater is blowing cold air. Isobel is three thousand miles away, in another world completely.

"Why did you bring me here? What the hell is this all about?" I ask.

"Black Magic... Voodoo... He'll put a spell on you, Mr. Carter. You better be careful from now on."

"And that's why you tracked me down at the St. Francis?"

She lets her hand slide down until it rests on one thigh between my legs. Good Lord. Heaven...

"I tracked you down because I recognized the seeker in you, one with good and pure intentions, but one who needs a helping hand to succeed in the valuable work you were put on earth to accomplish. All that is required of you is that you demonstrate the courage to stand up to your fated destiny."

It's hard to concentrate. She's running her hand up and down my thigh as she talks. If part of the definition of courage is resisting sexual overtures, I'm definitely toast.

"Are you ready to straddle your destiny?" she asks with a coy smile.

Then she leans over the gearbox and reaches up, circling her arms around my neck. We kiss. It's the first kiss I've received from a female other than my mother or aunts since I received a rather tepid one from Isobel when we parted. We kiss again.

My mind explodes. Is Heather's definition of fated destiny having a cousin taken into custody on a murder charge stemming from an insurance investigation assigned to me by the Big Boss and then being told to lay off trying to get Tony off the hook? Is it being locked in a cage with a full grown mountain lion in heat and then allowing Jane Preen to elude the cops? Is it having a tête-à-tête with a grieving, tormented mother in the St. Francis while discussing the dirty laundry in her family's closet, attending a Human Be-In in Golden Gate Park to interview a pampered rich boy playing games with obnoxious friends, breaking in on a drug-crazed Satanic ceremony, having a madman run at me with a knife, and, most immediately, allowing a seemingly spaced-out hippie girl in Indian garb, a total stranger, come on to me for no apparent reason (I'm no prize)? Is any or all of this part of Heather's definition of fated destiny?

"Where do you want me to drop you off?" I mutter.

"Your place is fine," she answers.

Lord, have mercy on my soul.

CHAPTER NINE

I, CHARLIE FOXHAWK CARTER, AM IN OVER MY HEAD

The phone is ringing.

We lie on the bed. Naked...She is lovely to behold. Shimmering white, soft skin in the silvery light of the bedroom... Shapely hips. Ripe breasts with taut nipples... Blond hair falling over her shoulders, down her back. Ganja haze electrifying my vision of her...

The phone is ringing.

She insisted we open the French doors. Traffic roars by outside. Not as bad at night as it is during the day.

The phone is ringing.

I turn towards her. She reaches into her purse and pulls out a pre-rolled joint.

The phone is ringing.

"Smoke some of this," she demands. "It's Panama Red."

The phone is ringing.

"Hold that thought," I answer, heaving myself up from the bed.

"Hello," I shout into the receiver, hoping the phone is dead, hoping against hope that this is not a reminder that I have neglected my duty for this blissful night of madness — sexual release, reefer madness, insane and passionate lovemaking.

Fuck my training — as a federal agent, as an insurance company employee, as a solid Richmond citizen, as a Christian soul, as an almost engaged person. This self-confessed outcast and seeker of truth and freedom shouts, fuck responsibil...

"Charlie. It's Tony. I'm free to go. Can you come down and get me?"

"I'll be there right away."

I slam down the phone, start tugging on my clothes. Heather is ready quicker than I am.

"Where do you think you're going?"

"With you..."

"Just a minute..."

I check with my service. I have two messages – one from Walter, the other from my father. Both want me to call back – urgent.

"You aren't invited."

"I'm going anyhow."

"I'll drop you off on my way."

"Let's get cracking. Tony's waiting."

She tells me a story to pass the time on our way down to the station. The radio is playing the Beatles' "'Tomorrow Never Knows."

"I was at 'The Matrix,' a nightclub over on Divisadero Street near Union. Musicians hang out there. Great place to get mixed up in an impromptu jam. Hangers on seem to shun the place, maybe because it serves alcohol, not cool, turns some of the purists off. Jack Casady was there. You know, the bassist for the Airplane. Real wild man...Bought me a drink. Let him pick me up. We were on our way out of the club. His Lotus Elan is parked right in front.

"Club's right near the bottom of a steep hill. Some idiot's brakes give out and he loses control. Smashes right into Casady's fancy sports car... He goes ballistic. Forgets I'm even around. Pulls a tire iron out of the trunk and threatens bodily harm to the middle aged drunk in the offending car. What a laugh. Good wind would blow Casady away. Him and his funny glasses..."

On the radio the Kinks are concluding "You Really Got Me." The next cut on the Kinks album comes on. KMPX likes to play long songs, even whole sides of albums. The rumor is the DJs sneak up to the roof to smoke a joint or whatever while one side of an album plays. I'm approaching the South-of-Market District. No place to drop off a lady.

"Is this going somewhere?" I ask.

Heather ignores me, carries on.

"I'm hysterical. Scene's ugly. Jack's ignoring me... Cops could show at any minute. Crowd starting to form...Drunk guy's car is blocking traffic. Trolley car coming down the hill has to stop. People on the trolley get off. Mill around... Drunk driver throwing up in the gutter... Loud music coming out of the Matrix... People pour out of the bar to watch the show...A real three-ring circus. Bobby pops up from nowhere."

"Your hero arrives."

"Offers me a ride... Jack can't be bothered. Adios rock-n-roll star. Just another kid who grew up in a nice, middle class neighborhood, copped a few licks from his favorite Delta blues musician, let his hair grow long, and made a big splash on the scene."

"Cool car, though."

"Bobby has beautiful manners, cultivated New England accent, obviously educated at the best East Coast boarding schools and college money and position can buy. But that doesn't stop him from snorting coke or doing H, getting down and dirty in the sack or on the dance floor. He's driving an old, beat up VW."

A light flashes in the back of my brain — a car passing in the night, a foggy night in a rear view mirror.

"What? Bobby had a VW?"

"Well, yeah. Why?"

I've shocked Heather from her reverie.

"Where is that car now?"

"He loaned it to me the day before he bought the farm. Why?"

"Why were you following me the night after the murder?"

"Following you?"

"Did I lose you going through the park?"

"Maybe you should let me off. Anywhere will do."

"You leave the keys in it when you get out? Can you lock the doors?"

Where is her oracle routine now? She nods – reluctant, half way between brought down and hostile.

"Well, yeah. Bobby gave out keys to his friends. Probably still some floating around. And I leave the door unlocked. Why not? It's just a junker."

I feel like Humphrey Bogart in "The Maltese Falcon." Damn. Double damn.

"What's wrong, Charlie? You think I'm a party to whatever it is you're tangled up in? Do you?"

She puts her hand on my shoulder. Out comes the oracle.

"It is necessary to move to a new level of awareness. Only from that altered space will you see things clearly. A new and deeper truth and peace will be yours."

Damn. Double damn.

"Don't get trapped in mediocrity, the feeding trough of the unenlightened."

Damn. Double damn.

"You stay here in the car. If it's going to take a while, I'll come out and let you know."

At Heather's request, I leave the key in the ignition so she can listen to the radio and keep the heater on. I pop the trunk. The knife Toucan was wielding is there, wrapped in a dirty rag. As I head into the station, I wave to Heather sitting in the car.

Is allowing her out of my sight while sitting in my car with the keys in the ignition a good move or a very bad one? What am I trying to prove? Who am I protecting? What kind of dumb fuck were you, Bob White, to go and get yourself murdered in the first place?

———————

"Coop. Got something I think might interest you."

I show him Toucan's knife.

The good news is that neither the handwriting sample Mrs. White sent over nor samples from Tony and Mr. White match the handwriting on the twenty thousand dollar check. And, with that revelation, there's no way even Mr. White's powerful friends can insist that Tony continue to be held in custody. He's free to go. Tony breaks Richmond customs and hugs me when we meet in the detective section instead of shaking hands. I ask him to wait for me in the car while I talk to Coop.

Coop gives a long, low whistle.

"You think this might be the knife used to stab White?"

"That would allow you to zero right in on a truly crazed individual perfectly capable of committing a multitude of heinous crimes – including murder."

"Where'd you come across it?"

"Bernie Toucan, Ronald Outrage's boyfriend, attacked me with it at Outrage's place. The two of them mix sex and satanic worship."

"Potentially lethal combination..."

"And how... Toucan was the leader of the band that played at the Straight Theater the night White was murdered. They only played a few numbers. Plenty of time for him to look good for the murder... Think your lab boys might be able to do anything with this?"

"Maybe... We've got some bright boys with some fresh ideas up in forensics that will, one day, revolutionize police detection."

Coop calls to one of his assistants. We're standing in his office. The door is open. It's an interior room. Could be any time of day or night... Coop's in his shirtsleeves. Wearing a spaghetti-spattered red and black tie...Shirt could do with a press. His pants look like he slept in them. Everything on him looks neglected, rundown. Not so his precision and care in handling his caseload.

"Take this down to the lab right away. I want every test in the book run on it. I want to know everything about that knife. Everything... Do you understand?"

"Yes sir," answers his assistant.

Carefully, he picks up the rag on which the knife lies and heads out of the room.

"You worked for a federal agency, right?"

"Right..."

"You guys use bugs?"

"That's safe to say."

"Mind if we put one on your vehicle?"

I weigh the pros and cons.

"If you're overseeing the case — why not..."

Coop calls out to another assistant and gives him instructions.

"What else you got?"

I'm not handing Heather over to the cops just yet. That means I don't mention the VW. If Tony is off the hook, I'm history on Coop's case anyway. Who needs the aggravation? Heather, then Isobel, race through my mind. An unkept commitment to be a questing seeker flickers on the edges of consciousness. I flop down in an empty chair near the door.

"Well…" I start, and then stop searching my mind for anything I want to pass along to Coop. He's been a solid guy in my book.

Coop stops pacing, looks at me, scratches his head, puts his finger to his chin, looks out into the main area where his subordinates work, closes the door, takes a seat at his desk chair, stretches himself, gives me a sincere look.

"If you're holding back the fact that your father has done work for Vitolinich's father, Bob White's father, Life Beneficial, and The Office, no need. It's a matter of public record."

That's more than I knew for certain. Coop doesn't fool around when he does a background check. That's reassuring – and unnerving. I'm glad he's in my corner. I only hope I can keep him there. He's a stand-up guy.

"So, what's bothering you, Charlie?" he asks with a sly smile.

First time Coop has called me by the first name. I like it.

"Mr. Robert Randolph White, Sr."

Coop sighs, tries to smile, shakes his head as he wags a finger in my general direction.

"He knows some very powerful people, Charlie. Tread lightly, very lightly."

Coop has nothing to offer that adds to my speculation but I can tell he doesn't think much of Mr. White either.

"He's got an eight-figure motive and, as the saying goes these days, he's got terrible vibes."

I don't include the fact that his wife suspects him as well or that he argued with his son over a deal of some kind or that he came on to one of his son's girlfriends or that he's gotten his hands very dirty carrying out special operations for the F.B.I. and J. Edgar Hoover and whoever the hell else are in the smelly fog of deceit and connivance called Washington, D.C. I try out a new approach.

"You find a VW parked in front of White's pad?"

Coop starts to say something, stops, then chuckles.

"Try a red, vintage TR2 for size. Nothing low rent about his taste or his pad. Lived up near Coit Tower…Telegraph Hill… You don't find anything there for cheap. Great view…"

"Mind if I take a look around there?"

Why am I doing this? I should be heading for the door, forgetting the shit storm this murder has created in my life. Maybe that's the reason. Have Tony and I, what the hell and Heather and Jane and the whole lightshow gang as well, really seen the backside of this tainted-with-evil tsunami? It might be wise to hold off on closing the claims investigation to give myself a reason for continuing to poke around where I'm not really wanted, it occurs to me.

"Be my guest." He looks at me then leans forward. "Vitolinich came up clean as a whistle but his girlfriend, Jane Preen, had a minor bust in LA for possession. Marijuana... Dismissed... Guess who she was busted with?"

"Bob White..."

"Bingo. Know where we might find Ms. Preen?"

"Search me. But let me know if you find her. I'd like to ask her a few questions myself."

Coop leans back in his chair, cups his hands behind his head.

"What about Green?" I ask.

"Just one of those society party boys living off of the fat of the land as far as we can tell..."

Coop un-cups his hands so he can rub with forefinger and thumb the place where his nose intersects his reddened eyes. I take my leave after writing down Bob White's Telegraph Hill address. I walk down with the lab assistant delegated to bug my car. My car is gone.

Damn. Double damn.

Coop has a patrolman give me a lift back to my apartment after I decline to file a stolen vehicle report.

Tony's out of the slammer. I have paperwork to fill out and big kahunas to kowtow to. There are some nagging loose ends I can cling to — the whereabouts of my car, Heather, the lightshow people, Tony, what's with my father, what has Walter at The Office come up with, what to say to Mrs. White. I'm sure there are more I'm not thinking of right now. Got to seem like I'm keeping all these balls in the air until, until, well until something convinces me I don't need to worry about this mess any more. I'll happily fill out the paperwork and kiss ass for Life Beneficial at that point.

Disgruntled, disgusted, cranky, I check my messages and discover I've got one from Mr. Meade, my San Francisco Life Beneficial boss; a message from Mrs. White, and two messages from Mr. White. Mr. Meade and Mr. White want the paperwork on my claim investigation handed in ASAP. Mrs. White just leaves a number to call.

I call the lightshow house. Molly has not seen or heard from either Tony or Jane. But she will let me know if she does. She has no idea where I should look for them. When I ask about the rest of the lightshow members, she laughs.

"The two Jims didn't go to Oregon as I suspected. They're staying with a friend over in Sausalito. So it's still just David and I and Rory alone here in this big old musty house."

What the heck? I call Jane's mom. She's cool but not unfriendly on the phone. She has not heard from her daughter or Tony. And she has no idea where they might be. But she does have a suggestion.

"You might check with her sister, Linda. She might know."

Of course, she has no idea how to get in touch with her. Then she asks, "The murder victim's father, you have any long conversations with him about what happened?"

That's a laugh, I tell her. All the murder mysteries I read, she replies, put relatives, particularly parents or siblings, at the top of their suspect list. They say truth is stranger than fiction, I reply. She says, don't count on it. And we sign off.

I call Walt at home. The phone rings and rings and rings in his apartment but no one answers.

I can't just let things slide, fill out the paperwork, let time heal. I've got friends involved here, well people I've gotten to know since moving to SF, people I don't want to get hurt because of this mess I'm calling an insurance investigation. What the fuck should I do now? Forget who killed Bob White and the tangled who-done-it? I just want to get on with my new life, hanging out with old and new friends, such as they are.

"Hi Mom, is Dad around?"

I've caught them at home. They have a very active social life. Business, family, friends, business associates, good works and board meetings all add up. Dad comes on the line. We get the preliminaries out of the way. Dad is cool, stern, business like.

"Mrs. Hancock, Edwina Hancock White's mother, became involved with a younger man after her husband died. That lover, a promising young chemistry researcher at the time, was appointed executor of the estate and Bobby the designated heir. The Whites - Bull and Edwina – seethed, to no avail. Bill Hancock does not involve himself. But everyone knows he was sweet on Edwina when they were youngsters."

"They had an affair?"

"Please. This happened in the 1930s, in Richmond high society. And Bill, despite his supposed passion for Edwina, has always had a poker up his ass."

My father, particularly around the family, is not one who is comfortable with profanity. Bill Hancock, I get by implication, is not very high up on my father's list of admired individuals.

"Anyway, this lover, Ronald Walker, no longer does research. He had what you might call a mid-life crisis. But Walker has kept control of the White family purse with an iron hand, primarily by indulging and dominating young Bob White. They were very close."

"Could that be a motive for murder?"

"For Walker... well..."

"Would Mr. White, do you think..."

"Bull White is a lot of things – many of them not very admirable. But..."

"Mrs. White thinks he might be involved somehow."

"She told you that?"

"Yes sir. Mr. White might have been having a fling with one of his son's lady friends."

"She told you that?"

"She told me she suspected it."

"Son, listen to me. Be very, very careful. There's definitely more going on than appears."

"We're already talking about murder here, Dad..."

"People who travel in the same circles as Bull White have extraordinary power and unlimited resources. So I repeat, play it very low key. Trust me..."

Just the tone of my father's voice, something, shakes me awake, allows me to ask him something that's been on my mind since I was hired to work for Life Beneficial.

"Dad... Why did they hire me at Life Beneficial? I had no real training. There must have been other more qualified applicants."

My father brushes away my question.

"How would I know?"

"For the same reason I got my job at The Office?" I persist.

"You need to pack it in for the night, son. Hit the hay. Rest is important. But before I hang up I want you to know that your mother and I both love you very much. And I will always give you the best advice that I can."

"Thanks, Dad, I love you too."

"I'm not done yet, son."

I am polite. I wait. I hear someone out. I don't fly in with my opinion, my position, my problems. That's being polite. It's also being smart. The Office taught me that.

"I'm advising you to let this thing drop. Fill out the paperwork and move on. Sleep on it tonight. See if you don't think I'm right in the morning. Both your mother and I hope you take our advice — because we love and care for you. Goodnight. Sleep well, son. And God bless."

"Dad, what about Tony..." I jump in to add.

The line goes dead.

My father — what does he know? How does he know it – through his connections to The Office? If so, is he trying to gently lead me away from a potentially fatal collision with flaky operatives and their arrogant and entitled superiors? And what about the Big Boss, Mr. Hancock, and the Whites and the minions at Life Beneficial, what kind of shit will they add to my life by closing the claim or not closing it? And Ronald Outrage and Bernie Toucan and others not yet known, how would they add to my grief? And, shit...I don't know.

I do know thinking about this whole ball of wax is not what I had in mind for my life. I want to be a seeker after Truth, a solver of puzzles that answer the big questions of life, not sordid secrets and crappy schemes.

I'm my own worst enemy. Maybe it's in my blood. Do I get that from the Vitolinich side of me? You see, I can't just let this thing go, let it take care of itself. I'm afraid what the consequences of not following through might be for other people involved in this mess, and for me as well. I have a bad feeling about what is going to take place and it would be nice, probably impossible but nice, if actions I take avert catastrophe, whatever that might mean. Is that vague enough for you? Well, it's weird enough to keep me in the game, a player, for now.

But I'm not sure how to proceed. One thing I could do is to get Coop to check out the approved signatures on the sign in card for the trust account – for comparison purposes. Maybe Walker was authorized to write checks and maybe he wrote that twenty thousand dollar check. If he did, why would he do so? And, if he did, isn't it likely that Walker is here in San Francisco? Would that make him a suspect in the murder? If so, why on earth would he want to murder Bob White? Jesus H. Christ, listen to me. I'm not the sleuth in a dime store murder mystery novel. I'm a claims investigator, a nice Southern boy from a good family assigned to work in San Francisco, a mecca for the youth rebellion. I'm interested in enlightenment, serious eternal questions. That's the kind of puzzle I'm eager to solve. Am I about to make things worse for those I hold near-and-dear instead of better by flying off on some suicidal tangent that sends us all right down the tube?

A click as the lock turns on my apartment door. It opens.

"I have returned bearing gifts," Tim Montgomery grandly announces.

"Oh?"

My low energy response fails to bring Tim down. He's a bundle of energy — wired to the max. A small brass toke pipe appears from his sport coat pocket. Tim holds it up.

"Perhaps you would like to partake of some Nepalese hash. It's laced with opium. First rate stuff... Guaranteed to clear your head and open up your mind."

Maybe it's Heather's influence. Maybe it's the fact I just got off the phone with my father. Whatever... The idea seems somehow to be right on target.

"Okay. If you're having some too..."

"Of course..."

We pass the pipe. We repeat the process. The hash does in fact clear my head and open my mind just as advertised. My basic problem is, I don't give a shit who killed Bob White and I'm not interested in trying to find out who it is. I mean, leave that to Coop and other professionals like him. I'm interested in settling into my new life in SF if I can just get free of this investigation, free and clear. That's the rub. I have a feeling the only way I can get free and clear is by going through it, keeping in the game, acting as if I'm trying to make sense of this mess. Does that make sense...no... but there you go...

"Want to take a spin? I've got wheels."

Tim is holding up the keys to his ride in front of my stoned out face.

The streets are not crowded at this time of night. We listen to Thelonious Monk on KJAZ after Tim hands me a Dexedrine.

We drive down 19th toward San Francisco State, then head up Market toward downtown. Our snappy little red sports car enters the vapor light zone of Market. Tim cuts over to Van Ness and heads towards the Golden Gate Bridge. But, instead of heading down Lombard towards the Bridge, we go uphill. At the top of the hill we find ourselves in a neighborhood filled with Spanish style homes.

Wham! We cross Hyde Street, cable car tracks still humming even late at night, and race down a street with hairpin curves, elegant townhouses flying past.

Poof! We are suddenly buzzing through North Beach, an Italian neighborhood transformed by invading Beatniks and Chinese families.

On Columbus Avenue - Italian restaurants, coffee houses serving espresso and sweets, a Catholic cathedral on the edge of Washington Square often used as a backdrop for major motion pictures, specialty and curio shops filled with exquisite handmade crafts and assorted debris, Bimbo's 365 where a mermaid swims in a tank above the bar, Tower Records on the corner of Columbus and Bay - a hive of activity now virtually deserted, trolley cars still in their barns this late at night.

Glide through the recumbent Marina Green.

We stop. Get out of the car. Float down to a five thirty am beach. Deserted — almost… Few hippies huddled together hoping to somehow avoid the chill night air. A hardy surf fisherman preparing to cast his line… A woman walking her dog along the lonely stretch of hard, damp sand… Wild, fierce wind…

The sea… Life is temporal but a part of eternity in just the same way a drop of water is finite in an infinite but limited sea. Only constant in life is change — trite observation or divine revelation? Depends on whom you ask… Response - rage against the coming of the night, continual prayer and meditation, wine women and song — take your pick. Can I pick them all?

Waves crash to the shore. Salt laden air, jutting headlands, a sun that is now struggling to make itself known… We're at the western edge of the continental United States. Can't go further without getting wet, going in over my head… Sink or swim. Long way to dry land if you take the plunge… I'm already beyond the grip of the undertow and swimming strong towards the fabled Far East - towards my fated destiny.

The sun breaks free of the horizon. It's cold as hell on the beach. Tim's already sitting in the car with the heater running… He's switched to the classical station. They're playing Mozart's Bassoon Concerto.

———————

Mama's, just off Washington Square, serves a mouth-watering breakfast. The doors open at six. We're the only ones around. But others come in in ones and twos while we order and eat.

"What's with the car?" I ask.

"A friend..."

"A girl..."

"If you must know..."

"And she let you appropriate her snappy red sports car?"

"She had to make a duty call to her parents down in LA. When I dropped her at the airport, she handed me the keys. I pick her up tomorrow – or the next day if she gets hung up."

"And the drugs..."

"Just some odds and ends she had lying around her pad."

"This sounds serious."

"Funny. That's the impression she has as well."

"Good grief."

"In a certain book, on the inside cover, there is a pledge she insisted I sign, a pledge to marry."

"Any particular reason for your signature..."

Tim, like my father, fails to answer. I'm brought back to my present — the need to file an insurance claim, the promise to Mrs. White, the responsibility I feel for my friends, the hope that I might make sense of all the ill-fitting puzzle pieces of my haphazard life — the need to prove something to my father, the need to quell my sense of obligation to Tony, the need to either carry Isobel with me into my new life or take up with the future in the form of Heather if that is an option. Is it? Probably not... And somehow, as I swim towards the rising sun, I am now audacious enough to believe in hopes and dreams, realizations...

"Say, would you mind swinging by this apartment I want to check out after breakfast?"

"I was thinking maybe we could head up Mt. Tam. Pretty cool view from there, I'm told."

Bob White's apartment is on the street that leads up Telegraph Hill to Coit Tower. Same road the tour buses use to spiral to the top. Glad I don't have to find a parking spot; glad I don't have to park. Don't forget to curb your wheels — or else. The landlord lives in the downstairs unit. Saves the view for a well-heeled renter... He's plenty pissed that the police haven't allowed him to put up a "for rent" sign yet. Time is money. I don't envy him his nut each month.

With a little convincing, I'm shown the garage. In it, the TR2 - it's red — naturally. White ragtop... Looks like it's not been driven in a very long time... A sparkling set of practically unused tools and a great workbench. Bobby must have liked to imagine he'd tinker in his free time... Too many other diversions captured his attention.

"Where's the black VW?" I ask.

The landlord speaks broken English at first. He's short, clean shaven, heavy set, sharp as a tack. He looks in both directions before he answers.

"What you talk about?"

"I was told Mr. White had a VW he used to knock around the city...It still around?"

"Who tell you that?"

"I don't recall." We regard each other with suspicion. I pull out my small roll of cash. The landlord turns up his nose but doesn't say no. "Did someone come by to pick up his VW after Mr. White passed away?"

"Not exactly," answers the landlord looking at my twenty with scorn. I hand him another twenty. He snickers. I fork over two more. His eyebrows go up. "Oh, you mean, the Volkswagen bug that Mr. White had. His guardian came by and picked it up. Oh, it must have been a week before Mr. White met his untimely end." His English has improved remarkably.

"What's this guardian look like?"

Landlord has fallen on hard times again. I hand him another twenty. He snickers. I shake my head. No more, chump. A hundred clams is enough. I'm not a bank. The landlord sighs. His English gets bad again fast.

"I no get good look...could be old man. All Europeans look alike. Was with a younger man...Hippie could be... Dark... Hard see."

"You know where this guardian lives or what his name is?"

The landlord shrugs. He directs me with his hand towards Bobby's living quarters. I'm expected to move on, take a quick look, then leave. Hundred dollars doesn't buy you much these days.

Bobby's pad is on three floors - the living area on the first floor, the sleeping area on the second floor, a study/observatory in the crow's nest on top. All three levels have windows, floor-to-ceiling. You can see laid out before you — North Beach in the foreground, a hill in the near distance covered with homes, the edge of Fort Mason, the Marina, and the Presidio. Right in the center of this cityscape is the Golden Gate Bridge in all its majestic splendor. On clear days you can see the Marin headlands, a smidgen of Sausalito and Tiburon, the Bay and Alcatraz Island. Dramatic is not sufficient to describe this view. Breathtaking, awe-inspiring, quaint, picturesque - it's all those things. Puts the pad to shame...

Place has little decks on each floor. Weather probably too cold to hang out on them for any length of time. Wind really whips around here. Place is damp. Probably doesn't hold heat well. Too much glass... Not double paned. Heating bill must be astronomical.

Very sparse furnishings... Bed, pillows for chairs and a beat-up sofa... Nothing in the refrigerator... Utensils must have come with the place. All bent and broken... Fantastic telescope in the observatory right next to a chair... Trained on the window of a building down the street... Bobby had other things on his mind besides star gazing. Built in bookshelves only have one book - Pilgrim's Progress. Joke book or a nod to Bobby's New England heritage? If so, where are Emerson and Thoreau, Walt Whitman and Longfellow? How about the Bible?

Bedside night table has a drawer. In it are some pictures. Bobby in front of his TR2... Bobby holding up a surfboard... Bobby on snow skis waving gallantly to the camera...And a picture of Bobby with his arm around Jane standing in front of a black VW bug... Next to them are Heather and Bernie Toucan. All smiling... All zonked.

VW's beat up. Got a lot of miles on it... Paint looks recent and cheap. There's a McGovern sticker on the front bumper. I can just make out the New York plate number. WJA 216...

Stuff the picture in my pocket. Split. A hundred dollars still buys something in my book. Pass it along to Coop when I get the chance. I'm still not interested in murder investigations. But who knows what's coming down the line?

What was that address I got if I needed to get in touch with Jane Preen?

Bob White's world — getting high, getting laid, getting away from dominating yet distant parents, creating your very own hustle and recreating your self-serving self – seems far away at 9010 Gough Street. The front door is ajar. I hear a raga playing on a record player. There are people chanting as they meditate in what must once have been the front parlor.

This is where I can leave messages for Jane Preen?

In the kitchen, monks in training are preparing a meal. The back door opens onto a magnificently tended backyard. A monk, obviously someone in charge, stops me.

"May I help you?"

I am struck by his seeming serenity, the depth hidden behind his tranquil eyes. I'd like to know more about these people and what they think.

"Yeah, ah your holy ah..."

"Please."

He directs me with his hand toward the kitchen door leading out onto a small porch that overlooks the bountiful backyard. A small pond complete with a waterfall and rocks that glow in the morning sun confronts me. The monk points to a bench. I follow his lead and try to sit cross-legged on it. My legs and joints scream. I ignore them.

"You are troubled," he states after we are settled.

I haven't got the hang of sitting cross-legged and fear I might never do so. A perfected lotus, even a half-ass half-lotus, is a seeming physical impossibility.

"Yes," I admit.

"You are seeking a car, a girl, the way to navigate toward a new way of life, in no particular order? How can your 'I' do all these complicated things at the same time?"

"Will you help me?"

A strange bird calls in the distance. We are far away – in some space that is familiar yet unexplored by me.

"If God wills it..."

"What should I be doing?"

"Listen. The answers are within."

I'm too unsettled to take advantage of the timeless moment being offered. It's not just the speed I'm high on. It's all the shit I'm tangled up with. Later...no time now later... I promise myself. Am I lying? The monk chuckles quietly, raises his hand, finger pointed skyward.

"Your worries are?" he asks.

"A car, a girl, old and new found friends — linked for the moment by a murder. I feel like I'm the only one who can untangle them from this predicament — not because I am clever but because of who and where I am in regard to them."

He points. I look. For the first time, I notice a small garage at the back end of the yard. Beside it is parked — my car. Heather is standing by the passenger side door, looking at the two of us. She has the keys — the key to my apartment, the key to my car, the key to my office. Does she possibly have a key that will allow me to unlock this complicated entanglement? Will she bolt if I rush towards her?

The monk slides off the bench and bows, bringing his hands together in front of him. I struggle out of my torturous half lotus and bow back in like manner.

"When the time is right, you will know where to go and what to do to seek fulfillment. Until then, allow me to present you with a gift."

I now notice that beside him is a book. He hands it to me, its title — the I Ching.

"I..."

"Hawk flies. Fox cries. Mighty wind," the monk murmurs. "Your private mantra to contemplate..."

Then he is gone. Heather has entered the garden through a gate. I wait for her on the porch, my heart suddenly pounding, my mind in a whirl.

"You have received a special gift," she states, looking over my shoulder.

I turn. The I Ching still sits on the bench. It's open. I glance at it and have only a moment to read the words that jump off the page at me before Heather continues.

"A wise but patriarchal book connected to ancient Oriental wisdom. I prefer 'The Tibetan Book of the Dead.' But receiving it from whom you did makes this book special for your progress."

"Is this where you live? Where did you take Tony and Jane in my car?"

"Look. Wait a minute." She puts her hand to her forehead. Pulls it away... Shakes her head, causing her blond tresses to jump back and forth over her shapely shoulders... Takes a deep breath and slowly releases it. I hear a long, low vibration, her chant, "Ohm."

She's still wearing her Indian costume. Is that get-up the only one she has? Well, it does fit her awfully well.

"So where are Tony and Jane?"

"Hiding out – until the coast clears..."

"Where..."

"Maybe this book will tell us."

Heather reaches down to pick up the I Ching and sits on the beach as she does so. I join her there.

Heather said she knew Jane well enough to know about a scar on her knee. Tony split with Heather from right in front of police headquarters.

I whirl about in the maelstrom of Heather's influence. Who is and what is the real Heather? One thing's certain - she's beautiful. Maybe we should consult the I Ching together - in private. Maybe the answers we receive from that consultation will make a difference.

She inches away from me. Sitting on our shared bench... Meditatively breathing...

"You are concerned for your friend Tony. I'm concerned for Jane. Can we leave it at that for now? Would that appeal to you - hanging out with me without any strings attached – in the Now?"

My mind is at a standstill. I try to formulate thoughts.

"There are too many things, too many people, too much happening in this Now..."

Heather's eyes plead with me. The cryptic comment I just noticed in the I Ching still open beside us jumps into my mind, "keep your stopping still means stopping in your place."

"I want to be with you in this Now, Heather, but..."

I pull out the photo in my pocket without holding it up for her to look at.

"But," I continue. "But Bob White's murder, Bob White's past, Bob White's present gets in the way. Fuck solving the murder and filling out some stupid paperwork. All I care about is helping out people I care about. But the black VW bug I asked you about. Bernie Toucan and his murderous knife... Ronald Outrage and how he fits in. Jane. Tony. How come it is that you disappear with Tony and now show up without him at a place Jane Preen told me to leave messages for her? I'm confused. I can't sit next to you without my emotions, my feelings, getting in the way of, getting tainted by..."

I look down at the photo. Heather is already looking at it.

"I mean you come on like a Delphic Oracle with your pronouncements and then we're in the sack smoking dope and making outrageous love. I try not to give a shit about this investigation stuff and then I find this photo at Bob White's pad and I...I don't know, I, I see you and Tony and Jane getting sucked back into this mess and you and I are what, an item, and how do you, how do you and I, fit into...Is this what being in the Now is all about..."

"I don't go into trances because I want to play games with your head. It just happens. Do you think I enjoy being labeled a kook?" Awkward pause... She crashes on. "As for the car, Bobby's murder, and all that other crap... Here's an oracle for you – all will be revealed – in the Lord's own sweet time. Have patience. Preserve. Be open. Let what you see in my eyes flower and come forth."

She's leaning into me. Her face goes out of focus. She's kissing me. Her body is pressed against mine. Reluctantly, inevitably, my arms encircle her. We carry on with our kiss. Then I push her away. Hold her at arm's length again.

"You cool with that?" she asks in the same soft voice from which her chant emerged.

I pull further away. Get off the bench and walk over to the steps leading down to the backyard garden and my car. I can just hear traffic buzzing in the background. Nothing would be easier than taking Heather in my arms. Nothing would be better than spending the rest of the day in bed with her. Investigating murders is not for me. Filling out paperwork is a chore I'm not ready to take on. Tony is no longer in custody. Heather is not on the police radar screen yet, maybe never, I hope. Mr. and Mrs. White will pack up and head back to the East Coast if this all blows over. Mr. Hancock and Mr. Meade will carry on with their lives and I will be a negligible part of it. My father and I will continue to struggle over our relationship. I will continue to have very ambivalent feelings about The Office, its mission, its operations and its methods. Life will go on with or without me. I will continue to swim towards the setting sun in the pacific oceans of my mind. Oh God, what the hell am I tangled up in, so tangled up I'm tangled up by myself? Everyone told me San Francisco was a crazy place but this...

Heather puts her arms around my waist from behind. I turn around. We kiss again. I look her in the eye.

"You're trouble, Heather. And you know it," I mutter into her sweet smelling hair.

"That's true. It's also true that we make a good team."

CHAPTER TEN

The bedside phone rings.

We got high on hash, coke, something else we snorted that Heather failed to describe. At Heather's command, we undressed ceremoniously in front of each other, one article of clothing at a time. She then proceeded to rub oil into my body from head to toe and directed me to do the same to her. Before I knew it we were making love, very intimate love. She moaned. I moaned. She writhed. I moved with her. She touched me. I touched her. She clutched me. I pushed harder and stronger.

The bedside phone rings a second time.

We got higher. We took a bath together, facing each other in the tub. The room was lit by one candle and filled with the smell of powerful incense. Afterward, we toweled each other off tenderly until we were dry. I entered her on the floor of the bathroom. We took a very long time to climax. We did so together. This is a woman, what a woman...

The bedside phone rings a third time.

We got highest. She ordered me to sit on the floor cross-legged while she turned off the lights and lit the candle and another stick of incense. From out of nowhere the I Ching appeared and three coins of unknown origin. They had a square hole in the middle and what appeared to be Asian characters inscribed on them. I threw the coins six times, concentrating on keeping my mind open and free. Heather made a note of each throw. Then we read the oracle including the change lines for Hexagram 39 (Obstruction) changing to Hexagram 15 (Modesty) with the fifth line changing. 'Here we see a man called to help in an emergency...should not seek to evade the obstructions, no matter how dangerously they pile up...strong enough to attract helpers... obstruction overcome...thus the superior man turns his attention to himself and molds his character...'

The bedside phone rings a fourth time.

We fell asleep in each other's arms. What time is it now?

Heather shakes her head, no. I pick up the phone. She rolls away to her side of the bed. Lights the joint already in the ashtray... Takes a big drag and offers me some. I shake my head as Coop comes on the line.

"Where'd you find that knife?"

"Picked it up off the floor after the guy who tried to kill me with it dropped it."

It's well after three in the afternoon.

"Get this straight, Carter. This knife is a ringer for the one used to stab the White kid. Makes a unique pattern at point of entry... Blade's crooked. Has some funny nicks in it that show up in the stab wound. So I'm asking you again. Where'd you find this knife?"

I'm sitting up in bed now...Lighting a cigarette... Heather puts out the joint after taking a second hit and heads off to the john.

"He was driving a black van — probably a Chevy — last time I saw him — one of those long-bodied deals. What do they call them — Chevy 10s? Probably registered in the name of the guy whose prints are all over that knife or to one Ronald Outrage, underground filmmaker in town to check out the decaying and dying hippie scene... He likes disturbed young men like Bernie Toucan, if that's his name. The knife play took place in Outrage's house, the old Russian Embassy over on Scott."

The toilet flushes. Heather comes out of the bathroom...Naked. Oh, she is a lovely sight to behold. Why do humans cover themselves? The human form is one of the most powerful forces on Earth. Maybe that's the reason - too powerful, too immediate, too honest...

"Good work, Carter. Bernie Toucan has now moved to the top of our list of murder suspects in this investigation," Coop answers as I hear the scratching of a pencil on paper, probably a notebook.

"I wouldn't be surprised if you found Outrage's place empty now."

"Got any bright ideas where we might find either one of them?"

"No. But I will certainly let you know if I find out."

"Oh and Carter," Coop interrupts me before I can hang up. "Be best if you give a call to the Whites. I can put up with them calling every five minutes but when my big boss calls as well - well, you get the idea."

"Screw the Whites and all the big bosses too."

"Okay. I'll grant you that. But it doesn't change the facts. People like the Whites have lots of juice. Enough said on that subject."

The line goes dead. Heather's giving me a hard look. Of course, I have neglected to tell Coop about the picture and Heather. I light a cigarette. Heather relights her joint.

"This is important. I want you to let me know where you are at all times. Leave messages with my service," I declare to her.

"So...That's the way it is," Heather answers, looking like a pin-up girl posed on my bed.

I'm pulling on my pants. I nod towards her pile of clothes, indicating she should put them on. She frowns but doesn't move.

"You ready to level with me...because Toucan's looking good for White's murder. And you were mixed up with him once. He's one crazy mother fucker, as you already know."

"Stay right here and protect me then. You don't really want to or need to find out about all the dirt surrounding this crime. You told me that yourself. Concentrate on us. Look, Tony and Jane are free-and-clear, aren't they? Just turn in your paperwork and take a holiday with me. The end of story... Time will heal all."

My shirt's on but not buttoned. I start shaving with my electric razor by the French doors.

"Okay." She smoothly changes course. "Together we can get to the bottom of this."

Me? I'm having a hard time keeping my mind on shaving. In fact, I have to adjust my suddenly uncomfortable shorts when I put down the razor. Heather has still not started to dress.

"You know Bobby's old man? Bull White? He came out here on a business trip a few months back."

Now she hops off the bed and heads over to her pile of clothes. My eyes are riveted on her. Why the hell aren't I hopping on her bones right now? Going on what will most likely turn out to be a wild goose chase, a potentially deadly one at that, forget about it. Just hold your nose and do the obligatory paperwork that will save my lowly and disgusting job and a whole lot of inconvenience, like the girl said. What's wrong with me? Do I have a death wish, a compulsive urge to sabotage myself and those close to me? Is this my destiny, my karma, to be a fuck up among fuck ups?

"It's time for a magical mystery tour around the city," she announces.

I stop tucking in my shirt.

"Did you sleep with Bull White? Is that it? Was he a rich guy accustomed to getting his way with an ego that always demands more, more, more and you came into his sights?"

"One baby step at a time, sweetheart. Give mommy a kiss first. She needs comforting."

After we kiss and she helps me straighten my pants, Heather heads into the bathroom with her clothes. I hear the shower go on. Looks like she's planning on staying for a while... I can see her form in the opaque shower curtain. The female form veiled...Classic...Mysterious. I shake it off...Got to go.

"When you go out, close the door. It'll lock automatically," I shout into the hissing shower noise.

She pokes her head out from the side of the shower curtain. She has on a shower cap to protect her hair. Where the hell did that come from?

"Pick me up in an hour. That should give you enough time," she comments.

———

Mr. Meade is in his office with the door locked. But I can hear him on the phone. I'm sitting at my desk in the near dark amidst an open-plan empty office waiting for my eyes to adjust to the low light. I need something solid, something I can use as a "get out of jail free card," something that will guarantee those nearest and dearest to me will escape this shit storm called a murder investigation should it become necessary. What do I care about all the rest of it – just messy politics of one sort or another?

I can now make out the messages on my desk. Big one on my blotter to call the Whites pronto or my ass is grass. Note from Hancock himself. Checking up on me... No need to call him back. Just talk to the Whites. Message from Mr. Meade wanting to know where the hell I am... Better let him know if I want to keep my job. And a message from Walt saying he called. I put my phone on the floor in front of my desk and kneel down to dial. Meade won't see me if he comes out of his office.

"Walt. How're they hanging?" I whisper into the phone.

"Charlie. I can barely hear you. What are you into, man?"

"Why? What?" I speak up, just enough for conversation.

"R.R. White, Bull to his friends, and somebody who has a folder in our files that no one, but no one, at my level and pay grade will ever see or even be able to ask about, period, that's what."

"That so... Is he one of ours?"

"He's so high up the food chain I can't sort it out. And I don't want to. Red flags popped up at every security desk in this office and the ones down the hall when I made my request for a look-see at the R.R. White file. I'm still fighting the questions off and am busy kowtowing to the powers that be. May they all prosper and flourish. So far, thank you very much, I have kept your name out of that questioning."

"Jesus H. Christ." A whole new world of possible dangers starts churning through my mind. I spent my time at The Office using my English major background to research and interpret, read that create a storyline or plot to neuter and defuse and confuse. All very hush-hush, all very Cold War, all very dirty tricks (dare I use the word – propaganda), each interpretation full of paranoia and intrigue – that's the way The Office likes their bedtime stories. I must admit it does spice up deadly boring field reports. And the operations I was called on to work this magic on, primarily stateside ops with the F.B.I. and J. Edgar Hoover attached, outraged and soured me on my job and The Office and the governing of my, our, country itself. Hey, I'm a member in good standing of the younger generation, aren't I? I mean, what did my work and the ops carried out in that secret agency do to the lives of individuals on the ground and individuals in general and what did it do to pervert the public's right to know? And what does and, most important, what did it have to do with "the Truth?" I shiver. Lastly, what does it do to what is happening to me and my friends and everybody else living in the Bay Area right now. "Jesus H. Christ," I repeat. "Walt, I'll understand if you have to give me up. Don't worry, I can handle it. I'm clean."

"Would that make any difference?"

No need for comment from my end so I move on.

"Anything of interest on any of the other names..."

"Lots of innuendo, lots to speculate about...Bernie Toucan is a wacko but you probably found that out from your cop friends. Jane Preen has a possession bust – dismissed, paid a fine. Ronald Outrage? There's something kind of screwy about him. I mean J. Edgar Hoover and his guys are all over his deviant behavior but I'm beginning to get this vibe that there's more to him than just his Satanic cult thing and his being a tenured professor at a major university. I'm thinking he might be a card-carrying member of a club we are more familiar with. And if that is the case, what does that say about this fucked up mess you indirectly asked me to check out? I mean, how far and how deep does The Office infection, uh connection spread..." Walt chuckles before continuing. "You'd have your creative work cut out for you to find an Office favorable spin on the shit you're into if you were still working with us. What a whopper you'd have to come up with, huh?"

"I have to admit I really am unable to wrap that bent theoretical assignment into a bundle and put it inside my poor innocent brain, partner."

"Hang on to that state of mind, pal. That's what makes you unique."

"Nobody wants an innocent fool on their side. Not in America these days."

We both think about that for a moment.

"And then there's your father's file – also off limits but no horrendous red flags jumped up to bite me for making the request. You, of course, have been vetted and re-vetted... You still come out squeaky clean. How do you do it? That's about it."

"What do you suggest?"

Mr. Meade is hanging up the phone is his office.

"I'd watch my back, watch my front, watch my sides and still not believe anything I see or hear. And then I'd pretend to go along with whatever the police or any mucky-muck had to say if you value your sanity, your future well-being, life as you know it. Then I would take a long, long vacation in a faraway land – with a nubile young hippie goddess eager to please if she's handy."

"How did you know?"

"Right... In your dreams..."

"Anyway, can't do it. I'm beginning to get the feeling job security is on the side of not closing this case. Keep the bastards nervous. Make 'em show some respect."

"Dangerous game for peons, particularly the innocent fool type..."

"Hey, when you're loose in the land of love, you always get a free pass. Always..."

"The source of this free love — you sure you can trust her?"

"That could be a problem."

"Oh boy..."

Mr. Meade comes out of his office. I'm not certain whether he hears me on the phone or if he's just heading to the can. He has on his suit coat, which he doesn't normally wear unless he's leaving the office.

"Talk to you later. Bogey at twelve o'clock. And thanks for the info."

I hang up the phone. The boss is heading in my direction and he doesn't look happy. He must have heard me talking on the phone.

"Where the hell have you been?"

I pop up from behind the desk to answer.

"Trying to tie this investigation up with a bow... Giving it top priority, sir..."

I stand up and dust off my pants.

"Dropped my pen, couldn't find it."

Neither one of us bother to mention that my desk light is off as are all the other desk lights in my area.

"Look, Carter," Mr. Meade continues. "I don't give a rat's ass what you do on your own time. I'm just here to see that the interests of Life Beneficial are seen to in my department. No screw-ups. Got it?"

"I'm a company man all the way, sir. Show me a butt and I'll kiss it. Tell me to jump and I'll only ask how high."

Stony-eyed silence. Cold audience here at old Life Beneficial...

"I don't like getting calls from Mr. Hancock unless it's to tell me what a great job I'm doing. He's concerned; I'm concerned. He's angry; I carry out his wrath. He's not quite over the edge - yet. I don't want to know what his mood might be tomorrow. You get my point?"

"Lovely place, the St. Francis... Like the smell of deep expensive pile carpets... Think I'll head on over there. They say no trip to Frisco is complete without it."

"That may be all you get out of this — a trip to San Francisco."

I don't know what he's been told. But my boss doesn't go for the kill. I can see that's his inclination.

Why is it part of the contract that all humans must earn a living? Why can't we just live off the fat of the land?

I shake my head and laugh at no one in particular. That hippie drivel — the last free ride — is rubbing off on me already. Mr. Meade jabs his finger at me. His eyes flash. He needs to go home and kick the dog.

"You think you're pretty damn clever, don't you Carter. Well, you just keep fucking with the big brass and you'll find out fast who gets the last laugh. And what sort of repercussions that has on your miserable life."

"I'm on my way, sir."

I stumble into my desk chair. It squeaks. Life Beneficial, standard issue...

––––––––––

"Carter. I thought we had an agreement, an understanding."

Cross-my-heart-and-hope-to-die, Bull is wearing a smoking jacket.

And he has a glass of champagne in his hand. He's freshly shaven and bathed. An ascot bulges from his neck, Cary Grant style. Well, he has moved up a rung on the Hollywood icon scale in my mind – from Peter Lawford to Cary Grant.

"I'm new at the game. Takes me longer to get the message about how things are done... Sorry, sir," I answer, still standing in the doorway to the sitting room, trying to keep my cool.

Despite the cartoon character Mr. White has made of himself, he has attained new stature in my mind after my conversation with Walt. Handling him with kid gloves isn't even an option. He's out of my league. But who asked me if I wanted to play in this league to begin with?

White does not invite me into the room. Mrs. White sweeps by, followed by a hotel porter. They head into the bedroom. I hear the clatter of boxes as they cascade onto the bed. Then the porter comes out of the bedroom. He's stuffing a healthy tip into his pants pockets. The Whites tip well. What kind of tip will I get if I close this case in their favor – the right to go on living?

"I understand from your immediate superior that you have not filled out the necessary paperwork on this case that will move it along," continues Bull pointedly.

"There're still a few loose ends that I'm looking into. Shouldn't take long at all... Just trying to maintain the high caliber of work done by Life Beneficial investigators, sir... Beyond reproach... Top drawer...And all that..."

"Screw the company line crap. Close the goddamn case. You got it?"

I'm thinking of Mrs. White, Jane, Tony, Heather, myself - a widening circle of people I don't want to see get hurt. And I'm having a hard time convincing myself right now that keeping this case open will benefit them – or me. So why not give in – pure cussedness, the old Carter/Vitolinich/Indian blood, the necessity to wear the white hat and "do the right thing" no matter the consequences just like in a Western movie, the desire to avert catastrophe, untie the damsel in distress from the train tracks, what?

No. I get it now. Because I don't trust, don't like, can't abide, won't back down in front of – Robert Randolph White, Sr. and the whole Office machine he represents. That brain flash comes to me loud and clear. I'm like Tony at that football practice in middle school, years ago when he went berserk. I know Tony paid for it later but, in the moment, he was glorious to behold.

"Can't do it just quite yet, sir... You see there's the police investigation to consider. It's an open case. We don't know who killed your son and why."

"You let me handle the police," White growls.

I find out immediately how Bull will handle them. He smashes his champagne glass in the fake fireplace. Heavily insulated walls and thick carpeting deaden the sound of the shattering glass but it rings loud and clear in my mind. That does it. No more fun and games groveling in front of Mr. Fucking White. White speaks softly.

"Listen to me and listen good... Close this case. Do I need to call the police commissioner and Bill Hancock again to make certain you do? You are history in every sense of the word, son."

Threats...Is that what you're offering, I think with much less emotion than I believe I have the guts for. Could panic and guilt lurk just below the surface of Bull White?

"Anything that will help me close the books on this investigation you'd like to tell me, sir? Something you might not like to become public knowledge? I'm discreet. I worked for The Office - remember? I can act with the proper discretion. Try me."

White laughs. Sees he's overplayed his hand.

"What have you got so far?" he asks.

Sits down calm as you please... Offers me a seat... Mrs. White stands in the bedroom doorway. She shakes her head, warning me not to play this game. I laugh with White, ignoring Mrs. White just as Tony would have ignored kindly warnings on that middle school practice field. Never mind maneuvers, go straight at 'em.

"I know that the executor of the White estate, Ronald Walker, is in San Francisco. He signed that check made out to Tony Vitolinich you were so worked up about."

Pure speculation...he does not react. I move on.

"I know that a crazy named Bernie Toucan is running around attacking people with a knife that matches exactly the one which stabbed your son multiple times after he was dead. I know that a college professor named Ronald Outrage is playing kinky voodoo games. He's mixed up with Toucan. And his likely connection with The Office could lead right to you. Am I doing all right so far, Mr. White?"

White doesn't move. He's quiet, attentive. I go on.

"Are you worried that I might start connecting all the dots about you and Walker and your trips to San Francisco and some little floozy you have tucked away in the free love capital of the world and whatever nefarious goings on you have instigated in San Francisco, all in the name of national security, the country's best interest? Are you trying to protect your son or cover up for yourself? Which is it, Mr. White?"

"Very clever, Mr. Carter, very clever, but your story is not compelling or convincing. Too much innuendo and very dull-witted... And your possible motives – how can you trust someone who would call Tony Vitolinich a friend, hop into the sack with someone who calls herself Heather Chicago, uses Jane Preen as an alibi witness? No, no, no, Mr. Carter. That will not do. Most important, you seem to have forgotten the accepted storyline. I'm the victim's grieving father, not a suspect."

White lights a Cuban cigar. He blows smoke in my direction.

"Tell me where I can find Walker. Tell me the mystery girl in your life does not exist or is not involved in your son's murder. Convince me that your son was not involved in Office operations gone haywire or family business that got messy. Convince me you had nothing to do with his murder. Help me settle this claim now - and in your favor. I want that. You want that. We all want this to end. And we all want to walk away winners. If you've got nothing to hide, which I would like to believe, what have you got to lose?"

Bull laughs pleasantly.

"I've got a news flash for you, son. If you don't settle this claim now, on the spot, I will see to it personally that Tony Vitolinich remains the number one suspect in the police investigation. A warrant will be issued for his arrest. And I will dog your movements and run you out of town - on a rail, as they used to say in the movies."

I shake my head.

"So, does that mean you are conceding you are mixed up in this up to your eyeballs and you will do everything in your power to come out of this smelling like a rose?"

Mr. White relights his cigar and takes several long drags on it. The cigar end glows red hot. It is well lit. He blows the smoke my way. I am unable to hold back a cough.

"Okay," I finally manage to cough out as I clear my throat. "You're a bigwig at The Office and call Mr. Hancock Bill or brother-in-law. You know lots of important people, people that run this great country of ours. Maybe some of them owe you favors or you are doing them favors heading up an ongoing operation in San Francisco. And I am a virtual nobody. Swell.

"If this nobody fills out those claim forms, what do I put on them? Do I deny your claim because you are possibly involved with the murder of your son? I do that and I'm dismissed as a lunatic with justification — because I don't have any proof to back it up. Okay, then do I, without proper substantiation, say the claimants have met all requirements? I can't do that either because I don't have proper substantiation. And the kicker is, if I did fill out the forms for the claim and close the investigation in your favor, would that be the end of it for me and people I hold dear or quite possibly even for you yourself? I don't think so..."

Robert Randolph White takes another drag of his cigar, heaves out a sigh as a smirk of a smile lights up a sparkle of malice and devilment in his eyes.

"No. No-can-do, sir..." I finish.

"Too bad, son because I like you... I really do. And not just because of your father..."

My father... You've hit the nail on the head with that one, Mr. White, hit the ball right out of the park. You and my father, you and my father... That's how I got involved in this mess and that's why I'm stuck with this mess until the bitter end. Do you think that's a contradiction, a flaw in my character? Think again. And for your information, I still say fuck this murder investigation. I don't care who killed your son or what shitty stuff is going on that makes this murder too hot to handle or that you get your double indemnity payoff. I'm just trying to see that my friends and I come out of this in one piece. And you, you and your connection to my father, you and your connection to my father... Shit. I love you, Dad. I really do. We went on camping trips together and you were scout master of my Boy Scout troop. We prayed together in church and we shared family meals. We went to all those Western movies together and we rooted for the guy in the white hat. We wanted to see him bring to justice the guy in the black hat. Okay, to put it a different way, the I Ching says somewhere, "what is great must also be right in order to be great." Please, Dad. Please... I want this story to come out right for all those we both hold dear. I'll try to hold up my end. And you, you...

I hear Mr. White pick up the phone and dial as I leave the room. I'm history with Life Beneficial, no matter how this case works out. That means I'm free and unprotected at one and the same time.

Wait, does Mr. White have people in the lobby, standing guard outside his hotel room? Didn't Tony get his ass kicked after that football practice for humiliating a fellow football player? I mean, doesn't the little guy get slapped around a lot in the movies? Thing is, in the movies they triumph in the end. Maybe not so much so in current day 1968...that can't stop me...for all of our sakes...Am I talking in ever tightening circles? Yes, I noticed that. Is that a trait inherent in all human beings on the edge of taking a very big fall, or just myself?

––––––––––

In the lobby of the St. Francis I'm doing just what Walt suggested, checking my back, front, both sides. I smile. Pop a cigarette out of the packet. Elevator man gives me a nasty look. I'm taking a nice leisurely stroll through the spacious St. Francis lobby. Everyone I see is a potential agent. Pass gigantic palm-filled porcelain urns strategically placed near marble columns that create nooks and crannies — and hiding places. Massive circular sofas covered in red velvet in these nooks with brass cuspidors and stand-up brass ashtrays. I'm radioactive — toxic. A sign set up on an easel directs guests to a debutante party in the lower lobby. Out of the corner of my eye I think I see an Indian maiden dressed in a leather-fringed jacket covered with beadwork. Heather descending the stairs... I make a break in her direction. Am I followed?

She's nowhere to be found below. The same can be said for the agents I assume Mr. White called to follow me.

Is Mr. White's influence and protection all pervasive? If I blow the whistle on him, will his game fall apart — just a house of cards? It's a certainty Mr. White thinks he's above the laws that govern most common mortals. I've got to believe Mr. White knows whereof he speaks. So it's time to make myself scarce. Where did Heather go? Or was she a figment of my over-stimulated imagination?

Surprise...The Great Northwest Phantasmagoria Lightshow is dazzling young debutantes and their escorts in a subterranean, low-ceilinged room where deafeningly mediocre music is being played. A tangle of bodies... The boys in rented tuxes. The girls in off-the-shoulder gowns bought at fancy stores or gowns used by mother or older sister once, then altered. Hormones and sweat glands are working overtime. Pimples and new-formed breasts collide. Teenagers... Watch out. Good grief.

I smile at a chaperone as she makes a beeline in my direction. I point to the lightshow platform trying to indicate I'm with them. She nods but continues to watch me carefully. Her daughter is probably somewhere nearby.

The lightshow guys are working furiously. The room is filled with flashing lights. It's impossible to make out the images the group has created because the assorted projectors are displaying the lightshow images on the crowd before they reach a convenient wall. The ceiling is too low for them to do otherwise. Looming shadows fill the walls, engulfed by abstract shapes, slivering amebic blobs, moiré patterns, strobing lights.

When the electrified clatter called music halts, the band, mercifully, takes a break. The crowd mills about. Nowhere to go really but this room or the outer lobby... The St. Francis is a terrible location for these kids to party. But it's a great bit of luck for me.

The lightshow members march down from their raised platform, shoulders hunched. Seeing me doesn't help relax them. Tony is not among those present.

"I thought Tony was out of the can," Dumas mutters.

Suspicion is mixed with hostility and fear. I shrug my shoulders.

"Any of you know where he is?" I answer.

No one responds. They just keep moving. I follow. They're headed toward a door used by the help. No trace of a tail that I can see. The door leads through a kitchen area and out onto a loading dock. Can't see anyone else around... If there was a tail put on me, they must have lost me in the crowd. The lightshow van is parked at the loading dock. The boys, without preamble, light up a joint and pass it around. No one has much to say. On the plus side, I am included in their ceremony. After a few minutes, the mood lifts – just barely. Harry takes me aside.

"You really don't have a clue where Tony is?"

"Last time I saw him he was headed out of police headquarters towards my car."

"And..."

"And he split in my car with a friend of mine who was waiting in the car."

"He must be really freaked out. Who's the friend, someone Tony knows?"

"Girl I met. Name of Heather Chicago – so she says..."

"Hey, Harry. We're on in fifteen minutes," Dumas shouts as the rest of the lightshow members head inside.

"Be right there," Harry answers over his shoulder.

Necessary work that keeps the hotel running smoothly takes place here. But no one wants to hang around. The odors, the vibes, the light, the air itself are uninviting.

"How can I help?" Harry asks.

"I don't know. Maybe you could put your ear to the ground and see if anyone knows anything about Bob White's father."

I hand him my card.

"I'll let you know if I get any feedback. Anything else?"

"I'd like to get in touch with Tony – soon. Know where he might be? Jane is probably with him."

"Have you checked with Jane's mother or her sister, Linda?"

"Mom's no help. How do I get in touch with her sister?"

"Good question. I haven't seen her in weeks myself. She's got a place on Potrero Hill...Vermont near Nineteenth. Back apartment on the second floor... But it's probably a waste of time looking for her there. And then there's always the ashram over on Gough Street. She and Jane both have spent time there."

"That so... What does she look like?"

"Blonde hair – long and straight... Around five-five...Slender...Looks like a fashion model. Has a tendency to make strange proclamations. Favors an Indian get-up..."

I should have known. What have those two sisters been up to since Jane moved back up to San Francisco? If it involves Bull White, it's making much more sense that he would want Tony out of the picture – permanently. I've got to find Tony right away – and have a heart-to-heart with those sisters too.

"Do me a favor, will you?"

"If I can..."

"If Jane's sister contacts you, have her get in touch with me. She'll know how to do that. Oh yeah, and if anyone shows up asking for me, you haven't seen me. Think you can get the other guys to go along with that too?"

"Are you kidding? Count on it."

———————

"Charlie Carter residence..."

"Tim? You got a car handy?"

"Well, yeah."

"Meet me out front pronto, car key in hand."

I hang up before Tim can answer and, hopefully, before any agents have arrived to stake out or wiretap my apartment. Tim is not alone when I approach him after carefully scanning the area. Don't see any tails but, then again, I never worked in the field for The Office. My training, such as it was, covered the basics and not much else. It did convince me, however, that I needed to keep myself in shape. Healthy mind, healthy body. Right?

"I just thought I'd visit my two favorite fellows," Isobel tells me when I approach.

We kiss – very awkward. Our arms don't really encircle; our lips meet but fail to caress. We do not make eye contact. Isobel gives me a tentative smile; my smile is unnatural.

"Surprised?" Tim asks.

"I...I am. Where's that car you were talking about?"

I ease both of them in the direction Tim points. They pick up on my mood – one advantage of old friends. It also could be a curse.

"I've been busy," I tell them as we scurry down the street with me trying to stay in the shadows as much as possible.

Isobel has done something different with her hair and her clothes. Looks more grown up – certifiable East Coast. She takes my arm in hers, wrapping her free hand around my arm. Why do I feel uncomfortable? Wasn't this one of my recurring fantasies only a few days ago – Isobel showing up out of the blue and giving me much desired attention?

"Maybe we could visit one of those famous San Francisco restaurants I've heard so much about," she puts forth.

"Well, ah..."

"Not a bad idea. Hit the tourist hot spots," Tim says.

I can't see his face but I'm thinking something besides Isobel's visit is motivating his agreeableness.

"Back together again - the three of us... Yes. Let's celebrate," Isobel continues. "We can share one of those famous bottles of California wine."

I try to smile and fall in line. What a shock it is to recall my first memory of her, only to discover I see Heather on that cliff top, not Isobel. I blush, then tremble with anxiety.

"Your flight okay... No trouble getting here?"

I try to put my thoughts aside. Isobel is right. All we need is a little time to re-establish contact. That has to be what it is...just nerves.

"The flight...oh yes...just fine...No trouble at all."

Am I imagining things? Is Isobel nervous too? Why? Is she part of the destiny Heather so pointedly mentioned on the first day we met? If she is, what does it indicate about my life path as I move ahead into the future? And, in the short term, how will it impact this mess I've gotten myself into?

"I decided to surprise you. Are you glad I came?"

"Oh yeah... You bet. Sure. But you've caught me at a kind of awkward time. I mean, you see, this case...well, it's kind of complicated, my first claims investigation really."

"That's for sure," Tim puts in. "I tried to fill Isobel in but I probably left out most of the good stuff — including that hot babe you came home with the other night. Am I right, or am I right?"

"Be serious, Tim." Isobel slaps Tim on the shoulder, then turns back to me. "From what Tim has told me, it sounds exciting, just like you see on TV or at the movies."

I can't help it. I look over my shoulder, scan in all directions, almost step off the sidewalk and smash my knee into a parked car. Isobel and Tim give me a funny look and go quiet.

"Is everything all right?" Isobel asks.

"Oh yes...I mean, well, not quite. Where's this car?"

We're walking west on Harrison Street now - towards the ocean. The street is a little too deserted, too quiet to suit my taste at the moment. And the streetlights are too bright. We need to get under some cover - fast - and get the hell out of here. I'm hot, exposed, endangering the lives of my two oldest friends, one of them the girl I have declared is the love of my life.

Shit. Heather — no, that's Linda — flashes through my mind. The case hangs like a weight around my neck in the damp night air. "Sketches of Spain" — moody, uncertain, surprising - that's San Francisco now.

We approach a nondescript American car - white with black wall tires, four-door, a Chevy. Isobel holds out the key.

"You want to drive?" she asks.

"Tim knows the city better," I answer, passing the keys along to him.

At least we're out of my apartment and into the perfect cover car - a rental. It won't be long before Mr. White's goons are targeting it - if they haven't already. A car passes slowly by. It's a Plymouth Belvedere, a cop car if I ever saw one. Is that them? Is our cover blown already? Tim puts the car in gear and pulls away from the curb.

"Where to?" he asks.

"Would you mind driving around the block? Give Isobel here a chance to see the neighborhood?"

I laugh nervously. Isobel sneaks a look at my profile. Tim drifts up and down streets near my house, goes down the main drag of the neighborhood. Some nice ethnic restaurants are beginning to open up alongside the market, the shoe repair, the cleaners, the laundromat. I add no commentary to this mini tour. I'm seeing some of these sights for the first time myself.

"Want to talk about it?" Isobel asks.

She's always been there for me – a sounding board, ready to give advice or just listen. Not exactly the kind of thing I'm looking for at present from her. But the awkwardness helps me lessen my attention on the big mess I'm in the middle of.

"What?" I answer too quickly, a rush of possible subject matters zooming through my head.

"You know, the case," Isobel answers.

"It probably wouldn't interest you."

"Try me."

"Rich kid named Bob White was murdered and his body was discovered on the stage of the Straight Theater down in the Haight-Ashbury district. A bunch of weirdoes rented the place the night he was murdered to hold some sort of satanic celebration. Music and voodoo rituals took place. Bob White may have been mixed up with the folks who staged the dance. One of them, the current number one police suspect, has a history of violence and was into black magic with his boyfriend. Guy named Ronald Outrage."

"Isn't he the one who made 'Satan's Blood'..."

"That's the one. Anyway, Bob White's father is putting the squeeze on me to sign off on the claim before I think I should. Mrs. White sits on the Board of Life Beneficial. There's still a very good chance my friend Tony Vitolinich might end up being charged as well. You remember him, my friend in Richmond — well, you begin to get the picture."

"That does sound complicated... So why are we driving around aimlessly?"

"Mr. White has put a tail on me."

"What? Why?"

"Well, there's my friend, Tony Vitolinich; his girlfriend, Jane Preen; her sister, Linda, she's helping me out — what they know or what Mr. White may think they know. And there's this whole twenty thousand dollar check thing. The Office comes into it somehow and maybe things that Mr. White doesn't want bandied about. And..."

"What you're saying is crazy, Charlie. It makes no sense. And it sounds like you are making very serious allegations. Have you talked this over with your father or brought it to the attention of the police or your employer?"

"Ah, well, that just doesn't seem to be a very good idea right now."

"Well, I think you should re-think your position. Don't you?"

She's looking at the side of my face as streetlights flicker by. I light a cigarette. That Dexedrine Tim gave me is wearing off. I'm having trouble organizing my thoughts, coming up with a good rejoinder.

"Well, er, you see, I..."

"Do you just want to keep driving around or what?" Tim cracks.

Mr. White - am I overreacting to him? No. It's more likely that I am under reacting. But trying to get buy-in from my closest friends from back home seems remote. What does that tell me about anybody else? I'm in deep, very deep.

"Scott near Divisadero... You know it?" Tim nods. "I'll direct you from there."

A ghost-like image, a wisp of a thought swoops through the car. It's an image of Heather. Is she a temptress, an oracle, a metaphor for a wild and disturbing possible future that awaits me...

Isobel takes my arm and gives me a softened look. Does she pity me? Does she think I'm having a nervous breakdown? Does she imagine it will pass like a case of indigestion if she's patient?

What is this thing called love? And how bestial are men when it comes to a relationship with the opposite sex? What bargains have I made? Which ones will I keep? I reach out into nothingness, looking for a guide, a reason, anything that supports. I connect with the first inklings of the quest I set myself before ever realizing the consequences of my choice – realization, true understanding, ultimate release and freedom - lofty ideals indeed for someone unable to convince my closest friends that I have a serious but very real problem.

A car passes in front of the Russian Embassy. A raindrop hits my neck and starts its way down toward my chest. I pull up the collar of my raincoat which, somehow, causes my tie to pop out. I push it back under my raincoat. Try the front door. It swings open. Inside, the hallway is empty, damp, deserted. Streetlight makes a swath of light on the dusty floorboards. Scrap of paper rocks back and forth in the wind, then flies off into the darkness. Atmosphere inside feels heavy, oppressive; drizzle outside is cold, menacing, yet cleansing.

My shoes make loud telltale thumps as I move down the hall. Hair on the back of my neck stands up. Place still smells like that g-d awful brew Outrage had bubbling on the stove.

Room that had the altar in it is empty...Cleaned out. Kitchen vacant... Up the squeaky back stairs. Look into each bedroom. One at a time... A broken floor lamp and an old mattress on the floor of one...Burnt down candles in ceremonial cluster in another. Mirror with a crack in it hanging from the ceiling of the master bedroom. Very dusty, dark curtains at the bay window... Looks like they came from a theatrical supply house. Spider web attaches itself to my face.

Outrage is gone. If he's not involved in this mess, would he be willing to offer me help getting clear of this toxic riddle, or would he only add to my problems?

Isobel and Tim have patiently waited for me in the car. To their credit, they allow me free rein. I'm grateful. Maybe there's a chance that we can re-connect. We move on – into the night.

———————

KJAZ plays Vince Guaraldi's "Cast Your Fate to the Winds" and then a Gil Evans cut on our ride over to the Gough Street ashram. Isobel puts her head on my shoulder. We're in the back seat. I put my arm around her. She snuggles up to me. I find myself thinking, I'm riding on a cushion of avoidance…Into the dark night towards eternity… Am I a romantic, a fool, a sappy hero about to do his good boy duty? Everyone is the hero in their own life, you idiot…

I'm out of the car after making it clear this visit is another solo performance. No sense in getting my friends involved. Shutter bangs somewhere. Dog barks. Strange winds howl. A cat screams.

Am I walking in my dreams?

A siren's song calls out to me in the deep recesses of my cranium. Is it Heather's inner voice calling, sending icy chills down my spine? An image accompanies the song. I am tied to a ship's masthead. We are ready to crash into a rock looming out of the briny sea. On top of the granite rock is a mermaid - Heather. She's the one singing the siren's song. I can't make out the words. My ship is sinking. She's smiling. I find I'm holding my breath. But I must have air. I must breathe. Am I awake or am I at home in bed? If I'm in bed, who is with me? My shoes make deadened thunks on the sidewalk as I make my way through the damp night air on a San Francisco street.

———————

No light in the Gough Street ashram. I circle around to the back. Tim moves the car and parks near the dilapidated garage… The backdoor is unlocked. I head inside. Candles light the hallway. An initiate looks up from his meditation, a question mark in his eyes.

"Jane Preen and her friend Tony…" I respond.

He points up the stairs without uncoiling from his half lotus position. I only have to open two doors to find them. They're in a back room overlooking the garden, sitting on a mattress held in position by a box spring. A candle burns on an overturned orange crate being used as a night table. On the bed, Jane, partially naked, her body bathed in sweat, thrashes about and moans. A distracted and very agitated Tony jerks his head up at my arrival. He does not let go of Jane's hand.

"Tony? You guys high on something?"

"You're working for the pigs…"

"I've got to get you out of here, now. Can Jane walk?"

Tony stares long and hard at Jane. A tear rolls down his cheek.

"She told me the moon was green. Then she told me it was on fire. That was...hours ago."

"No time for talk, Tony. Get up."

I take him by the arm. He lunges toward Jane. I am pulled onto the bed. I hear "Sketches of Spain" drifting in through the open window. Does Tim have the radio on? Is his window rolled down? Or is this an auditory hallucination partnering up with the mental vision of Heather the siren?

"Tony. Snap out of it. We've got to split. Now..."

"Charlie? Is that really you?"

"Come on."

I pull Jane by the arm. She offers little resistance. The agony she seemed to be experiencing moments ago has quieted. I throw the sweaty sheet around her shoulders and lead her to the door.

"Bring her clothes."

Tony does as I ask, just as he did when I coaxed him shoreward at our first meeting. Before we reach the stairs, Jane moans and starts her descent toward another bout with the demons her trip has created. She grabs her stomach and cries out. I ease her to the floor. Tony is useless. No one stirs in the house.

"Hurry," I command, pulling Jane to her feet again as her pain seems to pass.

We move cautiously down the stairs. My shoulder is soaked with Jane's sweat. She is leaning on me heavily. She's a bigger woman than I suspected. At the bottom of the stairs is the monk I talked with on the back porch of the ashram. He puts his hand on Jane's forehead.

"We can help her," he states.

"I won't leave her."

Tony clutches Jane's arm. The monk remains calm. He nods toward two acolytes who have joined us in the hall.

"Help them take Jane to the car. I will be right back with some herbs that will help." The acolytes gently take Jane from Tony just as she is seized by another rush of pain. She screams, grabbing her belly again. Her body goes into spasms. The acolytes ease her to the floor, waiting for her to regain composure. The monk disappears from the hallway only to return momentarily. He hands me a jar. I can't see what's in it.

"Brew this and have her drink it as a tea. It will soothe her pain and help her to sleep." I take the jar wordlessly. "Do not fear for her - or your friend. But be vigilant."

He cups his hands together at his chest and bows to us. I return his salutation. We exit through the back door — and are deposited into the questionable safety of the rental car. Isobel has moved to the front seat. Tim puts the car in gear.

"Where to — the hospital?" he asks, without bothering to ask about

Tony and Jane.

Isobel looks at Jane. Tony covers her with the sheet. I shake my head no. Tim turns back onto Gough. Jane moans as another rush of pain descends on her.

"You want me to just drive around?" Tim inquires.

"Is there anything I can do to help?" Isobel asks.

"Tony. Is there any place you guys could spend the night — some place where no one would think to look for you and Jane and you could get some help if needed?"

For a minute I think I've lost Tony. But he comes around.

"Well, maybe Campbell and his wife would put us up — for the night. Campbell's father is a doctor of some kind and..."

"Give Tim the address."

Tim doesn't have to be told to get to Campbell's house in a hurry. Jane is resting quietly for the moment. I feel confident that whatever is in the jar the monk gave me will help soothe her pain. This medical emergency will pass — whatever it is. Worst case scenario, Campbell can call his father. Sticking around at Campbell's house isn't the way for me to help them.

"Know of an all-night car rental place?" I ask.

"I remember seeing a sign in the place I rented my car saying they were open all night," Isobel furnishes.

"Drop me off at the rental place after you drop off Tony and Jane at Campbell's. Tony, you take this," I hand him the jar. "And make tea from its contents. Make sure Jane drinks the tea." I turn to Tim and Isobel. "You two go back to my place. I need someone there I can call — even if it's just to get a reality check."

Campbell and his wife take Jane and Tony in without any questions. We make our apologies, then head down to the airport.

"Charlie, I understand your concerns. But don't you think the authorities..." Isobel begins.

"The authorities..."

"You can still stand up for your friends. And if they've got nothing to hide like you say then..."

"You saw Jane — and Tony too. You think they'd get better care in a cell than at Campbell's?"

"I didn't say that."

"And if they're locked up and I cave, what kind of defense will they have if it comes to a trial?"

"But they aren't guilty, are they?"

"The innocent are always vindicated in this country, you're saying? We just sit passively on the sidelines hoping and praying that somehow... somehow...I can't...."

Isobel gives me a peck on the cheek and a pat on the hand when I get out of the car at the rental office. Did she really fly into San Francisco — to visit with me? And did we really end up having a fight about whether I should be a good boy, a good scout and do my duty? And did we ever hit on asking "what's the right thing to do in this situation for all concerned?" Guess the human condition involves, at some point, taking sides. I'd like to be able to say I'm on the side of humanity's highest aspirations. I guess that makes me a fool, an innocent, in a word a knucklehead.

CHAPTER ELEVEN

I, CHARLIE FOXHAWK CARTER, NEED LOTS OF HELP

Show me the way.

I pay for my rental car with cash. I am too paranoid to rent a motel room down near the airport as I had planned. It seems like a good idea to avoid San Francisco as well. A map of the Bay Area courtesy of the rental company takes me across the Dumbarton Bridge to the East Bay and onto the Richmond-San Rafael Bridge, heading directly for Marin County.

Show me the way.

I ran smack dab into conflict — moral, mental, emotional, philosophical — which caused me to leave The Office. Brooding and aloof, hoping to escape my inner turmoil, I returned to my parental home in Richmond and again smashed up against the push-pull of my mental state. I rejected my few friends...Didn't want to go out partying with them...Didn't want to go to the beach with them...Didn't want to hang out at the club with them...Didn't want to spend time in their homes with them. They were in quick succession hurt, sad, angry, dismissive. "Charlie's dropping out," they said. "Next thing you know he'll be growing his hair long, smoking dope and burning his draft card," my childhood friends asserted with a he's-no-longer-one-of-us-and-he's-in-for-it-now chuckle.

Isobel tried to talk some sense into me. I pushed her away. But she didn't give up. She told me to knock off the John Wayne act, that she was there for me — ready to talk things through with me or to just sit quietly. I remembered our failed weekend in D.C., the one into which Tim intruded. What was the point of our relationship? Why must I be so self-destructive, she inquired, her patience fast eroding.

That's when it first occurred to me — why am I here?

I yearned, yearned for my father's guidance, yet shied away from it. He was tied up in my mind with The Office and the signal I got from him was "sink or swim, kid. And don't make a mess of it." I was struggling, uncertain, lost.

Where can I find guidance?

Show me the way.

You can see for miles in every direction from the top of the Richmond-San Rafael Bridge. Behind me a massive array of storage tanks and loading docks for oil refineries toward which tankers steam. On my left, an open expanse of blue-black water shimmers in the moonlight, the San Francisco Bay. Glittering on the skyline...San Francisco...Must be ten, twenty miles away. Looks like a vision floating in space — some science fiction, fantasy city filled with magical towers and electric angles. Most striking of all — Marin

County — overseen by Mt. Tamalpais... Some say Tam was named for the "sleeping maiden," an Indian maiden, reclining in the heart of verdant hills and valleys. Oh boy, spare me the Indian maiden references. Housing projects have not marred this maiden's elegant form. Homes are beauty marks on her body, graceful dashes of light on the landscape.

A surprise in the foreground, San Quentin Prison, brings my mind snapping back into place. Looks like a Spanish fort with ominous towers and medieval-like walls. On a neck of land jutting out into the Bay...dank and dangerous...the very ground and air around the place permeated with what are now called "bad vibes." Would the word used in former times apply – Evil?

Why am I here?
Show me the way.
Despite my conflicted thinking, I felt duty bound to follow in my father's footsteps but struggled with the idea of conforming to the mold...a lawyer, me? When my father told me about the opening at Life Beneficial that would lead to my assignment in San Francisco as an insurance investigator for claims, I welcomed the suggestion and interviewed for the job. Was my father's idea that I needed some business experience before going back to college and getting my law degree? Or was he giving me an out, a graceful exit? I guess even then I knew his influence had something to do with my being hired at Life Beneficial and probably both his and my connection to The Office entered into the hiring decision as well. I didn't waste energy pondering; with cowardly relief, I took what I hoped was the easy way out and accepted the job. I was just a good boy, doing my duty, a good scout. But now -

Why am I here?
Show me the way.
Did a moment of fury send Bull over the top? Did he clobber his son and somehow convince Bernie Toucan to stab his comatose son? Doesn't make sense... Putting The Office into the equation does what? Starts to connect the dots for me but elevates my mental and moral conflict and adds sinister possibilities to every angle of this sorry mess I'm in... Fathers and sons, what's with that classic relationship — complicated...archetypical...combative... passing of the torch...of knowledge...of morals...of humanity...

Fuck solving the riddle of who murdered Bob White. Let it go.

Can't...
Are you getting an inkling of why?
Let me know if you are.

I'm sucked into San Quentin as I hurtle down the far side of the bridge into Marin. An evil quagmire that rivets my gaze... A place where tormented souls are sent to serve their time... There they rot and plot, waste their lives in torment. Dream nightmares; hatch murderous schemes. Fight with fellow inmates or try to become invisible. Guards always watching... Bars and barbed wire confining them...

Why am I here, thinking —
Show me the way.
Am I here because I am a seeker, a nut now mixed in with fellow nuts? To make myself whole, have I forsaken my puritanical Old World roots for a jazzier, hipper West Coast vibe that resonates with the Far East and mystery religions and attempts to bring into focus, into the "real" world, the invisible world, that place where ocean spray battered by the wind tingles and you can just catch a glimpse of — The Beyond?
The Bay Area is ideal for dreamers. Have I embraced them — and am I now drifting toward the nexus of their dream world? I feel as though I have passed through an invisible gate that, once passed through, obscures the exit for all of time. Heather is one of my guides.
Will Isobel join me in this new and uncertain world? If she does not, will Heather become my lover and companion? Heather knows about the necessity to always-look-straight-ahead in this perilous world in order to reach ultimate goals. I have no idea whether her goals will mesh with mine, whether Heather has any desire to link her future to mine. Hazards, hidden land mines, obstruct our path forward on this journey. Truthfulness, keeping vows, will be required, as I see it.
And is that what I am doing here —

Seeking a hedonistic ecstasy experience?
Lust and Greed...

Show me the way.
Lots of open space surrounding the prison grounds... Must be owned by the state... Road I turn onto, Sir Francis Drake Boulevard, follows Madera Creek, a muddy tributary of the Bay. The water is shallow. The tide low... The smelly mudflats are exposed. An unwholesome stench drifts by my nose from the spoil dredge boats have collected maintaining the narrow channel. Up near the entrance to the creek there is a small stand of houseboats, just like their more famous counterparts down in Sausalito in the Gates. They are dark shadows on the water.
A gravel quarry on the right... Run down but the open pit is still in use. Dusty and dry here, despite the fact it's been raining off and on for days, weeks...Tumbledown buildings await the highest bid from land hungry developers moving in for the financial kill.
Head on to highway 101 — a major north-south highway still alive,

living in the shadow of a partially complete super highway under construction planned to travel the whole of the West Coast.

The I Ching is a new tool I might use to seek guidance. What kind of augury would I receive now?

One that predicts exciting times or
Challenging, torturous, menacing,
Cold, deadly ones...

I turn south towards the city, surrounded by the nascent opulence of the "'Me" generation. They're grabbing land in paradise - Marin County. Is it a trap that'll tie them back into the American mainstream? If it is, they're too busy getting high, believing in youthful dreams and the Age of Aquarius to see potential pitfalls.

Could Outrage be the murderer? Got carried away with one of his satanic ceremonies... Toucan did his part post mortem. Sympathy for the Devil... Probably helped along by chemical substances modern and arcane... Learned from a voodoo cookbook...

Fuck solving the riddle of who murdered Bob White. Let it go.

Can't...
You know why.
I don't.

I veer off at the Route 1 exit and head for the beach via a turnoff that shoots up Mt. Tam. I need privacy, somewhere to crash — even if it's only for a few hours. I'm beat.

The road is treacherous at night even when there's a full moon. It twists and turns back and forth through innumerable switchbacks. Wind formed trees hug the hillsides, punctuated by large rock outcroppings and wide swaths of open space along steep hillsides - civilization has melted away. I'm dizzy, dizzy from the ride, from all that has transpired, from all that I am attempting to integrate.

A turnout appears. I pull in and shut off the engine. All I hear is the wind. I'm groggy, drifting off, terminal... I don't even know where I am. How could anyone find me? Fitful rest...

I am awakened by some hippies looking for a place to sleep. I'm too tired to complain, too tired to explain, too weary to give them the finger. After an awkward and indeterminate amount of time they melt away into the night. No cops show up to disturb me. Other nocturnal dangers lurk in the shadows but take a pass —

For Now...

In my dream, my father, in his study, is looking at a folder marked top-secret. I enter the room. I know I shouldn't but I ask him about the folder as he slides it under the heavy leather-sided blotter on his sturdy mahogany two-partner desk. He frowns at me and, with a sweep of his hand, directs my gaze to a darkened corner of the room. In it stand both Isobel and Heather. I must choose between them. Neither of them wants me to choose them. I am tongue-tied and duty bound. I am being dragged out to sea with the rip tide. Tony is standing on the shore with my mother. They can do nothing to help me. My father taps his foot to a snappy Lester Lanin tune that swings and sways like the movement of the tides. I take a deep breath and submerge myself beneath the waves, fighting, fighting to reach the shore. Panic, lack of oxygen, strangles my consciousness. There is no way out. I awake sweating, teeth chattering in the chilling night air.

In the cold pre-dawn light, it's time for me to make a move - even if it's a bad one. I curve down, down, down the mountain, roar up the Waldo Grade towards Rainbow Tunnel with Sausalito on my left side, the Marin Headlands on my right... Beautiful morning sun rising in the East Bay... From the ocean side, fingertips of fog roll down the hillside towards me... The mouth of Rainbow Tunnel, shrouded by vaporous gases, transports me into another world.

Isobel and Heather, Mr. and Mrs. White, Bernie Toucan and Ronald Outrage, Jane and Tony, my father — torment and assail me.

I am catapulted down towards the Golden Gate Bridge as fog eats up the road in front of me. It rolls through the Golden Gate and slowly spreads across the San Francisco Bay, bringing in more mists of uncertainty as my tires slap over joins in the bridge surface. Tall, reddish orange columns rise up into the foggy heights above... Below the crashing ocean...Rocky...Deep... Treacherous crosscurrents luring leapers into their welcome yet icy embrace. Death... Death... Death...

Why do flower children live here? Certainly not because Beats hung out in coffee houses and bookstores in North Beach or because Forty-niners had wild and woolly times on the Barbary Coast, but maybe because dreamers like me can separate themselves from the flow of the seasons and the rhythm of the world here. A portal...An opening... Unsettling...Yet liberating...In the seam between life and death...

Bernie Toucan wouldn't need any accomplices to kill Bob White, so he's the most likely suspect. Tie that theory up with a bow and deliver it to Coop and all my troubles go away - wouldn't they? Maybe, somehow, probably not...Toucan in custody, what foul smelling sight would that uncover?

I stop at a pay phone near the tollbooth after crossing the bridge to check my messages. Bull White wants to meet me at Golden Gate Fields this afternoon. Tells me – no tricks, no agents... Neutral ground where we can talk things over... I call my apartment. No one answers. I call Campbell's house. The phone rings and rings and rings... Coop has still not come on shift yet. I don't have the heart to make any more calls. Who will answer – where will that leave me? The Bay Area takes its own sweet time coming alive after sunrise. Thank you, Lord, for the breather. Onward and upward...

———————

Seems like almost all the residents on the hill leading up to the top of Potrero are Mexican or African American, just like in the Mission District down below. As I near the hilltop, I enter a land of small cottages that were built for the working class more than a generation ago. Mostly white hippies fleeing the scene in the Haight live here now. It's quiet...Pleasant...Sunny. You can't beat the view of the city skyline and the Bay. Enough empty lots to give the place an open, almost rural, feel.

I pull over near the intersection of Vermont and 19th Street... Location that Harry gave me of Heather's place. McKinley Park dominates the neighborhood. This surprisingly well-kept small park is surrounded by two to four story apartment buildings. Mt. Sutro and its many television towers fill the sky off in the distance, blocking an ocean view.

Canvass the mailboxes in the entry halls of the apartment buildings. Find Linda Preen. Ring the buzzer. No answer. I give the wrought-iron gate at the base of the stairs a push. It's open. Head up the lime green outside stairwell.

There's no light in the second floor interior hallway. Walk cautiously, feeling my way along the wall. Something scurries by my feet. A cat... I turn a corner. The glare from the window at the end of the hall makes it hard to see detail. Preen is in number three at the back.

I knock on the door. No answer. I try the doorknob. It's unlocked. Has someone been here before me? Is Heather inside – in what condition? Is this a trap? I open the door.

I am confronted by a cold, damp one-bedroom efficiency. The bed is unmade. Quilts are piled up on top of it. There's a hotplate on the floor near the bay window that looks out onto a small fenced yard overgrown in weeds. The backside of another dilapidated apartment building looms over the far side of the tiny yard.

The bathroom is a mess. Half-filled toothpaste tube still open. Discarded, rusty razor blades next to the hot water tap, a broken eyebrow pencil next to the cold water one. Facial cream jar open...Dried up contents.

Torn shower curtain. A toilet that continually runs... Encrusted ring in the bathtub... Inside the medicine cabinet, plenty of empty prescription bottles, mostly for uppers and downers...All in the name of H. Mendoza.

Battered desk next to the bed... Serves as a night table and breakfast nook...Cluttered with magazines. Scissors...Glue. Picture frames stacked neatly on the floor next to the table...In all sizes... Some of the frames look costly.

On the table are collages in various stages of creation...Use the magazines as source material. Most of the magazines are current. Some are European; the vast majority of them are American. All are esoteric. Mixed in are high quality magazines of the thirties, the twenties.

Finished examples of collages on the walls... The collages are cerebral, calculated, cold, removed...Almost clinical...Filled with charged colors. A feeling of intelligence and economy carefully concealed beneath shocking juxtapositions... One theme after another mentioned and seemingly discarded only to reappear... The collages are inventive, stark, disturbing, dark, surrealistic.

I get lost in them...For a long and seemingly endless time... The Heather Chicago who curled up next to me in my bed created them? I shake my head. The human condition... We are all part of it. Captured and tormented... Seeking release and connection.

On the table are cut out pieces ready for montage use. Sleek car with running boards from the 1920s... Some women in gauzy dresses; their hair tied up and feet bare...Look like goddesses...Running. Pair of 1930s women's spike heels... Microscopic views of unidentified cells in fabulous colors... Intense young men captured walking down Haight Street and lying half-naked in the park. A soap bubble... Two babies crying - one starving, the other with a wet diaper... A magician pulling a rabbit from a hat... Some Buddhists in deep meditation near sacred shrines... Clouds of burning incense obscure the view. The table is piled high with images. Some fitted together; others awaiting placement.

Is this therapy or does Heather sell these things?

I sit down in the desk chair. It's the only chair in the room. It is carefully placed to catch the view out of the bay window. I light a cigarette. See an ashtray on the windowsill nearby. Turn in the chair to face the bed. The collages...The room...The tone is monastic, contemplative.

A tired phonograph record player sitting on top of a speaker with a torn front is tucked in a corner between the desk and the bed. Albums lean against the speaker. She likes blues. Delta blues. Chicago blues. A Gregorian chant record... An album of Baroque music - Vivaldi... A record of ragas — morning and evening ones... A salsa album... Very eclectic...

I turn on the record player. The Blues Breakers begin to wail. Put my cigarette out in the ashtray. It's filled with her tightly rolled marijuana butts. I imagine Heather smoking weed as she works through the night...Listening to record after record. The player has an ejector. The albums would clunk, one on top of the other, as they change. Heather would fill the room with the smell of incense, marijuana smoke, herbal tea kept warm on the hot plate.

She would be bent over her work concentrating, cutting, pasting, discarding, rearranging, feeling her way to a solution, shaking her head in time to the music, relighting her marijuana cigarette, tireless, meticulous, involved, immersed. Maybe high on speed...obtained from Toucan or Bobby — a side benefit of the operation Mr. White has no intention of talking to me about?

The needle was on the last cut of the album when I turned the player on. The record ends. A Vivaldi album pops down in its place...Shakes me from my reverie. Get up and look through her closet...Filled with outrageous outfits. Mostly second hand stuff — from the Salvation Army? Her smell, her scent, her body oils have weight, deep affinity and attraction.

This is Heather's retreat...Her lair. She comes here to hole up, hide out, cool out, get away from men, the world...Away from any and all scenes... She puts on that old sloppy robe hanging on a hook attached to the back of the bathroom door. She's here for days...Alone. Lives on canned soup, hot tea and marijuana cigarettes...Creates her artwork.

Sometimes she sits reading, propped up in bed with her quilt wrapped around her, a small collection of favorites to choose from leaning against the chair. The Tibetan Book of the Dead...The I Ching... Book on Tarot card reading... Book on the Cabala and the Occult... Book of Romantic and Transcendental Poets... Whole Earth Catalogue... Herman Hesse... Kahlil Gibran... Jane Austen...

She would sit in the chair I am sitting in looking out the window waiting for a can of soup to heat up on the hotplate. Just thinking...Just being... Watching the sun rise over the corner of the adjacent apartment building...

All the while the record player is playing, playing.

Guests are unwelcome. Work...Discipline. The concentrated essence of Linda 'Heather Chicago' Preen...

In the desk drawer incense — rope kind and some of the stick type... Some Smith Brothers cough drops sticking to the wax paper wrapping. Yarrow sticks to throw the I Ching. Pack of opened, now stale, cigarettes...Pall Mall... Her brand. Token for the bus... Deck of cards... Tarot cards... And a little black book, in the back of the drawer, filled with names and numbers, weird notations - some sort of cryptic diary of sorts.

I leaf through it. No last names. Few addresses. First names and a phone number, all on one line. Many entries. Below the entries are some hieroglyphics. One example - 23 > 52 (3); Hanged Man; 37; Aquarius; White; 5,000...

Doesn't take a genius to figure out that one thing she keeps track of is the astrological sign of each entry, when she knows it. Hanged Man is a Tarot card. Is she noting age, race? What are the numbers all about?

Look for Bobby's name. It's there...In red. Very long entry for his name. Several Bernies...One in red...No phone number for that one...Underlined hieroglyphics below his name. No Ronald... No Bull. Luther gets a check mark. Some green notation... Jane, of course, gets a long green notation...Three checks. Long list of hieroglyphics for Jane... Notice most of the entries have several changes of phone number. Maybe that's why she left it behind. Waste of time trying to keep up with people and places in these ever-changing times. Or, maybe she got tired of playing whatever game she was playing...Moved on to other things.

I look out the window at the scruffy backyard, slapping the book into the palm of my hand. Heather's mixed up in this all right up to her pretty eyeballs. Was she involved in Bobby's death? In what way was she involved with Toucan? Did she and Bull make love? If they did, how do things stand between them? Is she involved in any Office operations? What kinds of operation take place in San Francisco? Do these operations have any connection to Bob White's death?

Jesus Christ, how can I offer her freedom if she's an agent of, or in collusion with The Office?

Heather. Heather. Am I crazy to let my desire for you tear me away from my childhood vision of the ideal – Isobel? Would you laugh at me for even bringing the subject up? With a murder and some very kinky dealings thrown into the mix I must be crazy to even consider it...Holy shit, I'm worse than the worst innocent. I'm a fool.

Heather. Did Bobby have you trapped? Did you smash him on the back of the head to get away? Was it self-defense? Were you one of Bobby's stable of concubines? Were you in cahoots with him dealing drugs? What?

Holy shit... I've plunged Tony and me in water fast rising over our heads. We're toast. Why didn't I just fill out the claims forms like Heather suggested? Too late now, someone else has probably been assigned the task. Why did I allow myself to blow my cool in front of Mr. White?

Shake my head in disgust...Must be this g-damn moody room. Mold going to my sinuses...Or, same thing, my upbringing... Have to see this thing through now. Clean up my foolhardy lunge... this mess, the tangle. Save what can be saved... Put the puzzle pieces in their proper place, work assignment pieces, moral and religious pieces, family obligation pieces, Office case, fuck the goddamn insurance claim and the goddamn murder investigation. Shit. There's no way. I have no idea what to do, how to proceed. Got to...now... No matter the consequences or who gets hurt? That's a point...try to avoid that...

I push myself up from the chair. Turn off the record player. Leave. Don't take one last look at her place. Don't look at the gloomy hallway. Don't look at the g-d damn darkened stairwell. Don't take a peek into her god awful mailbox or sneer at the peeling green paint. Don't look back at the tired apartment house. Don't think about the fact that I'm having nasty suspicions about the only female I've gotten close to in the last year.

I'm heading for my car, eyes looking straight ahead. Marching down the street...Disciplined...Angry...Fed up...When I'm brought up short.

Black VW parked on the street. It has New York plates, WJA 216. And it wasn't parked there when I went in.

I'm sitting on that car...As long as it takes... Maybe a useless move... But what else have I got that's more immediate? I take out the black address book from my pants pocket. Thumb through it carefully. Puzzle over the codes. Keep an eye on that VW. Read Heather's drug addled diary entries. It's sunny and mild on Potrero Hill. I'm icy cold within. A random page is a good place to begin.

'In the shadow of my Mata Hari mother taking my decidedly uncomfortable place... Beware the pleasure purveyors. They will enslave you with shackles made of your vices. You will dance the dance of the seven veils for industrialists, spies, the idle rich and their cronies. Ah, sweet cocaine. Ah, miracle morphine. Yes, speedballs that send you up, down and sideways, a little, no a lot of weed and hash thrown in. With the unexpected presence of your sister as a companion piece – something to keep the boys in the backroom entertained.

'Do not consult the oracle when you have already taken the forbidden trip, accepted the tainted path, downed the spiked agenda. You will not find relief. In fact, you will be required to continue your lap dance on middle-aged players and demented scions of the human race.

'Captured, imprisoned, condemned. But never ever give in. Reach down inside to find the message. Proclaim it. Let venom be one-sided. The objective eye of insight will not desert you. Take heart. All will be as you make it. Have the courage to live in dark times with the heart of a tigress. Roar even when you are not in heat. Lick your chops with your own secretions. Long live prophecy. Long live the 'Voice That Has Come Down Through the Ages.' Amen.

I need a shower. I need a good night's sleep. I need. I need. I need to move straight ahead without looking sideways for a mate, a blessing, an easy way out...

He comes out of Heather's apartment building. Male...Asian...Five ten...Twenty-two or three...Medium build... How...must be a back way into that building...

Asian guy fumbles with the key while trying to unlock the door of the VW I'm sitting on. The door is already open. Takes him forever to get the car started... Then he pops the clutch and kills the engine on his first attempt to pull away from the curb. The VW belches out a puff of dirty smoke. Car needs new valves. Maybe even a head gasket. Guy needs some instruction on how to drive a stick shift.

I turn over the engine on my car. Wait. Other driver finally gets it together and pulls away from the curb. Car jerks and lurches. I ease out behind him.

We head down Potrero Hill towards the Bay...Into Hunter's Point... Empty streets...Dying port...Poverty prevalent. Turn up Third Street. Head toward downtown... Cross the Fourth Street drawbridge at China Basin. Swing round to the Embarcadero. Pass a schooner up on blocks converted into a restaurant. Wharf after wharf; pier after pier. Empty but for a cruise line or two... Pass under a section of freeway feeding onto the Oakland-Bay Bridge... Cruise by the Ferry Building. Landmark at the base of Market Street... Seedy hotels, greasy spoons and bleak and empty piers give way to office complexes and hotels. Turn up Broadway and merge with traffic from the freeway off ramp. Crawl slowly down the Broadway strip... Topless joints with hucksters on the street trying to lure customers into the joints even at this early hour... Cage on a pole up above one club... Girl dancing in it... Left on Kearny... Cross Columbus. Pass the Flatiron Building as we head into Chinatown. Narrow streets...Packed with cars, crowded with people, festive lights. Park in the underground garage below Portsmouth Square...

Guy locks the car door. Bad move for the next occupant. Looks in every direction...Trying to remain cool, smooth - James Bond. A miserable failure...

We ride the garage elevator up...Together. I stare right at him. He's sweating big time. I nod to him and smile. He's defiant. Before I speak the door opens and he bolts. Give chase. Run through a park crashing through ancient Chinese men playing games of mahjong, checkers and chess. I follow at a polite distance, begging forgiveness from the undisturbed Chinese men still concentrating on playing their board games while I try to not lose sight of my prey.

The crowded streets are a perfect place for him to bob and weave. Plenty of alleys and obscure doorways... Vendors out peddling on the streets... Tourists stop and take pictures. Gawk and wonder.

I'm jogging now...huffing and puffing...Running into people. Colliding with fruit and vegetable stands set up outside of markets. Cars honk at me as

I race across the street. I'm acting like a damn fool. Real thriller stuff...Total nonsense.

Guy turns down an alley. I'm right behind him. Should have grabbed him in the elevator.

He ducks into a restaurant. I follow. Small dining area... Lots of tables and chairs...Cluttered...Almost empty... Head into the kitchen... Cook looks up at me...Says something in Chinese. I barrel past him, heading for the back door. Going to get this bastard...Piss ant... Back door leads to an alley. It's empty. High fence in one direction, the street in the other... I'm up the high fence and over. Office basic training and erratic daily exercise attempts try to keep me in the hunt...fails. I need to start running again...Got to get back in the exercise groove. Backyard...Into a building...Tenement...Filled with Asians. Dark...Cramped. Shit. I've lost him.

Find a pay phone. Check my answering service. Coop has left me a message — there's now a federal warrant out for Tony's arrest. If I don't back off, one for me won't be far behind, he has been informed. My San Francisco boss also has left a message – disciplinary action has been taken against me. I am to turn in all my paperwork on the White claim post haste. Read between the lines - you're fired and we will do everything in our power to make your life miserable for a very long time.

I have to ring Luther Green's doorbell several times, long and loud, before I hear someone stumbling down the hall. Door swings open. Green is a mess...Obviously just got out of bed.

"What the hell do you want?" he asks, glaring at me.

The place is quiet. Party animals are still in bed. Will they come back to play much later in the day?

"Want to talk to you about Heather and other things."

It occurs to me that Green might be mixed up with The Office somehow. Why would Outrage choose the Straight Theater for his satanic voodoo event? How come Bob White's body ended up there? Outrage must be connected with the Office; why else would he think I was one of their agents the day I walked into that Russian Embassy kitchen? So...I start to enter Green's pad. Green blocks my way. Not sure whether he's going to fall asleep or attack me.

"What's the matter, she dump you already?"

He motions me in. Follow him down the hall towards the back of the place. Turns out Green's kitchen looks out on a well-kept but tiny backyard. I'm impressed.

Green puts on some water to heat while he pulls out coffee beans from the refrigerator. I see Melitta filters in action for the first time that morning. Drip coffee... For those of us who like coffee, there's no better way to make it.

I sit down at the circular kitchen table.

"I assume you want some coffee," he comments, still half asleep.

He's wearing a robe. His hair is tousled. His eyes are crusted with sleep. But his mouth is curled up in a smirk. Green has never met a situation he doesn't think is ironical, camp. He's a dyed-in-the-wool smart ass. He'd be fun to have around. Always ready with a real hot zinger that would scald the skin off an armadillo.

He pours out cups of coffee for both of us. Water hasn't finished dripping through the filter. Green needs a java injection fast.

"So? Has she dumped you already?" he asks once more as he puts the sugar and milk on the table and sits down.

"We've gone from weird to wild and back again."

"Lemon tree... Very pretty..."

"How did you meet her?" I ask.

"Oh. She drifted in on Bob White's arm. Of course, that didn't stop her from playing the field. He didn't seem to mind. Bobby just eats up rejection."

"Thought you didn't know Bobby?"

"I don't think I said that."

"Ever run into Bernie Toucan or Ronald Outrage before they rented your hall?"

"Once or twice..."

Green is downing big gulps of coffee. His eyes are becoming more alert, less dazed. He's sitting straighter in his chair.

"Bobby ever show up with another date..."

"Yeah, Jane...Jane something..."

"Did you know Jane and Heather were sisters?"

"Guess Bobby liked a certain type – or had a fixation on their family." Green gets up and rummages through the refrigerator. He finds the remains of an old salad...Mixes it up with his finger. Smells it...Tastes it. Has his seal of approval. "You want some?"

"Never eat salads before noon."

"It's noon somewhere in the world," he responds. We both laugh. He sits back down at the table.

"Did Bobby ever talk to you about his family or any business dealings he had with his father?"

"I thought we covered that last time."

"I recall you blew me off. Does that qualify as answering my question?"

"You've got a point there."

I don't have time for bobbing and weaving today.

"Before I started working for Life Beneficial, I was employed by a little known and top secret governmental agency, The Office...you familiar with them?" Now it's time for my reappraisal. Green's eyebrows rise; his eyes do more than twinkle. They send me an 'ah-ha' look. "Well," I prod.

Green snorts. "So what if I have? The Office is listed in governmental directories if you know where to look and how to read, ah, interpret."

"You an agent?"

"No."

"But you've had dealings with them?"

"Yes."

"What kind?"

"Ask someone at The Office, someone in charge. You probably still have their number in your Rolodex."

"Fair enough..." The Office, front and center again. Everything about this mess keeps ending up in a mention, a connection to The Office. I don't see how Green's connection to The Office can help me right now. I return to Heather and her sister, Jane. "So what sort of scene was Heather into?"

"Oh, probably like most party-hearty hippie chicks – scenes where she has access to lots of sex, drugs and rock-n-roll, not necessarily in that order, while surrounded by men loaded with dough, eager to share a swinging lifestyle, essentially weak men, particularly where women are concerned. Control – that's what they all want, don't they?"

"No idea what any of her swinging friends were up to, not even unsubstantiated rumors?"

"Fuck I know," he says with a twinkle in his eye. "But I'm willing to take you to a place where you might be able to find out – one of the hippest places in the Bay Area. The Trident... Filled with dynamite waitresses and hostesses..."

"Why would they want to look at me? I'm just an ordinary guy, not one of your high roller types."

"No idea. But it'll do your heart good to see them. It certainly does mine," laughs Green, slapping me on the shoulder. "Won't take a minute... Take a turn in the yard. Looks like a good day for it. I'll be ready in a jiffy."

I light another cigarette. Finish my coffee. Maybe I'll take Luther up on his offer later, much later. Scribble a note of regret... Slip out quietly. Got an appointment to keep...

———————

Golden Gate Fields is in the East Bay. It's built to human scale. I like it. Easy to keep track of the horses...No big crowds at the betting windows... Plenty of room to spread out in the stands...The Turf Club for the high rollers is up top... That's, of course, where I find Bull White...

He's leaning against a rail smoking a stogie...Enjoying what I find out later is a real rarity, warmth and sunshine at this track. Wonderful day... Makes me feel like kicking back myself. This town has a style all its own, a style that I could grow to like. I mean, what's not to like. Fine women...Moderate weather...Beautiful views. A touch of moodiness and mystification thrown in to make everything perpetually enticing...

Bull studies his racing form, then pushes back in his chair. Relights his cigar...Blows smoke leisurely up toward the sky...Watches the start of a race, loses interest before they're beyond the first turn. Tilts his wide brimmed hat over his face...Tears up his stubs when the PA announces the winners...Gets up from his seat to take a stroll. Bull has an elegant, no, an animal grace, a relentless energy in all his movements. And, he's true to his word. I see no hint of anyone watching.

"Mr. White," I doff my hat and bow slightly in his direction as he walks towards me.

He looks up...Flashes me a cold, reptilian smile.

"Hard at work, Mr. Carter?" he asks with regal ease.

"I'm trying to do my duty, if that's what you mean."

"You've turned in your paperwork on the case to Mr. Meade then, I take it?"

"You fucked Heather Chicago lately?" I shoot back.

Is Heather just a swinging gold digger looking to get laid, to get pampered, to get all she can get, as Luther implied? Did Bull White hook up with her? Did his son find out about it, blow his top and, in the heat of the moment, did Bull White end up killing his son? If so, how does Bernie Toucan figure into the story? I was assigned to investigate an insurance claim and I've let personal feelings overrule my sensibilities. I ignored the ground rules: keep my nose out of an official police investigation, keep my eyes on what I'm supposed to be doing, investigating an insurance claim. My ass is grass now. I'm history at Life Beneficial and headed toward reading my name on a federal warrant. Wonder what the charge will be?

Bull snorts...Pulls me into a corner. Have I struck a nerve? Has my guesswork scored a hit?

"I beg your pardon," he mutters with as much contempt as he can muster.

"Heather. Heather Chicago. Or was she using that name then? You know. Dresses in an Indian costume...Great body...Really swell in the sack... One of your son's main squeezes... You know, that Heather, or would you prefer her given name – Linda Preen."

"If it wasn't for your father, I'd..."

"Leave my father out of this, Mr. White."

"No. Let's put him right in the middle of this, Charlie, because he and I are on the same side. You want to know what that side is..." Bull waits for me to answer but it's really a rhetorical question at best so I wait. He goes on. "The United States of America...That's right, the American Way...Truth-and-Justice...On our side...Remember..."

You're on a roll, partner. Hit me with it.

"We're willing to get our hands dirty in the service of our country.

We're patriots. And we don't take kindly to anyone, anyone or anybody you got that, who stacks up as someone trying to drag our flag, our values, through the mud. Principles, son, that's what holds this whole shooting match together – principles and the guts to stand up for them and stick by them when the going gets rough."

"So what is it that you are saying, sir? What exactly..."

"That you have no idea what you are dealing with here, son."

"Respectfully, sir, I'm just trying to do what is right. Keep people I care about out of harm's way. Enlighten me. Show me the error of my ways."

"Questions of national security come into play here. Need to know. Top secret and confidential material... You must have run across the concept during your tenure at The Office, remember that place?" Before I have a chance to answer Bull plunges ahead. "So what the hell does my private life, a life devoted to the service of my country, have to do with closing the books on an insurance claim? Can you tell me that? It's tantamount to treason, sedition, or at the very least obstructing a top secret federal operation. You've picked the wrong side of the law to stand up for, young man, and a federal warrant may be the end result of your laughable heroics."

"So I am to assume you are reacting the way that you are because of some top secret operation that has to do with national security – and that you have federal agents trailing me because of this – whatever it is – is that correct?"

"That is a yes sir sonny buck, roger, a big ten-four. And it's time for you to dutifully say, 'over and out,' suck in your gut, stand down and take whatever consequences there are like a man. I'm sure your father would stand behind me on that."

Grab the fucker by his arm with all my strength and pull him towards his box. He chomps on his stogie. Madder than hell at my affront to his dignity, I mean principles... Too fucking bad... That stogy is history...It looks like a Havana...Someone bumps into us and Bull is shoved up against me. We grapple, then Bull pushes me away.

The next race goes off. The announcer comes on the PA system, staccato delivery...growling monotone voice. The crowd explodes. Some jump from their seats. We're hidden from view. I'm holding Bull by the arm.

"The point is..." I squeeze Bull's arm tight to get his attention and talk through gritted teeth. "The point is, you son of a bitch, that you were fucking the murder victim's girlfriend and you are, as you have pointed out more than once, the co-claimant for the insurance policy I was investigating and the murder victim is your son, the same one whose girlfriend you were fucking. And to sign off on this case, as you were so eager for me to do, I had to prove none of the claimants were involved in any way with Bobby's death. Get it now?"

"Get this. Neither I nor anyone else in my family had anything to do with my son's death. So get smart, shut your mouth and back off. Got that..."

People around us go wild. The field makes the clubhouse turn.

"It's Pistol Pete and Maraschino Cherry. Pistol Pete and Maraschino Cherry," rumbles the PA announcer.

"And I should do this for reasons of national security – need to know – top security clearance eyes only – is that about right too, Mr. White?"

Snide son of a bitch... I want to flatten his nose. But I don't. Has the world on a string and still insists on hitting the sack with his son's girl. Heather. I loosen my grip on his arm so I can grab his shirtfront and pull him towards me. I glare at him with all the menace I feel.

"Maraschino Cherry by a nose... Pistol Pete second... Clubhouse Willy third..." concludes the PA announcer.

The crowd settles down. Bull brushes me aside. He outweighs me by fifty pounds and still has some chops. He lets loose with a terse, muttered monologue. I strain to hear him as we glare at each other inches apart. He's almost whispering.

"Listen, you little shrimp. For your information I had a nice long chat with my wife. And I was surprised, no, alarmed, to discover what she had been telling you."

Bull shakes his head like a you-know-what getting ready to charge then continues.

"And you know what she told me? She told me that she had let it be known to you that she suspected I was involved with the murder of our son because of some floozy. Our son – get that, kid?"

"And it makes a lot of sense, too. Bob Jr. was a spoiled brat holding the purse strings. Toying with you for being a bastard and probably making a nuisance of himself, mucking up the works in your noble Office operation... Then you screw his girlfriend. He confronts you. You fly off the handle. Bam! There you go. Accidental homicide... And no insurance money either if what you did is brought to light...Might even lead to some jail time...so you're hot to put a lid on it. Am I getting warm?"

Bull's eyes glitter lightning bolts. He grabs me by the arm and drags me along with him through the crowd. The announcer comes on the PA to introduce the next race. Some people are tearing up tickets; others are celebrating. The betting windows are a whirl of activity. We vamoose toward the paddocks. It's quieter there.

"All right... Bobby and I have not been on the same page for several years and I tried to help straighten him out by involving him in an Office operation. That was an unmitigated disaster. I should have known," White begins when we are by ourselves with no one to overhear. "Ever since he announced that he had just dropped out of college - for no goddamn good reason at all. His grades were fine. He was on the fast track. Suddenly he takes it into his head that college is for losers, people who can't hack it in the real world."

"You blew your stack?"

"You're damned right I did. He didn't know what the hell he was talking about. Never considered for a minute what it would be like if his trust money stopped rolling in. He just wanted to play the hotshot, the cool guy. A fuck up is what he was. I said, 'Fine. Screw up your life.' He laughed. I..I blew my cork. Yelled... Bobby yelled back."

Bull pulls out a fresh Havana. Walks further away from the racing crowd. Looking down at the ground...Rolling the cigar between his fingers.

"Bobby said he'd get even. Said he'd get the executor of my mother-in-law's estate to cut us off. You better believe I put the kibosh on that pronto. And then he takes it in his mind to...well, enough of that."

He stops walking. Bites off the end of the cigar...Spits out the stubby end... Sticks the cigar in his mouth...Lights it with an expensive lighter... His clothes are elegant; his bearing patrician.

Off in the distance the PA system comes on. Nearby, stable boys warm up horses for races to come. The wind off the bay is beginning to have a little sting to it. Wish I had brought along a coat. Every person I ever asked told me to dress in layers if you lived in the Bay Area. I'm beginning to be a believer.

"Was that before or after your little fling with Heather?" I ask.

The sky is blue up above. Bright flags flutter in the breeze. There's an amazing dearth of noxious insects in California. We should all be lucky enough to experience the abundant life affirming sensations on a day like today.

"I don't know what the hell you're talking about." Bull runs his hand through his hair. Straightens his coat with a small tug...Looks off into the middle distance...Then looks at me.

"So why sic federal agents onto my tail and issue a federal warrant for Tony Vitolinich's arrest if you have God on your side and no connection to your son's murder? And what's all the hurry about closing out the insurance claim, come to that? You strapped for cash? I don't think I can make myself believe that."

The wind really begins to pick up now. Horses paw and snort in the paddock next to us. We are alone. In a vacuum, a vacuum that is being pressed on all sides by questions that demand answers.

"You're right, Charlie. You're not worth my time and effort. You, my friend, are a fool. And fools, without knowing how they do it, put themselves in harm's way each and every day. Most of them end up with a knife in their back or worse, when all they expected was a slap on the wrist or better yet a shiny award for brave service."

White flicks a long ash off his cigar. Watches it drop to the ground... Grinds it with a deliberate motion of his very expensive shoes...Looks up at the horses warming up...Looks back at me.

"So what the hell is it with all that bullshit about national security —

and my father? How does that fit?"

White takes another long drag on his cigar...Blows the smoke into the wind. It slides by the tip of my nose.

"I can't believe you worked for The Office for two years and that you are your father's son," White finally answers.

I turn my back on him and walk away.

"Go ahead. Run. You can't hide. You can't escape from us —anywhere in the world. Game over...face it, kid..."

For some reason I am not panicky. Then again I wouldn't say I was cool, calm and collected either. I just know - I must be on my wayyyyyyy...

———————

"Tony here?"

"Upstairs in his room with Jane..."

I'm up the stairs and heading to Tony's room before Molly has a chance to continue — got no time to chat. I stop at the top of the stairs and call down to her.

"Oh yeah, there's a federal warrant out for him."

"What?" Molly exclaims.

"We've got to get them out of here — fast."

Their room is on the second floor of the big, old Victorian on Regent Street. The rest of the lightshow folk are out — as usual. The hallway is in shadows. I knock on Tony's door.

"Tony. It's me."

Long silence... Then the murmur of conversation followed by the sound of feet shuffling across the hardwood floor... The door opens a crack. Tony peeks out.

"Charlie?"

Tony's pupils are dilated. His voice is very far away.

"What the hell are you doing here?" No answer. "Tony. You've got to pull yourselves together and get out of here - now. There's a federal warrant out for your arrest."

"Far out..."

Over Tony's shoulder, candlelight flickers on the wall of the room. The window shades are drawn. A mattress on the floor, two orange crates as bedside tables with books inside them, a desk and a chair - these are the only furnishings in the room. Strange, hallucinatory vibes pulsate in a thousand fragmented directions in this their shared shadow world. Beads of sweat cling to Tony's forehead. His skin looks cold and clammy.

"You okay?" I ask. "Did you understand what I said?"

"Jane's bad," answers Tony pulling me by the arm into the room while partially closing his door.

Still?

There's nowhere to sit but on the bed. Tony pulls me down onto it. Jane's a lump in the quilt. Her blond hair tumbles out from one edge of it. I can't see her face. She's balled up in a fetal position.

"Jane. It's Charlie. He's come to visit us," coos Tony, rubbing her back.

Jane stretches out her legs in answer. Then she groans. I tense up but quickly realize this groan is not the same one that was connected to her spasms a little over a day ago. What happened to that pain? What happened to these two between then and now?

"You want some water. Anything..." I ask.

"Water?" she responds.

I get up and go into the bathroom the two share with Molly and her husband. I hear baby Rory cry out in his sleep. Look in the mirror. Turn on the tap. Look back at myself. What do I see – anxiety, guilt. These two could be on their way to a federal lockup and it would be my fault for allowing it to happen. I've got to get them out of here. Then what? Think about that later.

Tony looks at me with big, begging eyes. I'm adjusting to the light. Notice that incense is burning. A record on the phonograph plays Gregorian chants.

"We die over and over again only to be reborn," Tony explains. "Now we're dead."

I lift Jane's head. She struggles to sit up. The quilt falls away from her. She has no clothes on - again. I help her drink. Her lips are dried, cracked. Some of the water dribbles out of her mouth.

"What happened?" I ask.

Jane takes the glass from me. Presses it against her cheek, then drinks more water only to look at what's left in the glass as if it is a sacred substance — lovingly, longingly... What is she seeing...heaven or hell? Tony, for some inexplicable reason, has a moment of clarity.

"Campbell got freaked when Jane passed out in the bathroom after creating a bloody mess on the bathroom floor. But Jane wouldn't let Campbell call his dad. She called someone. I don't know who it was. A care package arrived. Some pills – for both of us... Jane's stomach pains stopped after that." I can almost feel Tony leaving his body again. There is a long pause before he continues. "This is the strongest shit I've ever taken, Charlie. This trip just keeps going on and on and on and on and on and on and on..."

"We've got to get you out of..."

"Charlie — is that really you, Charlie?"

Tony gently pulls the quilt up to cover Jane. Then he laughs a laugh of fear, a laugh of marvel, a laugh of sorrow, a laugh Tony will have to deal with the rest of his life. He has torn the fabric of his universe asunder — and all the while the temporal world is readying to strike, to take away his freedom, to turn his life to shit.

"Tony. Tony. Listen. We have to get out of here. Leave. Pronto. Do you understand what I'm saying?"

I shake him but he doesn't stir. Jane's body trembles. Her lips quiver. She goes into what seem like mini-convulsions. The glass tips over on the orange crate nightstand. A few drops spill onto the quilt... Droplets bead on its surface, then trickle off the edge of the mattress. Time freezes just when it needs to speed up. We've got to get a move on.

"Do you need any help?"

Molly is at the door.

"Help get Jane dressed, will you?"

Molly is a savior. Jane laughs riotously. Then she's silent. A hoot owl calls. Birds chirp in nearby trees. A car passes in front of the house. Tony, backed up against the wall, staggers, then regains his composure.

Without warning, Jane calls out.

"Charlie. Charlie."

"Yes, I'm right here," I answer.

Then I realize she is not seeing me in the flesh. She visits with me in her vision world even as her clothes are, with our awkward efforts, being put on her.

"Linda will be at the gig. You must meet her there." The urgency in her voice becomes conspiratorial. "They're holding all the cards, Charlie. Be careful."

"What...why?"

Jane does not acknowledge me. She groans. Molly and I have to hold her up.

"They lied. They play dirty pool. They're bastards."

Jane laughs, then moans once, twice more. It's hopeless to question her now. Who knows how long I'd have to wait for her to join the land of the living again. She's in the grips of a very powerful hallucinogen. At long last her clothes are on. We are still holding her upright. Tony's eyes continue to bug.

"The lightshow has a gig out at Muir Beach. Maybe that's where Jane wants you to meet Linda," Molly suggests as we guide Jane out into the hall.

Jane is steady on her feet despite her condition. She's innately solid, a sturdy woman despite her California go-go girl look. Tony follows us out of the room. Wherever Jane goes, so does he. He frowns, mutters to himself, glides into partial reality.

"Some stay high a week. Some don't come back. Ever...that's the word on the street," he declares with fervent intensity.

He looks at Jane and shivers. I can see his mind is reeling, spinning. The trip down the stairs is treacherous. The powerful sunlight shocks the two of them into a semblance of awareness. I repeat the reason for urgency again.

"You've got to hide out, Tony. There's a federal warrant out for your arrest. Who knows what kind of trouble Jane is in..."

We're standing by the car. Molly is on one side of Jane and I am on the other. Tony strokes Jane's hand, brushes some hair away from her face, cleans up some drool from the side of her mouth. He touches her so tenderly, with such warmth. He answers from far away.

"Got a gig... Need the bread. Have to go." He sighs, looks at the empty playground across the street, stifles a wave of emotion. "Charlie. What can I do? Jane and prison and death and...I'm scared, Charlie. Help me. Please."

A car door slams off in the distance. Several people begin laughing and talking. It's a balmy day in Berkeley. Feels like summer and it's the middle of the winter. Tony's life has been a constant series of gut wrenching changes since he moved to the West Coast. These new troubles have pushed him over the edge. I put my hand on his shoulder and try to look him in the eye without letting go of Jane. A police siren wails down on Telegraph Avenue.

Jane moans. Tony, forgetful of my presence, leans over and takes Jane in his arms. He pulls her to him. Jane leans against him, arms limp. He holds her tight, comforting her. This gives me a chance to unlock and open the back door of the car.

"A college chum of mine lives in the city," Molly offers. "I can give her a call if you want."

We have now shepherded Tony and Jane into the backseat of the car. They are still locked in a ludicrously furious embrace.

"If I haven't been followed, it should be perfectly safe."

"Is it that bad?"

"I've only managed to get a hint of what's hiding behind the curtain. What I've seen isn't encouraging."

"Wait here."

Molly hustles into the house. I sit down in the driver's seat. No cars on Regent Street as far as the eye can see. No pedestrians either. Tony loosens his death grip on Jane. I turn and look into his fearful blue eyes.

"Thank you," he says after a long quiet pause.

"We're not out of the woods yet."

"I know," he answers.

"You up for helping me decipher the notations next to these names?"

I open Heather's black book at random and hold it up in front of Tony's face. Tony kisses Jane tenderly on the cheek. Jane smiles, takes Tony's hand. Tony strokes her hair, smiles down at Jane, then looks at the book.

"Astrological signs: Aquarius, Pisces, Taurus..."

"The numbers..."

"The I Ching, hexagrams..."

"What else?"

Tony takes the book from me, studies it. Jane rests quietly at his side.

"Hanged Man, Tarot... Probably some numerology..."

He's lost in the ozone again. I take the book from him and put it back in my pocket. Molly scurries out of the front door.

"Here's my friend's address. Try not to freak her out. She's had a rough time with romance of late."

Haven't we all. Heather, Heather and Isobel... Seems like every way I turn I see nothing but troubles and complications, troubles and complications. People are getting hurt. People are taking sides. Not what I thought I'd run into on the West Coast – and what exactly was that? Realization, a new path, enlightenment?

I pull away from the curb and turn on the radio – this time to KMPX.

The Steve Miller Blues Band are singing 'Quicksilver Girl.'

"Jane okay?" I ask.

We're heading for the freeway and the Bay Bridge back to the city. Jane is nestled in the crook of Tony's arm, limp as a rag. In repose her face is sweet and innocent – angelic.

"She'll make it. She's strong. Much stronger than I am."

Tony. Tony. Tony. Tony and Jane, will they end up tying the knot if these troubles disappear? What about me? What Destiny am I propelling myself toward? Better start thinking about real short term goals – like keeping one step ahead of probable pursuers, keeping my razor and toothbrush with me at all times in case I get arrested, trying to eat and sleep and all the other necessities whenever it is possible. Wonder if Tim left any of those "mother's little helpers" around my pad? Is it worth a swing by on the off chance? Is it worth the risk? What the hell...fatalism is now my middle name. Paradise, realization, is a dream for real as of now.

CHAPTER TWELVE

"Charlie. We've been so worried about you. How are Tony — and Jane?"

"Safe — for the moment at least...Thanks for asking."

"Is Jane having female problems?"

"Huh?"

That stops me in my tracks.

"Stop standing in the doorway. Come in. Take your coat off. It's your apartment, isn't it?"

I step in and take my coat off. I will never cease to be amazed by women.

"I made beef stroganoff," she announces.

Female problems, does she mean pregnancy problems, as in aborting? Could that be part of what was happening with Jane?

"Beef stroganoff..." I say half aloud.

That was the meal Isobel served us at what I laughably describe as the high point of our relationship. We actually made out on the couch. She told me she had made a promise to herself not to have sex until she was married. I was the perfect gentleman, just like my mother had raised me to be. What was one more downer in my already-littered-with-rejection life?

"Any visitors...any calls? Anything strange or unusual happen?"

I realize how drained I am. Running – running in place and getting nowhere is very tiring – and vexing to the ego. I'll have to check with my psyche to find out how my soul is reacting if I can find the time or its location.

Isobel puts her hand on her hip and looks at me in a provocative way. To me that familiar look is not just a sensual one, believe me. In my mind's eye it says something fundamental about her. I see the reflective gaze she had on her face standing on that bluff overlooking the creek all those years ago on my first sighting of her. What was it she saw in that moment? Whatever it was, it is that which has held me captive to her all these years. That gaze...the object it sought out and clung to.

"Well, there were several calls. I answered. I hope you don't mind."

"Who called? What did they say?"

I see Isobel's neat handwriting on a pad near the phone. Nothing seems out of place in the apartment. Where is Tim? How did I get into this movie? The phone rings.

"Don't answer that," I almost shout but manage to keep my voice down to what I hope will be considered the normal range for conversation, free from panic and the need to make sudden moves.

"You need a good stiff drink," Isobel announces, opening and closing cabinet doors until she finds a bottle of Calvados. The phone stops ringing.

She pours a tall shot into a juice glass. My kitchen cabinet has a limited range of serving utensils, plates, silverware, pots and pans.

"As my mother used to say when we had to take medicine, send it right down the little red lane. And don't hold your nose, please," Isobel comments, handing me the glass.

I restrain the urge to pick up the pad and read it. I can't believe that I have been keeping at arm's length the girl of my dreams ever since she arrived on my doorstep. What the hell is happening to me anyway? Has San Francisco softened my brain? I throw down the shot.

"You said there were several calls," I begin while Isobel pours me a refill.

The apartment seems very bare – bare walls, unpacked boxes, a set of weights in a corner next to a pile of suitcases, rental furniture, ceiling light the only source of illumination in the front room. The stark lighting, harsh and unkind, seems to solidify my circumstances and make clear I am an outsider, a loner, a loser, consigned to the ash heap of humanity. I am camped out in a strange town, surrounded by unfamiliar and potentially threatening people, facing seemingly insoluble problems. There's nothing to hold onto, nothing permanent in my life. And it need never have happened if I had taken the easy path, the straight path that led toward registration in a top quality law school. Isobel pours herself a shot as well. She takes a small sip of it before she answers.

"Charlie. Please don't get mad."

"I won't."

"One of the calls was from your father; the other was from Mr. White."

I down my shot. Isobel pours me another. Why? She knows I'm not a drinker. What's changed between us? What's changed in her – anything, or just my perception of her? Isobel takes another small sip of her brandy and puts the glass down on the counter. We sit facing each other on tall metal stools that allow you to use the counter as a breakfast or snack area.

"You said something about beef stroganoff?"

"All I have to do is heat it up. The asparagus we can eat cold. I love them that way, don't you?"

She opens the refrigerator door as if it were her own. Out of it come provisions she has bought, including a chilled bottle of California white wine.

"The store owner suggested it. It's a California wine. You up for it..."

"Tell me about those phone calls while you heat up the stroganoff." Isobel nods. "Can I help at all?"

She smiles at me and shakes her head no.

"Well, we both know your father. He's very reserved."

"There is that."

"I admire him so much, as I'm sure you know."

"Very nice of you, too..."

"You do too. You know it's true." When I don't answer she continues. "He's very concerned. I could tell from his voice. He wants you to call him. He didn't say it was urgent but I could tell he had something important to say."

Isobel puts the Stroganoff on the stove to heat and puts the asparagus on plates along with a dollop of mayonnaise. I'm hungrier than I thought. My mouth is watering. I make it a point not to think too much about my father. Now is not the time to deal with our relationship. Or is it? Could it be the essence, the lynchpin that will solidify our new grown up relationship? I'm too tired to focus so I give up - for now.

"When did Mr. White call and what did he have to say for himself?"

Isobel stops what she is doing so she can look me in the eye, a mother hen expression on her face. And she again puts her hand on her hip. This time I remember where I have seen the hands on hips pose before: Isobel's mother uses it with remarkable success. "Watch out," her mother seems to say with that pose. "You are about to be steamrolled." Isobel is terrified of her and seldom breaks ranks with her mother's opinions, her mother's methods or her views. Am I about to be steamrolled?

"Charlie. You have been making some very bad decisions regarding Mr. White and the handling of that insurance investigation. He's a perfect gentleman, in fact very much like your father. You need to listen to him, take his advice."

I down my just poured glass of wine. I've never been much of a fan of wine. Beer is more my style when I do drink.

"I know what it means when you clam up like that, Charlie Carter. You are going to be stubborn and very, very stupid. Charlie, Mr. White really is concerned for your welfare - and he spoke very highly of your father."

"Leave my father out of it."

"Mr. White told me all about the situation. Shared with me that Mr. Hancock and he were related by marriage, that his son had been a grave disappointment to him, that his wife was having a few emotional problems and having her son murdered wasn't helping - and neither is the way you are handling this case. Why, Charlie, why are you adding to the grief of this very nice family into whose life this tragedy has come? It doesn't make sense. It's so unlike you. I must say I was shocked and saddened. And I told Mr. White just that."

I'm a stone, a Sphinx, a stubborn old galoot — just like my father, the one Mr. White admires so much. Yes, I admit it. My father and I are alike in many ways. And that too is a major issue that I still have to work out.

"My family is very close to the Hancocks, as you may recall. And, believe me, no one in the Hancock or White family would ever have anything whatsoever to do with this scandalous situation. Bob Jr., I am sorry to report, was just a bad apple who ran into trouble, probably of his own making."

I pour myself another big glass of wine. I find I have polished off the first glass. The beef Stroganoff is beginning to bubble on the stove. Isobel ignores it. She concentrates her attention on me. I can see now that it is useless for me to try to convince Isobel, to win her over to my side. Besides, that's not how I see this situation — as a contest where there are winners and losers. I shrug, then I sigh. Isobel takes it as a sign of weakening resolve. She approaches me and puts her hand gently on my shoulder.

"You've been under tremendous pressure. I mean Tony and his girlfriend getting involved in this sordid affair. And run-ins with hooligans and desperados — crazy people — San Francisco types of the lowest caliber — why did both Tim and you allow yourselves to get sucked up in all the outrageous and self-destructive behavior being perpetrated by people who never bother to think about cleanliness, morality, the overall good, just their own personal pleasure? I mean, you are both from good families who raised you to respect other people, their position on things, and their property. Your father is a lawyer for many important companies and people of high moral character, for goodness sakes. Don't you have any respect for that? I haven't had a moment's peace since I got here."

More silence. More drinking of wine...

"Charlie. We haven't had a chance to talk about other things, important things – and simple, everyday things too. I mean — Charlie?"

Isobel sighs but politely serves our meal. She'll not rest content with my silence. In fact, she's probably offended by it. Did Bull White see her as someone who could control me and did Isobel see herself in that role as well? I'm not having any of it. I'm into drinking my wine and downing some chow. Isobel watches me eat. Things get a little fuzzy. I'm off into a monologue before I know it. I don't know what I say but I have a feeling Isobel is having none of what I say in this monologue. Somehow KMPX comes on. Did I turn on the radio? Did I leave it on that station? Am I shouting? Man, oh man, am I drunk.

Isobel is grave, then maternal. I see her drifting away in a fog of exhaustion and drunken rage. Something new has been interjected into our relationship — unbridgeable distance. Will either of us close the gap? Do we want to? Is love and marriage, the whole nine yards, in our future? What did that look on Isobel's face mean all those years ago as she stood gazing off into the distance on the cliff above my sacred creek? Is the meaning of that look significant to Isobel or did its source reside only inside of me? Somehow I now...now...now...out like a light.

———————

My father, my mother, have never had occasion to shake their finger at me. They do not do it now, even in my topsy-turvy dreams. But they are there accusing me of disgracing my family, of failing to live up to the principles that I was raised to abide by. Isobel, naked, is in full support. She does a lascivious dance to show me the error of my ways. Heather just laughs and fades away in deep meditation. All my hopes for transcending human failings and traps are ludicrous. I am bogged down, chained to a rock in a sea that is rising. A gigantic bird is eating my liver. I am in pain but I cannot holler, cannot rid myself of this agony. No light that is blindingly bright shines. Nowhere to run; nowhere to hide... No need for an accusing finger, just the inner rings of Hell for comfort. The shut-off switch, the Void, is an impossibility considering the state of my eternal soul. Blackness comes, Blackness begins, Blackness ends over and over again and again and again...

There's a knock at the door. I jerk to attention. I'm sitting up in bed. A woman beside me... Heather? Good god, Isobel. What... Another knock on the door...Louder...

"I'm coming. I'm coming."

Isobel sits up, eyes wide open. She's still wearing her clothes. So am I. I must have passed out. I can't remember a thing. She must have put this blanket over me and curled up in it herself. Did we – did we make love? Whatever we did, our relationship is now in a new phase – whatever that means.

"I'll close the door. You can take a shower."

She nods. I rub my eyes, shrug mentally. I don't have a peephole. Fuck it. I open the door. It's Coop, not the hounds of the Baskervilles sicced onto me by Mr. White. Wonder where they are now, those hounds? Have they been called off? Is it safe to pick up my car and turn in the rental?

"I told you," Coop begins. "The only way this thing works is if you stay in touch – off the record. Keep going like you're going and I'm going to be forced to play it by the book if I'm still allowed to take part in the case."

I head over to the kitchen. Two glasses from last night and the wine bottle are still on the counter. The wine bottle is empty. I start up water for coffee. Light up my first cigarette of the day. Christ. What time is it? I look at the clock over the stove. Nine o'clock. Coop stands in the middle of the front room waiting for an answer. I'm still trying to decide if I'm really awake and up.

"I've decided to follow my dream...throw off my suit and tie and join a hippie commune. Turn on. Tune in. Drop out."

"Maybe this will revive your interest in the mundane world of current affairs. Bernie Toucan paid off big. We went back over the crime scene evidence. Found his prints on the tape used to bind White's wrists. Have an APB out on him. Any idea where he is..."

"Off in the ozone somewhere. What about Tony? What about me?"

"Federal warrant out on Tony...Yours is probably in the works. Religious types might call where you and Tony are Purgatory, or then again maybe the edges of Hell."

Is Coop privy to my dreams? Am I dreaming right now? What is real and what is not? How the hell do I know at nine o'clock in the morning with a horrendous hangover?

"So I should make myself scarce?"

"That's open to debate. What are your plans for the future? Do they include employment at Life Beneficial? Do they include pursuing leads in this very open case? Do they include spending time at a federal facility in Kansas? Take your pick."

"That bad, huh..."

"I'm pulling my punches. Must need a coffee jolt..."

The coffee water is beginning to boil. The smell of coffee brewing begins to fill the air. I have finished my cigarette. Life, the little details that are so vital, is good.

"Mr. Randolph White is not someone you want to cross."

"Thank you, Mother..."

Coop grimaces. Rocks on his feet... I'm not the only fish he's got to fry.

"So we figure Bernie Toucan looks good for the murder, but," Coop informs me again while we wait for the coffee. "But if you throw out the federal warrants, one real another forthcoming, I don't know hopefully they're just fishing expeditions and not some sort of vendetta, the sooner they disappear the better if you ask me... I mean they distract attention from what should be the focus, solving the murder of Bob White, Jr." Coop is looking at me but he isn't seeing me. He's trying to sort things out in his mind and with what he has he can't put the pieces together so they fit and will stand up in a court of law. "Sure, Toucan is a certifiable crazed lunatic, but is that all there is to it?" he continues. "What the heck was Bob White into that he got himself killed in such a dramatic manner?" I take down cups and pour hot coffee into them. The cavalry is on the way for our starving brain cells. Coop continues his rumination. "Had the LAPD question some of the White kid's known associates...We've got everything from 'he's a good kid' to 'he's a spoiled rotten prick used to getting his way.' One thing for certain — he was into drugs, big time."

Coop adds, "One thing that connects Toucan and the White kid - they know many of the same people."

Heather and Jane and Tony come to mind. That list also includes Ronald Outrage and Luther Green, of course. Would I be on anybody's list as a known associate? Are you kidding? I'm at the top of Bull White's list and that of his cronies. It seems I have a death wish that in some way is connected to the women I get involved with. Go figure, since I'm totally inept in that department.

Am I glad or sad Heather hasn't shown up? Where is she right now and what is she doing? Hope Tony and Jane are coming down from their high and are still safe and sound at Molly's friend's house. I hear the shower turn on in the bathroom. Isobel is up. Coop glances in that direction.

"Visitor..."

"Surprise visitor from back home..."

"You talk to Tony lately or his girlfriend? They have anything to add worth hearing?"

"I'm clueless..."

"They're still suspects in a murder investigation, you know."

"Oh, don't I know it..."

"Right..." Coop gives me a sharp look. I take a sip of my first cup of coffee for the day. "Listen, I've been working homicide long enough to take my hunches seriously. And I'm telling you this case is going to get nasty sooner rather than later. Maybe you better keep a low profile. Tell Tony and his friends to do the same."

The shower stops running. Isobel is readying to dry herself off. She's naked, naked and wet. That's a picture for you. Why can't things be like they were a week ago – when all my troubles were well accounted for and familiar? Can't I just get on with the business of asking myself "why am I here" and "what's the meaning of life" without all this drama?

"I'm not just being a good guy. For some reason you seem to be a magnet in this case. I stay close to people like that."

Coop allows himself a slight smile.

"I like you too."

The coffee is doing its work. I'm awake, sitting up straight. Alert. Wish I could have Coop ride with me on the case. I could benefit from his experience big time. But we've got different agendas. And, down the line, those agendas probably won't mix. Hope not. I might need a friend before this is over.

"There's going to be a three-day event out at Muir Beach starting today. I'm hoping to find some answers there. You going to be around..."

"You got anything definite?"

"Just like you – only hunches."

"All you have to do is file your report and you're free and clear. Nothing the Whites would like better. Might earn you some big time Brownie points, might even get you a raise, a promotion, a job and a desk rather than pounding the pavement... I don't know what all."

"Too late for that... I'm toast...and it wouldn't get me off the hook or my friends either."

"What's in the bathroom got anything to do with that?"

"A complication all right... But nothing whatsoever to do with this case..."

"I wish you luck then. It sounds like you might need it. What else you got, anything?"

I light a fresh cigarette. Force myself to think. Still very hard to do... Isobel might be listening. What the hell possessed her to show up unannounced anyway? And then what does she become – a spy for Bull White, his informant? Do I really mean that, do I? Back to business…

"Well, there is this girl. Told me her name was Heather Chicago. Real name – Linda Preen… Long, blond hair… Five-six… One ten soaking wet… Green eyes… A real looker… Hangs out with the artsy crowd - models, painters, rock musicians… Has a place over on Vermont Street near Nineteenth. If you haven't guessed already, Jane Preen's sister."

"And I thought Bernie Toucan was your main problem."

"Tell me about it."

"I'll check her out." Coop turns to leave, turns back. "You've got too many players in your game, Carter. Impossible to cover your back… Too many variables… You be careful. Meantime, I'll notify the Marin Sheriff's Department we might have need of their services this weekend. You ever been to Muir Beach, by the way?"

"No. Why?"

"Well, it may look like it's just across the bridge on the map but by the time you get there you'll think you're out in the middle of nowhere. And you are. Perfect place for an ambush… Take a hell of a long time for the cavalry to arrive."

"Thanks for the encouragement."

"Don't mention it. Oh, and by the way, take something warm to wear. It can get pretty chilly there, particularly at night."

———————

"When will you be back?' Isobel asks.

She looks so small and out-of-place standing in my San Francisco apartment, the one in which I can still detect the smell of Heather wafting in the air. Shit. Isobel is out of place in San Francisco, but so am I.

"It might be a day or two before I'm free."

We kiss. Not as exciting as the one we exchanged last night. Not as distant as the first kiss we exchanged when she arrived in town. Is this the sweet sorrow of parting, the end of a childhood romance, the beginning of a revised version of my future?

———————

I throw caution to the winds and exchange my rental car for my own at the parking garage across from the St. Francis. I need at least one security blanket. My car is the one I drove while living in Washington, D.C. I drove it across country. Isobel and I kissed in it. I have provisions stuffed in the trunk.

No one seems to tail me as I pull out of the underground garage. My head whirls round and round — a veritable kaleidoscopic explosion of disparate ideas and thoughts. My heart pounds irrationally... I have trouble keeping my focus on the road. Melt down, brain lock, too much for me to handle... I'm not ready for this. Why me? Why now? I need a break from myself.

Head straight up Mt. Tam rather than down towards Muir Woods and Muir Beach and the upcoming Tribal Stomp at which I hope to encounter Heather. I don't want to know what she knows just now. Some say there's magic in the air on Mt. Tam. I could use some of that.

CHAPTER THIRTEEN

Show me the way.

Massive granite boulders jut from the short grasses on the hillsides. Rushing water falls round the rocks, down precipitous hillsides covered with grass. Gnarled trees, contorted by the wind, embedded into the steep slopes. Paths crisscross in all directions, clinging to the sides of steep hills.

Show me the way.

Take in great gulps of fresh air. Brisk. Do a few deep knee bends. Run in place. Put on a sweater and parka from the trunk of my car. Part of my emergency stash... Pull out my all-purpose backpack put together during my Boy Scout days. Head out, flopping the pack onto my back. Glad I'm wearing my hiking boots.

I'm no longer wearing a tie. I have on a worn flannel shirt I used when I helped out in the yard back home.

Show me the way.

Follow an ocean side trail. Leads back into undeveloped territory. No one in sight for miles... The burden of my thoughts, reflections, preoccupations flies away. It's good to hike a nature trail. Hunted with my dad as a kid. Joined the Boy Scouts and went on camp outs. Helped my dad build a cabin on a piece of land he bought with some of his hunting buddies. In the heart of the Blue Ridge Mountains...We camped out there in a lean to for most of one summer.

This trail full of animal sign, all fresh: usual stuff — deer, rabbit, squirrels, voles... Raptors float high in the sky — vultures, hawks, one lonely eagle. Pull out my binoculars to check them out. Come back to the present moment. Drift along for an indeterminate period of time. I'm well over five miles from the trailhead and my car. Good. Maybe I'll pass through a seam in the present and make contact with an alternate reality. In this new world I will be free of all unwanted problems - those made by myself as well as those made by friends and foes alike. Will that mean I will be living in a world in which I am the only human and all needs are taken care of without thought? Is this world called — Realization — or simply self-indulgence?

Show me the way.

My chosen path has descended hundreds of feet. I've passed through several patches of woods, one with a stream that tumbles right across my path. I'm now in another open field making my way along a continually curving path leading me toward an obtruding hillside. Another patch of woods takes me into a cluster of evergreens that dim the surrounding glory of the day. Suddenly in the middle of a small glade up ahead — a cabin in brilliant sunshine. Thought this was public land. Now see this was once a retreat of some sort. Four or five small shacks on the side of the hill... Smoke rises from

one of them. Am I on the other side – well into my alternate reality?

Woman in front of the occupied cabin is splitting firewood. Wearing moccasins. Hair tied back with a leather thong. Looks fit. Mountain woman. Very healthy... Able to bear children, cook, nurse and make clothes - all at the same time. Dark hair and olive skin... Tall. Well built.

"Howdy," I holler when I am still twenty-five yards away.

On the porch next to which she's working, I see a baby trussed up in a carrying device on a frame with straps. Baby looks at me with serious eyes. Doesn't make a peep. Girl-woman stops in mid-swing. Looks me up and down.

"This is private property," she comments without rancor.

Tone that could move folks away from her in a hurry if she was of a mind — particularly when she's got an ax in her hands. Wonder how long she's been living in this cabin.

"Just wondered if you had any water. Didn't bring any with me," I answer, trying to look like a tenderfoot.

She shades her eyes with her hand. Looks me up and down again. Carefully. Before she can answer the door of the cabin opens. Man walks out on the porch. He's dressed in Eastern garb. Robe. Turban on his head... Barefooted. Costume looks a little breezy to me for this kind of weather. His voice is soothing, melodious. Chock full of calm, peace. A holy man... Is he from planet Earth — our part of the Galaxy? Am I outside the known universe? Where am I? Why am I here?

"Ah, you've arrived. The well's round back. Feel free."

He waves with his hand in the direction of the well. His body is relaxed, alert.

"Thanks. Thanks a lot."

He was expecting me? I make my way round the side of the house. The man follows. The woman goes back to her work.

"Would you care for some tea?" asks the man as I pump the well handle and dip down to drink. The water is cold, clear, invigorating.

"Well, thanks," I agree, even though moments before I wanted nothing more than a bit of solitude.

The inside of the cabin is primitive. Only one room... Has a bed, a wood stove, a table, a small open area next to a window used for ceremonies of some sort, maybe meditation. No indoor plumbing I can see.

As I start to sit down at the table, the man takes a seat on a pillow in the area I had thought was for ceremonies. Turns out that's the living area... He directs me to sit on a pillow across from him. The tea is already on a tray at his side.

"You will need help in solving your problems," he says after I am settled and he is pouring me a cup of tea. "Danger lurks in every direction. You must prepare."

He chuckles. His eyes twinkle. He offers me a cup of tea.

"Have we met?" I ask, accepting the tea.

He sits quiet and calm with crossed legs. Half lotus. Practice makes perfect, I guess. I'm leaning against the wall with my legs going every which way. Can't get comfortable. The wood stove doesn't really heat up the room. There are chinks in the wall that let in the wind. I am itchy in places I don't want to scratch.

"You are right that she is the key for you. But you are unprepared for where she will take you."

He smiles at me again. Kindly, friendly, open... His eyes are penetrating, yet playful. They have seen things beyond my imagination. He is ancient, fresh born, eternal, a rock. He takes a sip of his tea.

I do likewise. I have never tasted anything like it. It must be made of some exotic herb. Strange. I begin to feel light, strong, healthy. My head clears. Almost like the feeling you get when your sinuses clear after a long bout with a cold. Release.

"She will hurt you even though she means you no harm."

"Are we speaking of Heather or Isobel? Are they...known to you?"

There is a long silence. I hear the wind rattling the windowpanes. The wood burns; the stove steams, hisses. Mountain woman is outside whacking away. The baby coos. A bird calls in the distance. The sky is breathtakingly clear. The sunlight falls on the cabin floor. All is well. My shivering has stopped. I put down the cup. My legs have loosened. They find a position on the floor that is more natural. I look into the man's eyes. They twinkle and sparkle, are dark orbs of learning. I do not understand the forces within them but understand they are intended for good. After a long time, he answers.

"You wear your emotions, your thoughts, on your sleeve. I am only addressing them. Showing you a way, a path, how to put the puzzle pieces in their proper place perhaps?" he comments quietly.

I nod. Fate and Destiny — are they aligned with this encounter? I rationalize. We Westerners are so burdened by logic. Is that because of the climate we grow up in? If we are foolhardy enough to discard this seeming security, will we regret it? When? For how long? Eternity? Give me that old time religion. It once was good enough for me.

The man picks up a small leather pouch decorated with intricate Indian beadwork and held closed by a leather drawstring. He hands it to me.

"Think about what you have seen in my eyes when you are in trouble. Let this pouch be a reminder — in times of need."

"I..." I begin.

His eyes stop me in mid-sentence.

"That little black book will not help you. And remember, if you are in trouble, I will be with you - if you reach out for me."

In that instant two things happen. The door swings open and

mountain woman enters carrying her papoose on her back. She has firewood in her hands. A rush of air follows her in. At the same instant, the man goes into some sort of trance. He makes some moaning sounds that I realize are a revitalizing chant. The air around him tingles. Positively charged ions snap and pop. A bright, warm light surrounds him. He is not an old man. In the prime of life... Almost young looking... I'm amazed. Startled. The wood in mountain woman's arms clatters to the floor.

"It's time for you to be on your way," she comments to me, all the while looking at the man.

It is obvious now that she is his student, his disciple. I do not know or understand the practices they are trying to perfect. I doubt I ever will. I start to rise. She halts me.

"Did you finish your tea?" she asks. I look down at my cup. There is a swallow or two left. She continues. "Listen."

I finish my tea in one big swallow. I feel light-hearted, free. Then mountain woman repeats her command.

"Listen. Tamalpa says, without pride or anger, let Mother guide you."

Her baby holds my gaze as I pass them by, headed for the outside world.

CHAPTER FOURTEEN

I, CHARLIE FOXHAWK CARTER...DO OR DIE

They're playing volleyball without a net on the beach. There must be a dozen of them. The sun is toasty but I really think it's overdoing it to run around buck-naked. It's winter, after all.

The beach arcs around the edge of a cove, a crescent moon. Unimpressive waves make their way shoreward. Not likely to attract surfers worth their salt. From the parking lot, which is where I am standing, you can walk directly out onto the beach. Low-lying cliffs drop dramatically right to the water's edge at both ends of the beach near the tips of the cove.

I'm not tempted to go inside the rustic roadhouse where the Tribal Stomp will take place. It's long, low and rectangular...Hugs the sandy soil and scrubby underbrush surrounding it. It's painted dark red and has a dark roof. It's seen better days. Probably pretty beat up inside... Could it have been a hangout in its heyday for gangsters making bootleg runs up and down the coast or was it a revival, meeting hall, the Elks Lodge? Whatever it was used for is now a part of the distant past.

I stuff my hands in my pockets and look up at the sky overhead. To the north are high clouds. The edge of a front...Looks like it's moving in fast. Off the coast, far out to sea, is a dense fog bank ready to come ashore with the setting sun. My nude friends and I are living in a bubble, a dream, a lie. This sunny weather is a momentary aberration, an apt metaphor for the far out San Francisco scene.

Some of the nude frolickers are sunbathing. The more energetic ones playing volleyball without a net stagger around in the sand laughing like hyenas. Equal number of boys and girls cavort. None of them acknowledge me. It's as though I'm invisible. Is that because my vibe is alien to theirs or because I'm contained in a parallel universe in which the sole inhabitant is myself? Doesn't matter...Outcome is the same.

I hike up the beach as far as I can go where I spend a pleasant hour scaling rocks that block easy passage further along the coastline. I jump from one rock to another, inch down slippery surfaces, sit on one with the wind whipping through my hair, stare out to sea. Sun glare sparkles off the briny water. Surf crashes into the rocks, sending spray in all directions. Nature's power wears down the most resistant boulders...Pulverizes them into sand granules.

I take off my shoes and walk along the edge of the water, careful not to get wet. The water is frigid, hostile. A couple walking their dog passes me. First the dog sprints past. Then the middle-aged couple... Holding hands. Talking quietly.

The holy man I encountered on the mountain — what the hell was that all about — left field, totally off-the-wall and non-applicable, a hallucination? Or did I somehow make a connection, a breakthrough that will allow me to realize the "in" of an "in crowd" that pulverizes me-ness and us-ness and collapses them into the Universal All? Am I making sense even to myself? Why do I now feel like I'm on the other side observing my former self, a feeling very akin to my first experience of this kind when I was introduced to "my grandfather" by my father? What will this mean as I play out my hand, the hand that was dealt to me? Or did I deal the hand to myself?

Show me the way.
Show me the way, Mother.
I will follow.

———————

"Seen Heather?"

"Who?" answers Dumas, curt, all business.

"Why?" Harry asks.

"Jane said she'd show," I reply.

"That means we'll at least have an audience of one," puts in Bracken.

They're unloading the truck. I pull my leather jacket from the trunk of my car and put it on. I'm already wearing a sweater. The sun is disappearing into the fog and it's getting cold. The high clouds that were far away are moving our way fast. There is a distant rumble warning of weather in the making. The fog bank held offshore during the day must already be pouring in through the Golden Gate. The nude sunbathers are gone. There are two fires going on the beach. Some hardy individuals wrapped in blankets are sitting around them. A dog is running through the surf as it rolls into shore.

Why am I following through on a lead supplied by someone in a delusional state at best? Why on earth would Heather show up here? Why should I want to find her when I feel certain what would come next might have a very unhappy result? It's crazy. It's all crazy. I'm crazy. This situation is crazy – and suicidal. Meeting a holy man on the mountain who tells me Heather is the key is crazy. The fact that I somehow believe him is crazy. The key to what... I'm lost.

The top half of my brain tells me I'm wandering aimlessly; the lower levels, my intuition, the part of me that is in touch with the invisible world, is saying something else. I can't hear what that something else is. I need to get amplification, insight. Different...I feel different, altered. What was in that tea the holy man served? I try to shake it off, can't... Shit, might as well do something while I wait for the second shoe to fall. Hope I'm ready for whatever comes afterward, if I survive the impact.

"Looks like you guys need all the help you can get," I comment, picking up one of the projectors from the back of the van and carrying it into the hall.

How the hell are they going to transform this dump into a scene, a happening inflated by the excitement of illusion?

The lightshow guys are quiet, intent, focused. I do as much grunt work as they will let me. Harry, the one with the red hair and the New York attitude, checks out the electricity, a thing of primary concern for lightshow artists. No juice; no show. Blowing fuses in a ramshackle place like this could shut down the whole act...Disaster.

The door to the hall was unlocked. No one's around... No custodian. No dance hall manager. Harry doesn't seem to mind. He's cocky, confident.

I help the rest of the guys set up a riser on to which we place some tables. On the tables we place their equipment. By this time Harry has dragged power lines to this position. The risers are strategically placed at the opposite end of the hall from the stage, such as it is.

While Harry fiddles with the power, Dumas arranges the sturdy wooden boxes that contain lightshow images. David, Bracken and I unfold a gigantic sheet of highly reflective plastic called Mylar. It's their light and portable screen surface. It's seen some use. Duct tape will secure the screen to the wall behind the stage and on either side of it. This covers wood walls that would suck up light and image intensity and will provide a bright, relatively smooth surface on which to project lightshow images.

Harry sets up a strobe light in one corner of the room. Then he busies himself with several colored lights that will shine on a mirror ball. His final touch is setting up one projector near the refreshment stand. He loads Polaroid images that, when projected through a specially designed rotating wheel, will cause the image to glow like the aurora borealis.

Then they all check out the position of the projectors. Play around with image placement. Amazingly, the dank, dark room is transformed into a psychedelic wonderland. The whole space flickers, strobes, is ready to rock and roll. Tony is still a no-show.

I can see the lure of this profession - the power in visual imagery. The lightshow guys create a world filled with symbols of their own making, an electronic collage, a moving mural. This rapid-fire impressionistic display triggers synaptic firings that stimulate brain waves, or so the lightshow guys inform me. I have my doubts. The only limitation to their expression is their own imagination. That's why they think of themselves as artists, not crazed hippies, and feel affronted when people fail to recognize and attest to this, to them, obvious fact.

The boys retreat outside to smoke a joint prior to the show. It's dark, cold. The wind is blowing. I get the feeling the wind blows often, long and hard here at Muir Beach. The fog is rolling in, long, dense fingers creeping out of the sea.

"Who the hell thought a three day happening here would attract a crowd?" Harry asks.

"Same guy who hired us to work at the Longshoremen's Hall for our first gig – John Paul," answers David, as the rest of the guys give Harry a nasty look.

Harry is still an interloper despite what he brings to the table - his electrical knowledge, his unique visual eye and his considerable moxie, an attitude sorely lacking among the rest of the crew.

"Longshoremen's Hall... Was that a cool gig?" Harry replies.

"Just about as cool as this one looks like it's going to be," mutters Dumas.

"Well, at least it's a gig. We ask to get paid in front this time?" David queries.

No one has an answer for him. Bob White had a real point. These guys need representation, professional management, in the worst kind of way.

"Are we planning to leave the stuff here or will we set up and tear down each night?" Bracken groans.

He does all the driving and most of the grunt work.

"I'll talk to this John Paul if you like," offers Harry, finishing off the joint.

No one answers. They all look bleakly off into the uncertain night.

"We'll tear down and set up each night. And we'll camp out on John Paul's doorstep in Lagunitas until we get paid if he doesn't come through," Dumas proclaims.

The nude sunbathers, now clothed in hippie attire, writhe and wiggle on the dance floor. A handful of other locals make the scene. The band, The Flamin' Groovies, is loud, uninspiring. The lights flash without cessation. No refreshments that I can see. A rumor spreads that there's another gig in the city tonight - a big one with all the headliner groups playing - Jefferson Airplane, Grateful Dead, Moby Grape, Steve Miller Blues Band. Will this paltry crowd pull up stakes and leave? No. Too spaced out for that to happen. Turns out they're all part of a commune. John Paul has been making their scene. He had a fling with one of the women.

I'm huddled in a dark corner. Time crawls. I nurse a beer. Waiting... For Heather...For whatever it is that will happen. Holy man tea stimulating my mind...just trying to look out for the woebegone and forgotten, I tell myself... That must include me...I'm protecting myself by showing up and hanging out here...lost...crazy...

A second band, Canned Heat, comes on around nine and picks up the pace. More people arrive. Still waiting. Surrounded by a bunch of folks wearing outlandish get ups. What kind of game is this anyhow – and why should I stay? Can't take it anymore. Go outside for a smoke. Look up at the sky. Streaked with clouds. Few stars still peeking through... Rain nearing. Fog thickening. Driving conditions will be dangerous on Route 1. Plenty of accidents in weather like this, I bet, particularly when the drivers are stoned out hippies. The parking lot has fewer cars in it than celebrants inside. Guess some of these kids are here for the duration. Camping out at this low rent happening. Hope they brought enough food and plenty of warm clothes. There's no shelter available and nowhere to get provisions.

The few cars parked in the pot-holed, unpaved lot point every which way. One of the wackiest vehicles is a Ford Falcon covered with psychedelic drawings in DayGlo paint and objects – shells, toy horns, an assortment of tiny collectibles - epoxied to the body of the car. Of course, there is also the obligatory ancient yellow school bus with wild psychedelic drawings on it – an homage to the Merry Pranksters.

The music pounds away inside... Clover, the headliner group, is up next... There is a rumor that the Charlatans will show at some point.

I look at the pool of light created by a spotlight located at the edge of the parking lot. It shines on incoming waves. A fire still burns on the beach. Beside it one hardy individual gazes off into the void of ocean and fog. Easy to forget where you are, who you are, what is real, the dimension in which you exist when you're high as a kite. Am I in a better place? Am I any more centered or more aware?

Shiver slightly. Crush out my cigarette butt. Zip up my jacket. Walk out into the sand. It's cold and crunchy under foot, inhospitable. Foamy surf clings to the sand as the water rushes up the beach, creating dark icicle fingers along the shoreline. Music from the dancehall scene a distant memory here... I'm invisible to the battered roadhouse high up on the beach.

I look out to sea and into the dense fog. Hear a foghorn sound. Another. Then I see the barest outline of a light. For a moment I think it's just my imagination. But it reappears. Lighthouse nearby, a ship...

Could this cove still be in use by modern day smugglers? It's close to the city yet a very isolated location. Jam my hands deeper into my pockets. Look up and down the shoreline. Light is gone. Probably just my imagination...

Decide to stop by my car to get a snack out of the trunk before I go back inside. Rub my hands together against the cold before I open the trunk. Hear the sound of another car entering the parking lot: a Volkswagen, with a busted tailpipe, making plenty of noise. I blend into the shadows, trying to see where the VW parks, if it does. Can't quite make it out. Motor coughs once, then silence. Door slams. Whoever was in that car heads inside. I follow.

The intensity of the music has picked up. Clover is cranking it up another notch. Crowd has grown to about fifty which pretty much fills the place. Lightshow guys are completely transported by their work. Take a nuclear blast to get their attention. Smell of marijuana heavy in the air. Get high just being in the now hot, steamy room.

Strobe light shows skeletal children cavorting in its on-again-off-again light... The lightshow guys have created a moonscape on the wall, on the bodies of the dancers, on the spectral musicians on stage. Musicians totally captivated by their creative juices. Wailing rock and roll... The people in the room into a place that feeds on its own energy, taking everyone higher and higher...

Close. Breathless. Agitated. People begin to strip. Seems like the right thing to do. Bodies glow, drip with sweat, the body electric. Oily images on the lightshow screen make the room seem fluid, fetid, luxurious.

Heather. At the edge of the crowd...A glimpse of her... Then gone... An illusion? My own wet dream come to life or my worst nightmare? I'm out of the shadows that hide me in a hurry, heading toward her image.

Ahead of me, Heather's hair and the side of her face, in the strobe light, surrounded by dancers flashing off- on, on- off, off- on. The music loud, pulsating... The lights look like amebic couplings. Can't seem to pinpoint Heather's location. Like a frustrating dream...

She's leaving the hall. Looking for something or someone. I follow.

From the doorway I see... Off in the distance...Her...Standing in the parking lot. Heather, under the spotlight... Her hair blows in the wind. Her fringed leather jacket, her leather skirt, pressed against her body. She's oblivious to the cold, the wild night swirling all around her.

The beach fire still burns but no one sits by it. The weather has taken a distinct turn for the worse. Heather scampers out onto the sand. Into the dark shadows before I have a chance to call out – or wonder if it would be better to stay silent.

She stops, shines a flashlight out onto the water. It glances off angry waves pounding in to shore. Out of a particularly thick finger of fog emerges a long boat with a deep hull, coming to shore, on the choppy waves, filled with bundles. Cutting through the surf, man at the tiller, standing tall, leaning into the rushing waves, two men on either side of him... Stevedores. Smugglers... Heather's the lookout signaling that the coast is clear.

Boat rushes up onto the beach on the surge of a wave as the man at the tiller guns the engine. Stevedores, off in a flash, pull the boat up higher beyond the waves. A van pulls onto the beach from the parking lot. Whirls around, spraying sand high... Bernie Toucan's black van... He hops out of it. Throws open the back doors. Stevedores race back and forth between boat and van off-loading the bundles, stacking them in neat rows, kilo packages, bricks, marijuana. There are a lot of them. Load must be at least half a ton.

They're efficient. Have the boat unloaded in less than fifteen minutes. Toucan and the pilot of the boat confer briefly. Heather stands off to one side. She's in on it, up to her beautiful eyeballs. Why would she want me to see this? Why did Jane tell me that Heather wanted me to attend the gig at Muir Beach when this was set to go down?

Head back to my car. Going to follow Toucan and the dope shipment wherever the hell they go. No sense in trying to be a hero. Four against one — unhealthy odds... Someone stands by my car. Whoever it is has made me.

"Charlie. It's me. Harry." He nods in the direction of the beach. "What's going on down there? Some fool got himself stuck on the beach?"

It's impossible to see the launch from Harry's angle. Only the front of Toucan's van... Mist, fog, the halo of Heather's flashlight obscures the off-loading... Situation's crazy, surreal. Bunch of stoned out hippies partying right next to the landing of a major shipment of marijuana... They going to line up to buy the product tomorrow in the Haight, never the wiser? Pay top dollar for what they could have gotten here for little or nothing?

"Smugglers," I mutter to Harry.

That gets his attention.

"Smugglers..."

"Toucan and Heather are in on it."

"You sure about that..."

Harry's voice reverberates in my brain. Tingling sensation connected by a pair of holy eyes travels up my spine.

"We've got to help her. The cops won't..."

"I'm coming with you."

Open the driver's side door of my car, slide in and lean across to unlock the passenger side. Harry pops in. The engine turns over. None too soon... It looks like the launch has returned from whence it came. Toucan slams the door shut on his van. The flashlight beam disappears as Heather gets in on the passenger side of the van. Toucan's headlights come on and his van spits sand, wheels spinning, before making its way slowly back to the parking lot through heavy sand. The van's riding low... I'm poised to give chase. We pull out of the parking lot. Wind along Route 1 together. Pursued and pursuer.

I try to keep a respectable distance between us so I don't spook him. In no time at all, though, I'm right against his bumper. He's swerving wide and tail-heavy around corners with me in pursuit.

He's a better driver than I am. He maintains his speed despite the load and the continual horseshoe turns in the road. I slam into his rear end - once, twice. Sparks fly from scraping metal. Harry hangs onto the dashboard and the door strap.

"You got a gun?" he asks.

"You planning to use it if I do?"

"No. But Toucan might plan to use his if we ever stop his van."

I gun the engine. Ram Toucan's rear end hard again as we head into a corner. Sparks, dirt, fly as Toucan's van swerves erratically around the curve. I'm heading toward him again as we hit a straight stretch when Toucan slows down. Our bumpers lock momentarily. I manage to wiggle away. Toucan guns his engine as he heads into the next turn and almost loses control. I slide around the "s" turn, tires squealing. Nobody better approach from the opposite direction. We'd both be toast. Curves flash by with persistent regularity. Toucan weaves back and forth across the road. I try to ram him again. He swerves into the oncoming lane. Out of the mist comes a car headed right for him. Toucan cuts the wheel wildly and his van shoots back into our lane. I brake to avoid hitting him. A curve comes up fast - too fast. Toucan tries to react. Too late...Runs off the side of the road. Piles into a tree... Van's rear end pointed straight up in the air, wheels spinning crazily. Front end pointing downhill jammed into that tree. I slam on my brakes. Harry and I are out of the car before it comes to a stop.

Toucan's engine is racing. The headlights are pointed in contradictory directions. The grill of the van is wrapped around the tree. Steam rises from the radiator. I hear someone breaking through the underbrush, heading down the hill. Look into the cab of the van. Empty. Must be Toucan running downhill. Have to assume he's armed.

Wonder if Toucan has any idea where he is. I'm lost. All I can see is fog and the edges of trees. Pull out my backpack from the trunk of the car. Strap it on.

"Go for help," I shout at Harry, heading down slope John Wayne-style after Toucan.

"I'm coming with you," he answers, following me through the underbrush.

Lots of crumbled rocks to make the footing slippery... Underbrush that's hard to push through... Fog thick and filamentous all around us. I pull out my flashlight from my backpack and slow my pace. Flashlight's big enough to use as a club if I get into a tight spot. Run the light back and forth across the underbrush up ahead.

"Down that way," points Harry.

I see someone moving to our left. Near a large boulder covered with moss. I shout down the slope.

"There's nowhere for you to go, Toucan, nowhere for you to hide... We're going to get you."

"We'll see about that," he shouts back up at us as he continues his downhill scamper.

Then I hear it, a squeal. Heather. She's with him. A willing participant or a hostage? Harry and I bound down the hill in hot pursuit. Toucan's moving slower than we are. He's dragging Heather. She must be resisting. We're closing in on them, fast. They disappear into a patch of underbrush. Harry dives into the middle of it. I take a side path. Without warning we are through. And we're teetering on the edge of a steep drop. Heather breaks free of Toucan's grasp with a tug and an angry shriek. Toucan grunts, starts to grab her, gives up, hauls ass down a path that runs along the edge of the crevasse. I'm after him in a flash shouting back over my shoulder, "Take care of Heather."

Heather stands at the edge of the cliff. It crumbles under her weight. She's falling. Harry grabs her hand as she tumbles over the edge. I hesitate. Harry screams over his shoulder.

"I've got her. Get Toucan..."

I'm still hesitating. Harry's no Hercules, not even a Jewish version of one.

"Go. Go," shouts Harry, puffing and panting. Heather struggles to dig her heels into the side of the cliff. She grabs hold of a bush firmly embedded in the hillside. Harry's right. I go after Toucan.

He's waiting, crouched and ready, his back to a slope at a curve in the narrow path. I make a lunge at him. Succeed in bringing him down in a football-style tackle. I learned something that proved useful on that junior high school football team. But my chin hits the heel of his shoe, hard. Toucan falls with a thud. I'm dazed. Before I've collected my wits, he's up and holding a massive stick. He takes a swing at my head, trying to cut me down. Grim reaper... I jerk back. Fast. He's overplayed his hand. I take advantage of it. Pull him forward with his instrument of destruction. We collide. Go at it rough and tumble. Break apart. I assume a loose boxing stance. Toucan, his guard down, reaches into his pocket as I begin to deliver a right cross. Toucan tries to avoid my punch but it hits him solid. His hand flies out of his pocket and from it comes a powdery dust that attacks my eyes. It's an abrasive of some sort. Hurts like fire. Tears flood my eyes. Can't see clearly... I stumble forward. Toucan picks the stick back up and brings it down heavily on the back of my neck. Behind me I hear a shout of panic. It's Heather. Toucan kicks me in the groin. Whacks me with the stick so hard it breaks the stick. He's like a crazed animal, a mad beast from the depths of Hell. Blackness engulfs me.

I wake up. It's raining. My head...My face... My ribcage... My kidneys... Pain...ouch, fuck, fuck, fuck. Nothing seems to be broken. Not totally clear where I am or how I got here. No conception how long I've been out. Then it hits me. Heather. I heard her shout. Harry was with her. Toucan and I were fighting.

I struggle to my feet. The hard packed dirt path is turning to mud, making the footing difficult. Try to get oriented. Look up at the sky above. Rain drops splash in my bloodshot eyes: cleanses them, can almost make out the tops of trees. Feel like I washed my eyes with Twenty Mule Team Borax. Stagger up the path. Legs and arms begin to regain feeling.

"Heather," I shout. Nothing... "Harry." Silence...

Retrace my steps. Can't find where we broke through and joined this path.

"Heather. Harry. Can you hear me?"

Find my flashlight. Thank goodness it still works. The third location I check turns out to be the one where Heather lost her footing. Rain is coming down hard now. I shine the light towards the bottom of the precipitous drop. It's sheer but only goes down about thirty feet or so. If they landed right, they might not be badly hurt. But there are plenty of rocks to make any landing painful.

"Heather. Harry. Can you hear me?"

I'm shining the flashlight into nooks and crannies looking for arms, legs, bodies. At last, I locate what I think must be them. They're much farther down the slope than I suspected. Must have landed and then tumbled farther down, much farther down.

I pull out a rope from my backpack and tie it securely to a nearby tree.

Belay down the cliff. The rain, the activity, brings feeling back to my body and increased pain. No time for that now. Rescue Heather and Harry first.

The hillside is covered with fragmented bites of shale. See a body. It's Harry. Crumpled between a boulder and a small pile of rocks he collected from his downhill descent. Heather is a few feet beyond. Their hands are still linked.

"Harry, you all right?" I shout, fearing the worst. Life is fragile and tenuous. "Heather. Can you hear me?"

They are lifeless. Bloody. Rain pours from the sky above. How to rouse them... Afraid to shake them... Try to remember the first aid training I had in Boy Scouts and at The Office training camp. All I can remember is how to use a snakebite kit.

Gently prop them up against a rock so I can wipe off the blood, check them out. Heather has a nasty wound on her head. Harry's ribcage and leg look bad.

The ground around me is turning into a torrent of slippery mud and shale. I'm struggling just to keep from sliding farther down the side of the hill myself, breathing hard. Tears stream down my face. Blur the driving rain. I scream into the howling winds. Want to hold Heather tight. Breathe life back into her. Harry's body is lifeless. Limp. It's my fault. Somehow I should have been clever enough to keep us all free from harm. How?

Help. Help. Someone... Help.

Show me the way. Show me the way. Show me the way.

My hand, inexplicably, makes contact with the beaded pouch the holy man gave me. I see eyes. The eyes of the holy man...Boring into my brain. He tells me to calm myself. I understand I will do what is right.

Throw off my backpack. Get out my first-aid kit. Try smelling salts. Clean their wounds. Somehow this calms me. My energy, the energy in those eyes, is going into their bodies. I can feel it but wouldn't be able to explain it. It's really happening. They'll be all right. Still hurt. But stable. I'm doing my job.

I touch the pouch again - offer a silent prayer... Open myself to healing mysteries unknowable, to the puzzle that has taken one life and has brought mayhem into the lives of those for whom I care...which catapults me back to the present moment - Now.

I must get these two people out of immediate danger. Drape Heather over my shoulder. Struggle pulling us up the cliff. Hand over hand. Torturous... Thighs feel weak...Shaky...Head pounds. My ribs are killing me.

Yet I feel light, buoyant inside, sailing above my work, giving encouragement to myself, cheering the life-affirming game along.

After a timeless period I have made it. I gently put Heather down. She moans softly. The rain runs down her face. She looks angelic, shimmers and vibrates. I work fast.

Must get Harry up as well... When I reach him, a miracle, he's coming around but weak... Mumbles something I can't understand.

"Don't try to talk. Got to get you back up the slope... Think you can help me move you?"

Harry opens his mouth; rain drips into it. His eyelids quiver, heavy with rainwater. They open. He looks dazed at first but his eyes clear.

"Sorry. I..."

"Forget it. We'll talk about it later. You've got to help me get you out of here, now. Do you think you have the strength to do it?"

"Try."

"Okay. I'll help you up. Ready?"

"Ready."

I help him up. He groans. His left leg: can't put any weight on it. I hastily sit him back down.

"I think I need to take a look at your leg. Okay?"

He nods, lips blue, teeth chattering.

I don't think it's broken. I'm hoping it's a sprain or a hamstring pull...

I notice an open space, a path, between the cliff and the dense undergrowth that surrounds us. Get Harry to his feet again.

"Use me as a crutch," I direct.

I stagger repeatedly. Harry outweighs me by at least fifty pounds.

"Hold it," he commands.

As if it was left for him to pick up, there is a walking stick resting against the side of the cliff. He hefts it - pushes away from me so he can test it.

"This'll work," he mutters, seemingly to himself.

It's going to work, but how long will Harry be able to bear the pain? He grimaces with each step. We seem no closer to finding a way up to where Heather is. Then – there it is – a well-trodden path up the side of the cliff to the ledge on which I left Heather. When we reach the ledge, we stop as if by command.

"You wait here. Conserve energy."

"Cool...cool," Harry pants, trying to smile.

The rain drenches us. He's a burly hundred and ninety pounds of fighting-to-hang-in-there; I'm a hundred and thirty pounds of struggling-to-help. Good. Keep it up. I pat him on the back. He gives me another weak smile in return.

"I won't be long. You won't get too wet here."

Harry laughs from the shelter of the small nook he's collapsed into. It has an overhang. His legs stick straight out in front of him, protruding into the rain. He raises his hand to his forehead in a salute. I salute back.

Tony told me Harry dropped a tab of acid the day before he had to show up at the draft board to be examined. He rode the New York subway in the front car all night... They still classified him 1-A. Now he's on the lam –

avoiding the draft. That's the story, anyway.

Heather is still out like a light. I kneel beside her so I can kiss her forehead. Rain comes down in torrents, makes a roaring sound that seems to come from all directions. The temperature hasn't dropped but the dampness makes it feel colder. If I don't get Heather moving she'll start suffering from exposure. I pick her up and allow her to slump over my shoulder.

"Hey," she mumbles and begins to wiggle on my shoulder.

I almost fall down but manage to stay on my feet.

"Heather?"

I put her on her feet. Lazily she raises one hand to her forehead. It comes away bloody. Her eyes open further.

"Charlie?"

"Do you think you can walk if I help you?"

"Yeah...Sure..."

Harry is on his feet before we reach him. How he managed to get up unassisted I have no idea. It seems to take us an eternity to wind our way back up to the road. Fortunately, there has been little or no traffic. My car is still at the edge of the road with the passenger door open and the motor running. We help Harry into the car.

"That was a trip," Harry huffs, easing himself down into the back seat. "Slide the seat forward," he instructs, stretching out his leg with relief when we do so.

Heather joins Harry in the backseat. There's blood on her forehead. Her body looks battered and bruised. A high-speed chase, a car crash, a fall down a precipitous hillside, and she's still a knock out. Her eyes sparkle with animated liveliness; her being radiates energy and grace.

"You two are a sight for sore eyes," I comment, closing the driver's side door with a solid thud.

We are no sooner around the corner heading back downhill before we hear a car approaching from up above us. We stop. So does the car above. We wait. I roll down my window. Is it my imagination or do I hear a police radio? I take my foot off the brake and we slowly begin coasting downhill. How much time has passed since the high-speed chase? There's a turnout up ahead, a scenic overlook. I pull in. We all need to cool it even if it's only for an hour. I'm out like a light almost before the car stops.

The eyes...Those wise and benevolent eyes... The beaded pouch is in my hand. I open it. Inside are sacred and holy objects nestled within the embrace of unearthly blue powder. The feel of that powder: soft, restorative, energizing. I put a finger dusted in powder into my mouth. The powder has no taste, no sensation of dissolving or being taken in. That finger when I take it out of my mouth shows no sign of unearthly blue powder on it. Bernie Toucan's stick did not strike the real me on the back of the neck. His foot did not kick the real me. I am whole, untouched. I dip my finger into the beaded pouch once more and touch that finger to the foreheads of both Heather and Harry. They did not go tumbling down a steep hillside. Wait a minute. I'm performing these actions while evidently floating near the roof of my car. That's the perspective from which I observe my actions. Is this a dream? Have I somehow entered that other worldly state that comes upon me from time-to-time? An indeterminate time, a space that takes place outside our known world, a Void, nothingness that is everything-ness, that which is everything that is and that which is not a part of everything, All...Almighty...my being is purified, at rest, restoring self within Self...Almighty.

CHAPTER FIFTEEN

Sunrise... Storm a thing of the past. Temperature in the low fifties...

"Head down to the parking lot at Muir Beach," Heather says.

"What?" I reply.

"I need some things," she answers.

I head downhill in that direction.

"Charlie?"

I'm hugging the road, keeping my eyes straight ahead. But my heart is thumping deep, regular, as if I am in a trance, deep meditation. Those eyes... Those eyes...They have seared my heart and my brain, made me anew. It's really there. The beaded pouch, I feel it in my pocket. Unearthly blue powder, sacred objects within, healing magic, clear sighted, restorative guidance...

"We've got to get Tony and Jane out from under," she says.

"What?" I reply.

"They've got them."

"What? Who?"

"Some very bad guys up to some very dirty tricks."

I snap into "the real world" while inhabiting and observing in another.

Does she mean Toucan and Outrage? If Outrage is involved and Outrage is connected to The Office then that means Bull White almost without question is involved as well. And that would mean that Heather is suggesting we liberate Tony and Jane from the custody of federal agents who are executing a federal warrant for the arrest of Tony. The chances of getting ourselves away from the clutches of guys like them look very dim...

Bottom line of the moment... Heather wants to save her sister; I want to save my secret cousin, even if he doesn't know we're related.

Shouldn't I at least clear the air – get Heather's connection to this tangled mess straight? Somehow that seems secondary. Secondary to what, I ask myself, a personal crusade, tilting at windmills, exploring delusional suggestions, helping the woebegone and forgotten. Not purely an ego based rumination. That state I am in will not pass away soon. It will allow me to do what must be done. There are others, friends and lovers that can benefit from my unexpected condition.

"You all right..." I ask her tenderly.

"Harry and I — what a pair we are... But we made it. Good thing I've practiced yoga and meditation. I don't know if I could have made it otherwise."

"She sure looked like a goner there for a while," Harry interjects with a creaky chuckle from the backseat of the car.

Harry looks pale and drawn but he's toughing it out.

"Harry's leg's bad, Charlie. We've got to get him somewhere he can get fixed up."

"Any ideas..."

"Yes. But it's not close."

"I can hold out. I've made it this far, haven't I?"

Harry gives his tough guy grin. It looks more like a grimace to me.

"When your eyes didn't open, I thought you were a goner," Harry tells Heather, masking his concern with lighthearted wonder.

"They didn't open?" Heather asks.

"How do you feel?" I ask her again.

"Funny. I feel like I fell off a cliff."

She waits a beat for me to react. I smile a crooked smile. She pokes me in the ribs from around the seat. I wince from a very far away place. My body, this body, might feel better if it was taped up.

"How the hell can we help Tony and Jane when we need help ourselves?"

"Might kill two birds with one stone at this place I'm thinking about – get patched up and hook up with Tony and Jane."

"And if they aren't where we're headed?"

"I don't take kindly to people who mess with my kid sister."

———————

We look into each other's eyes. The sky has lightened with the dawn. Birds are calling. It's going to be a glorious day. We are cruising north on Highway One.

The VW is the only car in the parking lot when we pull in. The beach seems empty. The fires that had been burning so brightly last night are still smoldering. The lightshow guys must have packed up their gear and split.

"I'll just be a minute."

Heather is out of the car before it stops rolling. I remember all the unknowns about her that plague me. I remember Isobel. I observe all the elements of this crusade of mine. And I realize my mission – to discover my true self – is just as the monk forecast – something I can only approach once I have removed all the obstacles that are now before me, my ego included. Heather gets back in the car, stowing a crammed full leather shoulder bag she removed from the VW. Clear evidence she's lived out of the car on-and-off for some time.

"Let's get the hell out of here," she exclaims as she slams the car door shut.

Harry is passed out as we head into this new day. His face is still pale and drawn. His breathing is ragged and uneven. Heather puts a hand to his forehead. We both look at him. Then she looks at me.

"Just trust me. Can you do that?"

"Can I...trust you?"

"When it counts..."

She puts her hand on top of mine. I turn my hand over and squeeze her hand. She kisses me on the cheek. Harry mutters something in his sleep. The road winds and twists in front of us... Nobody is out and about at this time of the morning. We have the road to ourselves.

Heather whispers in my ear, "Answers will come. From dark nothingness they will spring into the light of day. The invisible world will be made manifest in the visible world."

Is she aware of the holy man living in a cabin on Mt. Tam? Are she and Mountain Woman both pupils of his? Is she talking to the interior observing being that is 'me' or to the Charlie that made love to her in the very real world not so long ago?

"I need some sleep. Wake me up when we get to Lagunitas."

Just like that she's out like a light. I turn on the radio. KJAZ is playing Monk cuts — very cool, very laid back, sounds found in down-at-heels backrooms in New York, the Village. Somehow this music reflects the fierce Zen-like silence of the landscape through which we pass. I can see what drew the Beat scene here. This is the place where East meets West. The West Coast is a freewheeling scene, wild and crazy - very cool, very hip — yet very connected to the untamed and magical space that surrounds us all.

———————

As my Volvo putters through Samuel P. Taylor State Park, my mind takes its own sightseeing tour. Heather is the tour guide in my fantasy world. She drives Bobby's beat-up black VW with the New York plates like it's a swaying seat in a topsy-turvy ride.

"Yes, I was ordered to follow you. That's how we met. Bull White, no, Ronald Outrage; no, Luther Green; no, Bernie Toucan; no, unknown people in a position of power (at The Office?) ordered me to do it. I won't tell you why that order was issued or even if that's true. Trust me."

She points to a moving mural by which we are slowly passing. In it I see myself at the Straight Theater, myself interviewing Luther Green, myself interviewing Ronald Outrage, myself entering the New Orleans House in Berkeley where the lightshow is performing, myself leaving with Jane after Tony is taken in for questioning, and so on.

She continues, "Who is responsible for Bob White's murder? Which one, are White-Outrage-Toucan the guilty ones? Yes or no? What do they do? They smuggle drugs. No, they worship God-and-Country. No, they are devil worshippers. No, they are pleasure seekers gone amuck. No, they are just like your father. No, they are the backbone of our society. To divert attention from their guilt are they willing to run roughshod over the Constitution and the laws of our country, put their interests ahead of any other priority. Are they now shouting with glee like fraternity brothers at a toga party, 'the ends justify the means...You must cheer us on and bow down as you turn a blind eye towards us.' Don't ask me to point the powder finger to the one who's responsible. Trust me."

She directs my attention to another diorama in which I see what seem to be clips from formulaic TV cop shows and excerpts from tabloid journalistic pieces on the decay of moral values among the young in this wine-women-and-song era, fiddling while Rome is burning, while our brave soldiers carry on a war no one wants or cares to participate in to keep our country safe and strong and our beyond-drafting-age citizens far removed from the jungles and muggy heat of Southeast Asia. In our great nation where might-makes-right, oil and big business in league with the military industrial complex are the only victors in this Vietnam proxy war conflict.

These formulaic cops are asking questions like "Who killed Bob White, a bird, Cock Robin? Or could it be Bernie Toucan? A case could be made with the means and the opportunity nailed down. But what is the motive? Go down the list – Bull White, Ronald Outrage, Luther Green perchance– can we lay out a convincing case for any of them?" I am speechless with horror and cry out, "Stop concentrating on the stupid murder. I'm not interested. I'm a seeker seeking realization." Heather turns my way to answer, "It's just another one of your silly puzzles you're trying to solve. Haven't you got that yet? Turn on, tune in, drop out. Trust me."

Again Heather points to an approaching diorama. In it, she and I are working on a very intricate puzzle. I am struggling to figure out how to put pieces together when there are no guideposts, no blocks of colors, no recognizable structures or forms, no defining edge pieces. Heather shrugs off these obstacles. She is busily cutting up the pieces so that they fit no matter whether the piece belongs where she is forcing it to fit or not. She's telling me, it's easy if you already know the solution. Trust me.

Is that true realization, the solution, the answer? Stop. Stop mixing metaphors, dreams, reality. Stop....stop...stop...

———————

I wake Heather up as we enter Lagunitas from the west. On the main drag, particularly around the grocery store, it's obvious this is a hippie retreat. A hitchhiker with long hair and colorful clothes, a dog at his side, has his thumb out at the side of the road. Up in the hills on either side of the road, there must be places ideal for communal living. Do these hippies feel glamorous when they tell their friends they live here or in places like it - Woodacre, Forest Knolls, San Geronimo, Point Reyes? They drive a beat up truck or Volkswagen bus if they can afford it. Live in the bus if they have to. Camp out on somebody's property. Better than panhandling in the city...Live off the land, and the generosity of well-heeled members of this generation's elite - musicians, drug dealers, dance promoters, poster artists, record company executives, disc jockeys.

"I've only been here once. And it was at night," Heather mutters.

Harry's eyes pop open. He's in obvious pain but refuses to acknowledge it.

"Turn here," she directs.

We head up Manzanita Avenue, another one of the many back roads just barely wide enough for two cars, typical in Marin County, right down to the endless twists and turns, the potholes and shoulders that drop off into thin air.

"Pull over and park."

A sensation takes hold of me. This place, it's unsettled, troubled.

Heather points at a driveway just ahead. I crane my neck up the hill. There's a tangle of shrubs and bushes nestled beneath a young stand of redwoods. I can just make out a rooftop.

"Wait for my signal before heading up the driveway."

Heather disappears up the steep hillside. It's very quiet, peaceful. Birds sing in the trees. Wind rustles the leaves. Did the storm hit here? Something untoward has gone down here...

Heather waves me up the driveway. I park in front of a garage when I get to the top of it. Harry struggles to pull himself up as he grabs his homemade crutch. There's a garden in the front of the house done in the Japanese style. A small concrete pagoda... Plants that look like a Bonsai arrangement full scale. Rocks inserted into the tableau... Raked gravel... Large circular stepping stone path... A pond filled with koi. Moss in profusion...

Harry finally gets the door open on his side of the car. Heather helps him out. The house is low lying. It caresses the hill. A series of decks and porches extend from the multiple levels that flow down the hillside. Hard to tell just how big the place is. It nestles suitably into the mixture of created and natural landscape.

"Sarah lives here. She's the house sitter... Mostly likely just finished her morning meditation or is lounging in the hot tub. You'll like that part. She's got humongous boobs."

Heather smiles, heads inside. We follow – slowly – and enter an almost empty entry area. There's a low table against one wall on which there is a vase filled with dried plants. Poster of some swami or other on the wall behind the table... He's floating in a red and yellow sea of weird demigods. A mandala pattern with him at the center... Oriental rug on the hardwood floor... Open sliding glass door at the opposite side of the room through which I hear in the distance water splashing against wood. Harry takes a seat in the lone chair. Heather motions.

"Let's take a look around."

I have my heavy flashlight in my hand, ready for use as a club. We look in every room. See nobody. Last stop - down a short flight of stairs to a lower level... Open a door, then another. We're in a dark hallway.

"Got something you can pop open a padlock with?"

Heather points to a padlocked door ahead. Will we discover Tony and Jane behind that door, bound and gagged, dead, mutilated? Whose house is this? Why are we searching through it? Boy Scout training or just dumb luck - I have a bolt cutter in my backpack.

"Be prepared," I comment with fanfare after I have cut open the lock.

Heather flicks on the light switch. We are standing in the doorway of a chemist's lab. Little bit of this, that and the other neatly stacked on shelves. No windows or outside doors in this part of the house. The stacked items are chemical ingredients. They're labeled. Large bottles filled with pills. Several long surfaces to work on... Fancy lab gear all about...

"For a community college chemistry class..." I ask flippantly, not daring to step too far into the room.

Not interested in touching anything or breathing too heavily either. Getting high and tripping on some malevolent substance is not on my agenda at the moment. Heather is unconcerned.

"Outrage's playground: mixes up special batches of acid, STP, DMT, crystal meth and his own creations for unique occasions. You've seen the results of his work in action."

"Outrage..."

"His real name is Ronald Walker."

"Ronald Walker?"

"One and the same..."

The lover of the elder Mrs. White and executor of her estate, Bobby White's mentor, college professor metamorphosed into what – mad filmmaker, madder drug cocktail maker, maddest Office dirty tricks collaborator, murderer of Bobby White? Why would the executor of the estate want to kill his pledge, the golden goose?

"And that concoction that spilled onto Bernie Toucan which sent him running from the room?"

"He probably thought Walker had doctored it. I mean, after all, Bernie did steal all the musical instruments and the van after the Straight Theater ceremony."

"Jane and Tony..."

"Jane's miscarriage followed by their mutual trip to outer space, both courtesy of Mr. Walker and his designer drugs. Who knows if Walker knew what his concoction would do to Jane but he certainly knew it would fuck them up and put them out of commission for an indeterminate period of time."

"Why are you telling me this?"

"It's the first stop on the magical mystery tour I promised you a few days ago."

"You've got to do better than that."

"I will. Be patient. Trust me."

"Trusting you and taking this tour will solve the puzzle and free Tony and Jane and ourselves from this madness?"

"Did I tell you that Sarah was a nurse?"

I follow Heather back to the upper level leaving the lab door open, the broken padlock on the door handle. A lively raga, drums and stringed instruments wailing away, greets us. Sunlight shines on the hardwood floors. Dust motes dance to the musical rhythm.

Harry is no longer in the entryway. Heather steps through the sliding glass door. We're on a wooden deck. A bench around its edge... Under the overhang of an impressive live oak tree branch sits a huge hot tub. Sarah is steaming away in it. She smiles at us. She's talking to Harry, who's sitting in a deck chair by the hot tub.

"Hi Heather... Who's your friend? Looks like a cop."

Sarah has her arms propped up on the rim of the tub. Her large, pendulous breasts bob on the surface of the bubbling water. She has long brown hair which, at the moment, is twisted up into a bun on the left side of her head. There's something lopsided about her face besides the off-kilter bun. Has kind of a goofy but friendly look. I wonder if she's all there. Too much acid... Too much something...

"Insurance investigator...Harmless...Eager to learn the local customs... Give him a chance, will ya'?" Heather laughs.

"Well, he is cute. Wanna join me?" Sarah asks, partially rising from the tub.

Her breasts lift as she rises. They're taut, erect. She has a beautiful figure. Getting naked and jumping into a hot tub with Sarah and Heather would be...

"No. Thanks. Not just now..."

"How's Harry? You able to fix him up..."

"No problem. But he won't be making any sudden moves in the near future. Anybody else need fixing up besides Harry here?"

Harry has more color in his face but it's obvious he's hurting.

"I think I might need taping up. My ribs..."

Sarah hops out of the hot tub, agile and helpful.

"Oh, and bring something to patch up this cut on my forehead," Heather adds.

"I'll be back in a jiffy."

Sarah scampers into the house, still naked. Observing her in retreat is like seeing the subject of a famous Renaissance painting come to life depicting a serving maiden, a carousing goddess, taking flight. But, when she returns with supplies, her grip is firm and her knowledge thorough. I am taped up right and proper; Heather's cut is stitched and bandaged neat and professional.

"Fancy spread. Whoever owns it must be really well connected," I comment.

"That cottage over there is my place. Cozy, huh?"

"Bernie Toucan and Ronald Outrage your only visitors?"

"I never ask people their name. It's healthier that way."

———

The tide is out. Takes most of the charm away from the houseboat scene, stinks for one thing. Exposes dry rot and other major imperfections is another. Gate Five in Sausalito is a dump. The modern equivalent of gold rush shantytowns that grew up around San Francisco back in 1849...

This go-around, the hovels are occupied by hippies hanging out and hanging on in the domain of the last free ride... Free rent, who but a stoned out hippie would want to live on most of these ready to collapse and/or sink shacks...Boats, many of them, are deserted and free for the taking....Free food...They pick up out-of-date produce from the discard bin at the nearby Big G grocery store...Free clothes...They go to the flea market at Marin City or Alameda and trade for clothes and other essentials...Free dope...They grow their own marijuana in planter boxes on their decks...Free transportation... They ride bicycles around Sausalito and hitchhike into the city...Free love... They're open and willing, man...Free as a bird...Flying high, all the way.

Heather has wrapped a bandanna around her head. It covers her bandaged cut and holds in place a feather she popped into the band. She played the radio all the way from Lagunitas to Sausalito, rolled down the window, took deep breaths of air, smiled up at the cloudy sky overhead, leaned back in the seat... Closed her eyes, sang along with Jimi Hendrix, smoked a joint, and ignored my feeble attempt to pump her... Just commented, "Later, alligator..."

I know what Humphrey Bogart would do. Smack her around and lay it on the line. Heather is playing a dangerous game. Somebody is likely to get hurt. And, good boy and innocent fool that I am, I'm tagging along with this wild woman whose motives are not clear, tail wagging, hoping she will come across with some affection for her loyal companion. And how do I rationalize my actions? I tell myself that with her help the puzzle will be solved and the cloud of suspicion hanging over Tony and Jane will be removed and Heather and I will somehow be liberated as well. Do I also imagine the two of us riding off into the sunset together? Is that my ultimate dream – true love? Is all the high-minded stuff I've been feeding myself crap, a cover for my real intentions? And what does that do to my relationship with Isobel? I'm just as bad as the Gate 5 crowd - confused, hopeful and self-involved.

Heather hops into a rowboat tied to one of the scattered docking areas like she owns it. I join her. The only other way to approach the cluster of isolated and exposed houseboats we are heading towards is by a series of aging walkways. They are primed to collapse, in my estimation. If they did, they'd send you flying into the muck below. Just as soon jump in a sewer.

I put the oars in their locks and shove off. I've had plenty of experience rowing — at Boy Scout camp and on hunting trips. I take pride in clean strokes with the minimum of splash. We glide toward the pitiful houseboats around

Toucan's place. One of them is on its side, sunk. Another has a weathered tarpaulin over the deck... Some tired deck chairs... Toucan's place is trim, neat, cold, moody. Temperature seems to drop ten degrees as we drift closer.

No one seems to be around. A dog starts to bark. Not idle growls and yowls. Angry, crazy, constant, fierce attack yelps. The animal is tied up on Toucan's deck. A pit bull... Vicious looking creature...

I slowly circle the houseboat. Can't see any movement inside through the windows... Then I tie up a safe distance from where the dog is chained and we hop onto the flimsy wooden walkway that goes around all sides of the houseboat. The dog continues his frantic barking, complete with lunges. Make careful moves to avoid him. Look in the windows. Spartan... Crates stacked neatly beside a sturdy single bed, just right for a security guard to crash on. A trim galley and head... Potbelly stove heats the place. On deck plenty of firewood. Great place to read Edgar Allan Poe on a foggy night... But...no Toucan...no Outrage...no Tony and Jane...nobody....just that damn attack dog.

"I need to make a few calls. We'll come back later – after it's dark," she states.

Much closer to shore, a young girl with a baby strapped to her back floats along on the flimsy walkways. The baby's sound asleep. The mother looks to be twenty years old tops. Out on the bay, expensive sailboats tack back and forth...

"Tony and Jane aren't here. We'll be spotted in a minute if we try to stake this place out. What's the point?" I ask.

A bell dings in time with the gusts of wind that roll across the muddy inlet. The tide is coming in. In time, the mudflats will be covered over. The nauseous smell will be mercifully and measurably lessened by wind and tide.

"To free Tony and Jane...We'll have to risk it."

"Why...because I trust you...because I'm willing to be patient... What kind of fool do you take me for?"

I guess I know the answers. The shuttle helicopter takes off from the nearby heliport. People in a hurry to get to the airport are aboard, well-wishers and ride givers watching and waving their departure... Heather has already hopped into the rowboat. It'll be harder going back. The wind will be against us. Bucking the wind, that's what we're attempting to do. Crazy...illogical... the eyes of a holy man gleam just out of sight...a monk's prophetic utterances remotely ring in my ears...

We park the car in a dockside parking lot in downtown Sausalito. It's full of tourists – all looking for something to take a picture of, something to buy, something to eat, something to drink, something to do. But there is no there

there in downtown Sausalito... The days when it was a fishing port are long gone, as are the days when Sally Stanford ran a fancy bawdy house. Even the days when Beatniks congregated have passed. All that's left are shopkeepers paying exorbitant rents, trying to make their nut and a healthy profit.

Heather makes a beeline for one of the two on-the-water restaurants set apart from all the others by Bridgeway, the main drag through town. She opens the door of the restaurant with authority and strides boldly towards the hostess. We have entered The Trident Restaurant.

All of the tables and chairs, the wrap around booths, the bar, the walls and the ceiling are constructed of lush, lavish wood. The rumor is that the woodwork was handcrafted by cocaine inspired craftsmen. The wooden floors are waxed until they glisten. The music is hip, groovy. The waitresses and hostess, as Luther had forecast, are sensational. Heather fits right in, with good reason. She used to work here, it turns out.

"Is he around?" she asks the hostess.

When she gets a sullen but discreet nod of assent, she asks me to wait for her.

Doesn't take me long to figure out that I was right about my assessment of myself in regard to The Trident Restaurant crowd... I'm more anonymous than the potted plants – not hip, not cool, not with it, not part of the scene. Of course, the view is spectacular. Beautiful cityscape rising up from the waters of the Bay – makes the city look like it's a mirage, a fabulous creation. Across the street from the restaurant, steep hills that rush down to the Bay are covered with expensive homes above and chic shops below. The guests of this establishment are decked out in stylish mod outfits suitable for the location.

I sit down at the bar near the waitress station and, just to pass the time, order a drink. Before it comes, I spot a pay phone near the restrooms at the entrance. I slap a five on the bar and say, "I'll be right back." The bartender turns up his nose pointedly and notices a patron beckoning at the opposite end of the bar. My answering service tells me I've got two messages. One is from Walter; the other is from my father. Both callers say call back, urgent. Not on my agenda right now; they'll have to wait.

"Tim. What the hell are you doing at my place?"

"Isobel asked me to hang out in case you called."

"Okay, I've called. What's up?"

"Isobel is down at the police station with the police detective in charge of your murder case and I'm getting ready to blow this pop stand in a drive-away car parked out front. Last chance to speak in person, if that's your pleasure, is just after the Fillmore West closes, at 10 Colusa Alley. It's near the Fillmore. I've got some staples I need to pick up. "

"I'll give it some thought. That's Detective Cooper Isobel is visiting?"

"Right..."

"Gotta go..."

I put in another dime. The switchboard operator connects me right away. Who knows how much time that gives me.

"Carter. Your ears must have been ringing."

Coop is more chirpy than usual. It turns out the reason is he's playing to an audience of one.

"There's someone here who was so worried about you she came down to the station. Here she is."

Shit. I don't need this right now. Too late.

"Charlie. Are you all right?"

"Isobel... What are you doing at the police station?"

"I was trying to do what I thought was best. People in authority need to be involved. And you proved it by making this call."

"If by people in a position of authority you mean Detective Cooper, great. If that includes Mr. White, not so great..."

"I came out here to visit with you – and Tim. And that could still happen if you'd just listen to Mr. White." I don't know where to start. Haggling time is over; consequence time will arrive directly after the trust me and patience phase ends. "Are you with that girl, what's her name – Heather?"

"It's not like that, Isobel."

"Like what, Charlie?"

"You know."

"Charlie. I'm putting you back on the line with Detective Cooper."

"Isobel... Isobel... Isobel..."

"Carter."

"Coop. You filled Isobel in? She understands the dangers, the complications?"

"You have yourself a very perceptive, very intelligent house guest there, Carter."

"Thanks."

My heart is in my mouth. Is this the way I want things to end with Isobel, my childhood sweetheart, my ideal come to me in a vision, and one of the few people that has always been in my corner? I can't help it if I need Heather's help. Well, I admit, it's more complicated than that...

Coop clears his throat. I jerk to attention. I have been unconsciously looking out at the hedonistic scene before me. Not even the Romans could have matched it for laid back intensity. Me? All I see and feel is emptiness. That's why I'll never be a part of the in crowd, the revelers at the bar, those that succeed in this kind of lifestyle. There's something else, something I like to think is more worthy of contemplation, worthy of striving for. Or is that a rationalization for my deficiencies? Anyway, I'm calling what I'm seeking realization. And its current guiding form has come to me in a vision of piercing eyes, the eyes of a holy man who connects in my mind with a Hindu monk. And Heather is somehow a part of that mix. Am I bullshitting myself? Most likely...

"So Carter, what have you gotten yourself mixed up in now?" Coop resumes.

I picture him taking out his notebook and pencil, pulling his mustache vigorously, tapping his foot, humming a fragment of an almost remembered tune from the late fifties. The other cops in the room will give him an amused look. Is Isobel still in the room?

"Went out to Muir Beach... Jane Preen, Heather's sister, told me that Heather, that is Linda Preen, would attend this three-day musical happening. The Great Northwest Phantasmagoria, Tony's group, would be doing the lightshow."

"You think Heather is the key?"

"That's the way I'm playing it. She tells me Tony and Jane have been taken."

"By the feds..."

"I'm really not sure. It's complicated... She claims only the two of us can free them."

"Think long and hard about that."

"I'm not in this to find out who murdered Bob White. My only interest is getting Tony and Jane, well Heather and me too, off the hook, free-and-clear, out of this bad news game."

Coop's a good man. When this is all over, if we're both still standing, I'm going to treat this man and his lady to a real feast. Get plastered. Whatever...If I'm a free man...

"You think Linda Preen is involved somehow?"

"I know she is and I think that's why she has a mighty compelling reason for wanting to spring Jane. And springing Jane, I'm thinking, will bust this mess wide open."

"Like the alert you asked me to pass along to the Marin Sheriff's Office – the one that led to a half a ton of weed, a car crash and a manhunt stemming from it..."

"That's the tip of the iceberg..."

"Give."

"Heather did show up at the dance all right. I followed her outside. Lost sight of her for a minute and then saw her down on the beach. Turns out the beach is a drop site for smugglers — your half ton of weed came ashore. She signaled them with a flashlight. Toucan pulled out on the beach in the black van I turned you onto and had the stuff piled into the back of it. Landing craft shoves off as Toucan's pulling away. All under the cover of fog, wind, rain. Real slick operation..."

"You hear anything they said? Get close enough for a good I.D. of any of the others?"

"Too far away... Beach is too open. Might be able to identify the skipper of the shore rig, I don't know. Anyhow, I follow Toucan's van in which Heather's riding shotgun... She arrived on the scene in a beat up black VW registered to Bob White. Last time I saw it, it was still in the Muir Beach parking lot. Might have something of value in it, pile of crap in the back seat, a real junker, the one with the New York license plates..."

"I'll get somebody on it right away."

"Anyhow, I try to follow them at a safe distance but the fog is thick and the road windy. I get too close. Toucan reads my tail. He tries to shake me. He swings a little wide at a turn. A car is coming from the opposite direction. He loses control. Probably all that weight in the back of his van threw him off... He's one hell of a driver. No sooner is the van wrecked, though, than he's out of the car, pulling Heather with him. We all rush down a very steep hillside. Toucan ends up giving me several good whacks with a rather stout stick and a kick or two in the ribs for good measure. He slips away. I come to...make good our escape before anybody else is on the scene, not without difficulty."

"Where are you now?"

"I'm sitting on a houseboat down at Gate 5 in Sausalito packed to the rim with suspicious heavy duty boxes inside. I know, we paddled out and checked it. Pitbull watch dog, thank goodness on a sturdy leash, barking and lunging while we check. Tony and Jane aren't there - yet. But Heather must think they will be. Wants to go back after it gets dark... We're hanging out in downtown Sausalito until then."

"Not to make life more difficult than it already is for you, there's a federal warrant out now in your name, sedition, conspiracy to obstruct justice, assorted other misdemeanors."

"Just what I needed, but it figures..."

"There's something going on — and you better find out what it is fast — or you're going to end up in the same kind of trouble as Vitolinich and Jane Preen."

Heather appears at the hostess desk. She has yet to spot me.

"I've got to run. Talk to you later."

I slip into the nearby bathroom and use the facility.

Eat when you can.

Sleep when you can.

Clean up when you can.

Relieve yourself when you can.

We sit in my car looking out from the Marin Headlands towards a magnificent cityscape that includes the Golden Gate Bridge. Over the city, it's clear. Leading tendrils of fog blanket the bridge. The bridge towers poke through the top. Cars rushing over the bridge are momentarily revealed as the wind buffets the fog. A cargo ship emerges from the fog into the open sunlight on the Bay. A foghorn sounds, a clarion call that draws my attention toward the center of the luminescent Bay where Alcatraz Island, a rock littered with the remains of a maximum-security prison, molders, dark and sinister.

In the middle of light, darkness...In the heart of good, evil...San Francisco, a metaphor for life and my current experience - or am I just being melodramatic?

Heather sits beside me looking down at her hands. I start the car and head away from the bridge and late afternoon traffic. As we go downhill, the fog flips by the front windshield in denser and denser waves.

"Charlie. No matter what happens I want you to know that I was and am very fond of you."

"Sounds like the beginning of a 'dear John' letter."

We're on the grounds of a military base. Fort Cronkite...Looks more like a low-rent, government-run retirement community.

"It's for the best. You'll see, having me around, my world, you deserve something better, finer, more attuned to higher spheres."

"You meditate and make oracular proclamations.'"

"You are a seeker at heart. Seekers make more progress unattached. You'll see the wisdom. Look deep within."

A beach in a small cove, private and clean surrounded by lots of open space, appears up ahead after we pass by family housing, primitive but durable. Barracks for single folk... Rifle range... Mess hall... Commissary...

For the first time since I've known her, Heather hasn't turned on the radio. She looks out the window in silence watching the camp float by.

"The owner of The Trident and I were having a fling. Unfortunately, he also smuggled in 268 pounds of marijuana and got arrested. So was I - by the feds. Since then I've been working for them as an informant. They had me dead to rights, Charlie. And then, of course, there's my mother..."

"Your mother..."

"She was, is, one of them, a field agent, only used now on special assignments...whatever..."

I don't say it but I think it, my father too. I don't want to divert her from this line of conversation. We can get into all that when and if, in the future, I tell myself.

"Bull White..."

"He runs all the West Coast operations and others as well so I hear.

Only shows up when and if it pleases him."

"What kind of operations?"

"I don't know. I get told what to do and that's about all I get clued into... Only had contact with Mr. White a few times and believe me that was enough. Mostly get my marching orders from Outrage, well Bernie gets the orders and he passes them along to me. Sometimes Bernie and I work as a team, also not my idea of a good time."

"Bobby..."

"That's where the real trouble began. Bobby wasn't really supposed to be involved at all. His father was very clear about that. But, you know how it is, the boss's son and all. Anyway, for my money, this whole shitty mess begins and ends with The Office and their partner in crime Mr. J. Edgar Hoover. They're vindictive, protective, vengeance is theirs. And they are suspicious of, disgusted by, this whole scene, they call us, our generation; hippies, revolutionaries, terrorists or some such, unpatriotic traitors for Christ sake. And Jane and Tony..."

"Why did Bob White..."

"Oh you know, everything was always about his father to him, no matter how hard he tried to convince himself and others it wasn't. 'Hey dad, I'm over here, I'm over here and I exist. See, I know how the game works. I can not only handle it, I am a master at it,' something like that, until he got in over his head. I don't know. I was just a peon."

Lots of silence... We pull up and stop at the entrance to a single lane tunnel. There's a stoplight on the right side of the entrance. It's red. We wait for it to change. A car emerges. After a long interval a Jeep disgorges itself from the tunnel. It's a very long light.

Where are these vehicles coming from? Where are we headed? Is there no way to stop time, stop time and get off of the wheel? I have no appetite for the future we are preparing to enter.

"We have to get Tony and Jane safely away from them. These guys play for keeps and they don't care who they have to hurt or how to protect - their precious operation, their equally precious own asses, their slimy partners in crime. They wrap it all up in the flag, the same flag radicals are burning along with draft cards and bras. The same subversives these federal agents earn their keep trying to discredit, subvert, infiltrate, destroy. They're kids, Americans, the future solid citizens of the good old U S of A. It would be funny if it didn't get innocent people screwed over and thrown in jail."

"You let yourself be a part..."

"Not now. Let me finish."

The light turns green. I pull the car into what looks like a sewer pipe. It's an aging, bare bones tunnel. We are swallowed up, surrounded by concrete walls lined with pipes illuminated by dim orange-glowing lights. Water sweats out onto the walls and drips to the roadway surface below, creating rivulets.

The tires of my Volvo make a splashing, then a humming sound as they pass through them. A hypnotic view confronts us out the front window, a tiny dot of light ahead, the end of the tunnel. Bleak, monochromatic, dreary... My foot involuntarily slackens up on the gas and the car creeps along. We have entered a timeless place somehow, one from which none of us will escape.

"I — it's true - hear voices, see things, make prophetic statements. Not just because of the drugs I take but because I am possessed — by hell or heaven I don't know. And that gift, that problem..."

"It's a gift..."

"Wait. My mother..."

"I know, she worked for The Office. My father too..."

I can't help myself. I blurt it out. Fool, there's no future for yourself with her, I tell myself, even as visions of our future life together flourish. I guess that's another thing that sets me apart from my father. I'm more of a romantic at heart, a dreamer, not a pragmatic intellectual.

"She...I guess Jane and I have been trying for a long time to get away from her influence. She loves us in her own way. I want to believe that. But..."

"I hear you, but that's easier said than done."

"I thought I was seeking my destiny. You know – with my gift..."

We both contemplate that for a time.

"Maybe my mistake was that I sought guides, help, rather than looking within, someone to help me make sense of what was happening to me. That was a bust. I took up meditation, sat at the foot of a local guru. You met him. I hung out with the intellectual crowd down at the Art Institute. That's where I met Luther. That crowd was glib, droll, hollow. I drifted down to North Beach looking for poets, philosophers, the Beats. Where had they all gone or what had they become? Nowhere, nothing left. I kept going and ended up completely out of control, working at The Trident. I just wanted to understand the voices I was hearing."

"There's still time, still a path. There must, there will be..."

"Wait. Hold on. And then there was my baby sister, Jane, a lost soul if I ever saw one - got tangled up in dangerous games with troubled individuals she latched onto. I'm not trying to make excuses, understand. I just want you to understand. I want you to understand because I need you to buy into the play I'm proposing."

"You don't have to..."

We burst into the shocking glare of daylight. Our pupils contract. I swerve to avoid cars waiting to enter the tunnel. Our voyage through the underworld is over. We wind down Alexander Avenue, descending into Sausalito. A tour bus in front of us belches rancid fumes into our faces. Heather looks on with glazed, unfocused eyes.

She was just trying to understand her relationship to her inner voice, her family and friends complicating her desire for freedom to make her own unique way. Then she gets busted for being mixed up in a big weed buy and ends up playing stooge for Office fun-and-games. And then there's me. I was groping along too, an innocent with vague inklings of some nature god or otherworldly presence, a good boy who signed on at The Office purportedly to fulfill my military commitment and ended up working for Life Beneficial. We meet up, not by accident. She was on assignment. Our meeting is tied to a murder, the murder of an Office chief's son under suspicious circumstances. What a fool I have been. I'm a babe in the woods. I wouldn't have it any other way. I'd never have met Heather otherwise. I couldn't stop Heather from finishing her say now, even if I wanted to. The words come tumbling out of her.

"It may be too late for me, the jury is still out on that one, but I'm determined to free Jane of all that...of all the Bob Whites, all the Bernie Toucans, all the Ronald Outrages, all the Bull Whites...and all their cooked up crazy-ass schemes, dirty tricks, that have nauseating variations. I'm tired of mind games, games about control, controlling events, spinning them to suit the powers-that-be. Of course, they are convinced their direction is the Right Way, the Way of Truth-And-Justice, the American Way, a matter of national security cleared at the highest level right up to the throne of God, the power elite and beyond. Being a conniver above the fray corrupts as certainly as does the need for power that motivates their skuzzy antics. And the capper..."

"You don't have to..."

"But I do. I do. I have to. Someone must understand - why. I want..."

"No. It's not neces...."

Heather plows on, needing to tell someone about the darkness that has made her life a living hell. And something more, something else...will we get to that part as well?

"Coke, meth, smack, weed, weapons - they sell them to innocent victims. Then they flip them or put them in jail. They infiltrate, that's what they call it, the scene and corrupt innocent intentions. They introduce us-versus-them thinking and build walls that brand people speaking their minds with labels like radicals and worse. They talk up violent protest that alienates these young people from parents and society at large. Isolated and reviled, they are eliminated as players. Oh, they are so clever, so devious, so duplicitous. There's more. The weed that came ashore last night...it's been sprayed with Paraquat. That's a herbicide, and it makes people sick. Gives them respiratory problems. How do I know? How do they know? It was sprayed on those fields of weed by the very same Office operatives that are getting ready to distribute this tainted stuff. Their idea of just desserts, their idea of defusing radical elements among our youth, their idea of a hearty joke, their idea of the American Way, their idea of a job well done. And that's just the latest of their sick gambits."

"I'm tired of all that. Tired... I've had enough. All I want is out...for myself and my little sister..."

Heather is bathed in sweat. Her eyes are glazed, her face pale and drawn... Head down, she's looking at the floor boards of the car.

"Let what is within you guide you, Charlie. It will show you the way. No matter what happens to me."

Her voice has changed. It is deeper, solemn. The car moves very slowly. My God, my foot is off the gas pedal. Heather passes out. Cars stack up behind us. There's nowhere to pull over but in the dividing strip constructed so that ambulances can use the middle of the road in emergencies during heavy traffic jams.

I turn left at the first available street. Princess Street... Dump off into Princess Lane. Stop the car. No parking signs on both sides of the narrow lane. Slide across the seat. Take Heather into my arms. Press her to me. Her arms hang at her sides. Feel her forehead. She has been under tremendous strain, must have survived enormous upheavals during the last year...head-over-heels for her, the possibly of us...male seeking mate desperately...I'm a fool... and what else...

I lay her back against the seat. Her breathing is normal. She seems to have passed the crisis. I start the car and head up the hill on Buckley, park beyond the Alta Mira near a set of stairs that heads back down to the main drag. Listen to birds chattering and the sound of the wind.

Heather comes around, smiles up at me, takes my hand in hers. I avoid her eyes.

"How long was I out?"

"Not long. A few minutes..."

She makes as if to brush my hair from my eyes. Our eyes meet.

"Promise me you'll go back to your sweetheart when this is over. Don't let whatever happens keep you apart. Promise..."

"I thought I needed to be unattached."

"It's not too late for you. Reach out and grab happiness. Now..."

"That's crazy, Heather. Nonsense... We're going to beat this thing, together... We make one hell of a team."

Darkness comes early in Sausalito during wintertime. The sun dips behind the coastal range before it disappears into the ocean well before five o'clock. The chilly night air approaches. I roll up the car windows. We should get something warm into our stomachs before we head back down to Gate Five.

"You up to some steps?"

"Sure."

Before we get out of the car, she pulls out from her shoulder bag a pair of jeans, a white cable-knit sweater and tennis shoes. As she slips them on I pull out a pair of heavy pants, a beat up sweater and a pair of deck shoes. For good measure, I pull out an insulated coat.

She dons a blue woolen cap as we descend the stone steps that lead to downtown Sausalito. Disquieting shadows fall across them. Steep hillsides deep in shadows on either side of the steps create a tunnel that leads ever onward and downward towards the depths.

"Want to play a game of chess?"

We are in the no name bar. It's right out of Kerouac. Beatniks can play chess while KJAZ sides play for their listening pleasure. Anchor Steam beer, a local product, on tap. Right next to a fantastic bookstore...

"Want to play?" the man sitting next to us repeats.

Heather nods encouragement. He's looking at me. We sit at a table on a bench seat attached to the wall that runs the length of the bar across from it. There's more seating at the back of the room and on an outside patio in the back. Small tables spaced in front of the bench seat allow for a semi-communal feeling, cozy. Heather nods again, looking at me.

"Ah, okay. But I'm not very good."

"Neither am I. Just something to pass the time..."

He's smoking a pipe, Meerschaum, a genuine Sherlock Holmes model... He's stringy, fit and tall; has long blond hair, a beard and mustache; wears a tan pullover sweater, jeans and a black cap.

We set up the pieces. He takes black. I move several pieces back and forth in the air above the board reminding myself how the pieces move.

"Don't worry. It'll come back to you," comments the man as he sucks on the end of his pipe. The pipe bubbles. He lets a trickle of smoke slip out of the side of his mouth. He's had some practice with that pipe. After he makes his move, he looks up. "Name's Jacques by the way... You live around these parts?"

"In the city...The Avenues... My name is Charlie. This is Heather."

Heather has retreated into the shadows. She leans forward when I introduce her and takes my arm. Smiles sweetly at Jacques...

"He's my old man," she puts in.

"Love is a wonderful thing," Jacques throws back, chuckling. He points to the board. I shrug my shoulders. Move my castle. Jacques takes another tug on his pipe, laughs, makes his move. I'm already in trouble.

"I live on my boat. Just a few minutes away... Been living on it for almost a month now... Dream of sailing somewhere far away, maybe France or Xanadu..."

I look at Jacques with interest, imagining him crossing the Atlantic in heavy seas, rounding the Cape in winter, sailing up the South American coast. What an adventure.

Jacques has me in check on the tenth move. I shake my head. "Sorry, not much of a challenge for you."

"Let's go again," he answers. "You're improving."

Jacques is patient. So am I. The odds are if Tony and Jane show up at the houseboat, it won't happen until late. My backpack sits on the bench next to me. In it I have matches, rope, knife, first aid kit, heavy duty flashlight, my trusty bolt cutters, a little of this and that...stuff that might come in handy. I've seen it happen before, mostly on camping trips.

Heather watches the game with interest. She asks about the pieces — how they move, what they're called. I like the way she hangs onto my arm and looks up into my eyes. I'm distracted in a big way, not making excuses, you understand.

Jacques wins another game. "I don't think I'd do any better with this pretty lady on my arm," he comments with a wry smile. Heather flushes. I clear my throat to relieve the tightness. "Want to go again?"

"Why not..."

I try to concentrate, plan each move. Game is like my situation. Whatever Outrage and Toucan and White are up to, I'm always ten steps behind. They're in control of the board. I move a chessman and get blindsided shortly thereafter. Heather is my queen but she works both sides of the street. Tony is my castle — plucky and innocent. Jane and Isobel are bishops — knowledgeable, even formidable on home turf, but shaky when taken out of their element. With a rush, the rest of the players in my current drama offer up suggestions about their place on the board — the Whites, Bill Hancock, Mr. Meade, Walter, Coop, my father. Christ, this mess is out of control. So is the chessboard when I try to impose my will.

"Like to get some fresh air?" Jacques suggests at the end of the third game.

I look at Heather. She nods. "Something to eat wouldn't be a bad idea," she surprises me by saying.

"You game?" I ask Jacques. "Our treat... To the victor go the spoils."

No name is my kind of scene. The best of a bygone era where relics come to hang out... That's me all over. If I stick around in the Bay area, I might just move to Sausalito when this whole thing is over. There must be an affordable place that isn't a beat up houseboat.

"Why not?" agrees Jacques.

"If you gentlemen will excuse me for just a moment," Heather asks, getting up, not waiting for us to agree.

We watch her as she heads towards the necessary. What a delightful sight. Jacques takes his pipe out of his mouth. I clear my throat. The babble of subdued conversation mingles with smoke rising lazily towards the ceiling.

"Detective Cooper sends his regards," Jacques states, out of the blue.

"Huh," my head swivels in his direction, I meet his eyes. There's an amused twinkle in them.

"Sort of an off-the-books protective service was the intention, as I understand it. The way I interpret it is, I can be as involved as you need me to be," he adds as he cleans his pipe bowl with a tool, taps the pipe on the edge of an ashtray to empty the bowl and then stores the pipe in his coat pocket. I finish the last of my Anchor Steam beer draft and light up a cigarette before putting on my coat. I don't need to look at Jacques for him to understand I've gotten the message. And I don't need to speak for him to understand that I'm mulling over what he just told me. We sit in silence side-by-side. My hands are hanging loose between my legs and I'm looking vaguely at our small table, reminding me that Heather was in a similar position in my car. That was shortly before she passed out. That's not going to be my reaction, quite the opposite. I'll let you know when I get a handle on it, my reaction that is. Jacques doesn't seem to mind the silence. It's almost companionable between the two of us. Well, not really. Queasy feelings of doubt and apprehension in equal parts disturb the moment for me. We both see Heather returning at the same time and rise in unison. I pull on my backpack. Jacques pats me on the shoulder and smiles.

I wave Heather towards the front door as we link arms and promenade. Jacques precedes us. He moves with fluid ease... He might be a handy man to have around when the chips are down. The ambivalence I'm feeling is probably just the ever present anxiety and wariness that's been draped over my shoulders like a shroud for most of the time I've been investigating this damn insurance claim.

Outside, the weather is damp. A light mist has taken over along with the fog which is rolling down the hill. It's going to be a cold, wet night. I turn in the direction of the stairs, planning to get a parka for Heather. When we reach the base of the steps, I see a cop car with its light flashing parked beside my car. Am I about to be towed away? "Hey," I shout.

Heather squeezes my arm, holding me back. She's right. Looks like we're going to have to finish off tonight on foot... We don't need a run-in with the cops about now. Coop is cool and maybe Jacques is too but that federal warrant...

"Your car?" asks Jacques.

He speaks without intonation but there's something in his lack of inflection that puts me on guard.

"Thought so for a minute...But I remember now we came over on the ferry. Silly how you forget things, isn't it..."

"Right," mutters Jacques taking his pipe out of his pocket and feeding fresh tobacco into it. "We better get that bite to eat. You need something filling inside you on a night like this." We look down the near-deserted street towards the square in downtown Sausalito. When the tourists disappear the town reverts to a sleepy village. "I've been told the bouillabaisse and the abalone sandwiches at the Seven Seas melt in your mouth," continues Jacques, now our guide to Sausalito.

I nod, thinking of the night ahead and the sudden appearance of our new friend Jacques. Why would Coop dispatch Jacques to watch over and/ or assist us? Would he really do that, and do it off-the-books? I've had a good feeling about Coop from the first and I think he feels something too. So maybe, it's possible. Come on, Charlie, don't look a gift horse in the mouth.

The Seven Seas turns out to be an excellent place to eat. We take a seat in the front room. A bar along one wall limits seating. But, on a night like this, this is where the regulars congregate to chew the fat with the owner and each other. We take one of the tables... I recommend the fried oysters. Well, they're not as good as oysters from the Chesapeake but they'll do. Heather lets me take a bite of her abalone sandwich. It's delicious. Jacques eats his bouillabaisse slowly, thoughtfully, watching us without seeming to. At last he breaks our silence.

"Look. I know it's none of my business, but you guys look like you could use some help. And, well, I've got nothing but time on my hands right now and I could do with a little excitement."

Heather's eyes widen. I look at her and then at Jacques.

"Trust me," mutters Heather under her breath.

"What," say both Jacques and I at the same time.

Heather looks from one of us to the other. Is Heather aware she says some of the things she says? We both wait for her to continue. But she doesn't.

"Well... " I say rubbing my chin. "We could use a lift on a boat."

Coming at the houseboat by water is a whole lot more appealing than walking out on those flimsy and exposed walkways.

"Where to..."

"Friend's houseboat, way the hell out from Gate Five..."

"Tides willing, my runabout would work. Low tide they're all mudflats, you know. When?"

"Oh, around midnight would be good."

"That'll work."

I pause here, trying to calculate just how far I should go. Jacques waits, impassive. "You got a flare gun you could bring along?" I finally ask.

Jacques nods. Pulls his pipe out of his pocket... He's finished his soup.

"Put my hands on a lot more than that if it's wanted," he answers.

Jacques drops us off in dark shadows surrounded by murky midnight water, just down a walkway from the target houseboat. The guard dog is gone. Inside? I wave to Jacques. He shuts off the engine on his boat. Ties onto one of the numerous poles stuck into the muddy bottom.

Going to have a little fireworks display to greet our friend, I tell Jacques. Scare the shit out of him. Big joke, I say. Jacques just nods and tugs on his pipe. He's dressed warmly. Loaned Heather some foul weather gear...

Heather and I are next to a piling near the houseboat. A bicycle is parked next to the piling. An improvised bench made up of weathered boards, a discarded anchor and some engine parts hides us from view. We try to make ourselves comfortable on top of a smelly tarpaulin. Not bloody likely. Anger, violence, fear lurk palpably in the cold and still night air.

All hippies are long gone from the scene. Sensible people are at home in bed with their loved ones. Fog clumps in pockets. Small bursts of wind disturb distant patches of water. Keeping your extremities warm and not getting damp are major preoccupations. Heather presses up against me. I put my arm around her.

"Why are we here again?" I ask as quietly as I can.

"To get Jane and Tony out of this mess..."

"And they are likely to show up here?"

"If they don't, there's only one other place I know of that they might be."

I look out over the monochromatic nighttime waters, slowly at first and then with ever increasing power and intensity. The penetrating eyes of my holy guide rise up from within me. The warmth of their white-hot gaze comforts me.

Heather and I are quiet, removed from time and space yet powerfully in the present as well.

"When a soldier shoots someone during battle, who should be blamed? Is it the gun maker, the bullet manufacturer, the soldier's company commander, the planners back at headquarters? Should the soldier be judged as a murderer or rewarded as a hero?"

More Delphic, no, Socratic riddles in the middle of this frigid wait... I can't quite convince myself that I am actually here, that I should be here, that this body I inhabit is really my one true self. From far away yet very near I observe.

"We're talking about murder here if you are referring to Bob White and his killer is a murderer not a soldier or a hero," I reply.

"So you come down on the side of judgment, assessment of blame?"

"My parents, my elders, have always been able to depend on me to 'do the right thing,' to suck it up and do my duty, to be a good and obedient Scout," I answer, again diverting my comments away from her philosophic query.

"Do you do your duty out of love or out of fear, weakness?"

"Am I truly a seeker after truth, after self-realization? Do you see that in me because you are a seeker too? What is it that motivates your actions?"

"Jane. She got pregnant, don't you know. And something snapped inside of Bobby – with a little chemical help that fanned up the troubled flames of guilt, family loyalty and honor – and…but you never answered my question."

"You probably won't answer mine either."

Heather pulls away from me, looks off into the mid distance and then down at the planks of the dock. She starts, very cautiously, to pull a splinter of wood away from a plank. Waves slosh against the pilings below us. There is no moon in the sky above. The wind's workings have been suspended for the moment as well. We are alone and distant in our faraway space, Heather and I.

"You believe in astral travel? Vision states? Seeing the future?"

Her eyes are hollow, dark pools of blackness. I tumble into them and find myself in a void of infinite proportions. The all-seeing eyes of my holy guide are all that ground me.

"Well, I've had a few weird moments but, up 'til now, I've never had what I would consider a true vision. But somehow, some things have happened and I…I can't really explain."

"This world is not…" she starts, then freezes.

We both hear insistent footsteps on the dilapidated walkway, crushing footsteps that bring us instantly back to the moment. An unearthly dog howls in the distance. Clouds begin a march across the sky above. The fog hangs like icicles over the thick and viscous water. Darkness and uncertainty are on the prowl. Don't look; don't move. Be cautious. Trust me.

"Bernie."

It's Outrage. He's a number of yards behind the menacing footsteps. Those footsteps stop. They're Toucan's.

"Get the lead out, Ronnie."

Toucan stands no more than ten feet from us.

"Fuck off," answers Outrage.

We've barged in on what seems to be a well-worn private argument.

"Tell me again why it is that we both needed to come here?" Outrage whines, as his footsteps slow to a stop beside Toucan.

"To cover our tracks, you fool… That hack rent-a-cop you said we could control showed up with Linda at the Lagunitas house looking for Vitolinich and Jane after running me off the road. It's a cinch they'll show up here looking for them. The local cops are sure to follow," snaps Toucan.

"I should be giving the orders here. And I don't take them either, unless it suits my pur…"

The conversation breaks off abruptly as a houseboat shifts against the pilings of the boardwalk, causing a loud creaking sound. A door opens and closes somewhere. Footsteps echo in the night. They seem to stumble in our direction, then recede. There's a long silence. Good, Outrage and Toucan are on edge too. But Tony and Jane are not with them. What now?

"Come on," says Toucan irritation in his voice. "We've got to clean this place out."

"Bernie," pleads Outrage as Toucan's footsteps retreat. "Why can't we get someone else to do this for us?"

Toucan's footsteps turn back towards Outrage.

"We have to clean up our own mess, not leave any loose ends. Outsiders getting involved would only create more loose ends. Get it?"

"You're right, of course," mumbles Outrage but he doesn't sound convinced, doesn't move.

I discover that I have broken free from Heather's restraining arm and am hurtling from concealment towards Toucan and Outrage. Toucan turns towards the noise I make; Outrage is oblivious. I slam into Toucan while delivering an arm tackle on Outrage. Toucan and I land with a thud and bounce apart. Outrage tumbles away from view. Heather jumps to her feet and screams, "Jacques. Now..."

Jacques' boat comes to life as he fires his flare gun off into the night sky. The boat's spotlight comes on and a siren blasts. Then his loudspeaker switches on.

"Give it up, Carter. You've got nowhere to go."

Great, Jacques is an Office agent and he's blinding me with his spotlight. Toucan, with a howl of rage, comes at me, his knife in his hand. Before I can do anything to stop her much less change my forward motion, Heather leaps between us. Toucan's long steel shaft slashes into the meaty part of Heather's arm.

"Idiot," Heather grunts, grabbing Toucan's knife-wielding arm and jumping on top of it.

Her weight, slight as it is, rips the knife from Toucan's hand. Blood gushes from her wound. I hear Jacques's loudspeaker click on again and he makes another proclamation. But it is meaningless in my present state of consciousness, as purposeless as background static wafting in deep space through the universe.

I am consumed, possessed...Taken beyond rage, beyond fury. I've been seized by a glowing power that radiates from those all-encompassing holy eyes.

Toucan, seeming to sense my new-found energy, whirls round and runs. I dive towards him. No one, nothing, can stop my approach. I am riding on the wings of angels. I slam into Toucan again. We barrel into the side of his houseboat. Toucan bears the brunt of the impact.

Jacques's boat draws near, his spotlight targeting our struggle. "Preen is down. Preen is down," he announces.

There must be other agents nearby. I've lost track of Outrage.

I take a swing at Toucan, a swing of righteous vengeance. His head snaps back but he doesn't go down. He's been in a few street brawls in his life. His knee comes up into my groin. I stifle an agonized groan. The flimsy walk way sways, bobs up and down. We teeter uncertainly on the slippery surface. Toucan stumbles forward. I grab his elbow and wrench it out and upward. I hear bones snap in his shoulder. Toucan yelps in pain. We almost go into the water. The flimsy walkway buckles and bends in unpredictable ways. On the upswing of a wobble, I give Toucan an unstable karate chop with my booted foot that sends him flying onto the walkway of his houseboat.

Jacques bangs up against a dock near a stair-like walk that leads to where Heather had been. She is nowhere to be found. I vault onto the houseboat walkway as Toucan opens its door. I swing a wild roundhouse in his direction. He ducks and tumbles inside. My fist smashes into the wall of the houseboat.

Jacques announces, "Give it up. It's over."

Toucan has a gun. I don't care. I close in on him, awash with power from blinding beams of light from all-seeing eyes. His bullets won't stop me. His magic can't overpower mine. Bernie Toucan is going to take a fall.

Toucan sees this in my eyes. Probably for the first time in his life, he hesitates. He's not the wild man, the possessed one, in this fight. As I grab the wrist of the hand holding the gun, a hissing sound passes by our heads. It's a flare.

Jacques announces, "Give it up. Now..."

First amazement and then intense fear flicker in Toucan's eyes. His gun drops out of his hand. I have not relaxed my grip. With a fierce howl, the two of us lock in mortal combat. I grab him around the neck; Toucan returns the favor. We're in a death dance.

A fire breaks out on the houseboat behind us as Toucan pushes my chin back with the heel of his hand. His face reddens from the pressure of my vise-like fingers around his throat. He is forced to relax his grip on my chin, throwing me off balance. He gives me a short jab to the face. My head bangs into a piece of metal on the deck, probably what Toucan uses as ballast. Without warning, Toucan stumbles and, in an instant, is over the side. I follow.

The water is dark, murky, foul smelling - just like the man I have again clutched by the throat. Toucan has me by the throat as well. We sink in a gagging, whirling struggle into the icy, slimy water. Toucan lets out a bubbling scream. I realize I am screaming with him...Baying at the fast approaching eternal beyond. His strength surges, allowing him to break away from me. He takes a big, slow- moving swing. I dodge in slow motion. Too late...My head rocks back. We're running out of oxygen. I deliver a hard right to Toucan's jaw that seems to put him out for the count. No time to check. I race for the surface, trying to pull Toucan with me. He's too heavy. I let go. Toucan is lost to sight. I explode above the water's surface and suck in air in big gulps. Toucan is nowhere to be seen. It's as if he never existed, as if the Devil has taken his own back to subterranean grottoes too distant to penetrate.

A horrendous explosion erupts in the still night. Toucan's houseboat vaporizes. Whatever was stored in that houseboat was extremely volatile. Shards of wood, clothing, kitchen utensils - fly in all directions. A fireball illuminates Gate Five. Peace and love hippies are rocked out of their beds by the all-encompassing blast.

I tread water. Jacques' high- powered boat flashes past me, its running lights off. How the hell he missed me I don't know. I dive under water. Hopefully the water is deep enough so I won't be taken apart by his outboard motor blade. When I can no longer hold out, I come up for air. The nearest dock is still fifty yards away.

"I see him. I see him," Outrage shouts, pointing at me.

I take a chance and dive down, heading towards the raging inferno and away from the nearby dock. I have never stayed under water as long as I do this time. I go beyond endurance and into the misty arms of those piercing eyes. They are my strength, my salvation. Miraculously, I come up near the same landing where Jacques came ashore to manhandle Heather. Jacques's boat with the spotlight moving back and forth covers the dock and pilings towards which Jacques and Outrage thought I would swim.

"Mother Hen…This is Up-With-America Enterprise reporting. Do you read me?"

Some strange acoustic anomaly allows me to hear their radio transmission across the acrid waters clear as day.

"The Gate Five houseboat has been compromised and destroyed. I repeat compromised and destroyed. Toucan is lost and believed dead. Preen is wounded and at large, as is Carter. Should we continue to pursue? Repeat, should we continue?"

"Copy that, Up-With-America. We will dispatch a helicopter and a search team to Gate Five and alert the local authorities. You will return to home base with Agent Walker. Maintain radio silence."

"That's a roger, roger and out."

Jacques's boat turns and speeds across Richardson Bay towards downtown Sausalito. I am surprised to be taken by the arm. It's Heather, looking pale but determined.

"My mother should be here somewhere," she states, not waiting for me as she turns toward the parking lot, many walkways away.

"What?"

"She's a field agent, remember? I called her rather than using the ladies at the no name," she fires back over her shoulder.

A fire engine arrives on the scene. The police shouldn't be far behind. We join the stragglers that are making their way towards the gathering crowd on shore. No one takes any special notice of Heather and me.

"Linda. Over here."

And without another word spoken we get in Mrs. Preen's waiting car.

Then we go bumping and weaving, avoiding the crowd, as we head out of the dirt parking area and shoot out onto Highway 101 heading uphill towards Rainbow Tunnel.

———————

High above, mighty, massive clouds are livened by swirling bolts of lightning. Voices speak in them as thunder. The forces behind the 'real' world are being made manifest all around the car on our upward nighttime freeway journey.

"There's a first aid kit under the seat, Mr. Carter. See to my daughter."

Mrs. Preen is driving fast, fluidly, toward Rainbow Tunnel.

Coming into view out of the rear window of the car overseeing in the midst of this turmoil a mountain – Tamalpais...

I apply ointment and a dab of otherworldly blue powder, then wrap up Heather's arm, tight, secure.

From our rear the goddess of the mountain, Tamalpa, walks toward us, arms raised.

Toucan's knife just grazed the fleshy part of Heather's upper arm. The tight-wrapped bandages take care of the bleeding.

The goddess of the mountain is Heather, hair streaming behind her, face radiant, naked body glowing. She approaches never arriving.

Heather's face is pale but she seems okay.

The goddess Heather speaks, "Mother."

"Where to, my dear?" Mrs. Preen asks, calm and assured as if we were taking a Sunday drive.

Mrs. Preen is the mountain itself, the very peak. She oversees the normally reclining and now ever approaching Tamalpa, her court maiden and daughter.

"Haight Street between Cole and Clayton... The Straight Theater," Heather directs, with equal assurance and calm.

"I'm going to assume the back entrance would be more to our liking."

"Yes ma'am."

The Marin County Sheriff's Department is doing The Office's dirty work for them at the scene of the Gate Five debacle. Toucan's body will be found, if he is dead. What will be reported - his death or nothing at all? The explosion and fire will be the lead on TV's morning news.

Where is Coop? Is there a chance he might somehow help free Tony and Jane or will he be, willy-nilly, another pawn of The Office?

Electrified eyes penetrate, are superimposed over the Tamalpais vision. I, other awestruck humans in the foreground, bow in supplication.

I'm hunched down in the backseat of a powerful, shiny piece of Detroit steel. Pavement flies by under our feet.

We worship the sacred moment where the visible world and the invisible world connect and a synaptic flash occurs.

How could we not reach the Straight Theater before Jacques and his henchmen, who have to make the choppy watery crossing of the San Francisco Bay?

Time stands still.

Rain has cleared out the fog. The city glistens. Lights sparkle, like stars in a vast inky black universe.

How long will it take to reach Heather's last likely hiding place of Jane and Tony? Eternity... An instant... It's all the same.

We take the 19th Avenue exit after crossing the bridge and zip past my apartment. All its lights are ablaze. We catch all the stoplights at green and snap off the main thoroughfare at Anza only to head back across Park Presidio on Balboa. We turn onto Masonic. Valuable puzzle pieces will be put in place tonight.

"What don't I know that I should know?" I ask.

Heather smiles, concentrates on our surroundings.

"Be prepared. Trust me," she at long last answers.

"Remember your Office training and don't discount hunches," Mrs. Preen adds.

"There's a back alley on the Page Street side," Heather instructs her mother.

Mrs. Preen guns the engine as she backs into the alley, then shuts the engine off. Even without power steering, she holds us steady in the narrow confines of the alley as we coast toward the stage door I used just a few days ago to investigate a murder scene as an insurance claims investigator. The apartment buildings on either side of the alleyway are darkened, spectral against the never-quite-dark night sky of the city. Our footsteps when we get out of the car echo off the sides of the buildings. Making our way through puddles, we make small splashing sounds.

Heather must have a key. She opens the stage door. We hear footsteps receding from us across the empty stage on which Bob White's body lay last time I was here. The footsteps head up a set of what sound like metal stairs... Is it my imagination or do I hear voices? Could be just the wind whistling through the now opened stage door...

A trolley car rumbles down Haight Street and comes to a stop. A police siren sounds off in the distance. We are about to step into a confrontation during which hidden dark and destructive secrets will be exposed to view. Murderers might no longer be able to elude detection; covert operations might be exposed. Death is on the prowl, death and certain suffering.

We move cautiously forward across the deserted stage toward this new reality.

Heather, Tamalpa, greets Mother, the mountain's peak, at the edge of a sacred grove of redwood trees no mere mortal human can approach and live.

The high-ceilinged space above the stage is a lattice of light grids, ropes and wires. High up, along a wall in shadows is a lighted window, maybe for changing rooms or an office.

Within the interior of these tall, straight redwoods that stab forever upward into the infinite blue sky, holy guides sit, deep in a meditative trance.

Exterior metal stairs and an outside walkway lead to several rooms, all with closed doors. The light is on in an office. We can see the ceiling inside from below.

Mother, our present holy guide, is one among the gathered meditative guides. She is holding forth.

We take the stairs one step at a time. Dark forces clog my lungs like gritty clots of asbestos — in killing coatings that line the soul, trying to scar it for eternity.

Heather, Jane, Tony, myself bow down before the nurturing force of Mother.

We cautiously head along the outside corridor toward the lighted office.

Our holy guide and Mother proceeds and protects us, like a cross held up before us as we move toward the unknown.

Down below, through the grated metal walkway, what is lurking? Have the feeling I'm sinking into filamentous, life-choking slime. Its odor makes me want to gag...Turns my stomach...Makes me light-headed and dizzy.

Am I Orpheus? Is Heather Eurydice? Is this the Underworld? While trying to escape will we make the mistake of looking back?

———————

Mrs. Preen, handgun well out in front of her, cocked and ready, swings round and up from her crouched position and steps through the open office doorway.

"Thelma. What a pleasant surprise. Our mutual friends at The Office tell me you've been busy trying to dig up dirt on me and my most recent operations. Have you figured out yet that you and the rest of the has-beens are out of the loop and have no need to know?" Mrs. Preen remains neutral but alert and does not bother to engage with or contradict Bull White's opening gambit. "Do come in. Sit down," he continues after allowing her an opening to respond. "I feel confident we older folks, with calmer heads, can sort this whole thing out."

Bull White is warm and cordial. But his eyes are cold and hard. A shiver runs up my spine. Tiny shock waves from my mountain vision tingle in my brain. It's a good day to die. Bull White has greeted us — the boss of this operation, the agent in charge it seems of not just this operation but possibly The Office as well. He has a unique look for each of us. In the aggregate, we are universally beneath contempt, not worthy to be the mud on his well-heeled shoe. Displeasure is too mild a word to describe what he thinks about how things are panning out — and somebody, not Bull White, is going to pay dearly.

We spread out in the room but remain standing. White is seated at a desk lit by a gooseneck lamp, casting ghoulish shadows about the room. Tony and Jane, handcuffed to an ancient radiator, are crouched on the floor just behind White. Two flunkies rise, offering Mrs. Preen a seat, their hands poised just above their holstered weapons.

"I'm afraid I'll have to ask that you discard your weapons – with your left hand and very slowly," Mrs. Preen states, cool as a cucumber.

"After so many years and so many cases, I must admit you surprise me, Thelma. Your maternal instincts have overwhelmed your good judgment."

Bull White tosses his gun on the floor in front of the table. The two agents follow suit.

"Thank you. Now if one of you gentlemen will kindly take the handcuffs off your captives."

The two agents look at White. He nods. One of them steps over and takes off the handcuffs. Tony rubs his wrists. It's obvious he has not been holding up well; Jane, still looking weak from her ordeal, is alert and defiant.

"The shit he's responsible for stinks so bad there's no way it will stay hidden for long. No need of a rescue," Jane comments as she struggles to her feet, pushing away the offered hand of one of the agents.
Tony stands up too, following her lead.

"Step over behind us," Mrs. Preen orders Jane and Tony.

"Thelma. Let me remind you that you are interfering in Office business," Bull White comments causally, without moving. "Mr. Vitolinich and your daughter, Jane, have conspired to obstruct a federal operation. And, who knows, local authorities might find that they have enough evidence to charge Mr. Vitolinich here with murder and Jane as an accessory. Alarming and unwelcome news for a mother, I would imagine..."

Mrs. Preen has added up the score using her own calculations.

"All right, children, back out of the door."

"And down the stairs?" asks Jane, an edge of uncertainty in her voice.

"Follow Linda to the car, dear. It's right outside the door."

"Mr. Carter will be fleeing from a federal warrant. I would hate to have to issue one for a highly respected emeritus agent like you, Thelma. The charge would be conspiracy to overthrow the government, double agent. Very unfortunate indeed..."

Bull White slowly gets up from his chair as we back out of the room. The agents and Bull White move forward as one. Mrs. Preen fires once at their feet. They stop.

"Throw your weapons through the door and over the landing," Mrs. Preen orders.

"Did you know when Bobby first shacked up with Jane I had no idea she was your daughter? We'd lost touch...Hadn't exchanged Christmas cards in years. Or did we ever?" Bull White picks up his gun and throws it over the landing. Then he nods to his agents to do the same. We have stopped just outside the door, awaiting the disposal of their weapons. "Then when your slut of a daughter got pregnant, I must say I was no longer amused by Bobby's youthful sowing of wild oats. The fool wanted to marry her. That would never do."

The two agents toss their weapons over the landing. Each weapon makes a solid thud as it hits the stage floor far below.

"Stay together and walk very slowly behind me," Mrs. Preen orders.

We obey. Mrs. Preen begins backing down the stairs, gun in ready position in front of her. White and his henchmen follow right behind her – at a respectful distance. Mrs. Preen is an excellent markswoman and has kept herself in fit condition. We are nearing the bottom of the stairs when Bull White launches, once again, into amiable but threatening chatter.

"Oh, by the bye, if it is allowed that Vitolinich didn't kill my son and neither did Mr. Toucan, an interesting alternative and popular scenario that's been tossed around is that Linda murdered Bobby. The proverbial blunt object to the back of the head...Oh my, that scenario would end with the whole Preen family behind bars."

Jane looks drawn. Heather, ferocious, protective, jumps in.

"With Bobby and Jane getting married, how does that work?"

"She tried to trap Bobby with the oldest trick in the book," White states quietly. "And Bobby got wise. You took umbrage and lost your California cool, sweetie."

Mrs. Preen steps in to the conversation, cool, calm, collected...

"Bobby, with his usual inept behavior and poor timing, threw a serious monkey wrench into your precious operation and then he had the effrontery to call you on it when you made moves on his girlfriend. How did you react then, Bull? What did you do and what did you have done for you by others?"

The backward procession proceeds down another step. Mrs. Preen continues with her speculations.

"What changed Bobby from a love sick puppy into an addled madman, was it drugs Walker developed for future Office operations, operations you were setting in motion, Bull? Did you also authorize one of your henchmen to dose Bobby? Did you?"

"He was out of his mind attacking Jane; I hit him once from behind with the first thing that came to hand. He staggered around a little and then collapsed going into convulsions before going still. That's when Bernie came in and stabbed him," Linda jumps in to add.

"There — the confession. Mr. Carter, you can close the file on our claim and do a good deed for all concerned by turning Linda Preen in to the authorities," answers White, unruffled.

We stop our downward descent as if by command. There is more, more from Linda.

"You and your precious family reputation... You and your even more precious Office operations... God and Country... Bunch of old white men puffed up by pride, pride and self-importance, heavily influenced by the need for power, power that is so corrosive. It will all come out now, out into the open, if we do go down for Bobby's murder. You can bet we'll see to it, my mother and the rest of us." Linda finishes.

"Too bad you and your boyfriend didn't both get blown to smithereens along with some of those smutty shacks called houseboats. Two less loose ends we need to take care of," Bull White responds without emotion.

"Girls... Gentlemen," Mrs. Preen purrs, still holding her gun steady. We reach the bottom stair and begin backing across the stage towards the back door. "There will be a time and place for this when we've all had a chance to cool down. Cooler heads will prevail, particularly after the results of the independent tox screen and full autopsy I have ordered are made public."

"That tox screen and full autopsy will prove nothing... Neither of them will ever see the light of day."

"So it's not just your precious Office operation you need to protect then, is it. It's the double indemnity payout. Some very speculative investments you made gone south, the cookie jar running low on cash?"

"Did you hear what your daughter said, Thelma? She's just crucified herself with her own words."

"Bobby went berserk. Linda was protecting both herself and me. Bobby kept right on coming after she clobbered him like Linda said until he screamed and collapsed..."

Mrs. Preen soothingly shushes her younger daughter, Jane.

"You can run but you can't hide. We will find you. This will be the final episode of a sad family story."

Mrs. Preen stops, reaches into her pocket, pulls out a mimeographed letter. She holds it out to White. He takes two steps forward to retrieve it.

"Very colorful," White allows with a sour tone after he has read it. "And pointedly scandalous..."

"Much more damning than that for you and your career, as I am sure you will agree if it is sent to the people on this list I have created."

Again White takes two steps forward to retrieve the list and again he reads it.

"And what might your conditions be?" White asks after perusing the list intently.

His expression has changed from sour to a cold, blank wall, all in a minute. No one moves or speaks. Mrs. Preen has the floor.

"Without prejudice or harm to my children and their friends, they will be allowed to leave, immediately. And you will allow me to retire without intrigue or subterfuge. Of course, the future whereabouts of all of us will be no concern of yours or The Office. And all charges against us will be expunged."

White answers without hesitation.

"Done and done."

He bows to Mrs. Preen. Then he turns to me.

"Mr. Carter, I sincerely regret our parting. The debt I owe your father must, unfortunately, remain unpaid… And you and your friends must remain fugitives from justice."

Jacques and his henchmen burst from the shadows. One goes for Mrs. Preen and Jacques hurtles himself at our group. White and the two agents are a step behind. Mrs. Preen's gun discharges. The henchman approaching her grabs his shoulder. Tony throws himself in front of Jacques, delivering a perfect block. Jacques's gun pops out of his hand. I give him a kick to the head and retrieve his gun. This is no time for pleasantries.

"Run for it," shouts Mrs. Preen as White and the two agents head in her direction.

The Preen sisters hesitate. We stop.

"I'm okay. Go," Mrs. Preen, infuriated, roars kicking one of the agents in the groin.

"After them," Bull White roars, breathing hard.

"Go now," Mrs. Preen commands, delivering a wicked karate chop to another agent.

I am backing toward the door gun at the ready. Jane has the stage door open. Heather holds a sturdy metal chair up as a shield in front of Jane and herself. Tony is mobile but is holding his shoulder. I fire three quick shots at the feet of our pursuers. We are through the door. Heather props the chair under the door handle, neatly locking the door, a temporary measure at best but one that will buy us a few precious seconds. I fire the remaining three shots at the door, then discard the gun.

Mrs. Preen left the keys in the car. Jane is behind the wheel. Racecar driving must run in the family. No sooner have we slammed our doors closed than the shiny black car bolts from the starting block like it's on fire. We jet through and out of the alley. Jane slams the gearshift lever into drive. The car tires burn rubber. We make a one eighty and fly away down Page Street.

"Any suggestions what to do next?" asks Jane looking at us in the rearview mirror after exchanging a quick look at Tony to see if he's all right.

"Anybody know…" I offer holding on for dear life by the door rest. "Anybody know the quickest way to 10 Colusa Alley? It's somewhere near the Fillmore West."

We fishtail wildly onto Market Street. Artificial daylight, bright yellow and harsh, assails us.

"I'm ditching the car. Get the hell out," Jane hollers, slamming on the brakes after bouncing up onto the curb and back down again.

The car is past the intersection of Market, just beyond the boundary of the glaring streetlights. It will be noticed – soon. We're out of the car and on our way in a hurry.

"10 Colusa Alley... Tim told me to ask someone in front of the Fillmore West where it is."

"I know where it is."

Heather leads the way. I'm on her heels. Tony and Jane keep pace just behind us. Jane has a thin jacket wrapped around her. Tony has his arm around her waist, keeping her close, keeping her warm. The first order of business is to get Tony, Jane and Linda away to a safe place.

Market Street to Gough Street; Gough Street to Stevenson... None too soon... A police patrol car rolls by, spotlight searching in nooks and crannies. They've been dispatched to track us down and bring us in. And, if we're not careful, they'll succeed. The back alleyways we hurry through are ramshackle, littered with hole-in-the-wall businesses that have signs which are partially obliterated or hanging on by a thread, battered and overturned trashcans and barrels, broken streetlights at their entrances.

"That's Colusa up ahead," Heather announces.

10 Colusa turns out to be what was once a small metal work shop. The door is open. We go in. There are a dozen or so work positions with various pieces of equipment at each position, a lathe at one, a drill press at another, and so on. In the back of the room we see a scruffy hippie with an unkempt beard and Tim. They motion us to a seat. It's obvious what the function of the scruffy hippie is; he's a dealer.

"Tim," I start.

"We're waiting for the rest of the stuff," he interrupts me to say.

"And we were just about to sample some of this," the dealer states, picking up a slender brass toke pipe.

He takes a hit himself and passes it to Tim. Tim takes a long hit and passes it to Jane. She obliges without hesitation. Tony's eyes are bulging.

"What is it?" I ask.

"DMT, man," he answers. "All the way to the top and back in fifteen minutes... What a trip. Far out..."

Are we that crazy? Yes, apparently.

"We may have to make a fast exit," I comment.

Tim does not acknowledge me. Nor does Jane... Tony takes a tentative toke and coughs almost immediately. Heather is not shy. She takes a hit and passes the pipe to me. I mentally shrug and take a hit as well.

The dealer is right about the quality of his dope. We shoot right to the top of a full blown acid trip in a blinding flash, a New York minute. That state of consciousness does nothing for me. Those penetrating eyes and the mountain vision still hold sway. The mountain/penetrating eye vision only gets more colorful, almost cartoonish compared to what I have already experienced in my altered state.

While we are lost in the ozone, the door of the shop bursts open. A young hippie, a young woman, probably fresh from the Fillmore West, trots in... On her heels is a beat cop. Instantaneously, the hippie takes in the scene, turns, and heads back out the door. There seems no way that the beat cop has not seen us. He shakes his head, makes as if to scratch it, then turns and follows the hippie out the door, leaving it open...

In slow motion we look at each other, stoned out, locked in our seats. A crackling sound seems to hang in the air as if our collective synapses are exchanging the last vestiges of an excited communication. The dealer is the first one to return to the here-and-now.

"We were invisible," he comments, then chuckles with delight.

Maybe it's Mother. Maybe it's those penetrating eyes. Maybe it was the DMT. No matter. I know what needs to be done.

"Is there a back way out of here?" I ask with as much urgency as I can muster in the present circumstances.

"What? Well, yeah," the befuddled dealer finally manages to reply.

"Everybody... Use it. Now..." I'm up out of my seat, the signal for everyone else to snap to. "Tim, take my friends with you in your drive away car. I'll create a diversion."

"My care package," Tim begins.

It's too late for care packages, partner.

"Hurry," I holler.

Heather and I exchange a look. There's no more to be said, even if this is the last time we will ever see each other. She spirits Jane and Tony into action. The dealer needs no additional prompting. The back door, well concealed, is opened. They all race through it. Heather is the last one out. She turns back and gives me a kiss on the cheek. I am left to close the front door. From the outside this shop will look nondescript just like every other shop on the block, shut down for the night. Before I do, I watch Heather and Tony disappear into the strewn junk in the narrow passageway between the dilapidated, low slung buildings.

Then I pull up my coat collar and light a cigarette just before stepping out the still open front door and slamming it shut with a bang. All hell breaks loose. Police concealed behind trash bins, light poles and strewn debris leap from their hiding places. I tackle the nearest cop as the others raise their guns. After I am subdued, the machine shop door is unnecessarily smashed open. I find myself face down on the street looking at a police car pulled across the street with its lights flashing.

"You are under arrest. Cuff him," I am told by a policeman.

"We'll take charge of the prisoner," Bull White announces as he steps into view.

Coop is right behind him. There's no way he can object. The federal warrant was the reason for the all-points bulletin.

"Are the others in there?" White shouts over his shoulder.

Muffled sounds of men knocking over and smashing things inside the shop can be heard. After a long pause an answer comes back.

"They're not here."

"Where are they?" White demands, cool and hard.

"Read him his rights," Coop orders, stopping the answer I had no intention of making.

I can no longer feel the beaded pouch in my pocket. I'm suddenly very tired and cold but my heart is pounding pleasantly. My friends have eluded capture.

_____

My father is my first and only visitor. I am being held at an undisclosed location somewhere near the city. I still wear my own clothes, not prison garb. I have been well fed. I have been supplied with cigarettes, my favorite brand, Murad. I have had plenty of time to think things over — in a solitary room. I try not to show my father how much what he will say means to me.

He is already in the large, Spartan room, empty of all others when I enter. He nods as I approach and stands up. We shake hands leaning across the table where our interview will take place. We take our seats on opposite sides of the table. We sit in silence. My father clears his throat, then launches into our interview.

"Charlie, you are not doing the right thing. But there is still time to rectify your mistake."

He pauses. I wait in silence.

"Where are your friends?" he continues.

"I don't know and if I did I wouldn't tell you."

"But I am your father — and your appointed attorney."

"I don't remember requesting one. Who appointed you?"

"Charlie, you have let the attentions of a beautiful woman go to your head. That will not take you far in this world. In point of fact, it will lower you in the esteem of people who could matter to you a great deal as you pass through life."

After another long silence broken only by the distant dripping of a water faucet and the calling of the wind...

"I've spoken to Mr. White. In all his actions, he was merely trying to bring you to your senses, make you come to terms with the dangers of your position."

I light a cigarette. A door clicks shut somewhere in the building. Footsteps walk down a hall. A toilet flushes on another level.

"If this federal warrant in your name and a possible indictment are allowed to become permanent on your record, it would be a death knell for you professionally and personally. You would be ostracized for life."

I take another drag of my cigarette and pick some tobacco from my lip. Far off in the distance I hear a hawk cry, followed closely by the calling of the wind. I find I now have a response.

"If the son of your fellow agent was murdered, would you help cover up the murder by framing a childhood friend?"

My father is now silent, careful, giving nothing away. He's a great poker player and a first-rate lawyer. I elaborate.

"How does what you are asking of me square with what I understood you to tell me as I was growing up?"

My father sighs and seems to look at me anew.

"I worked for The Office during the war before it was a recognized and top secret operation. The Geneva conventions, your duty to serve your country, were our guiding principles. Surely, you can't be equating your situation to that?"

"World War II was a special time; so is this. Each time is unique; both require clear thinking and firm beliefs. Were the operations Mr. White oversaw here in San Francisco related to war?"

"I can't comment on that. You know that, son."

"It seems to me that infiltrating organizations made up primarily of young people exercising their right of protest, their right to assembly, their belief that free speech is part and parcel of being an American citizen, has more to do with politics than it does with national security."

I take another drag on my cigarette. My father choses to ignore what I want to believe are his doubts.

"Let's get back on track here," he begins, putting a hand on the table as he leans slightly forward. That outstretched, beseeching hand reaches to my side of the table. His eyes bore into my brain; no penetrating eyes are there to engage with his. Yet the influence those penetrating eyes has had on me remains, constant and firm. "Bernie Toucan killed Bob White," my father discloses, beginning his laundry list of due diligence, the summing up of the situation. "The knife wounds were the cause of death, not the blunt object to the back of the head or any substances in Bobby's body. That will be the conclusion of the Homicide Department of the SFPD and all courts of law. The view is that we may never know the why of Toucan's actions but we do know how and when he acted. He must have hit Bobby from behind with a blunt object and then stabbed him multiple times somewhere in the Straight Theater building. Then, for unknown reasons, decided to leave his body center stage for the police to find. That is what will be the essence of the police report when it closes the murder case. Your friends will have nothing to fear about charges resulting from..."

We both know that Bernie Toucan did not hit Bob White with a blunt object even though he did stab Bob White multiple times. We also know that if this murder investigation were allowed to continue another murderer might be identified, particularly if leads from the additional tox screen and the full autopsy are followed. The problem is these new conclusions would most likely bring into the light of day the dirty tricks our own government has been perpetrating on its citizens - most likely for political gain.

"A very convenient conclusion for Mr. White and The Office, wouldn't you say?"

"Well, yes, you could put it that way."

"So why are the federal government and Mr. White still pursuing my friends?"

My father chooses to ignore my question and the obvious oversights and likely problems that new conclusions might cause.

"I have spoken to Mr. Hancock. He is willing to turn a blind eye to your shenanigans. Youthful impetuosity, being a little green for the job... Of course, you will have to return to the home office for reassignment and possibly some disciplinary action, minor at best."

"Is that where my duty lies, a path that will take me directly back to the hypocrisy and blind deceit practiced at The Office and evidently at Life Beneficial as well?"

My father doesn't bother to remind me that I was raised in a world where this way of thinking holds sway, that my mother and he still live in that world, that most of my childhood friends have chosen to live by those same conventions. My childhood experience – feeling like an outsider, different, flashes through my mind. Turning away from my question, my father tries a different approach.

"Isobel has returned to Richmond. She's a fine woman, son, with a good head on her shoulders. She will help you to find the right way. Of course, you will have to fight for her, convince her that you have mended your ways. You're not the only one who has his eye on her, you know."

I've never felt that my father wanted to hear me talk about any girl I've dated. I find it unlikely he really wants to get off on that tangent now. I sit in silence, which seems to irritate him.

"You screwed up, son. Admit it like a man. Take your medicine. Work with us and not against us to bring this mess to a satisfactory, no, a win-win conclusion. We'll stand behind you. We're family. Your true friends will stand with you as well. Those who don't, you really don't want to know."

"Mrs. Preen is someone I would be proud to have as a friend. Would that still be possible if I turn her daughters in?"

"Thelma Preen is a professional. She reacted with emotion, something very much out of character for her. Understandable, as Linda and Jane are her daughters."

My father pulls out some papers from the briefcase on the table in front of him. He tamps the papers down with a tap, tap, tap so they make a nice neat package before putting them on the table beside his briefcase. A tower clock strikes two. I get up from my seat.

"Dad, I'm sorry to say that you and I differ on where my duty lies on this one. Give my love to Mother."

"I came here to help you, son," my father says to my back as I knock on the door for the guard.

I turn around and face him.

"I've always sought your blessing, Dad. I've always tried to live up to what you taught me. I'm hoping now you will see your way clear to give me a hand."

I hear the guard's footsteps coming down the hall.

"Dad, I...I love you, Dad."

The guard unlocks the door.

No one else comes to visit me that day or the next day or the next. I wait...

EPILOGUE

I, CHARLIE FOXHAWK CARTER, REMEMBER...FULL STOP

Spring 1969

Spring is an elusive season in San Francisco. There is no wide-scale and joyous transformation from barrenness to budding leaves, from bitter cold to warm, gentle rains. The snow that melts in the Sierras ends up in the Bay but it does not bring warm sunshine in its wake. No lightening of the heart occurs after the introspection of winter.

The winter rains slow, then stop. Fog at morning and night commences. The average temperature goes up ten degrees. The hillsides, green from the winter rain, will start to look worn; they will be parched and pale by summer.

After spending over a month in jail, I am released, only to discover the world has changed.

As if by magic, the newspapers and the public have forgotten about the Bob White murder. Bernie Toucan, even though his body is never found, has been officially declared dead and the incriminating knife with his fingerprints on it allows the Bob White murder case to be closed. The half-ton of marijuana seized by the State Highway Patrol on Route 1 between Muir Beach and Mill Valley is removed from their property room by federal marshals. Hippies suffering from lingering chest colds begin surfacing at free health care clinics soon thereafter. Could Paraquat laced marijuana be the cause of this health crisis? The Gate Five houseboat, smashed to smithereens, is sold 'as is' to a savvy developer, setting off a boom in Gate Five real estate prices. Hippies, living on the cheap or for free, are being driven out of their "last free ride" neighborhood and are being replaced by well-heeled swingers looking for a pad in which they can indulge their whim to mix with the natives without sacrificing their names or their reputations. No mention of the Lagunitas house has ever been made public.

The federal warrants that were issued for the detention of Tony Vitolinich, Linda Preen, Jane Preen, and myself have disappeared into thin air. For reasons of "national security," all records relating to the Bob White murder investigation are seized by federal agents.

I hear through my contact at The Office that the future of all San Francisco operations conducted by The Office was debated at a regularly scheduled monthly meeting of bureau chiefs. Officially there is no longer any local presence; unofficially the jury is still out.

Ronald Outrage makes a surprise announcement that he is stepping down from his college teaching position and has no plans to make more films. He disappears from view, only to reappear as Ronald Walker on the scene in Rome as winter turns to spring in 1969 with a companion, a young man of questionable character. It's unconfirmed but probable that this companion is Bernie Toucan.

An undisclosed buyer purchases the Straight Theater, voiding Luther Green's lease. Rumors circulate that Green moved to Hong Kong to take a position with an international financial operation looking to invest in overseas ventures.

Bob White is buried in the family vault in Boston. Afterward, Life Beneficial, with no fanfare or publicity, settles its claim with the Whites.

Bull White and his wife Edwina move down from Boston to Washington, D.C., where White resumes his lofty position at an undisclosed branch of the CIA. Mrs. White becomes one of the most sought-after hostesses in Washington. An ambassadorship is mentioned in their future.

Tony Vitolinich shows up unannounced at his parents' house just as his father is coming home from work three weeks after his disappearance. His father looks older and tired; his mother greets Tony with reserve but is tearfully appreciative that he has returned.

Shortly thereafter, Jane Preen materializes on the doorstep of Tony's just-rented apartment in Richmond, Virginia. Wedding bells are in their future.

The lightshow goes belly up and disbands while I'm in jail. The lightshow members are turned out into the street, suitcases in hand. They scatter to the four winds. Harry, now hale and hearty, as well as David and Molly stay on in the Bay Area, moving to Marin County.

Tim Montgomery sets up camp in the Richmond Fan District near RPI, Richmond Professional Institute. There's a small scene of arty folks to which he attaches himself. An uptick in the sale and consumption of LSD is noticed after his arrival. Among my belongings at my apartment, he left a hefty tome, The Urantia Book. Inside on the back of the front cover is a signed declaration that he will marry a certain former resident of Los Angeles that he impregnated.

Isobel returned to Richmond shortly after informing Coop about my potential meeting with Tim at 10 Colusa Alley. She still does not return my phone calls or my letters. I have been told that she is "seeing someone special."

Heather, it is rumored, has gone to live with Nick Reynolds, a former member of the Kingston Trio and a part owner of the Trident, on his Oregon ranch. We really were taking our leave of each other when she and the rest fled through the back door of that deserted Colusa Alley workshop.

My mother is there to greet me when I am released from jail. Dad is unable to come. Pressing business... Mom presents me with a gift - an heirloom from her side of the family. It is a cured hide stretched tight with leather ties to a wooden frame. On the hide is painted - a hawk flying; a fox crying; and, on the far side from the bird in flight and the fox, a wind god blowing a mighty gust of wind towards them.

I thank my mother for her offer that I return home and, instead, move to Mill Valley. A former college chum, Tom, and his wife have purchased a massive three-story Victorian. He's just been made partner in a law firm that has an office in San Francisco. They offer their basement, rent free, until I sort things out. Since I'm living on unemployment insurance, I graciously accept their hospitality.

One day, after collecting my unemployment insurance in San Rafael, I fill out forms and pay fees at the Marin Civic Center, taking the first step towards opening a one-man private investigation agency - Foxhawk Investigations. I wander the streets of Mill Valley, Larkspur, San Rafael, and San Anselmo, telling myself I am looking for office space and envisioning the shingle which will hang outside my office on which will be inscribed – 'Hawk flies Fox cries Mighty wind.' I vow I will cater to 'the woebegone and forgotten.'

Over coffee and a sandwich at a dive near the police station, I tell Coop I'm planning on opening a private investigation agency. Coop downs the last dregs of his coffee and pulls out his pipe before he smiles at me, chuckles and asks.

"Okay. Let's see if you're cut out for this career change. Give me your take on the Bob White case." I look at Coop with a startled, then a troubled look. Coop smiles reassuringly and adds. "Reason I'd like to know is I'm not so sure we got it right."

"Well," I begin. "Well, I think I've already told you I never approached this whole mess trying to solve a murder. I really didn't care 'who done it.' I just wanted to get myself and my friends out of harm's way, out of the situation entirely." Coop nods then puts his pipe in his mouth and lights it. "Okay then... I'll be sort of winging it because I've never really tried to put the whole thing together. And most of what I have is pure speculation with little hard evidence to prove it." Coop nods again and takes a drag on his pipe.

"So, Bobby for whatever reason downs one or more of Outrage's concoctions. That was a no-no; the drugs were not offered or intended for him. The concoction sends him beyond the moon and into outer space. He goes berserk. He is either already in the room with Jane or comes upon her. Who knows what he thinks or thinks he sees but, in his addled condition, he attacks Jane. Linda either comes into the room at this point or was already in the room and comes to the rescue. She bonks Bobby on the head with whatever. Bobby does not go down but keeps on coming at Jane. He staggers, stumbles around, falls. Then he goes into convulsions before expiring. Meantime, Toucan comes into the room and, after Bobby has expired, stabs him numerous times. Then Toucan hauls Bobby down to the stage after the gig and stages a very flashy murder scene, after which he hightails it in Outrage's van filled with the band equipment Outrage bought and paid for.

"Here's the thing. Why did Toucan do what he did? And why did Mr. White and the Office try to stick Tony Vitolinich with the murder rap? Both good questions... I say Toucan was trying to remove Outrage from suspicion. Creating confusion and alternate theories of the murder seemed like a good idea. Mr. White and the Office were trying to keep the Office and its operations out of the crosshairs of an investigation which could blow their cover and might possibly point to questionable behavior. Okay. How did it come to pass that Bobby took this lethal cocktail of drugs. Was he fed them intentionally? I don't believe Outrage would intentionally do this to Bobby and I don't think his father would either. Maybe Toucan would but I don't think he did. No one else comes to mind. I also say neither Linda's blow to the head nor Toucan's knife wounds killed Bob White. My theory is that Bob White was not murdered. His death was due to natural causes. Bobby self-administered that lethal cocktail. Somehow this triggered a heart attack or stroke, the cause of death. Of course, there are mitigating factors which might blow my conclusion out of the water and lead to a murder charge. I leave that to hotshot lawyers. Anyhow, the tox screen and the new autopsy might have offered some definitive proof. But..."

I've run out of gas. Neither of us has anything to add. Besides, Coop needs to be heading back. He puts out his pipe and pulls on his battered raincoat. We shake hands.

"You'll do," he tells me, patting me on the shoulder before heading back to his office.

I beat rush hour traffic on the Golden Gate and make good time to Mill Valley. In the next few weeks I share family meals with David and Molly and hang out with Harry, catching up on their lives and plugging into the Marin County scene.

On many days, though, I brood, walking the many trails that lead up, down, along, and over the voluptuous shoulders of Mt. Tamalpais contemplating Tamalpa, Mother, the holy man in his mountainside cabin, penetrating eyes, the shining light of sunshine. When daylight fades and the moon rises above the top most peak of Mt. Tamalpais, I retreat, carrying out my brooding, introspective contemplation indoors. Hand poised high above the card table on which the half-solved puzzle and the loose pieces lie, I, the seeker, search out the rightful place of the piece I hold. I, with a face expressionless but full of intense concentration, sit without moving, back straight and head slightly bowed.

From the place of the observer I ask: why am I here...there?

THE END

Thank You for this day, oh Lord.
I place myself in Your Hands.
Please give me the strength, courage and dignity
to face my own Death and Life.
In the interim, help me through this night
of dreams and illusions.
On the morrow, help me to find that Essence
which will put me in Harmony with Your Will.

ACKNOWLEDGMENTS

First and foremost, I want to thank my wife, Margaret, for editing and helping promote and market this novel and for being by my side to offer encouragement and critical input throughout. I want to thank Bob Campbell for photographing cherished moments and images. And I want to thank Kayleigh Montgomery-Morris for her caring and attentive approach to the design of the book.

I also want to thank my daughter, Rachel, and my son, Frank, for their support of and belief in me.

I would also like to thank those people, through the years, who have influenced me or have been good and loyal friends through thick and thin. Particular mention must be made of my college writing instructor, Clifford Dowdey; fellow creatives, Tom Gidwitz, Bill Jersey, and Patrick Prentiss; my brother, Sid, and his wife, Gail; and my cousin, Judy Spencer Merrill.

And I want to give particular thanks to those people who were a part of my life during the formative times of the late 1960s, most notably the members of the Great Northwest Phantasmagoria Light Show, the Peacock family, the David and Sharon Litwin family, the folks at Mind Reels, Jim Samans and the ever vibrant and evocative San Francisco/Bay Area and its inhabitants. You are in my thoughts and dreams always.

ABOUT THE AUTHOR

Frank Cervarich was born in Richmond, Virginia but left his heart in the San Francisco/Bay Area. He has written, edited and produced numerous programs for television, film, and video during a forty plus year career in the business. He lives with his wife, Margaret, in Maryland.

Looking to read more books in the Charlie Foxhawk Carter series?

MAKING THE SCENE: MARIN

is scheduled for release in 2020.

———————

Want to know more about
FOXHAWK?

Visit **www.foxhawk.org**
and
www.remembertimeneverwas.com